Spell on Wheels™

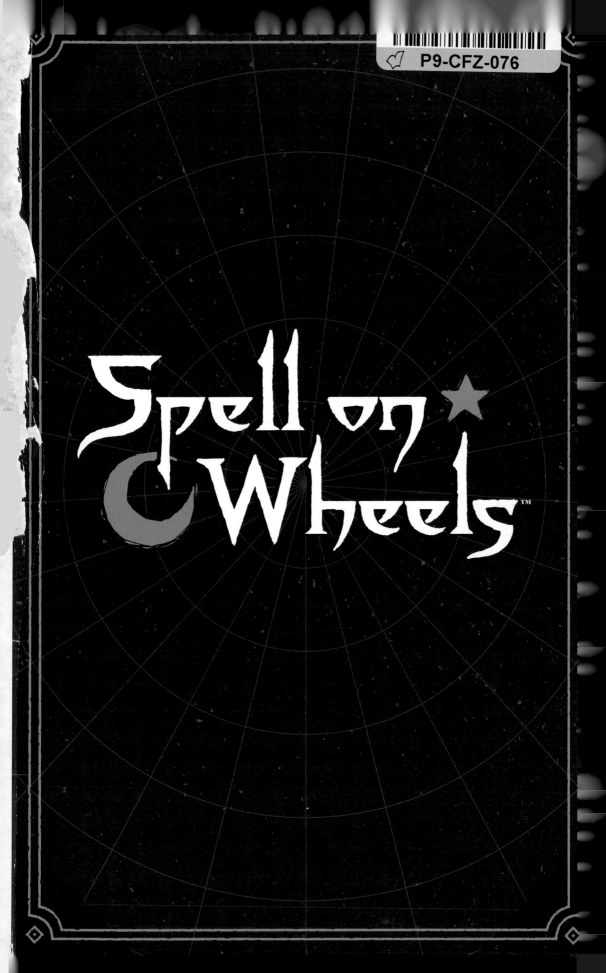

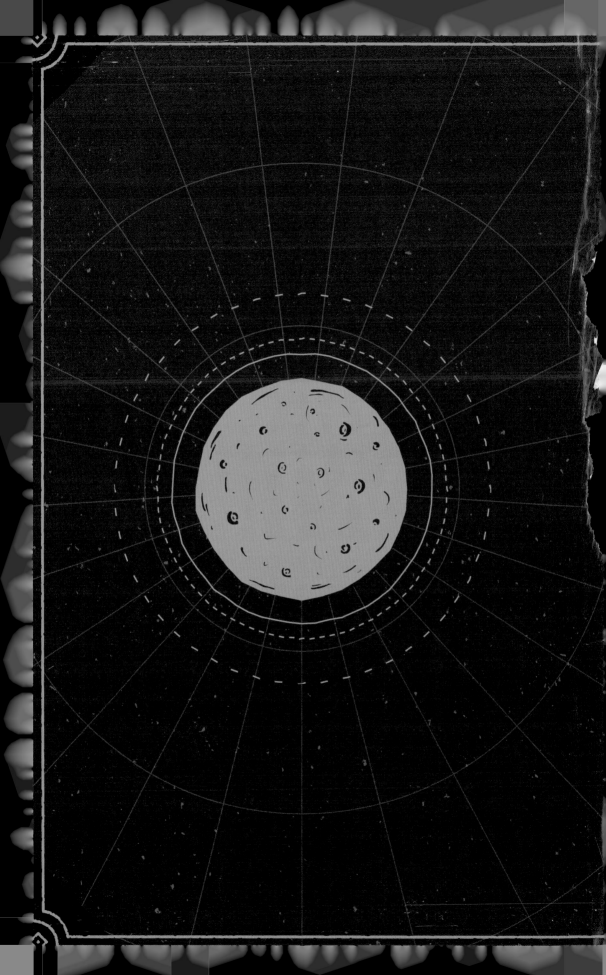

Spell on Wheels™

Story by ★ **KATE LETH**

Art by ★ **MEGAN LEVENS**

Colors by ★ **MARISSA LOUISE**

Letters by ★ **NATE PIEKOS of Blambot®**

Cover by ★ **JEN BARTEL**

Chapter Break Art by ★ **MING DOYLE,
PAULINA GANUCHEAU, MARGUERITE SAUVAGE,
JEN BARTEL**, and **JOE QUINONES**

DARK HORSE BOOKS

President and Publisher **Mike Richardson**
Editor **Shantel LaRocque** | *Assistant Editor* **Katii O'Brien**
Designer **Sarah Terry** | *Digital Art Technician* **Melissa Martin**

Published by Dark Horse Books
A division of Dark Horse Comics, Inc.
10956 SE Main Street | Milwaukie, OR 97222

First edition: June 2017 | ISBN 978-1-50670-183-7

1 3 5 7 9 10 8 6 4 2
Printed in China

International Licensing: (503) 905-2377 | Comic Shop Locator Service: (888) 266-4226

This volume collects *Spell on Wheels* #1–#5.

Library of Congress Cataloging-in-Publication Data

Names: Leth, Kate, author. | Levens, Megan, artist. | Louise, Marissa, colourist. | Piekos, Nate, letterer. | Bartel, Jen, artist. | Doyle, Ming, artist. | Ganucheau, Paulina, artist. | Sauvage, Marguerite, artist. | Quinones, Joe, artist.
Title: Spell on wheels / script by Kate Leth ; art by Megan Levens ; colors by Marissa Louise ; letters by Nate Piekos of Blambot ; cover by Jen Bartel ; chapter break art by Ming Doyle, Paulina Ganucheau, Marguerite Sauvage, Jen Bartel, and Joe Quinones.
Description: First edition. | Milwaukie, OR : Dark Horse Books, 2017. | "This volume collects Spell on Wheels #1-#5"
Identifiers: LCCN 2016056237 | ISBN 9781506701837 (paperback)
Subjects: LCSH: Comic books, strips, etc. | BISAC: COMICS & GRAPHIC NOVELS / Science Fiction. | FICTION / Fantasy / Paranormal. | COMICS & GRAPHIC NOVELS / Fantasy.
Classification: LCC PN6728.S596 L48 2017 | DDC 741.5/973--dc23
LC record available at https://lccn.loc.gov/2016056237

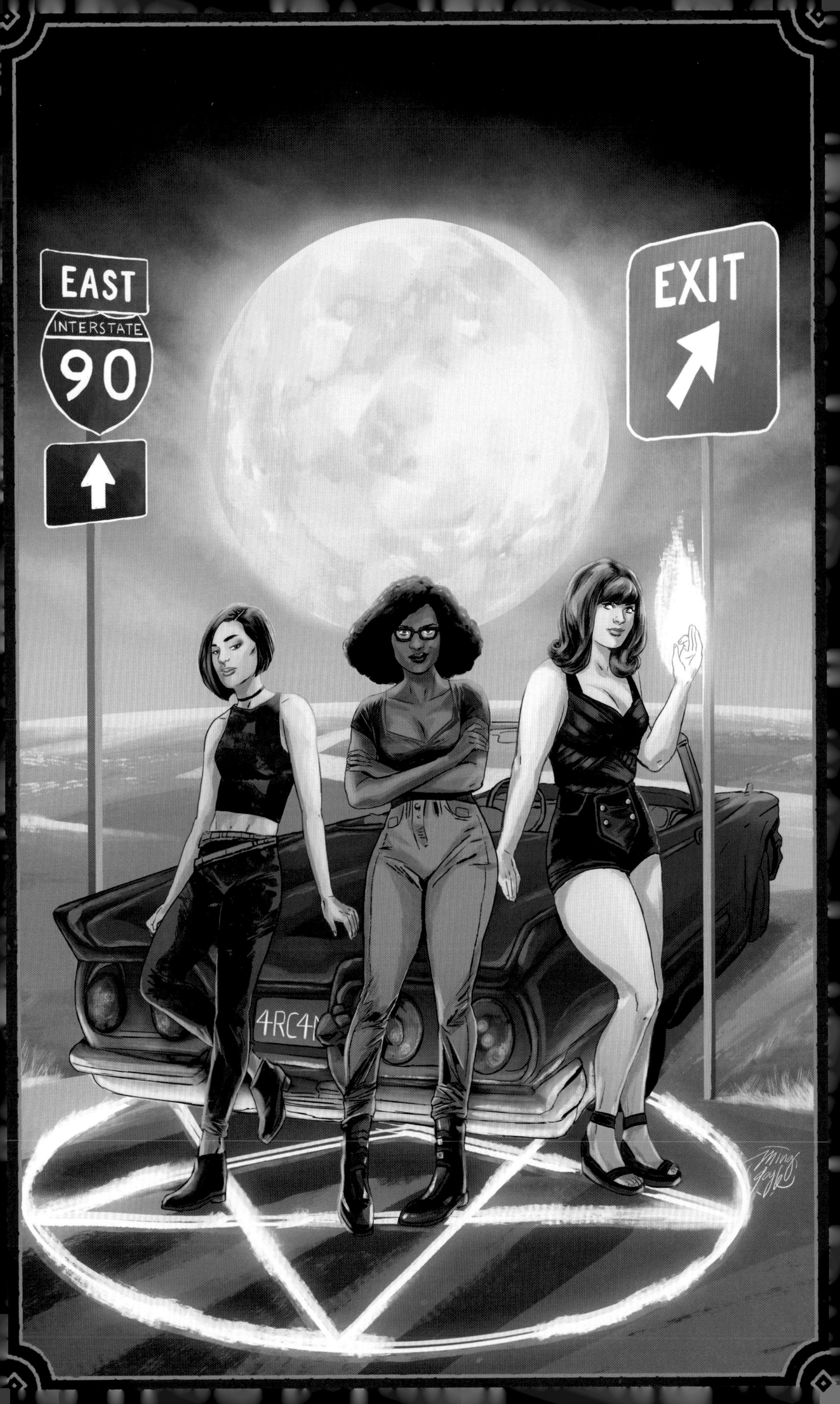
EAST
INTERSTATE
90
EXIT

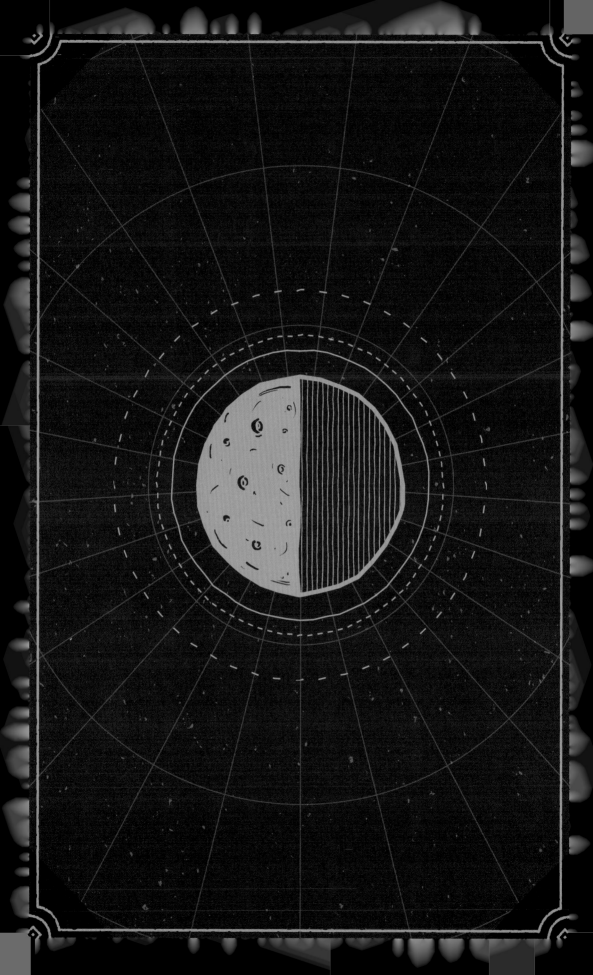

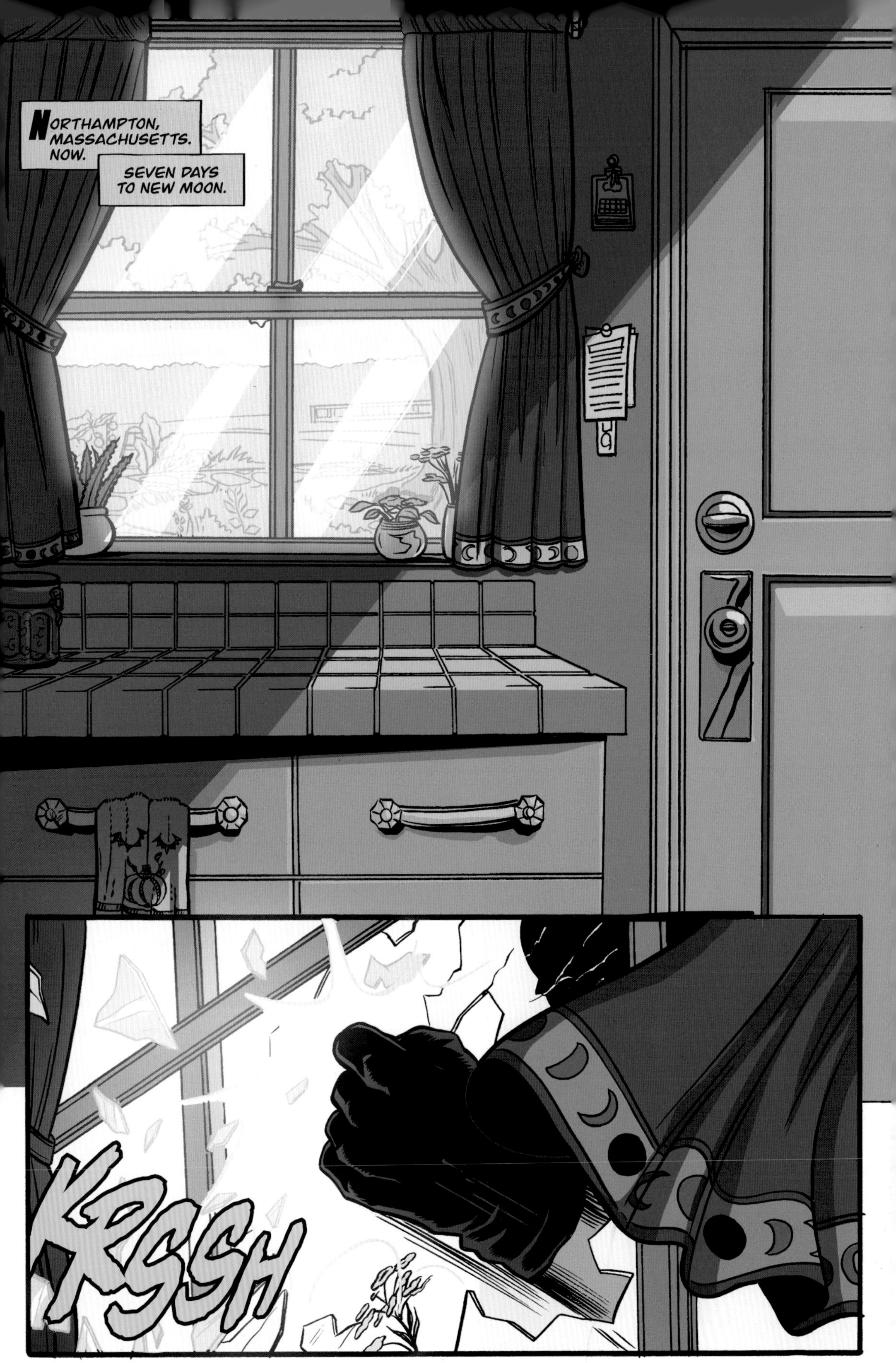
NORTHAMPTON, MASSACHUSETTS. NOW.
SEVEN DAYS TO NEW MOON.
KRSSH

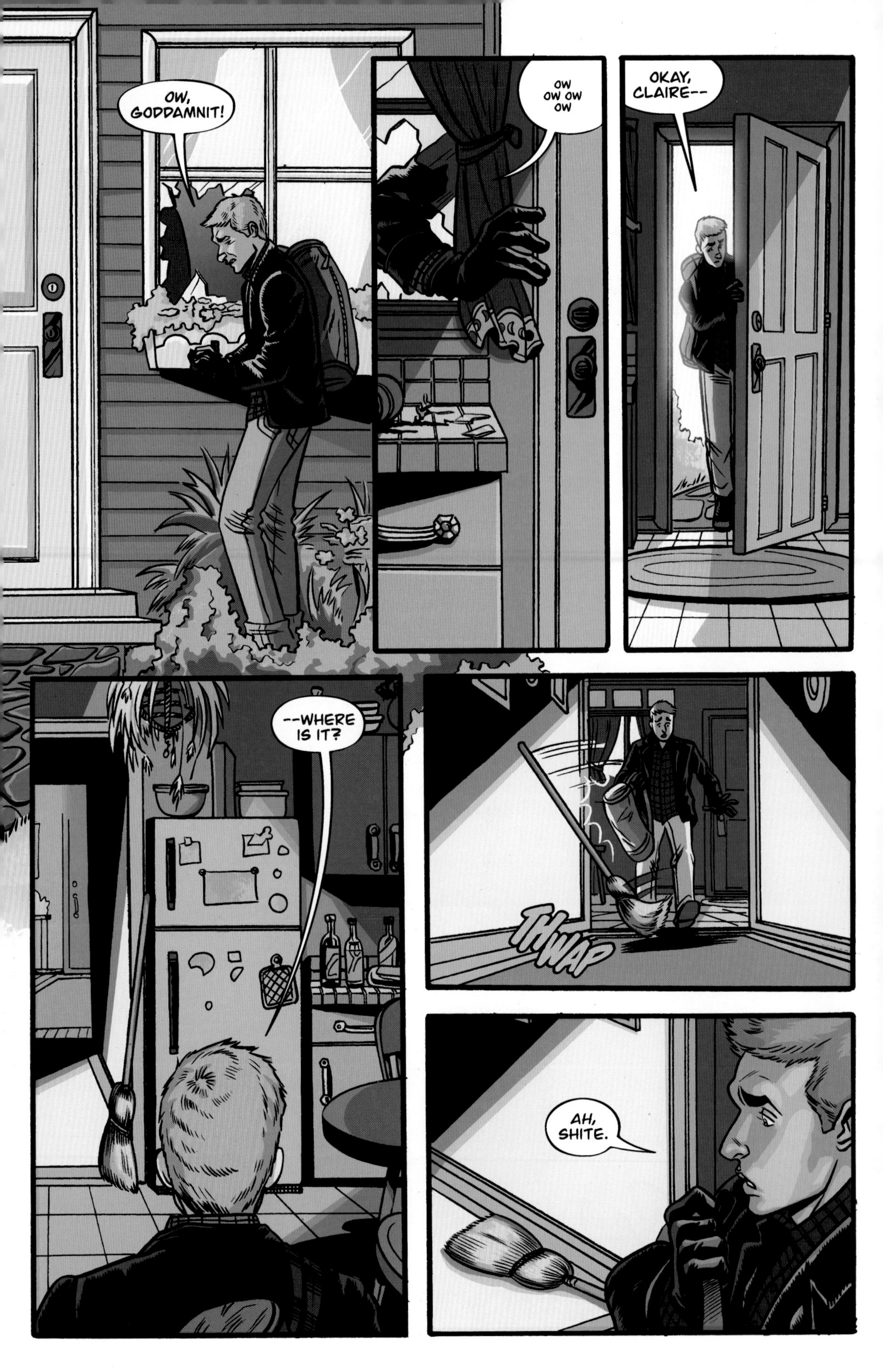

OW, GODDAMNIT!
OW OW OW OW
OKAY, CLAIRE--
--WHERE IS IT?
THWAP
AH, SHITE.

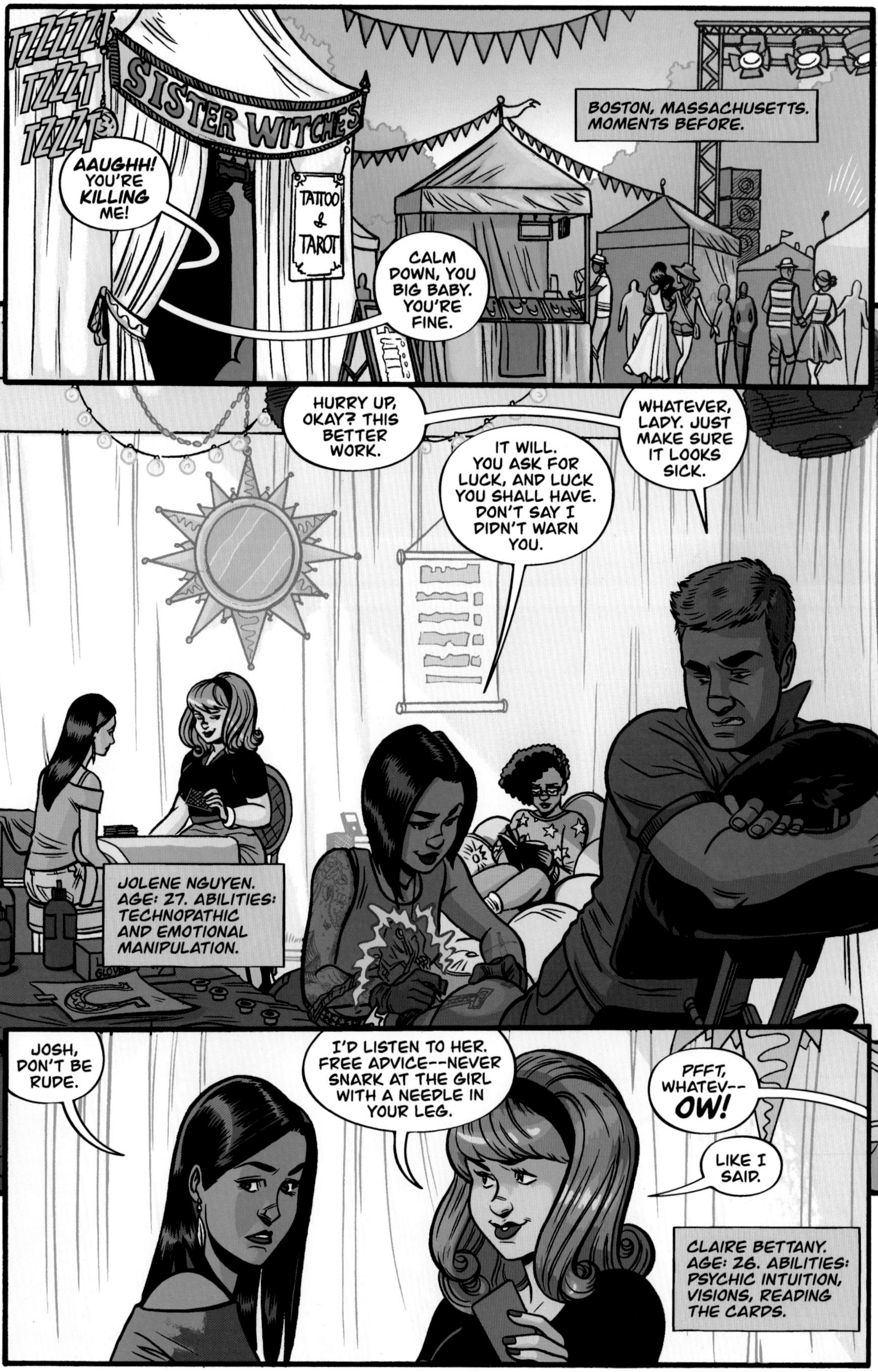
TZZZZZT TZZZT TZZZT
SISTER WITCHES
TATTOO & TAROT
BOSTON, MASSACHUSETTS. MOMENTS BEFORE.
AAUGHH! YOU'RE KILLING ME!
CALM DOWN, YOU BIG BABY. YOU'RE FINE.
HURRY UP, OKAY? THIS BETTER WORK.
WHATEVER, LADY. JUST MAKE SURE IT LOOKS SICK.
IT WILL. YOU ASK FOR LUCK, AND LUCK YOU SHALL HAVE. DON'T SAY I DIDN'T WARN YOU.
JOLENE NGUYEN. AGE: 27. ABILITIES: TECHNOPATHIC AND EMOTIONAL MANIPULATION.
JOSH, DON'T BE RUDE.
I'D LISTEN TO HER. FREE ADVICE--NEVER SNARK AT THE GIRL WITH A NEEDLE IN YOUR LEG.
PFFT, WHATEV--OW!
LIKE I SAID.
CLAIRE BETTANY. AGE: 26. ABILITIES: PSYCHIC INTUITION, VISIONS, READING THE CARDS.

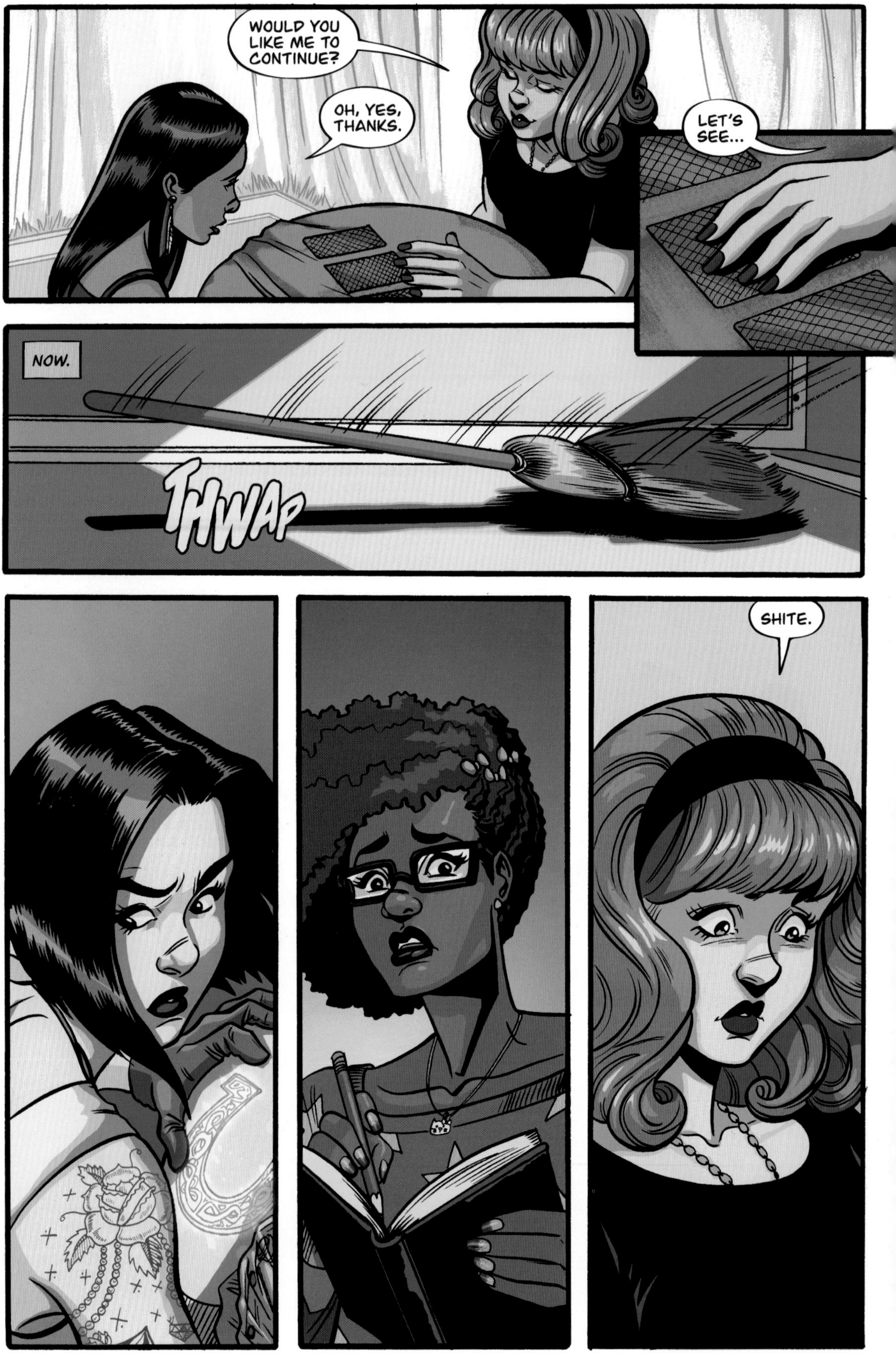
WOULD YOU LIKE ME TO CONTINUE?
OH, YES, THANKS.
LET'S SEE...
NOW.
THWAP
SHITE.

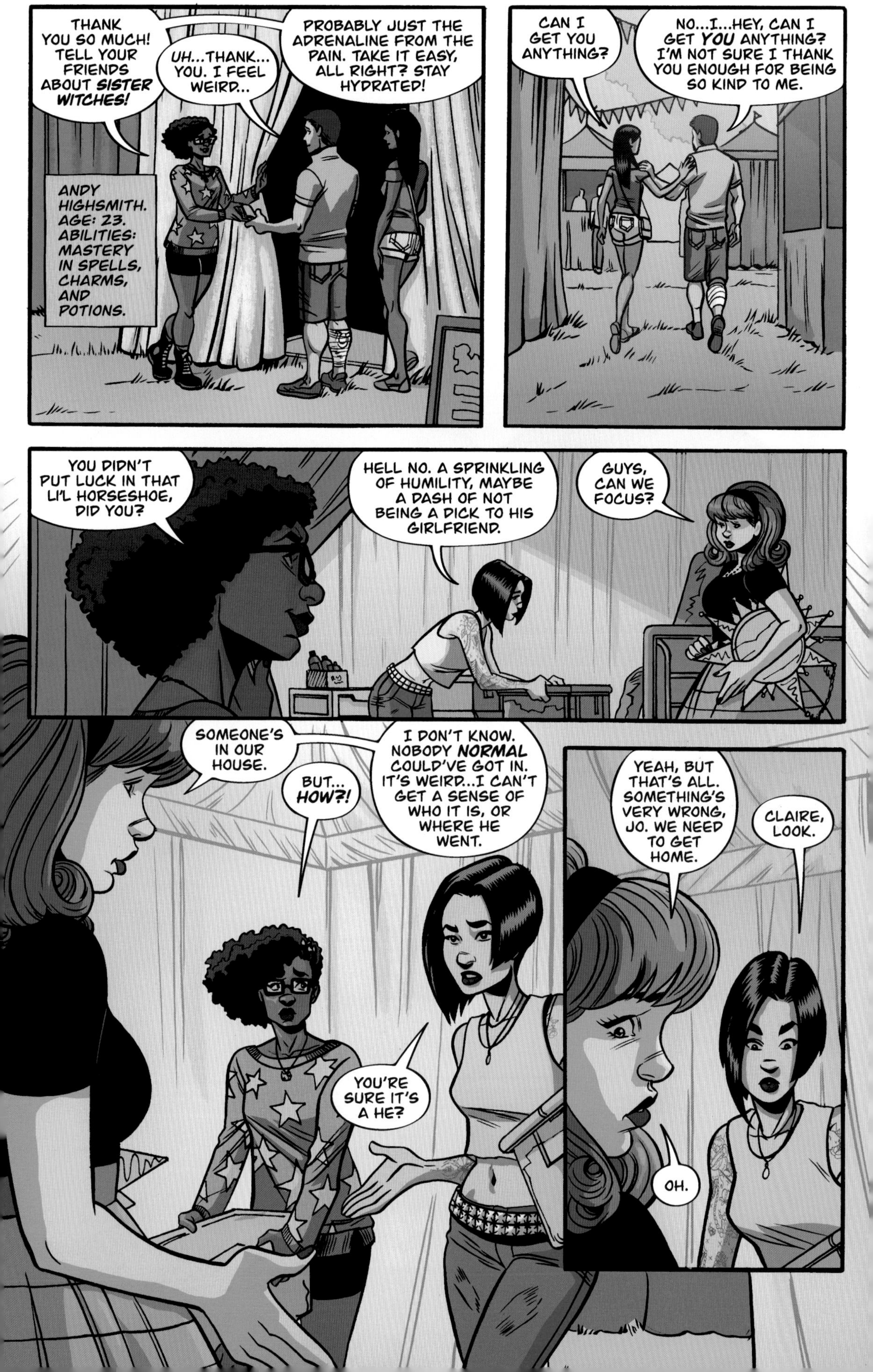
THANK YOU SO MUCH! TELL YOUR FRIENDS ABOUT SISTER WITCHES!
UH...THANK... YOU. I FEEL WEIRD...
PROBABLY JUST THE ADRENALINE FROM THE PAIN. TAKE IT EASY, ALL RIGHT? STAY HYDRATED!
ANDY HIGHSMITH. AGE: 23. ABILITIES: MASTERY IN SPELLS, CHARMS, AND POTIONS.
CAN I GET YOU ANYTHING?
NO...I...HEY, CAN I GET YOU ANYTHING? I'M NOT SURE I THANK YOU ENOUGH FOR BEING SO KIND TO ME.
YOU DIDN'T PUT LUCK IN THAT LI'L HORSESHOE, DID YOU?
HELL NO. A SPRINKLING OF HUMILITY, MAYBE A DASH OF NOT BEING A DICK TO HIS GIRLFRIEND.
GUYS, CAN WE FOCUS?
SOMEONE'S IN OUR HOUSE.
BUT... HOW?!
I DON'T KNOW. NOBODY NORMAL COULD'VE GOT IN. IT'S WEIRD...I CAN'T GET A SENSE OF WHO IT IS, OR WHERE HE WENT.
YOU'RE SURE IT'S A HE?
YEAH, BUT THAT'S ALL. SOMETHING'S VERY WRONG, JO. WE NEED TO GET HOME.
CLAIRE, LOOK.
OH.

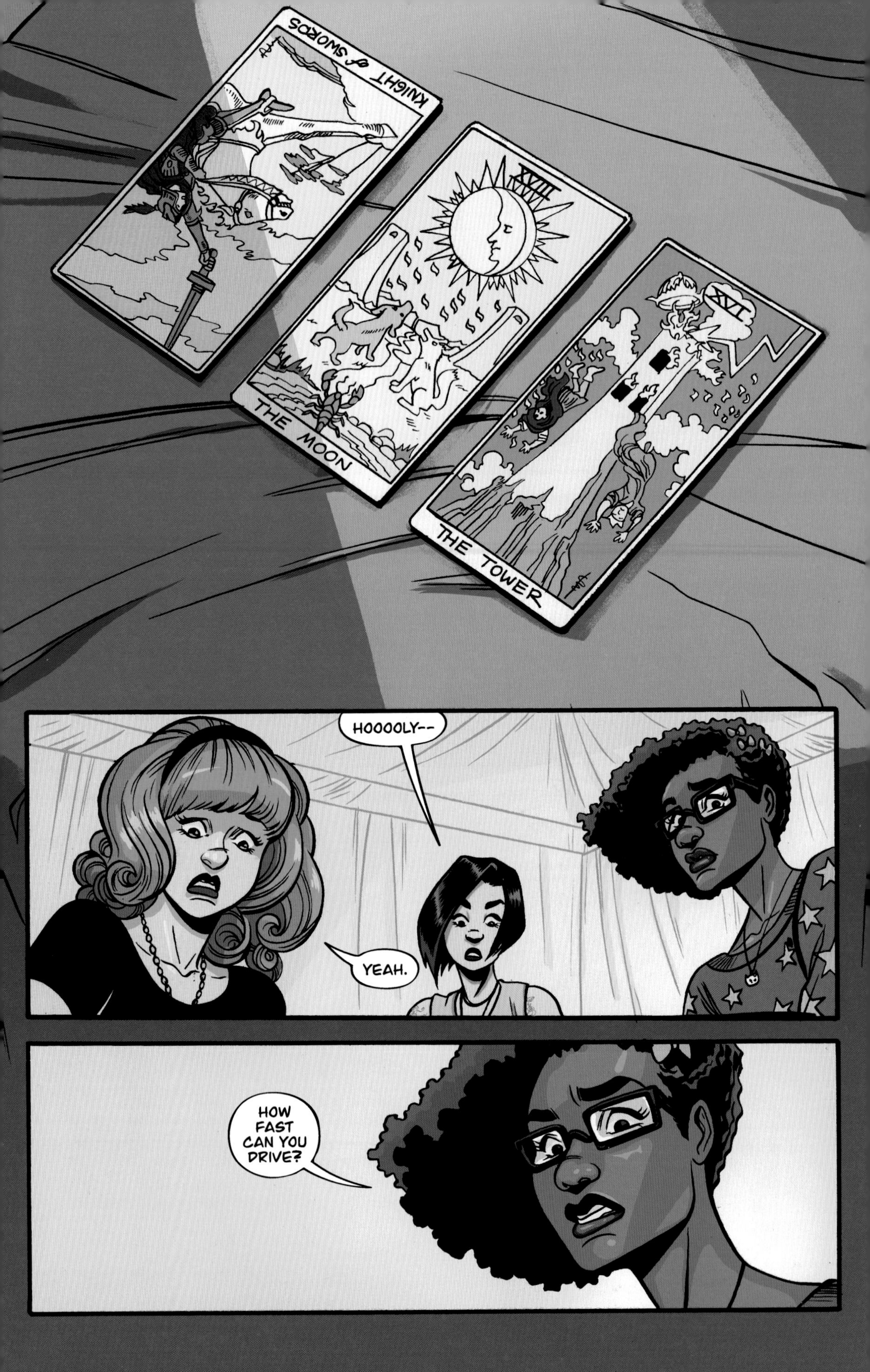
KNIGHT of SWORDS
XVIII
THE MOON
XVI
THE TOWER
HOOOOLY--
YEAH.
HOW FAST CAN YOU DRIVE?

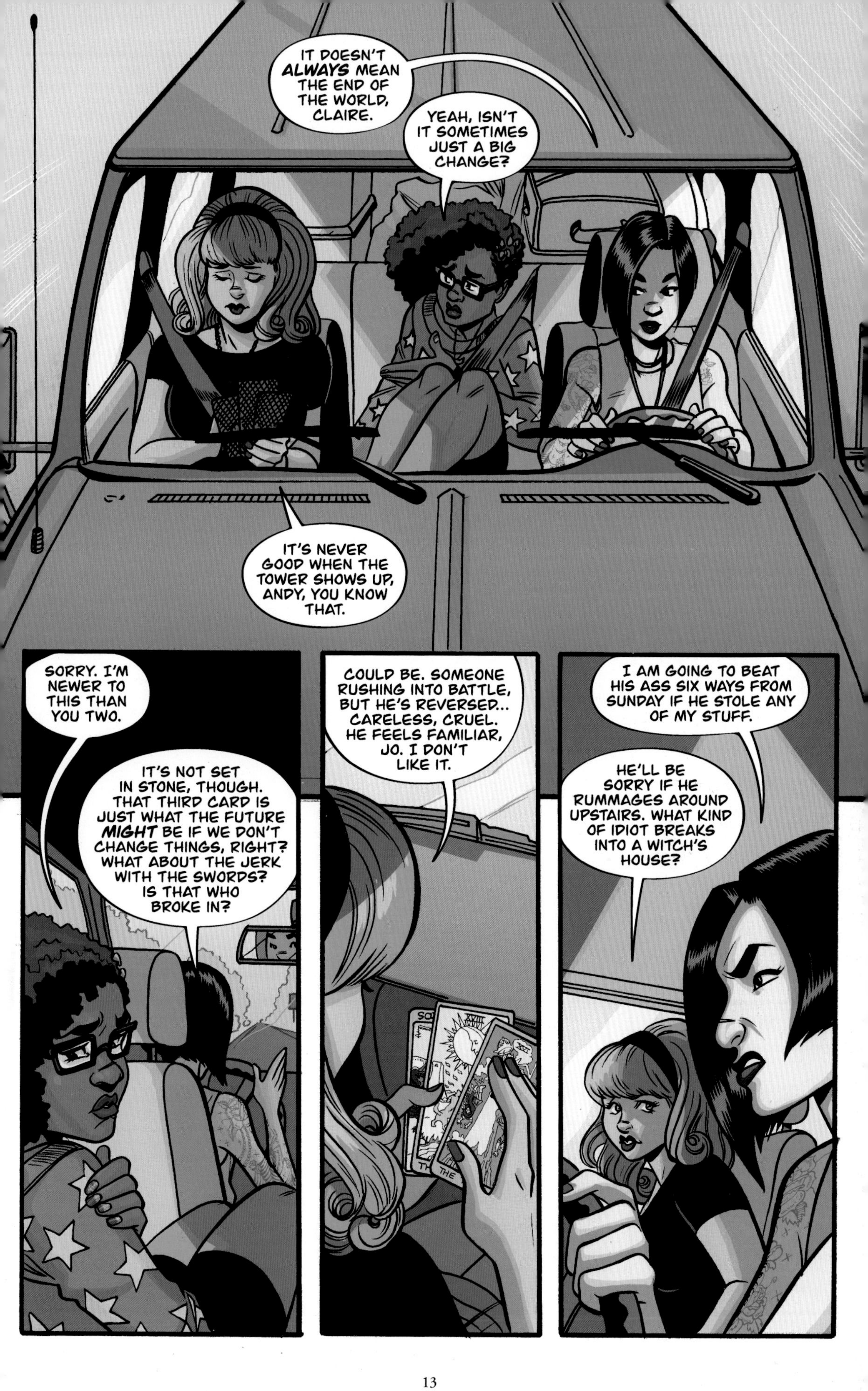
IT DOESN'T ALWAYS MEAN THE END OF THE WORLD, CLAIRE.
YEAH, ISN'T IT SOMETIMES JUST A BIG CHANGE?
IT'S NEVER GOOD WHEN THE TOWER SHOWS UP, ANDY, YOU KNOW THAT.
SORRY. I'M NEWER TO THIS THAN YOU TWO.
IT'S NOT SET IN STONE, THOUGH. THAT THIRD CARD IS JUST WHAT THE FUTURE MIGHT BE IF WE DON'T CHANGE THINGS, RIGHT? WHAT ABOUT THE JERK WITH THE SWORDS? IS THAT WHO BROKE IN?
COULD BE. SOMEONE RUSHING INTO BATTLE, BUT HE'S REVERSED... CARELESS, CRUEL. HE FEELS FAMILIAR, JO. I DON'T LIKE IT.
I AM GOING TO BEAT HIS ASS SIX WAYS FROM SUNDAY IF HE STOLE ANY OF MY STUFF.
HE'LL BE SORRY IF HE RUMMAGES AROUND UPSTAIRS. WHAT KIND OF IDIOT BREAKS INTO A WITCH'S HOUSE?

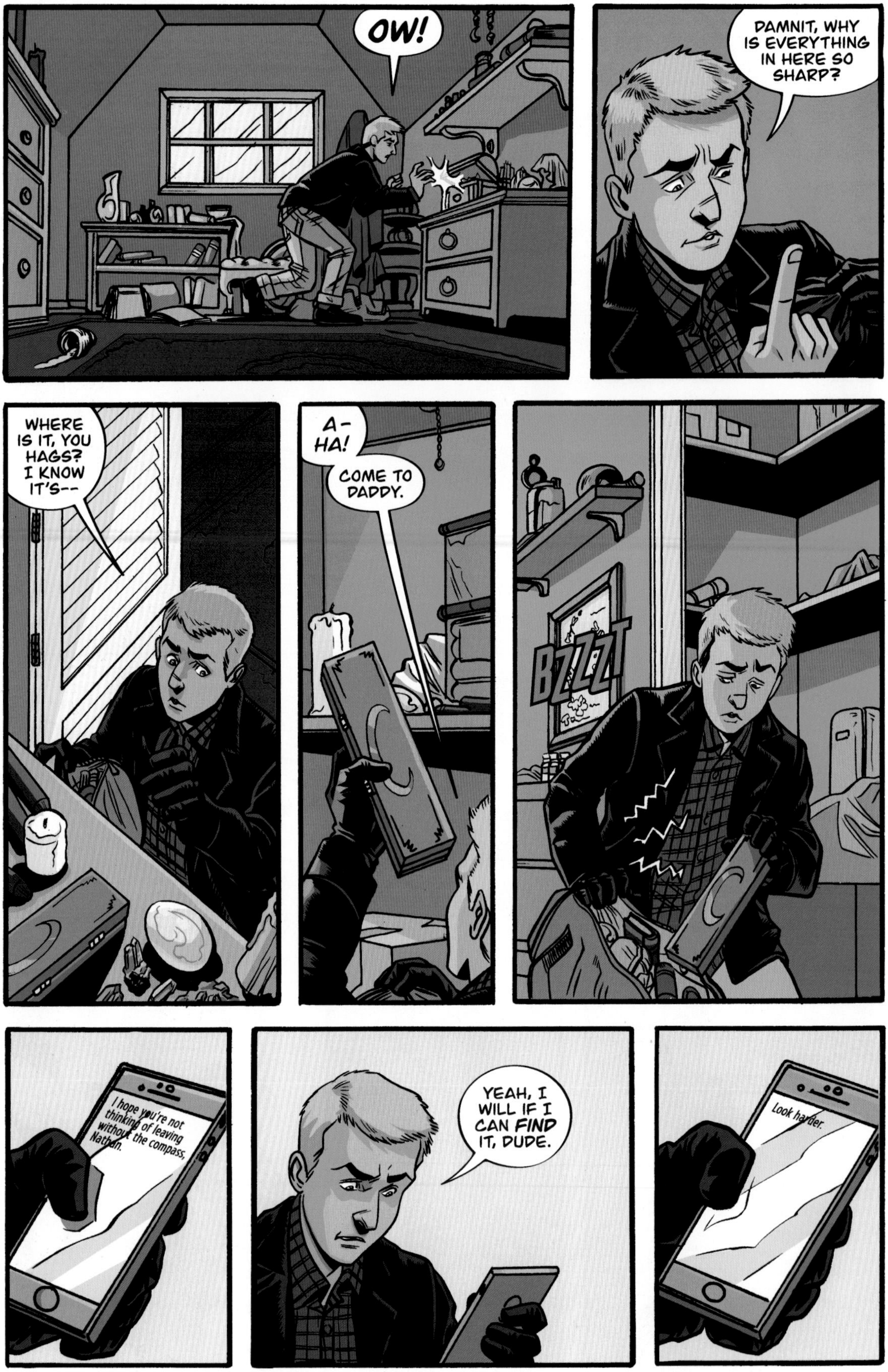
OW!
DAMNIT, WHY IS EVERYTHING IN HERE SO SHARP?
WHERE IS IT, YOU HAGS? I KNOW IT'S--
A-HA!
COME TO DADDY.
BZZZT
I hope you're not thinking of leaving without the compass, Nathan.
YEAH, I WILL IF I CAN FIND IT, DUDE.
Look harder.

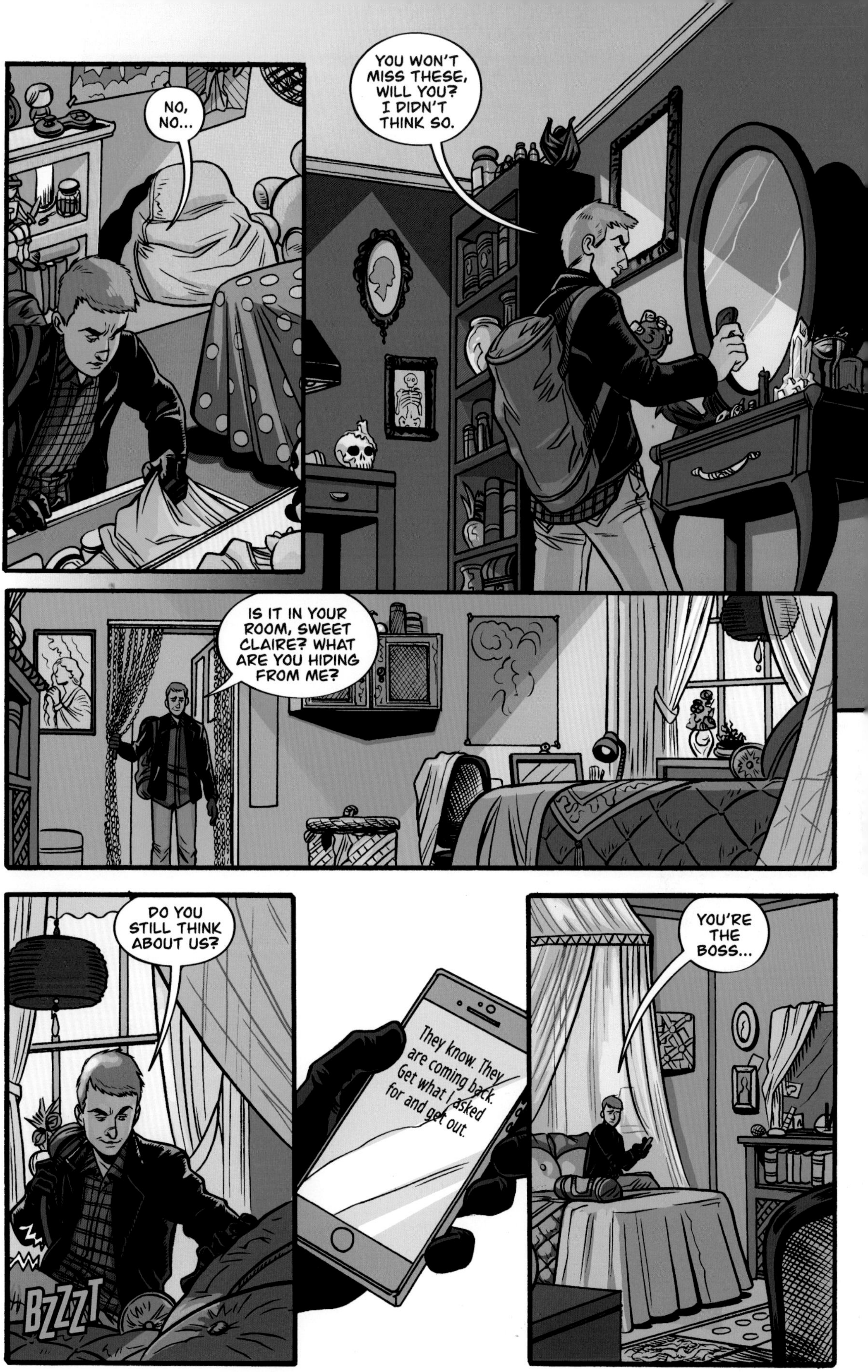
NO, NO...
YOU WON'T MISS THESE, WILL YOU? I DIDN'T THINK SO.
IS IT IN YOUR ROOM, SWEET CLAIRE? WHAT ARE YOU HIDING FROM ME?
DO YOU STILL THINK ABOUT US?
BZZZT
They know. They are coming back. Get what I asked for and get out.
YOU'RE THE BOSS...

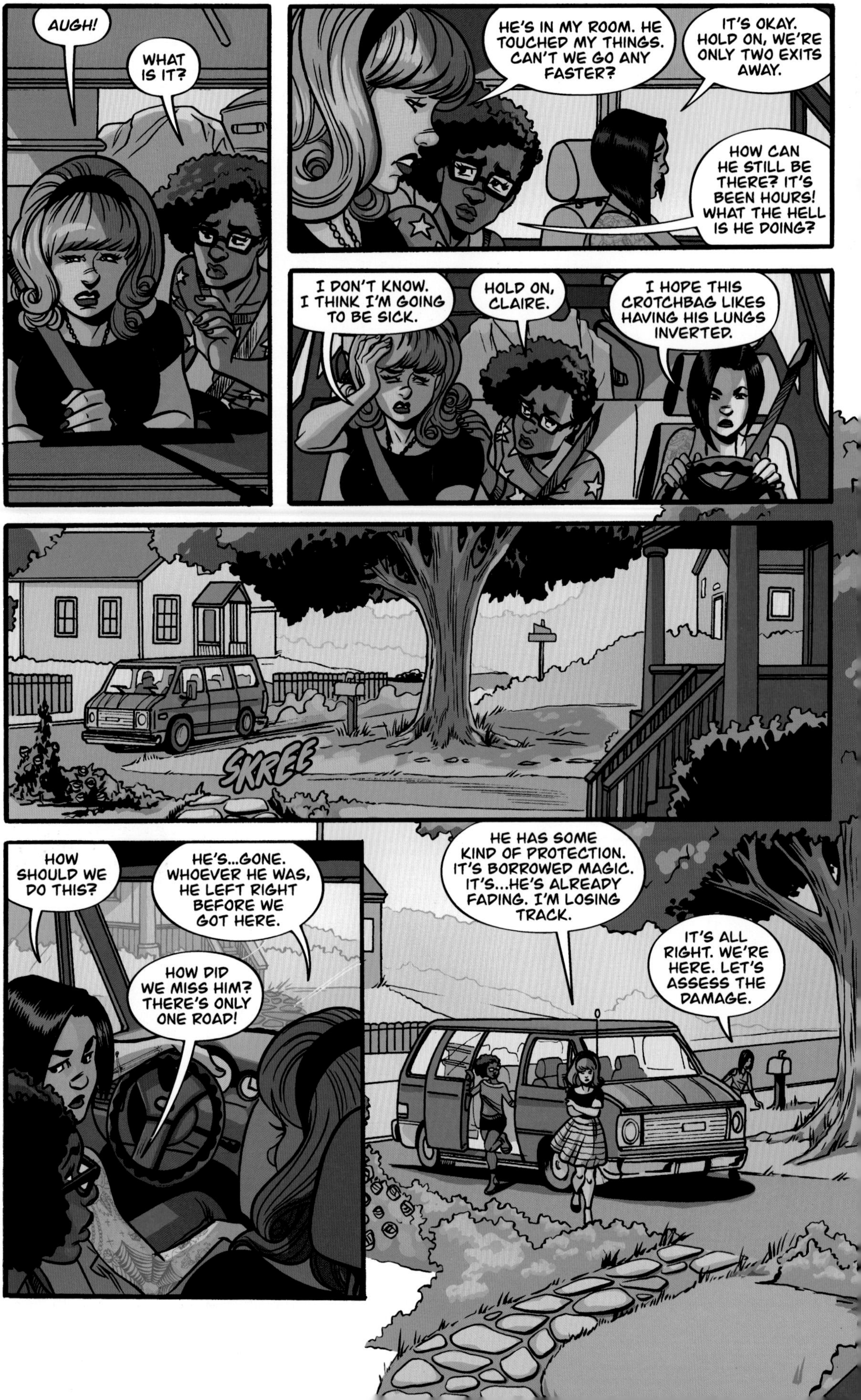
AUGH!
WHAT IS IT?
HE'S IN MY ROOM. HE TOUCHED MY THINGS. CAN'T WE GO ANY FASTER?
IT'S OKAY. HOLD ON, WE'RE ONLY TWO EXITS AWAY.
HOW CAN HE STILL BE THERE? IT'S BEEN HOURS! WHAT THE HELL IS HE DOING?
I DON'T KNOW. I THINK I'M GOING TO BE SICK.
HOLD ON, CLAIRE.
I HOPE THIS CROTCHBAG LIKES HAVING HIS LUNGS INVERTED.
SKREE
HOW SHOULD WE DO THIS?
HE'S...GONE. WHOEVER HE WAS, HE LEFT RIGHT BEFORE WE GOT HERE.
HOW DID WE MISS HIM? THERE'S ONLY ONE ROAD!
HE HAS SOME KIND OF PROTECTION. IT'S BORROWED MAGIC. IT'S...HE'S ALREADY FADING. I'M LOSING TRACK.
IT'S ALL RIGHT. WE'RE HERE. LET'S ASSESS THE DAMAGE.

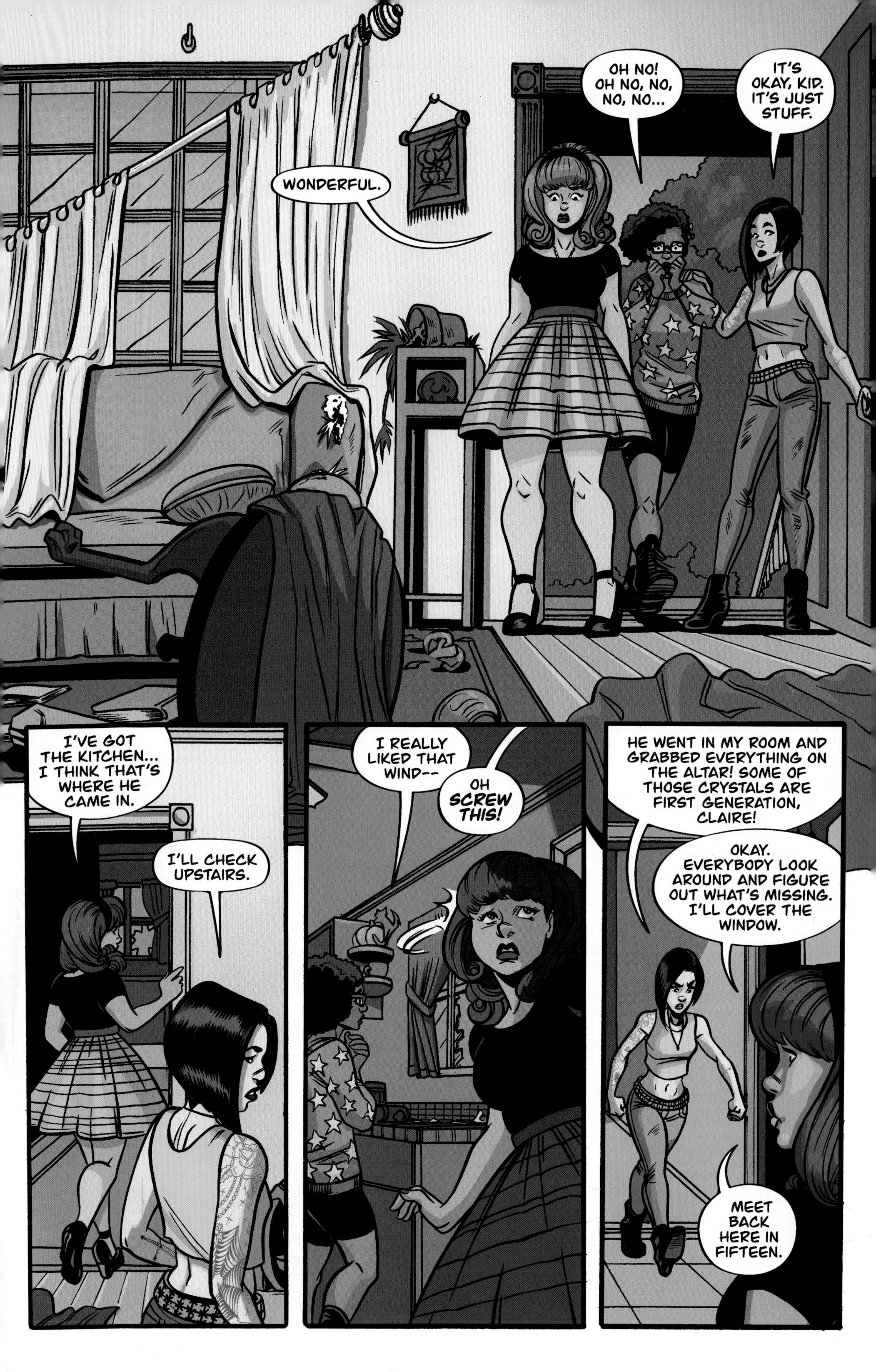
WONDERFUL.
OH NO! OH NO, NO, NO, NO...
IT'S OKAY, KID. IT'S JUST STUFF.
I'VE GOT THE KITCHEN... I THINK THAT'S WHERE HE CAME IN.
I'LL CHECK UPSTAIRS.
I REALLY LIKED THAT WIND--
OH SCREW THIS!
HE WENT IN MY ROOM AND GRABBED EVERYTHING ON THE ALTAR! SOME OF THOSE CRYSTALS ARE FIRST GENERATION, CLAIRE!
OKAY. EVERYBODY LOOK AROUND AND FIGURE OUT WHAT'S MISSING. I'LL COVER THE WINDOW.
MEET BACK HERE IN FIFTEEN.

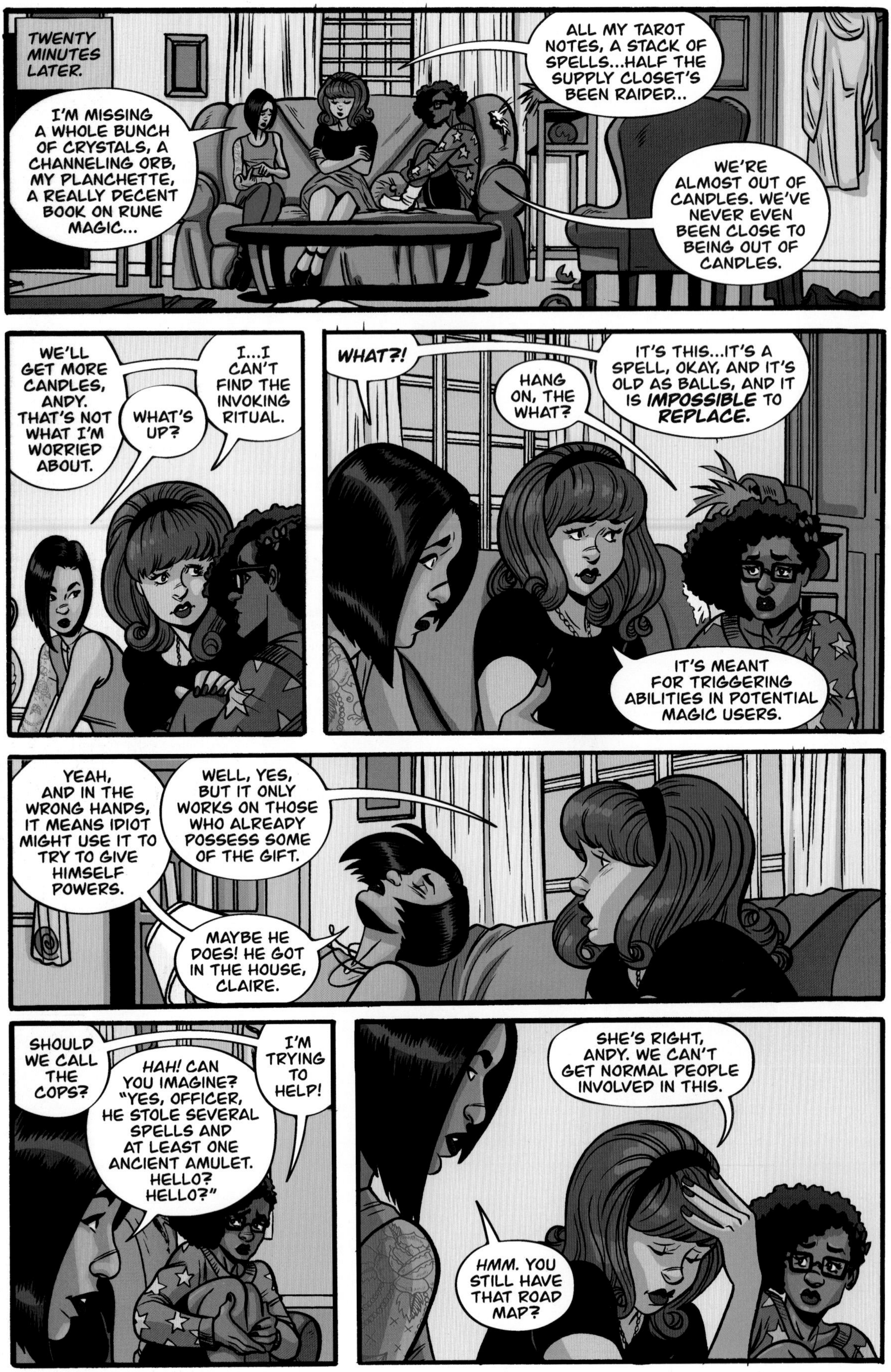
TWENTY MINUTES LATER.
I'M MISSING A WHOLE BUNCH OF CRYSTALS, A CHANNELING ORB, MY PLANCHETTE, A REALLY DECENT BOOK ON RUNE MAGIC...
ALL MY TAROT NOTES, A STACK OF SPELLS...HALF THE SUPPLY CLOSET'S BEEN RAIDED...
WE'RE ALMOST OUT OF CANDLES. WE'VE NEVER EVEN BEEN CLOSE TO BEING OUT OF CANDLES.
WE'LL GET MORE CANDLES, ANDY. THAT'S NOT WHAT I'M WORRIED ABOUT.
WHAT'S UP?
I...I CAN'T FIND THE INVOKING RITUAL.
WHAT?!
HANG ON, THE WHAT?
IT'S THIS...IT'S A SPELL, OKAY, AND IT'S OLD AS BALLS, AND IT IS IMPOSSIBLE TO REPLACE.
IT'S MEANT FOR TRIGGERING ABILITIES IN POTENTIAL MAGIC USERS.
YEAH, AND IN THE WRONG HANDS, IT MEANS IDIOT MIGHT USE IT TO TRY TO GIVE HIMSELF POWERS.
WELL, YES, BUT IT ONLY WORKS ON THOSE WHO ALREADY POSSESS SOME OF THE GIFT.
MAYBE HE DOES! HE GOT IN THE HOUSE, CLAIRE.
SHOULD WE CALL THE COPS?
HAH! CAN YOU IMAGINE? "YES, OFFICER, HE STOLE SEVERAL SPELLS AND AT LEAST ONE ANCIENT AMULET. HELLO? HELLO?"
I'M TRYING TO HELP!
SHE'S RIGHT, ANDY. WE CAN'T GET NORMAL PEOPLE INVOLVED IN THIS.
HMM. YOU STILL HAVE THAT ROAD MAP?

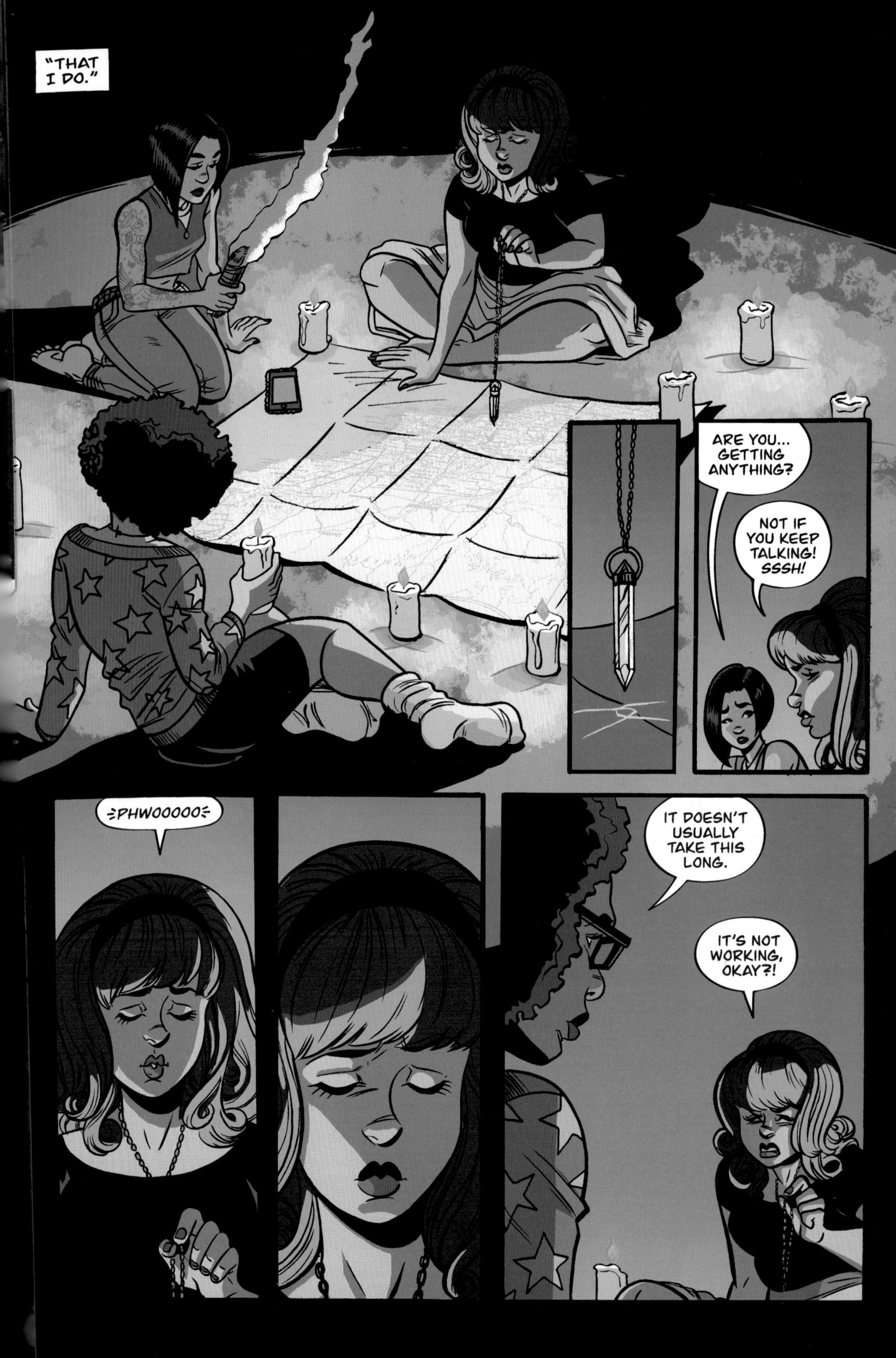
"THAT I DO."
ARE YOU... GETTING ANYTHING?
NOT IF YOU KEEP TALKING! SSSH!
PHWOOOOO
IT DOESN'T USUALLY TAKE THIS LONG.
IT'S NOT WORKING, OKAY?!

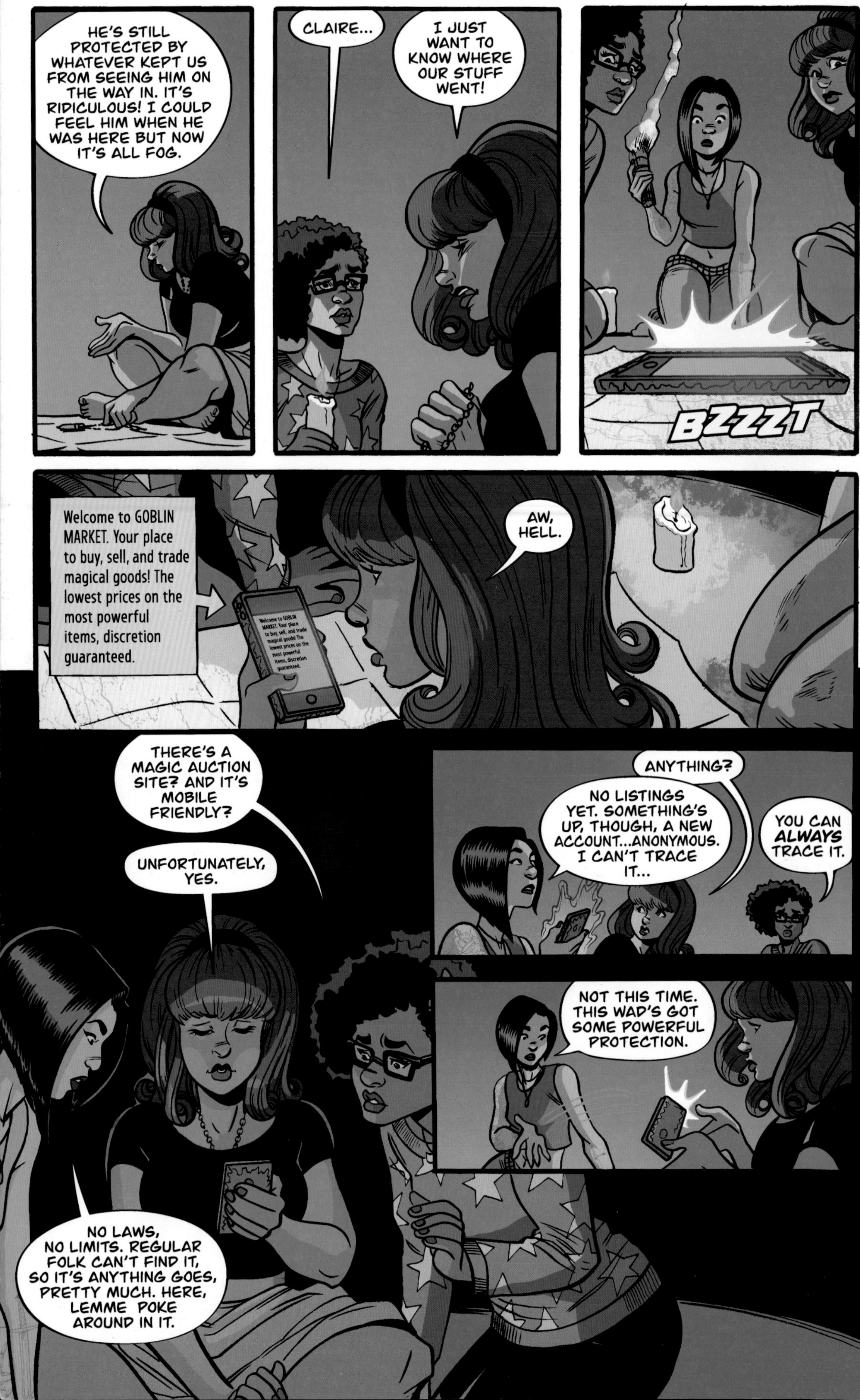
HE'S STILL PROTECTED BY WHATEVER KEPT US FROM SEEING HIM ON THE WAY IN. IT'S RIDICULOUS! I COULD FEEL HIM WHEN HE WAS HERE BUT NOW IT'S ALL FOG.
CLAIRE...
I JUST WANT TO KNOW WHERE OUR STUFF WENT!
BZZZT
Welcome to GOBLIN MARKET. Your place to buy, sell, and trade magical goods! The lowest prices on the most powerful items, discretion guaranteed.
AW, HELL.
THERE'S A MAGIC AUCTION SITE? AND IT'S MOBILE FRIENDLY?
UNFORTUNATELY, YES.
NO LAWS, NO LIMITS. REGULAR FOLK CAN'T FIND IT, SO IT'S ANYTHING GOES, PRETTY MUCH. HERE, LEMME POKE AROUND IN IT.
ANYTHING?
NO LISTINGS YET. SOMETHING'S UP, THOUGH, A NEW ACCOUNT...ANONYMOUS. I CAN'T TRACE IT...
YOU CAN ALWAYS TRACE IT.
NOT THIS TIME. THIS WAD'S GOT SOME POWERFUL PROTECTION.

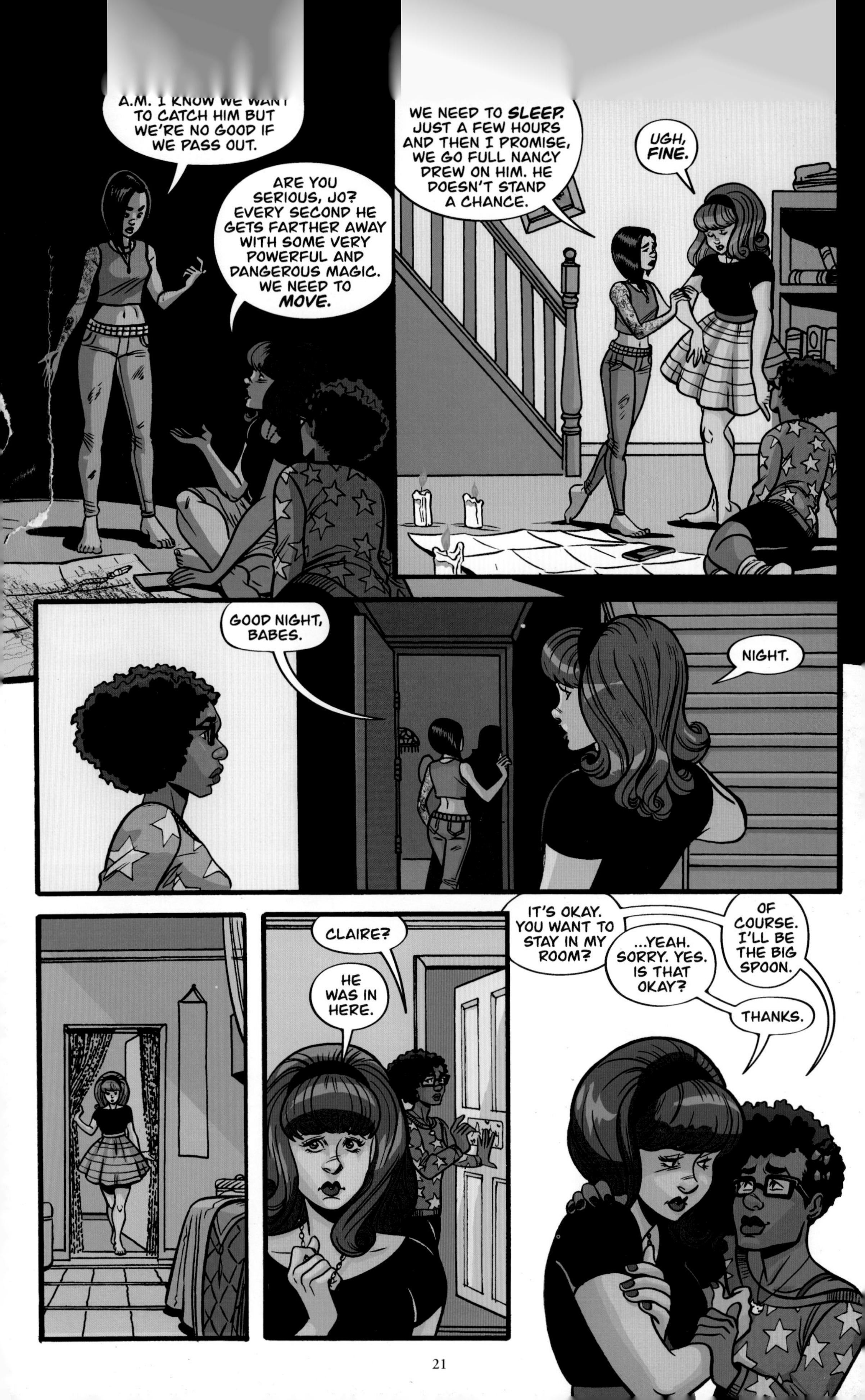
A.M. I KNOW WE WANT TO CATCH HIM BUT WE'RE NO GOOD IF WE PASS OUT.
ARE YOU SERIOUS, JO? EVERY SECOND HE GETS FARTHER AWAY WITH SOME VERY POWERFUL AND DANGEROUS MAGIC. WE NEED TO **MOVE.**
WE NEED TO **SLEEP.** JUST A FEW HOURS AND THEN I PROMISE, WE GO FULL NANCY DREW ON HIM. HE DOESN'T STAND A CHANCE.
UGH, **FINE.**
GOOD NIGHT, BABES.
NIGHT.
CLAIRE?
HE WAS IN HERE.
IT'S OKAY. YOU WANT TO STAY IN MY ROOM?
...YEAH. SORRY. YES. IS THAT OKAY?
OF COURSE. I'LL BE THE BIG SPOON.
THANKS.

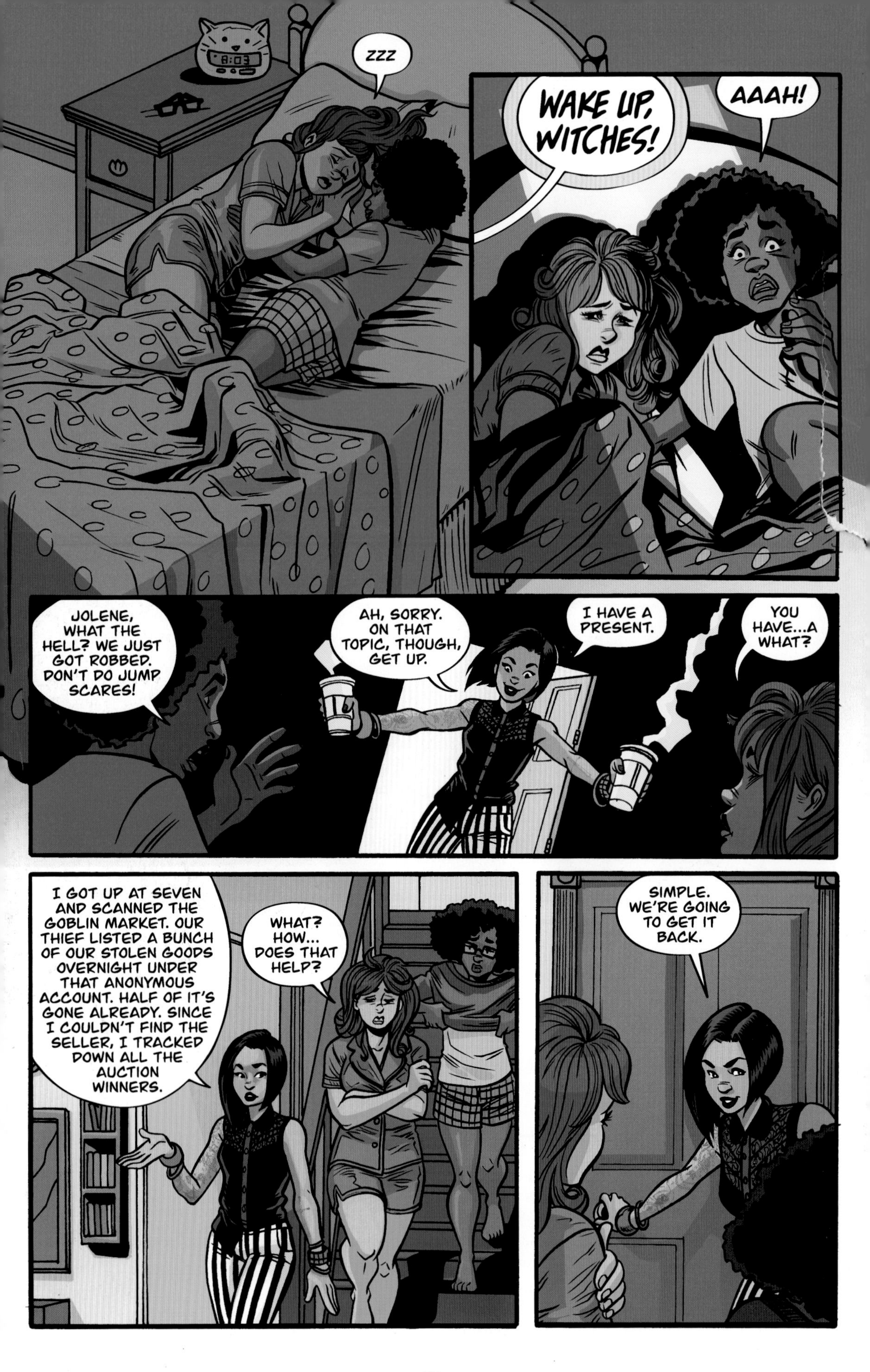

ZZZ
WAKE UP, WITCHES!
AAAH!
JOLENE, WHAT THE HELL? WE JUST GOT ROBBED. DON'T DO JUMP SCARES!
AH, SORRY. ON THAT TOPIC, THOUGH, GET UP.
I HAVE A PRESENT.
YOU HAVE...A WHAT?
I GOT UP AT SEVEN AND SCANNED THE GOBLIN MARKET. OUR THIEF LISTED A BUNCH OF OUR STOLEN GOODS OVERNIGHT UNDER THAT ANONYMOUS ACCOUNT. HALF OF IT'S GONE ALREADY. SINCE I COULDN'T FIND THE SELLER, I TRACKED DOWN ALL THE AUCTION WINNERS.
WHAT? HOW... DOES THAT HELP?
SIMPLE. WE'RE GOING TO GET IT BACK.

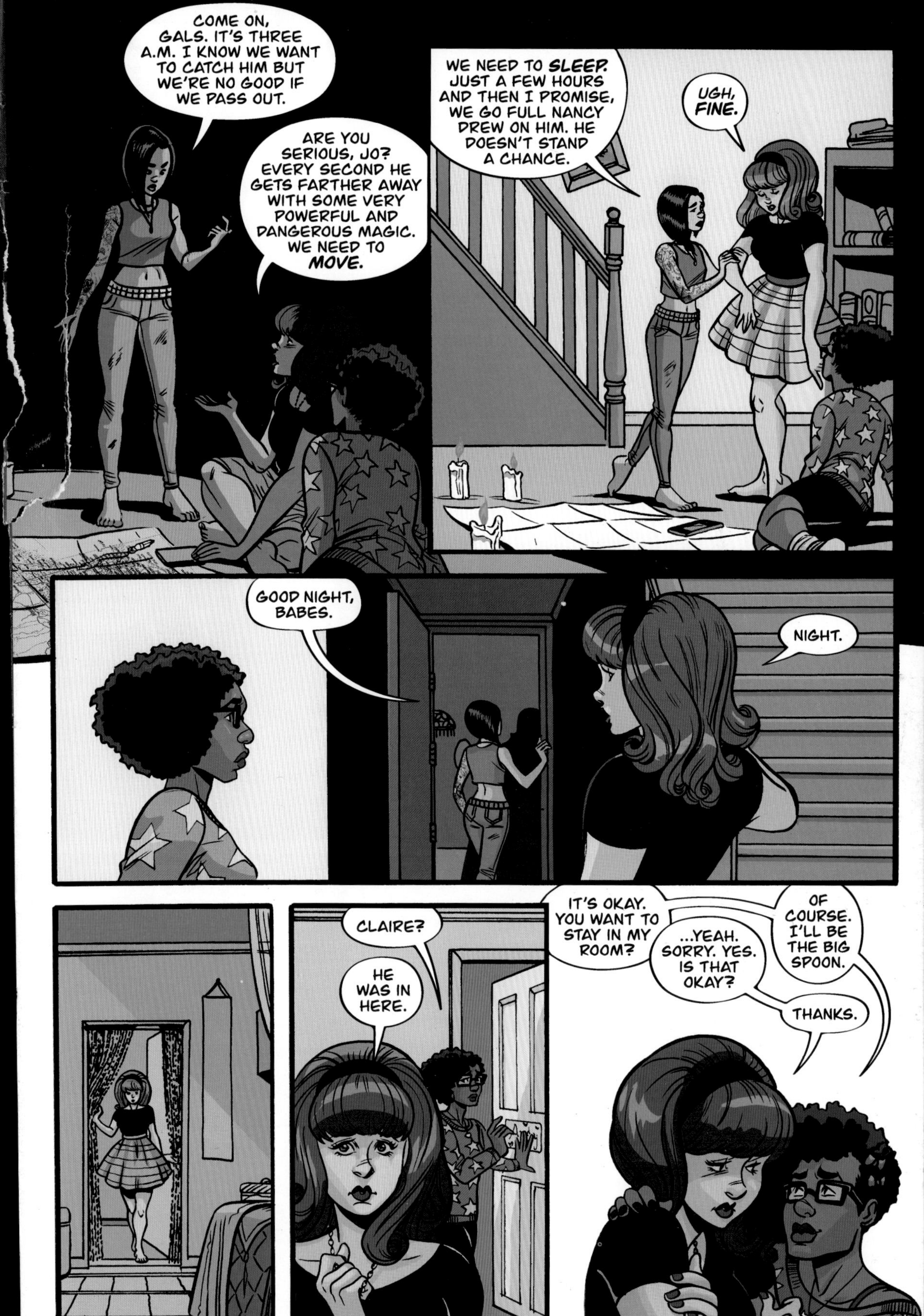
COME ON, GALS. IT'S THREE A.M. I KNOW WE WANT TO CATCH HIM BUT WE'RE NO GOOD IF WE PASS OUT.
ARE YOU SERIOUS, JO? EVERY SECOND HE GETS FARTHER AWAY WITH SOME VERY POWERFUL AND DANGEROUS MAGIC. WE NEED TO MOVE.
WE NEED TO SLEEP. JUST A FEW HOURS AND THEN I PROMISE, WE GO FULL NANCY DREW ON HIM. HE DOESN'T STAND A CHANCE.
UGH, FINE.
GOOD NIGHT, BABES.
NIGHT.
CLAIRE?
HE WAS IN HERE.
IT'S OKAY. YOU WANT TO STAY IN MY ROOM?
...YEAH. SORRY. YES. IS THAT OKAY?
OF COURSE. I'LL BE THE BIG SPOON.
THANKS.

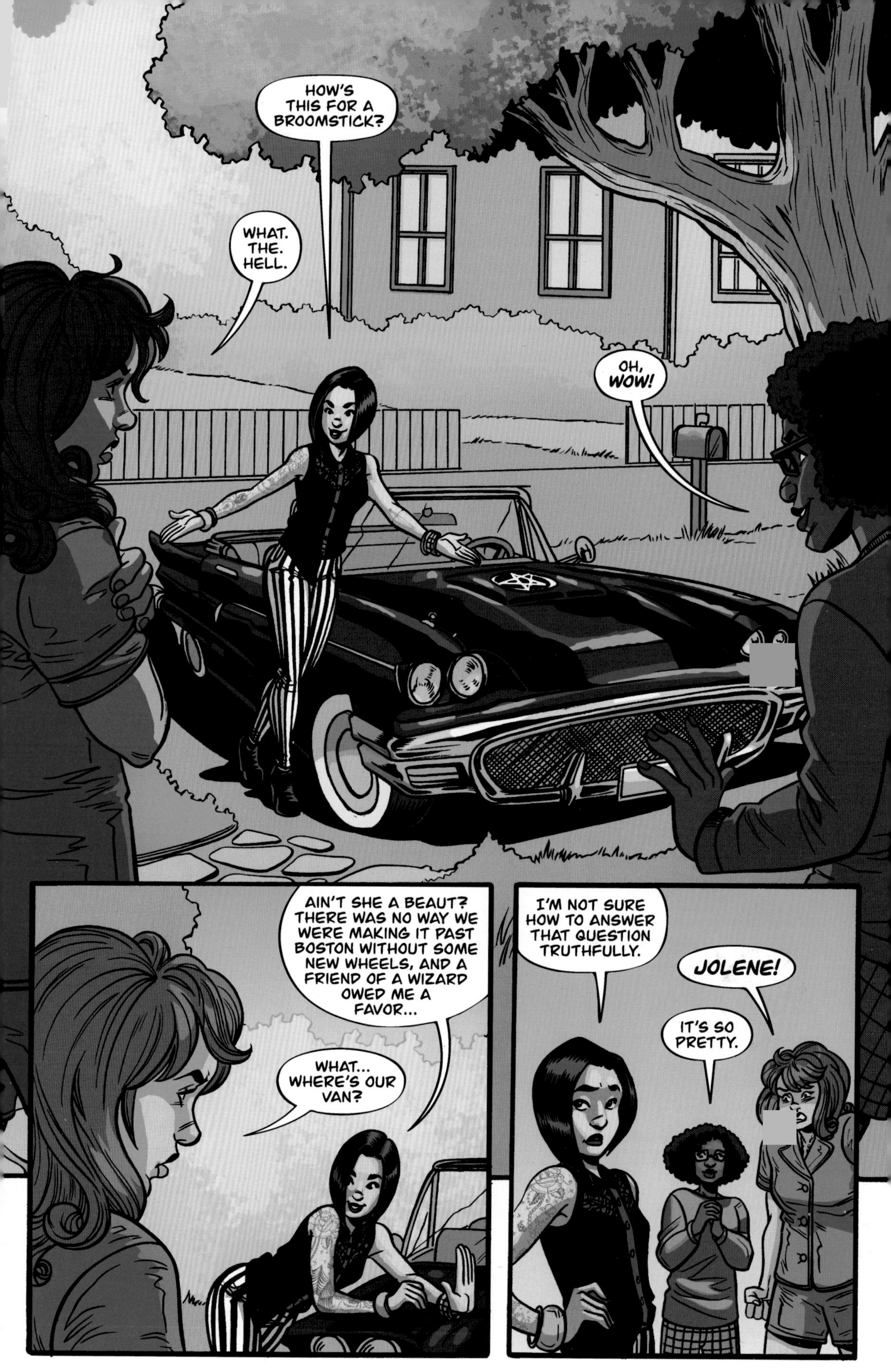
HOW'S THIS FOR A BROOMSTICK?
WHAT. THE. HELL.
OH, WOW!
AIN'T SHE A BEAUT? THERE WAS NO WAY WE WERE MAKING IT PAST BOSTON WITHOUT SOME NEW WHEELS, AND A FRIEND OF A WIZARD OWED ME A FAVOR...
WHAT... WHERE'S OUR VAN?
I'M NOT SURE HOW TO ANSWER THAT QUESTION TRUTHFULLY.
JOLENE!
IT'S SO PRETTY.

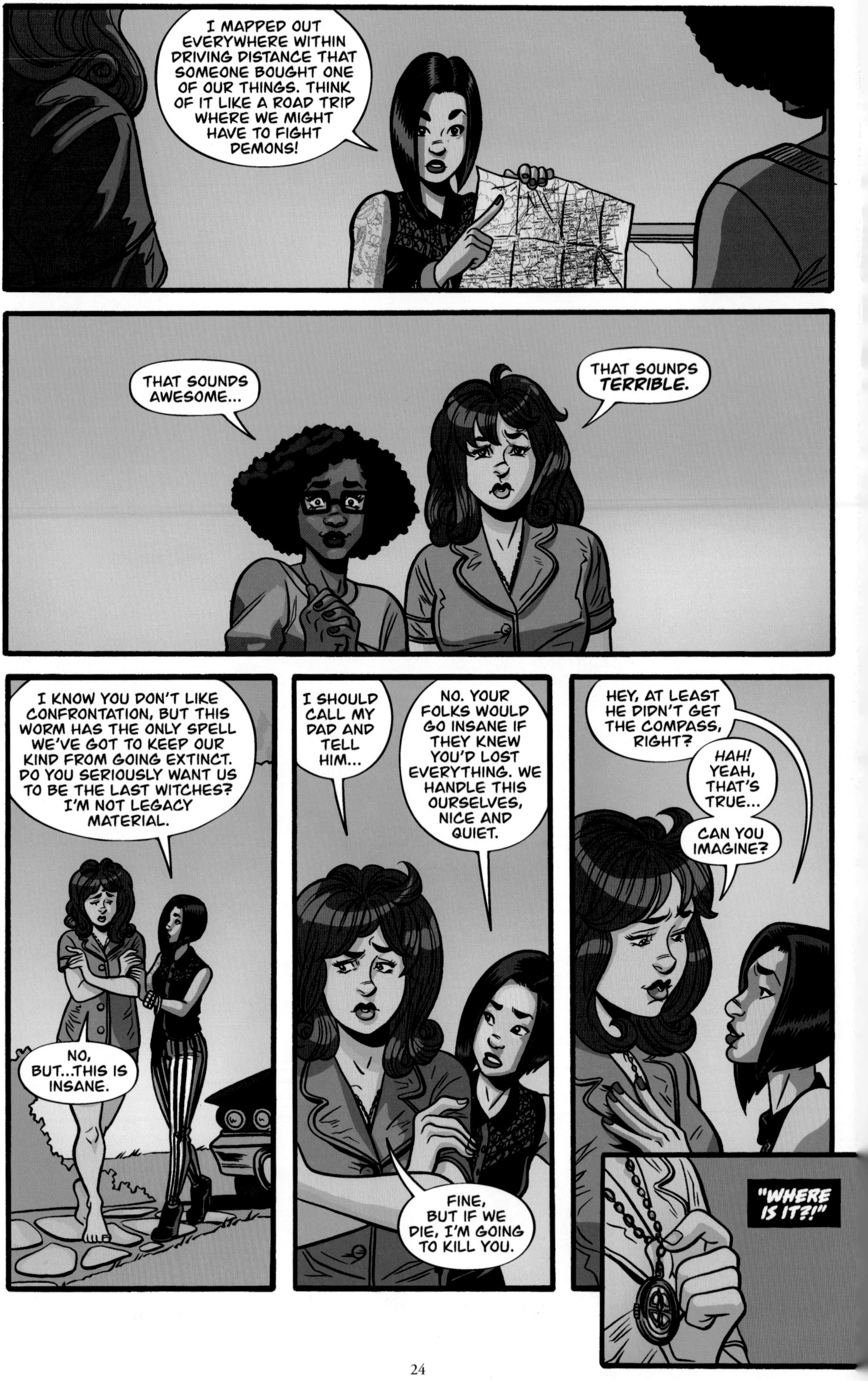
I MAPPED OUT EVERYWHERE WITHIN DRIVING DISTANCE THAT SOMEONE BOUGHT ONE OF OUR THINGS. THINK OF IT LIKE A ROAD TRIP WHERE WE MIGHT HAVE TO FIGHT DEMONS!
THAT SOUNDS AWESOME...
THAT SOUNDS TERRIBLE.
I KNOW YOU DON'T LIKE CONFRONTATION, BUT THIS WORM HAS THE ONLY SPELL WE'VE GOT TO KEEP OUR KIND FROM GOING EXTINCT. DO YOU SERIOUSLY WANT US TO BE THE LAST WITCHES? I'M NOT LEGACY MATERIAL.
NO, BUT...THIS IS INSANE.
I SHOULD CALL MY DAD AND TELL HIM...
NO. YOUR FOLKS WOULD GO INSANE IF THEY KNEW YOU'D LOST EVERYTHING. WE HANDLE THIS OURSELVES, NICE AND QUIET.
FINE, BUT IF WE DIE, I'M GOING TO KILL YOU.
HEY, AT LEAST HE DIDN'T GET THE COMPASS, RIGHT?
HAH! YEAH, THAT'S TRUE...
CAN YOU IMAGINE?
"WHERE IS IT?!"

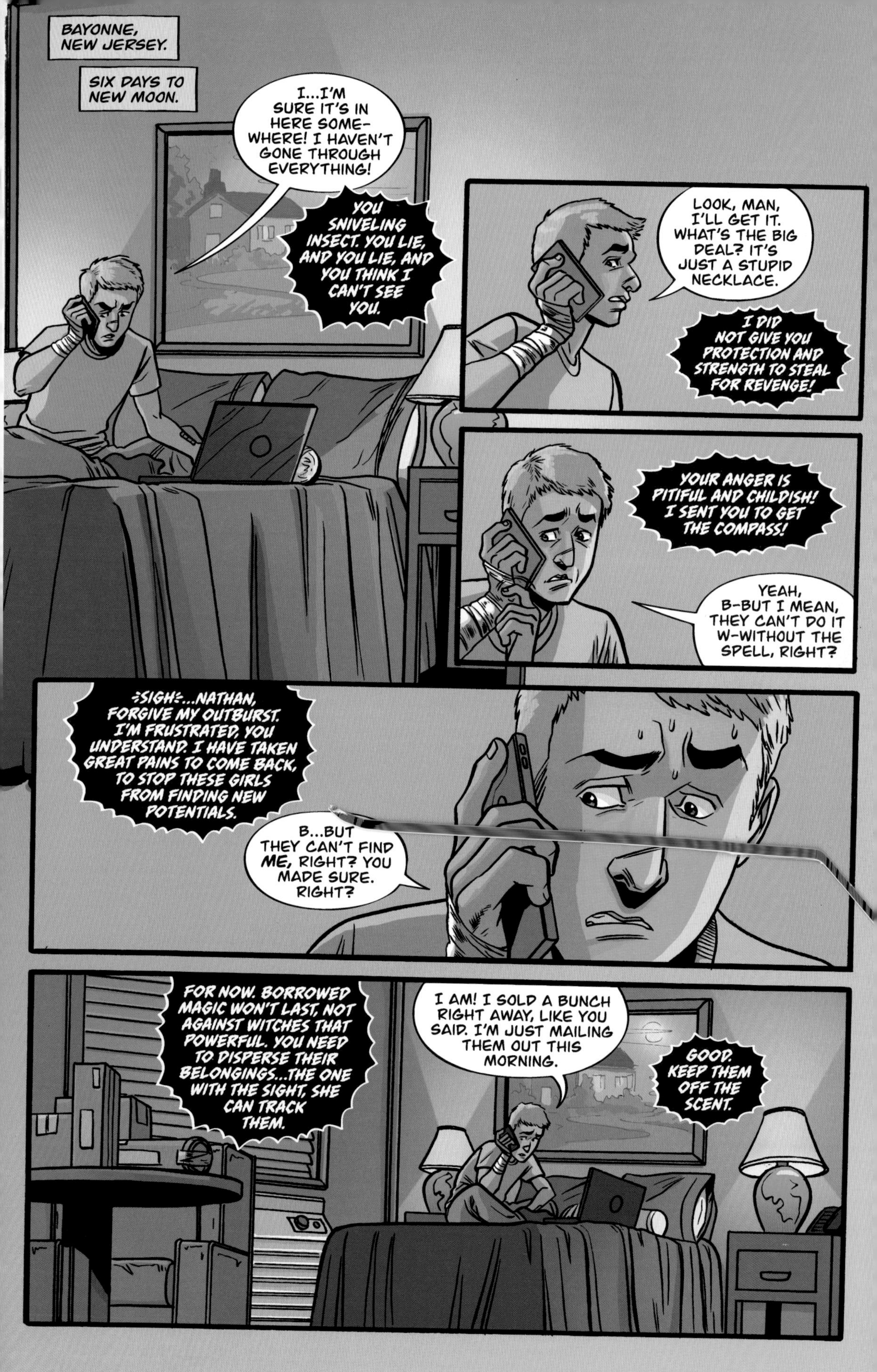
BAYONNE, NEW JERSEY.
SIX DAYS TO NEW MOON.
I...I'M SURE IT'S IN HERE SOME-WHERE! I HAVEN'T GONE THROUGH EVERYTHING!
YOU SNIVELING INSECT. YOU LIE, AND YOU LIE, AND YOU THINK I CAN'T SEE YOU.
LOOK, MAN, I'LL GET IT. WHAT'S THE BIG DEAL? IT'S JUST A STUPID NECKLACE.
I DID NOT GIVE YOU PROTECTION AND STRENGTH TO STEAL FOR REVENGE!
YOUR ANGER IS PITIFUL AND CHILDISH! I SENT YOU TO GET THE COMPASS!
YEAH, B-BUT I MEAN, THEY CAN'T DO IT W-WITHOUT THE SPELL, RIGHT?
SIGH...NATHAN, FORGIVE MY OUTBURST. I'M FRUSTRATED, YOU UNDERSTAND. I HAVE TAKEN GREAT PAINS TO COME BACK, TO STOP THESE GIRLS FROM FINDING NEW POTENTIALS.
B...BUT THEY CAN'T FIND ME, RIGHT? YOU MADE SURE. RIGHT?
FOR NOW. BORROWED MAGIC WON'T LAST, NOT AGAINST WITCHES THAT POWERFUL. YOU NEED TO DISPERSE THEIR BELONGINGS...THE ONE WITH THE SIGHT, SHE CAN TRACK THEM.
I AM! I SOLD A BUNCH RIGHT AWAY, LIKE YOU SAID. I'M JUST MAILING THEM OUT THIS MORNING.
GOOD. KEEP THEM OFF THE SCENT.

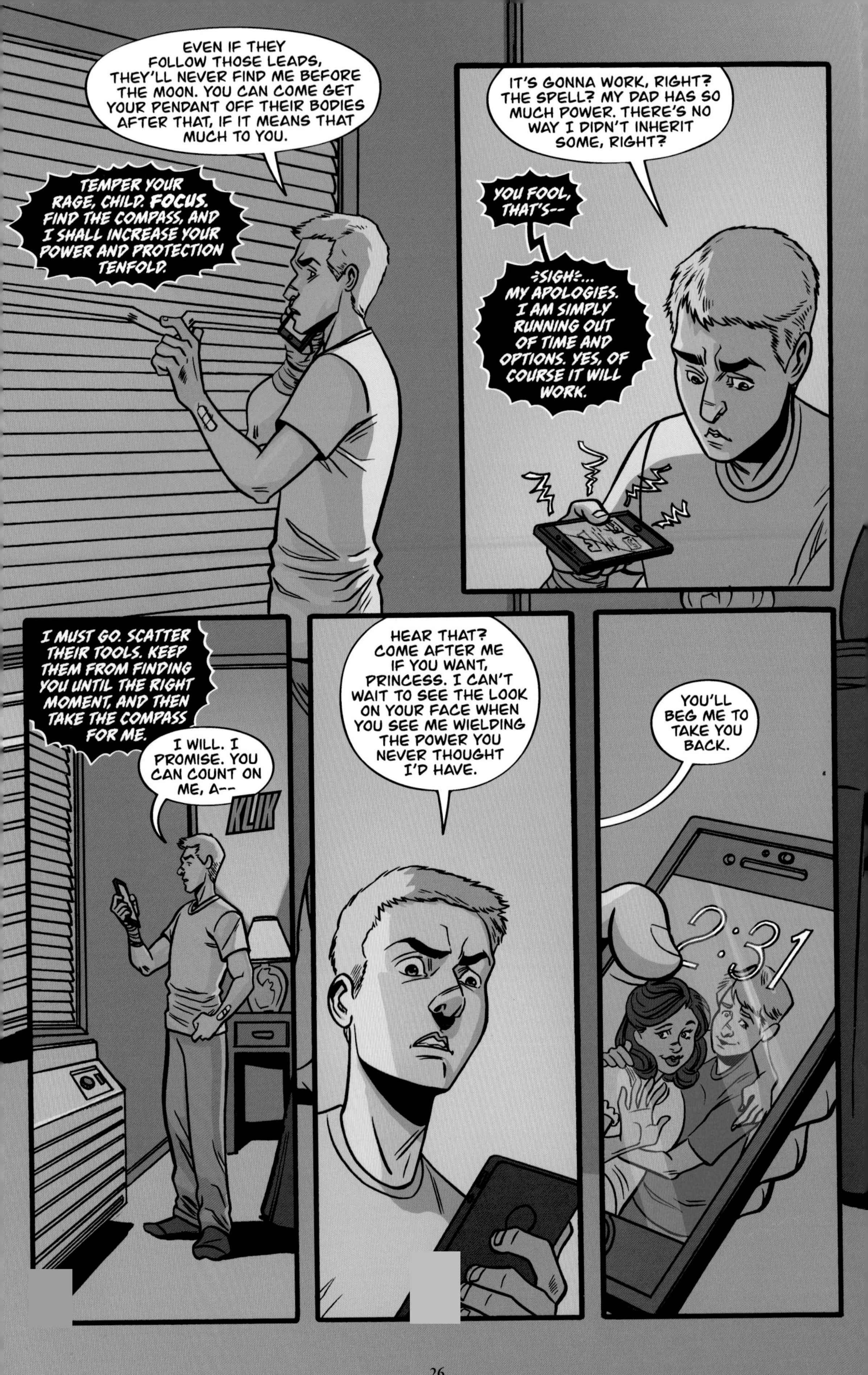
EVEN IF THEY FOLLOW THOSE LEADS, THEY'LL NEVER FIND ME BEFORE THE MOON. YOU CAN COME GET YOUR PENDANT OFF THEIR BODIES AFTER THAT, IF IT MEANS THAT MUCH TO YOU.
TEMPER YOUR RAGE, CHILD. FOCUS. FIND THE COMPASS, AND I SHALL INCREASE YOUR POWER AND PROTECTION TENFOLD.
IT'S GONNA WORK, RIGHT? THE SPELL? MY DAD HAS SO MUCH POWER. THERE'S NO WAY I DIDN'T INHERIT SOME, RIGHT?
YOU FOOL, THAT'S--
=SIGH=... MY APOLOGIES. I AM SIMPLY RUNNING OUT OF TIME AND OPTIONS. YES, OF COURSE IT WILL WORK.
I MUST GO. SCATTER THEIR TOOLS. KEEP THEM FROM FINDING YOU UNTIL THE RIGHT MOMENT, AND THEN TAKE THE COMPASS FOR ME.
I WILL. I PROMISE. YOU CAN COUNT ON ME, A--
KLIK
HEAR THAT? COME AFTER ME IF YOU WANT, PRINCESS. I CAN'T WAIT TO SEE THE LOOK ON YOUR FACE WHEN YOU SEE ME WIELDING THE POWER YOU NEVER THOUGHT I'D HAVE.
YOU'LL BEG ME TO TAKE YOU BACK.
2:31

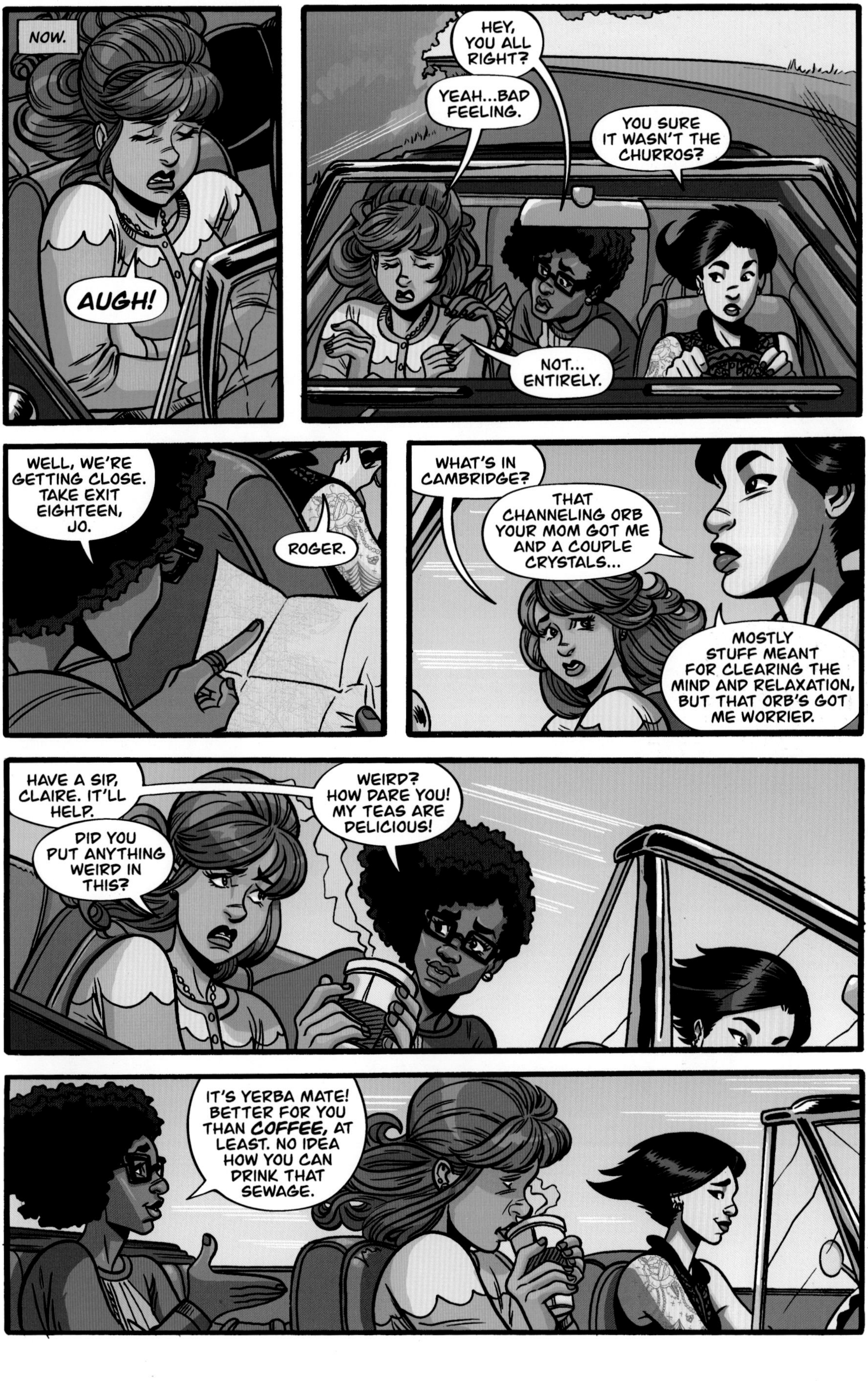
NOW.
AUGH!
HEY, YOU ALL RIGHT?
YEAH...BAD FEELING.
YOU SURE IT WASN'T THE CHURROS?
NOT... ENTIRELY.
WELL, WE'RE GETTING CLOSE. TAKE EXIT EIGHTEEN, JO.
ROGER.
WHAT'S IN CAMBRIDGE?
THAT CHANNELING ORB YOUR MOM GOT ME AND A COUPLE CRYSTALS...
MOSTLY STUFF MEANT FOR CLEARING THE MIND AND RELAXATION, BUT THAT ORB'S GOT ME WORRIED.
HAVE A SIP, CLAIRE. IT'LL HELP.
DID YOU PUT ANYTHING WEIRD IN THIS?
WEIRD? HOW DARE YOU! MY TEAS ARE DELICIOUS!
IT'S YERBA MATE! BETTER FOR YOU THAN COFFEE, AT LEAST. NO IDEA HOW YOU CAN DRINK THAT SEWAGE.

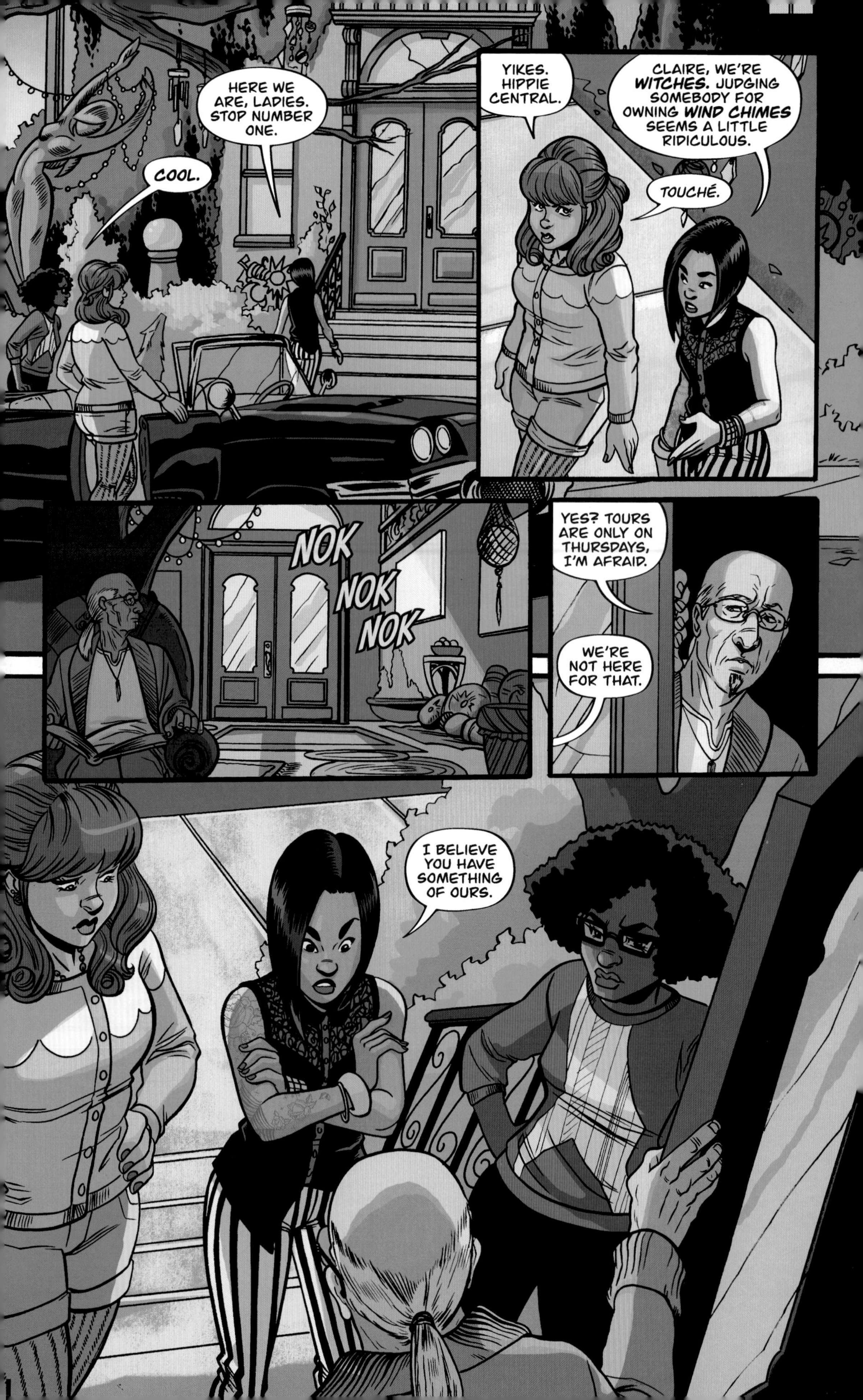
HERE WE ARE, LADIES. STOP NUMBER ONE.
COOL.
YIKES. HIPPIE CENTRAL.
CLAIRE, WE'RE WITCHES. JUDGING SOMEBODY FOR OWNING WIND CHIMES SEEMS A LITTLE RIDICULOUS.
TOUCHÉ.
NOK NOK NOK
YES? TOURS ARE ONLY ON THURSDAYS, I'M AFRAID.
WE'RE NOT HERE FOR THAT.
I BELIEVE YOU HAVE SOMETHING OF OURS.

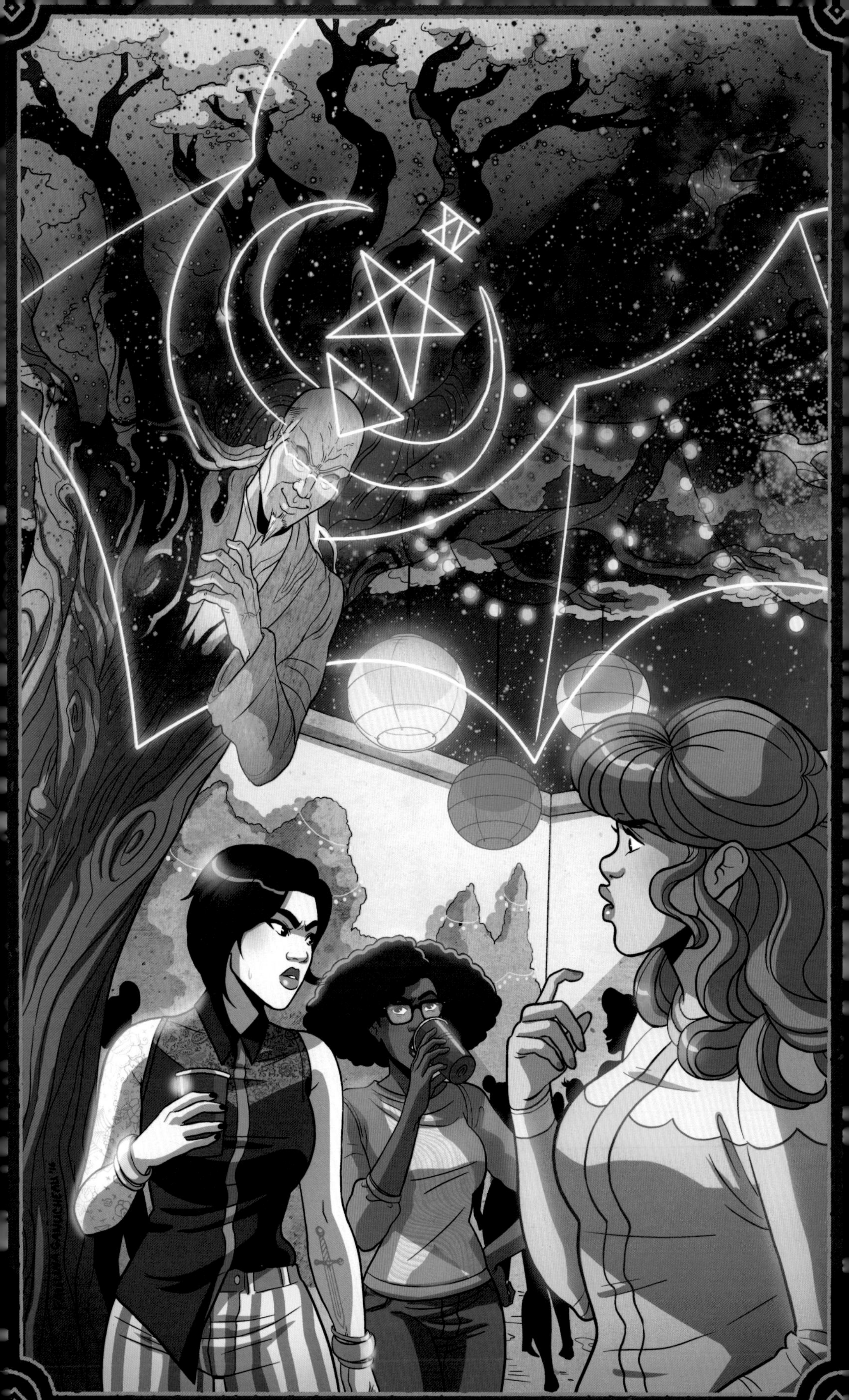
XV

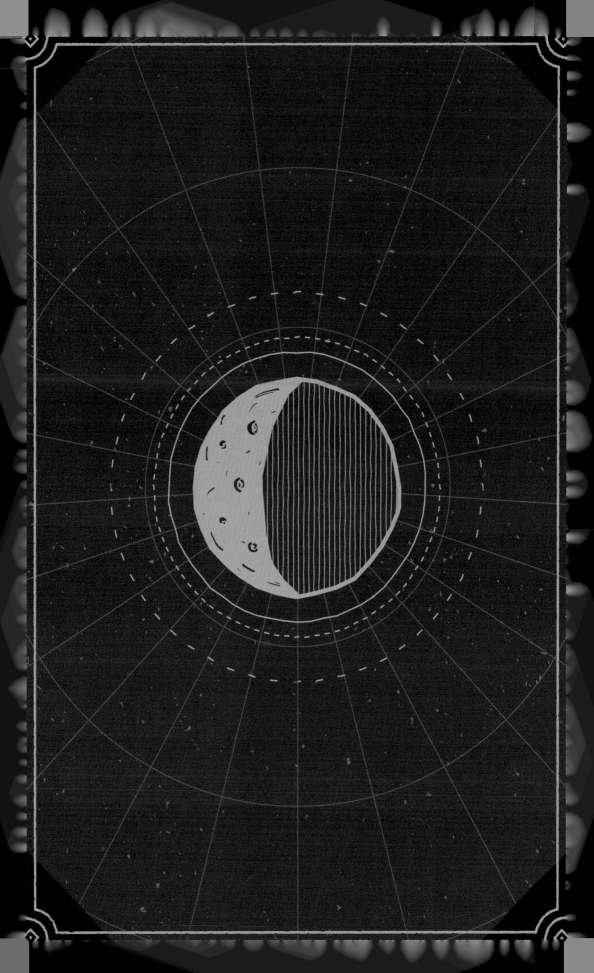

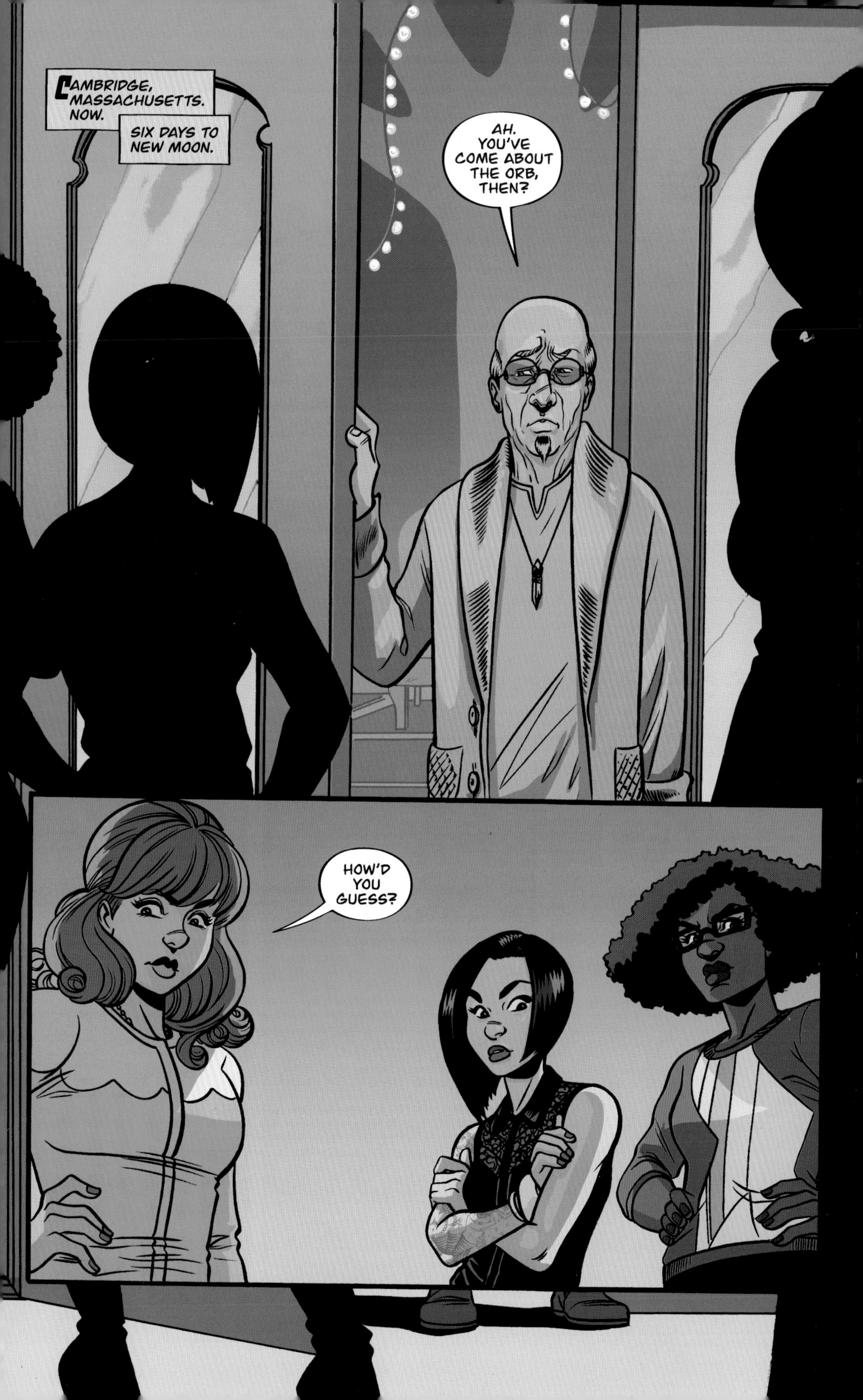
CAMBRIDGE, MASSACHUSETTS. NOW.
SIX DAYS TO NEW MOON.
AH. YOU'VE COME ABOUT THE ORB, THEN?
HOW'D YOU GUESS?

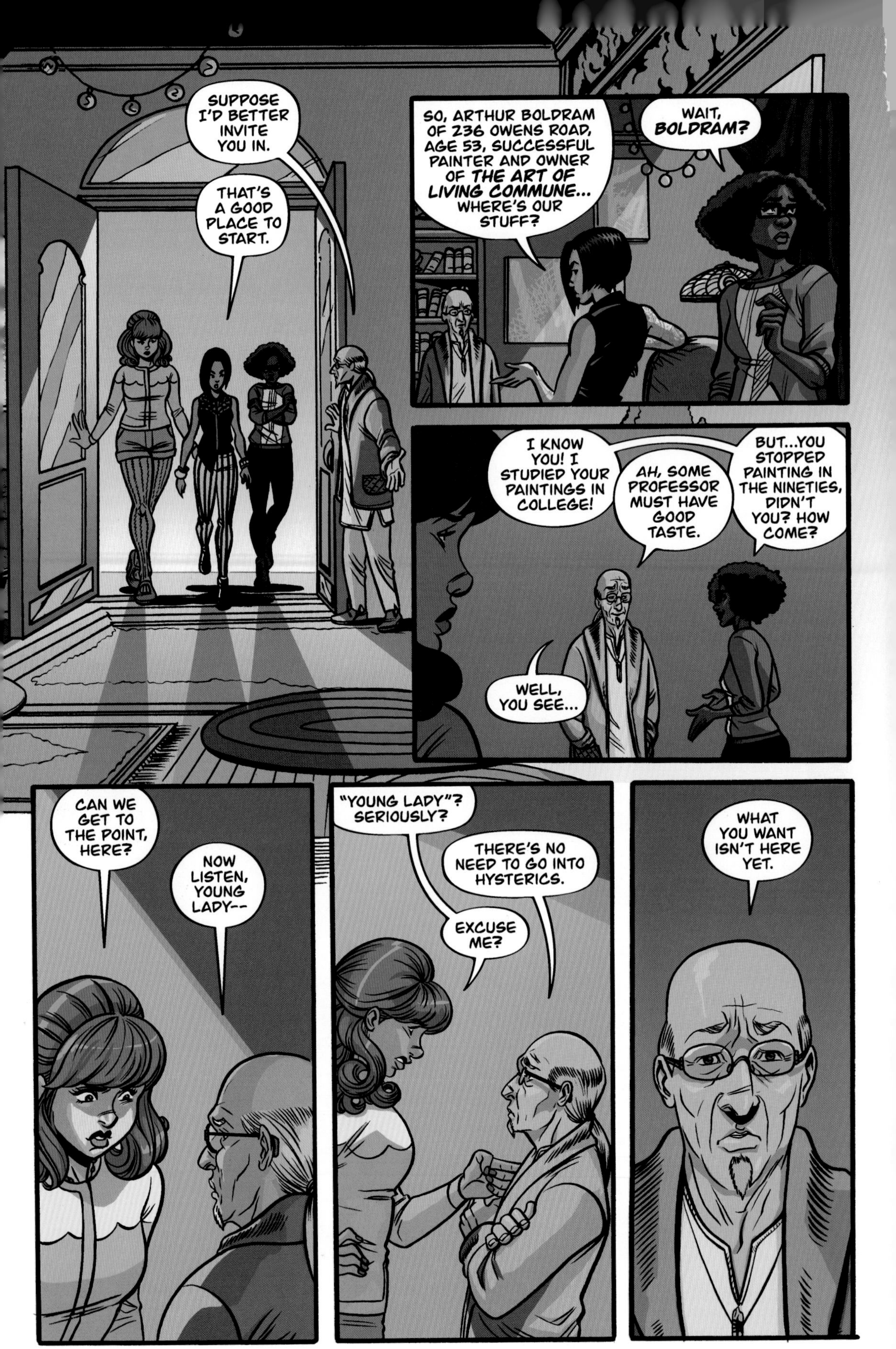
SUPPOSE I'D BETTER INVITE YOU IN.
THAT'S A GOOD PLACE TO START.
SO, ARTHUR BOLDRAM OF 236 OWENS ROAD, AGE 53, SUCCESSFUL PAINTER AND OWNER OF THE ART OF LIVING COMMUNE... WHERE'S OUR STUFF?
WAIT, BOLDRAM?
I KNOW YOU! I STUDIED YOUR PAINTINGS IN COLLEGE!
AH, SOME PROFESSOR MUST HAVE GOOD TASTE.
BUT...YOU STOPPED PAINTING IN THE NINETIES, DIDN'T YOU? HOW COME?
WELL, YOU SEE...
CAN WE GET TO THE POINT, HERE?
NOW LISTEN, YOUNG LADY--
"YOUNG LADY"? SERIOUSLY?
THERE'S NO NEED TO GO INTO HYSTERICS.
EXCUSE ME?
WHAT YOU WANT ISN'T HERE YET.

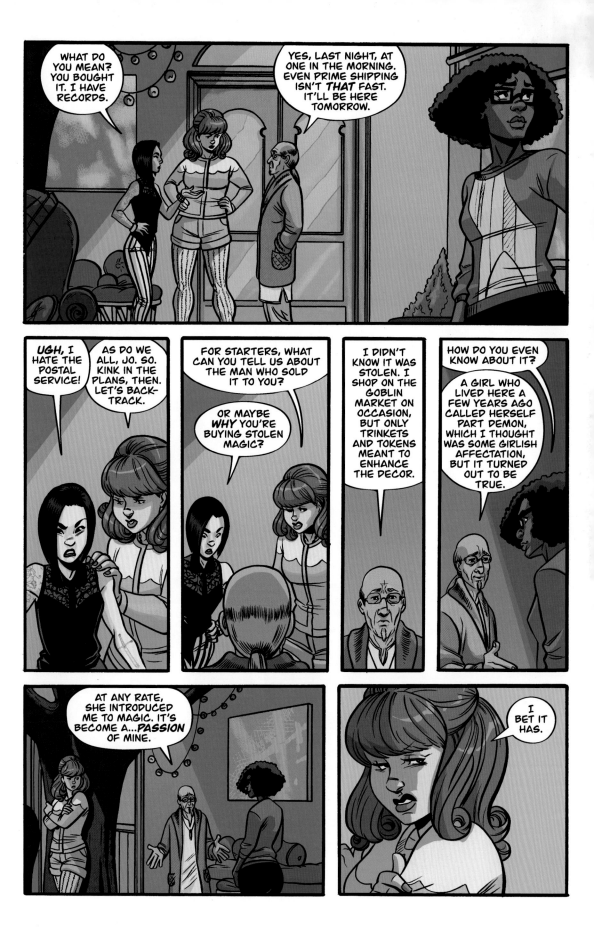

WHAT DO YOU MEAN? YOU BOUGHT IT. I HAVE RECORDS.

YES, LAST NIGHT, AT ONE IN THE MORNING. EVEN PRIME SHIPPING ISN'T *THAT* FAST. IT'LL BE HERE TOMORROW.

UGH, I HATE THE POSTAL SERVICE!

AS DO WE ALL, JO. SO. KINK IN THE PLANS, THEN. LET'S BACK-TRACK.

FOR STARTERS, WHAT CAN YOU TELL US ABOUT THE MAN WHO SOLD IT TO YOU?

OR MAYBE *WHY* YOU'RE BUYING STOLEN MAGIC?

I DIDN'T KNOW IT WAS STOLEN. I SHOP ON THE GOBLIN MARKET ON OCCASION, BUT ONLY TRINKETS AND TOKENS MEANT TO ENHANCE THE DECOR.

HOW DO YOU EVEN KNOW ABOUT IT?

A GIRL WHO LIVED HERE A FEW YEARS AGO CALLED HERSELF PART DEMON, WHICH I THOUGHT WAS SOME GIRLISH AFFECTATION, BUT IT TURNED OUT TO BE TRUE.

AT ANY RATE, SHE INTRODUCED ME TO MAGIC. IT'S BECOME A...*PASSION* OF MINE.

I BET IT HAS.

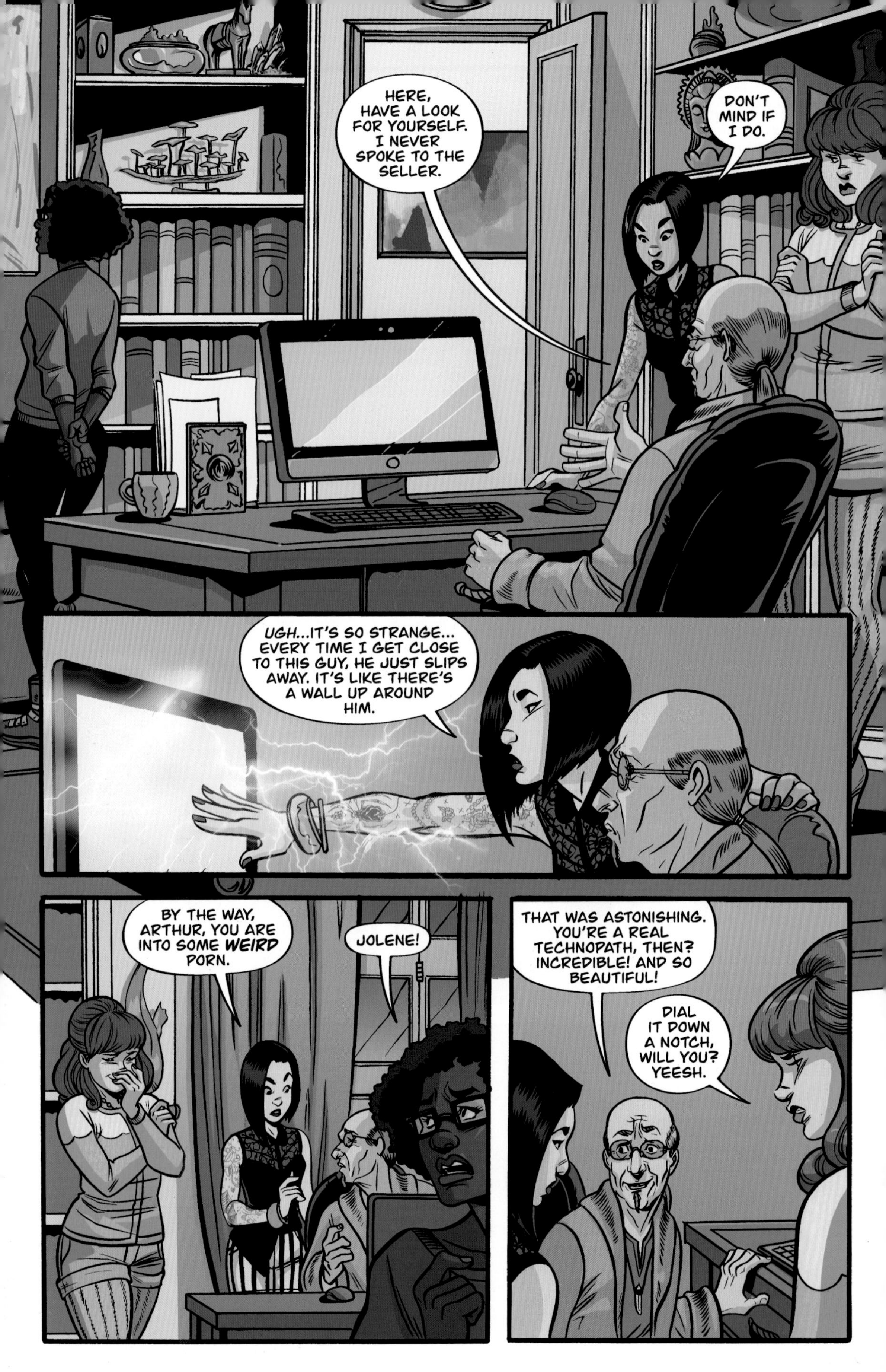
HERE, HAVE A LOOK FOR YOURSELF. I NEVER SPOKE TO THE SELLER.
DON'T MIND IF I DO.
UGH...IT'S SO STRANGE... EVERY TIME I GET CLOSE TO THIS GUY, HE JUST SLIPS AWAY. IT'S LIKE THERE'S A WALL UP AROUND HIM.
BY THE WAY, ARTHUR, YOU ARE INTO SOME **WEIRD** PORN.
JOLENE!
THAT WAS ASTONISHING. YOU'RE A REAL TECHNOPATH, THEN? INCREDIBLE! AND SO BEAUTIFUL!
DIAL IT DOWN A NOTCH, WILL YOU? YEESH.

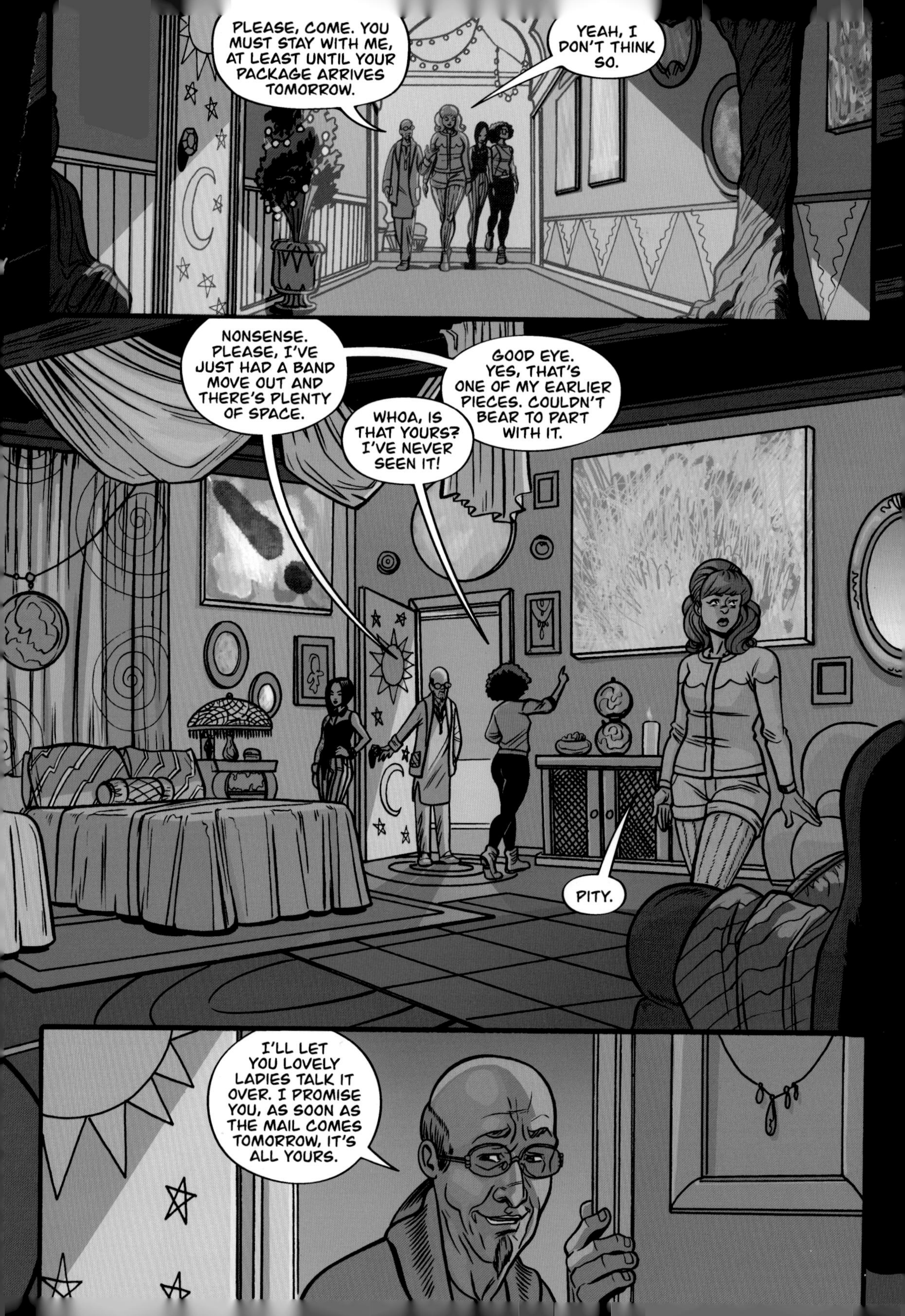
PLEASE, COME. YOU MUST STAY WITH ME, AT LEAST UNTIL YOUR PACKAGE ARRIVES TOMORROW.
YEAH, I DON'T THINK SO.
NONSENSE. PLEASE, I'VE JUST HAD A BAND MOVE OUT AND THERE'S PLENTY OF SPACE.
WHOA, IS THAT YOURS? I'VE NEVER SEEN IT!
GOOD EYE. YES, THAT'S ONE OF MY EARLIER PIECES. COULDN'T BEAR TO PART WITH IT.
PITY.
I'LL LET YOU LOVELY LADIES TALK IT OVER. I PROMISE YOU, AS SOON AS THE MAIL COMES TOMORROW, IT'S ALL YOURS.

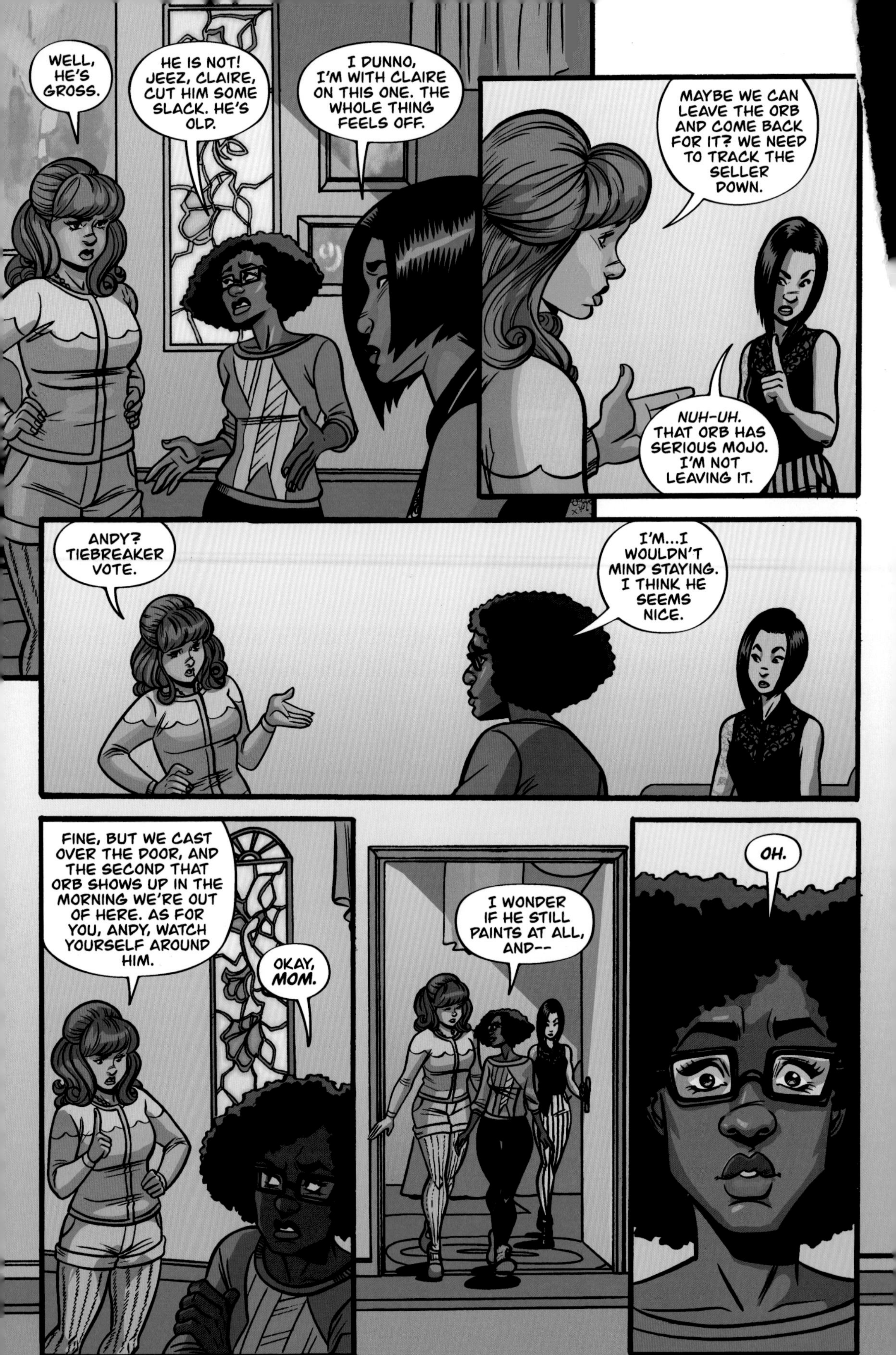

WELL, HE'S GROSS.
HE IS NOT! JEEZ, CLAIRE, CUT HIM SOME SLACK. HE'S OLD.
I DUNNO, I'M WITH CLAIRE ON THIS ONE. THE WHOLE THING FEELS OFF.
MAYBE WE CAN LEAVE THE ORB AND COME BACK FOR IT? WE NEED TO TRACK THE SELLER DOWN.
NUH-UH. THAT ORB HAS SERIOUS MOJO. I'M NOT LEAVING IT.
ANDY? TIEBREAKER VOTE.
I'M...I WOULDN'T MIND STAYING. I THINK HE SEEMS NICE.
FINE, BUT WE CAST OVER THE DOOR, AND THE SECOND THAT ORB SHOWS UP IN THE MORNING WE'RE OUT OF HERE. AS FOR YOU, ANDY, WATCH YOURSELF AROUND HIM.
OKAY, *MOM.*
I WONDER IF HE STILL PAINTS AT ALL, AND--
OH.

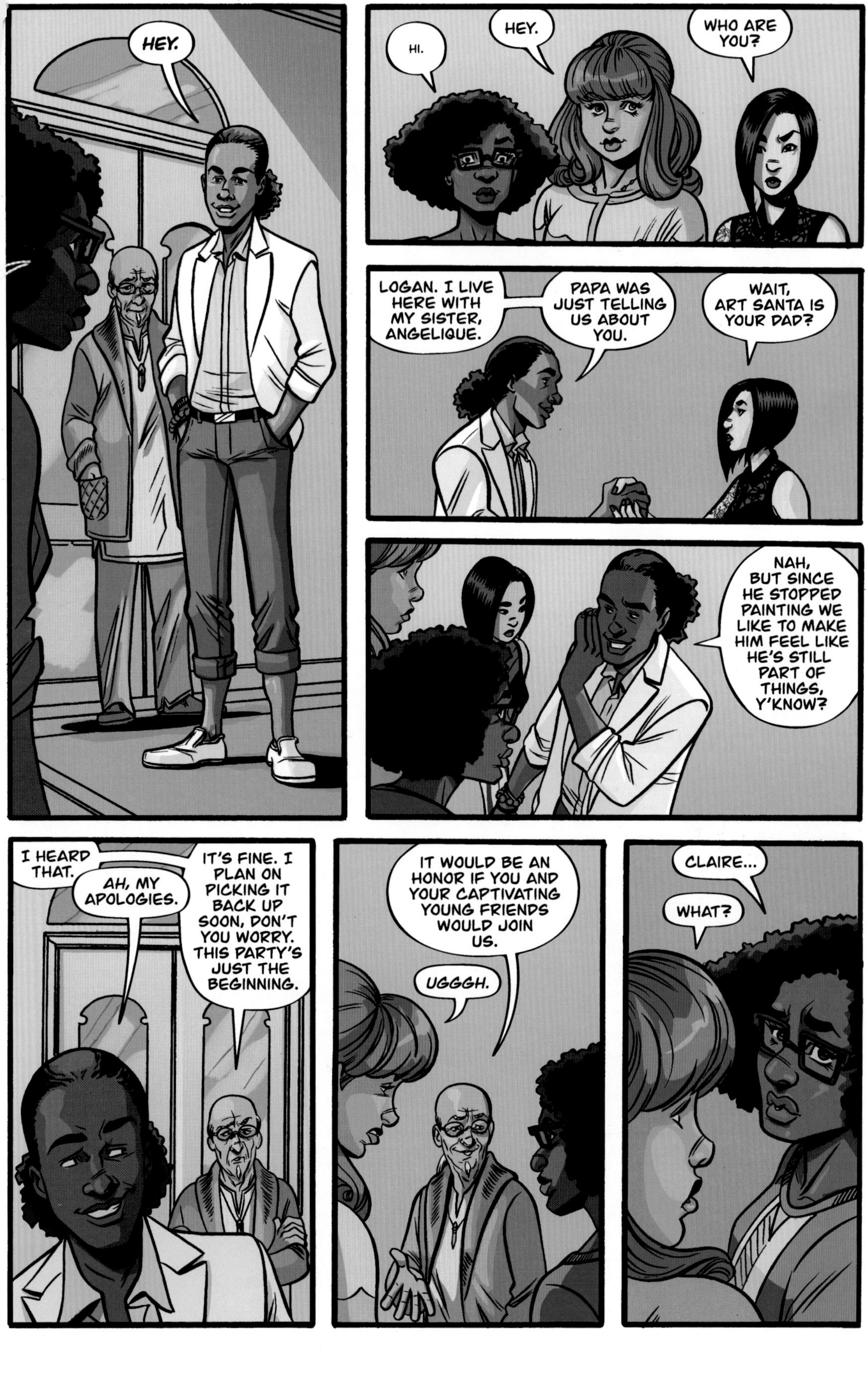
HEY.
HI.
HEY.
WHO ARE YOU?
LOGAN. I LIVE HERE WITH MY SISTER, ANGELIQUE.
PAPA WAS JUST TELLING US ABOUT YOU.
WAIT, ART SANTA IS YOUR DAD?
NAH, BUT SINCE HE STOPPED PAINTING WE LIKE TO MAKE HIM FEEL LIKE HE'S STILL PART OF THINGS, Y'KNOW?
I HEARD THAT.
AH, MY APOLOGIES.
IT'S FINE. I PLAN ON PICKING IT BACK UP SOON, DON'T YOU WORRY. THIS PARTY'S JUST THE BEGINNING.
IT WOULD BE AN HONOR IF YOU AND YOUR CAPTIVATING YOUNG FRIENDS WOULD JOIN US.
UGGGH.
CLAIRE...
WHAT?

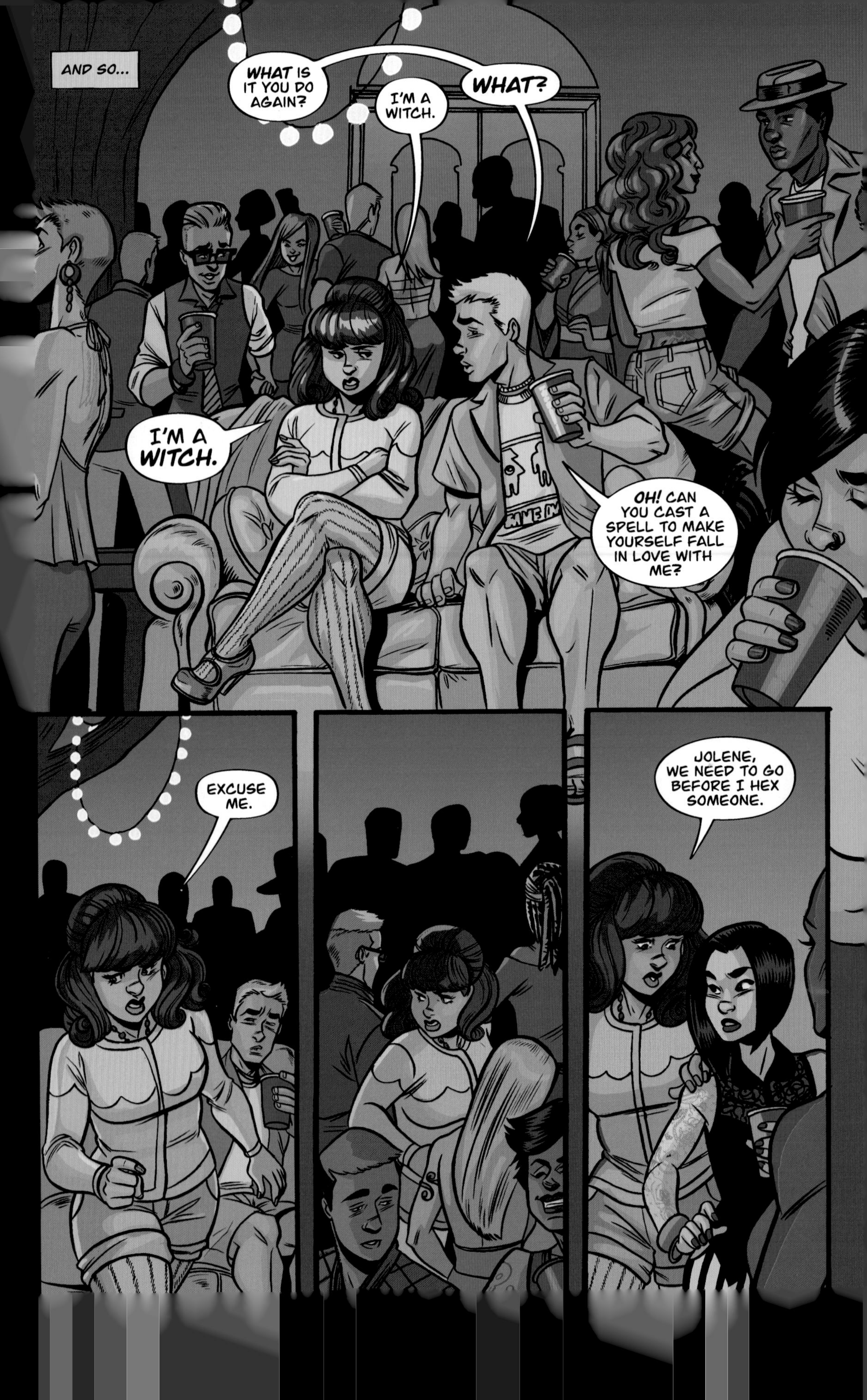
AND SO...
WHAT IS IT YOU DO AGAIN?
I'M A WITCH.
WHAT?
I'M A WITCH.
OH! CAN YOU CAST A SPELL TO MAKE YOURSELF FALL IN LOVE WITH ME?
EXCUSE ME.
JOLENE, WE NEED TO GO BEFORE I HEX SOMEONE.

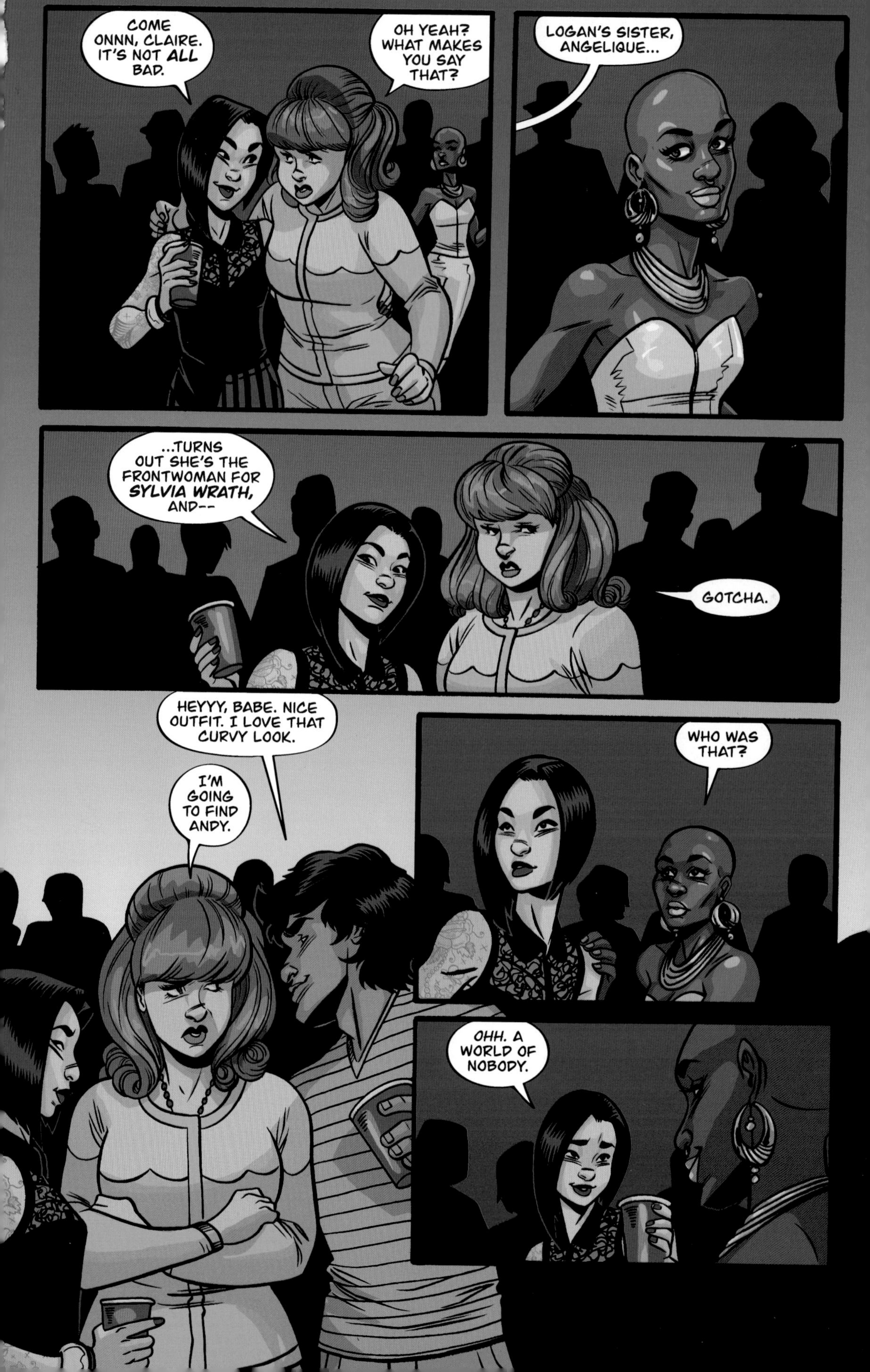
COME ONNN, CLAIRE. IT'S NOT ALL BAD.
OH YEAH? WHAT MAKES YOU SAY THAT?
LOGAN'S SISTER, ANGELIQUE...
...TURNS OUT SHE'S THE FRONTWOMAN FOR SYLVIA WRATH, AND--
GOTCHA.
HEYYY, BABE. NICE OUTFIT. I LOVE THAT CURVY LOOK.
I'M GOING TO FIND ANDY.
WHO WAS THAT?
OHH. A WORLD OF NOBODY.

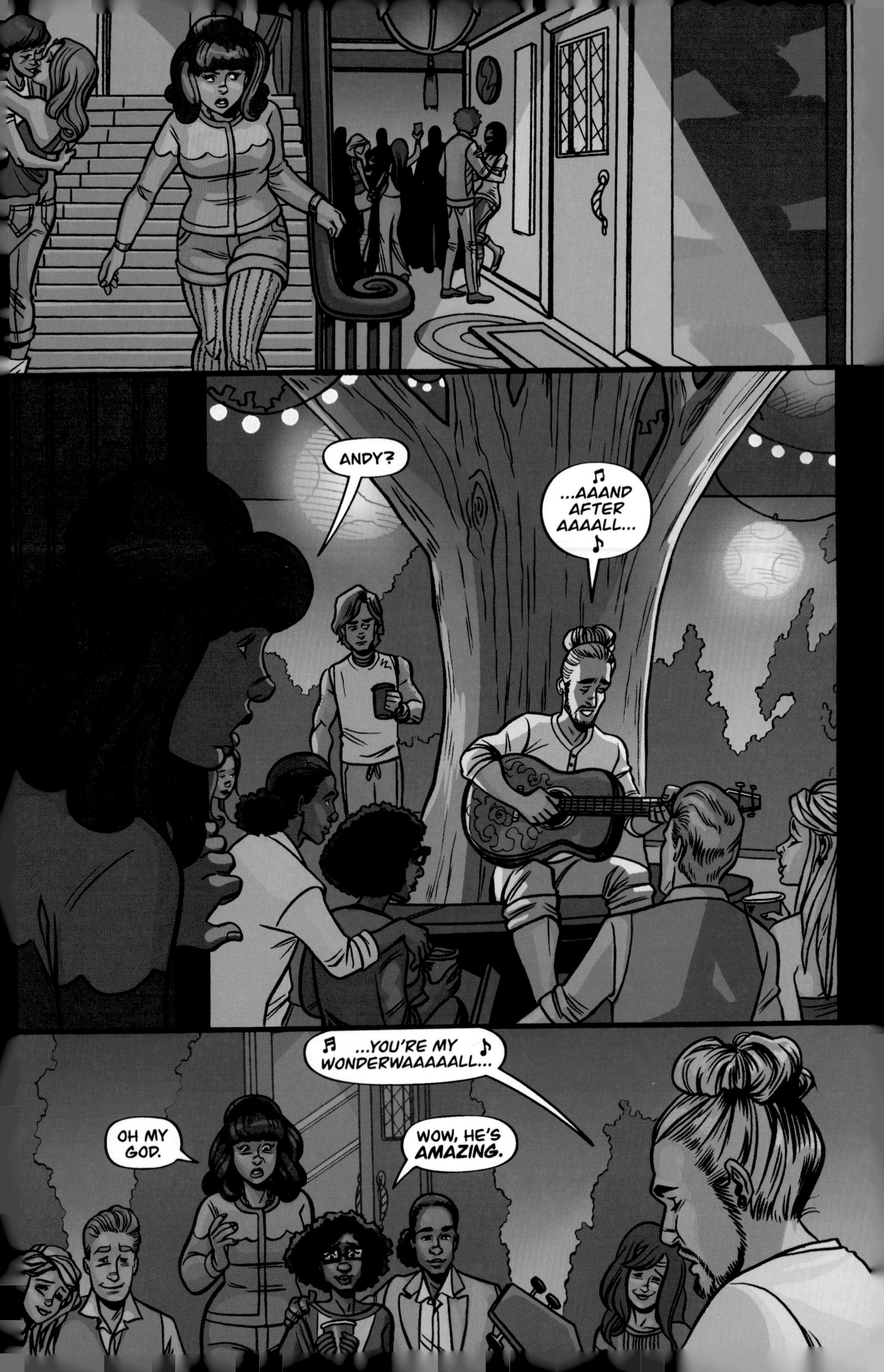
ANDY?
♫ ...AAAND AFTER AAAALL... ♪
♫ ...YOU'RE MY WONDERWAAAAALL... ♪
OH MY GOD.
WOW, HE'S **AMAZING.**

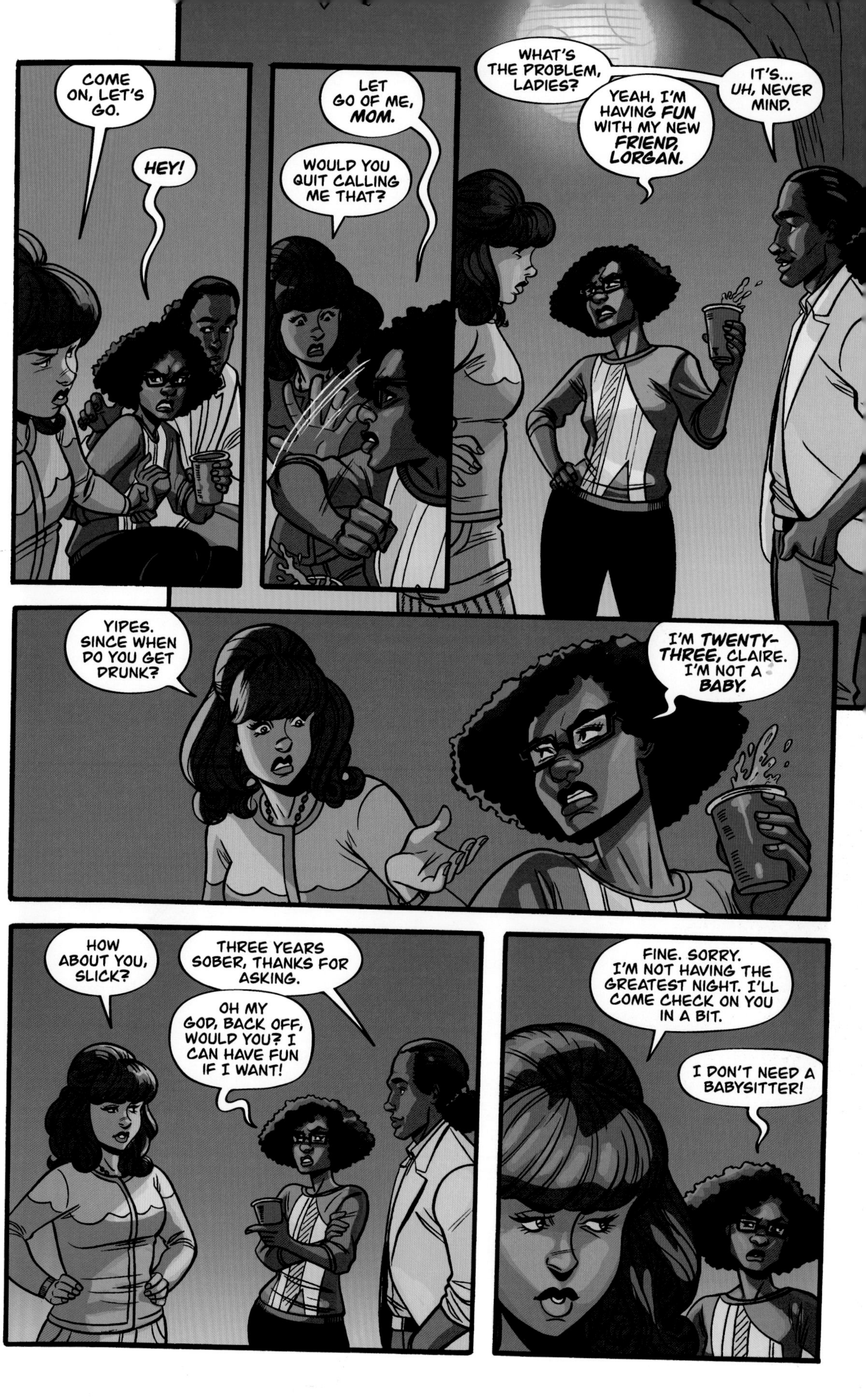
COME ON, LET'S GO.
HEY!
LET GO OF ME, MOM.
WOULD YOU QUIT CALLING ME THAT?
WHAT'S THE PROBLEM, LADIES?
YEAH, I'M HAVING FUN WITH MY NEW FRIEND, LORGAN.
IT'S... UH, NEVER MIND.
YIPES. SINCE WHEN DO YOU GET DRUNK?
I'M TWENTY-THREE, CLAIRE. I'M NOT A BABY.
HOW ABOUT YOU, SLICK?
THREE YEARS SOBER, THANKS FOR ASKING.
OH MY GOD, BACK OFF, WOULD YOU? I CAN HAVE FUN IF I WANT!
FINE. SORRY. I'M NOT HAVING THE GREATEST NIGHT. I'LL COME CHECK ON YOU IN A BIT.
I DON'T NEED A BABYSITTER!

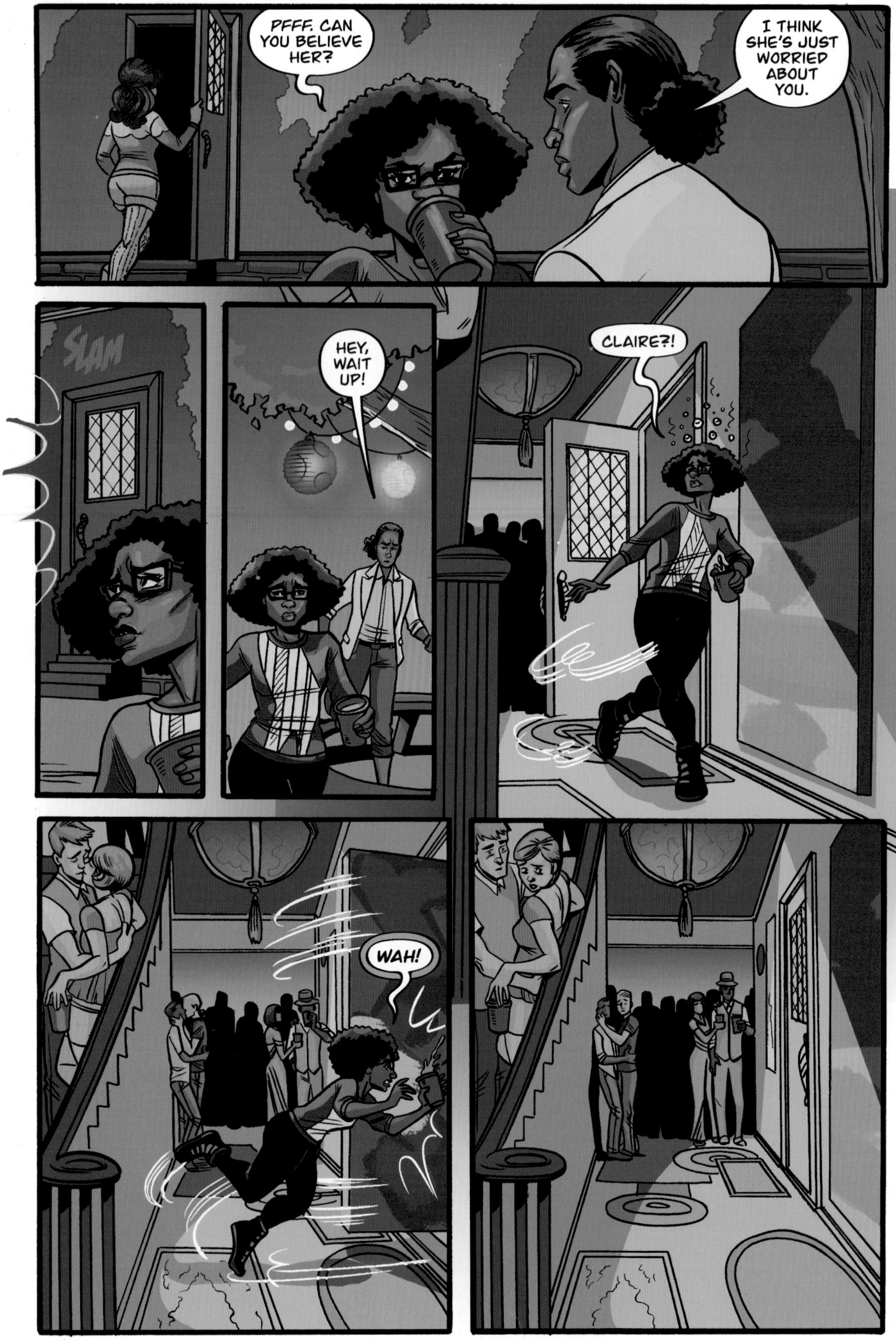
PFFF. CAN YOU BELIEVE HER?
I THINK SHE'S JUST WORRIED ABOUT YOU.
SLAM
HEY, WAIT UP!
CLAIRE?!
WAH!

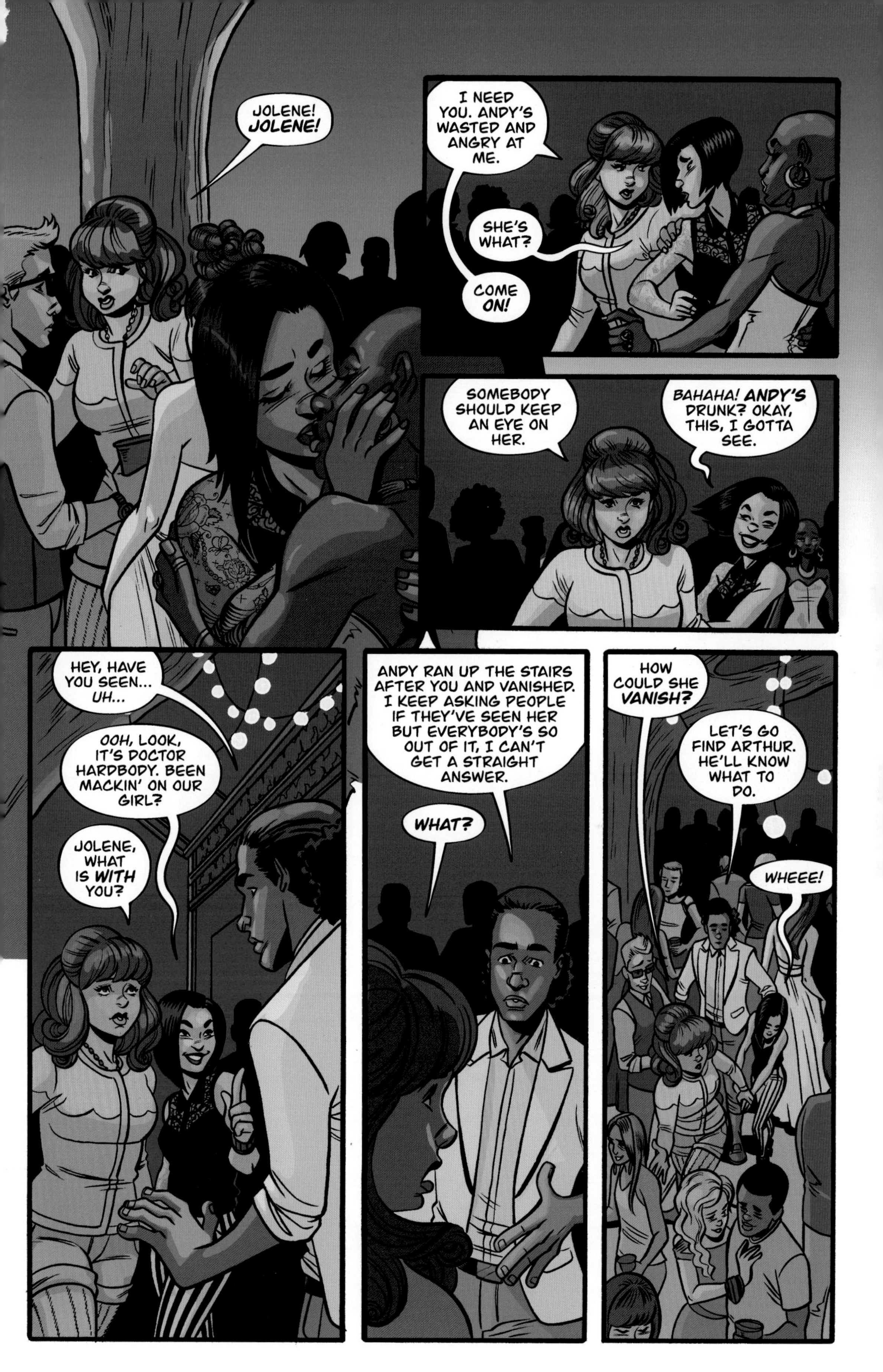
JOLENE! JOLENE!
I NEED YOU. ANDY'S WASTED AND ANGRY AT ME.
SHE'S WHAT?
COME ON!
SOMEBODY SHOULD KEEP AN EYE ON HER.
BAHAHA! ANDY'S DRUNK? OKAY, THIS, I GOTTA SEE.
HEY, HAVE YOU SEEN... UH...
OOH, LOOK, IT'S DOCTOR HARDBODY. BEEN MACKIN' ON OUR GIRL?
JOLENE, WHAT IS WITH YOU?
ANDY RAN UP THE STAIRS AFTER YOU AND VANISHED. I KEEP ASKING PEOPLE IF THEY'VE SEEN HER BUT EVERYBODY'S SO OUT OF IT, I CAN'T GET A STRAIGHT ANSWER.
WHAT?
HOW COULD SHE VANISH?
LET'S GO FIND ARTHUR. HE'LL KNOW WHAT TO DO.
WHEEE!

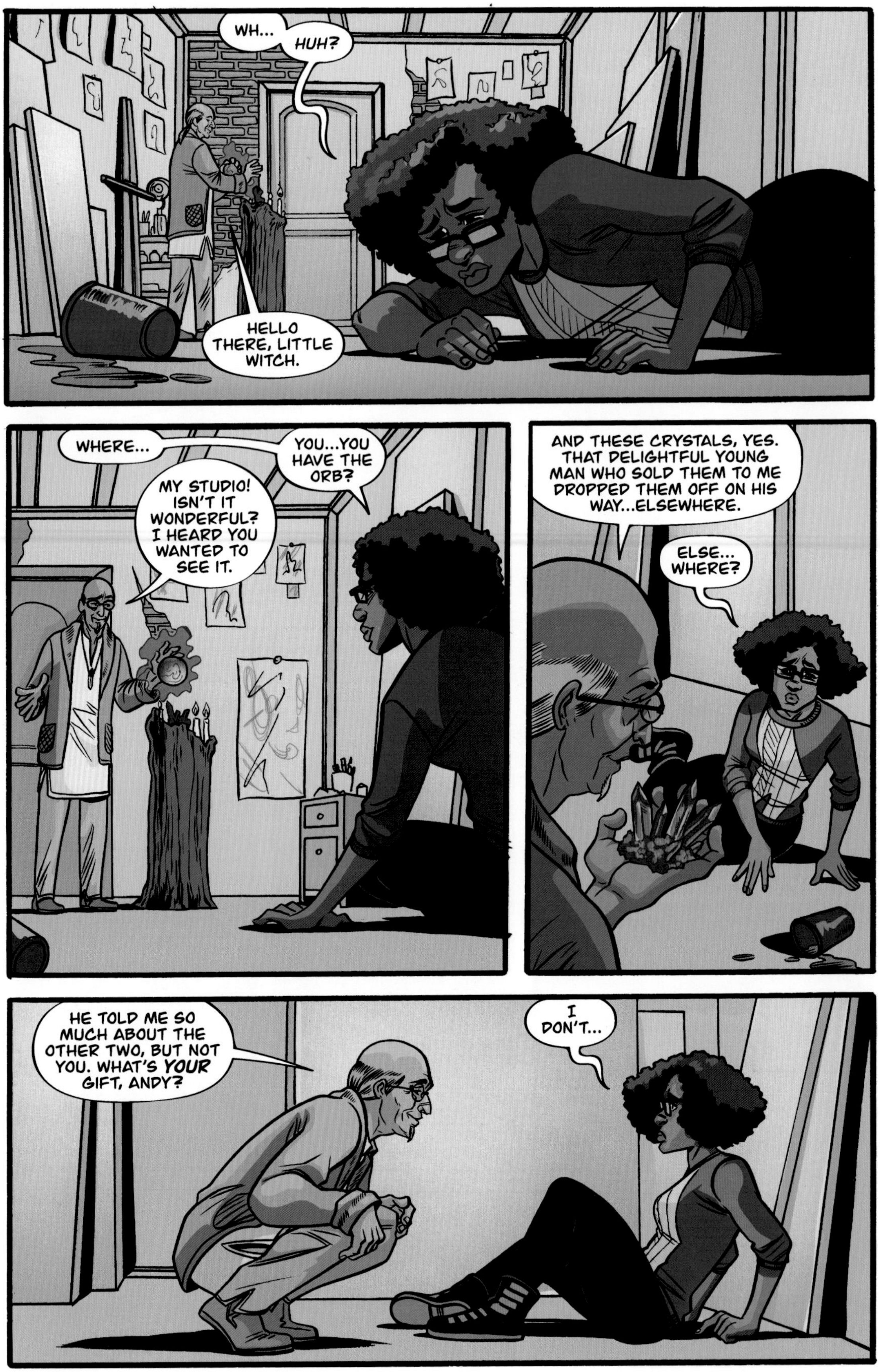
WH...
HUH?
HELLO THERE, LITTLE WITCH.
WHERE...
YOU...YOU HAVE THE ORB?
MY STUDIO! ISN'T IT WONDERFUL? I HEARD YOU WANTED TO SEE IT.
AND THESE CRYSTALS, YES. THAT DELIGHTFUL YOUNG MAN WHO SOLD THEM TO ME DROPPED THEM OFF ON HIS WAY...ELSEWHERE.
ELSE... WHERE?
HE TOLD ME SO MUCH ABOUT THE OTHER TWO, BUT NOT YOU. WHAT'S YOUR GIFT, ANDY?
I DON'T...

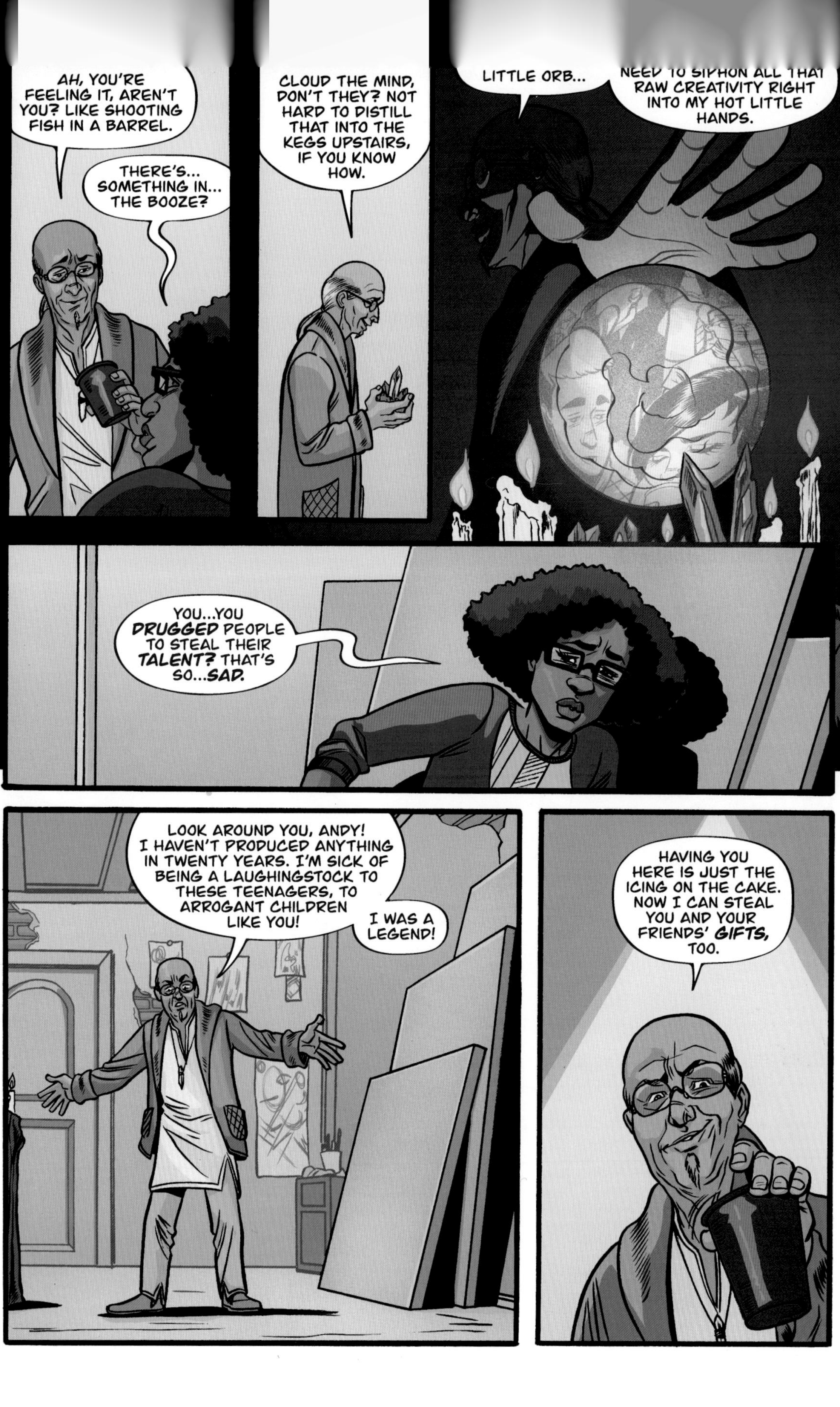
AH, YOU'RE FEELING IT, AREN'T YOU? LIKE SHOOTING FISH IN A BARREL.
THERE'S... SOMETHING IN... THE BOOZE?
CLOUD THE MIND, DON'T THEY? NOT HARD TO DISTILL THAT INTO THE KEGS UPSTAIRS, IF YOU KNOW HOW.
LITTLE ORB...
NEED TO SIPHON ALL THAT RAW CREATIVITY RIGHT INTO MY HOT LITTLE HANDS.
YOU...YOU DRUGGED PEOPLE TO STEAL THEIR TALENT? THAT'S SO...SAD.
LOOK AROUND YOU, ANDY! I HAVEN'T PRODUCED ANYTHING IN TWENTY YEARS. I'M SICK OF BEING A LAUGHINGSTOCK TO THESE TEENAGERS, TO ARROGANT CHILDREN LIKE YOU!
I WAS A LEGEND!
HAVING YOU HERE IS JUST THE ICING ON THE CAKE. NOW I CAN STEAL YOU AND YOUR FRIENDS' GIFTS, TOO.

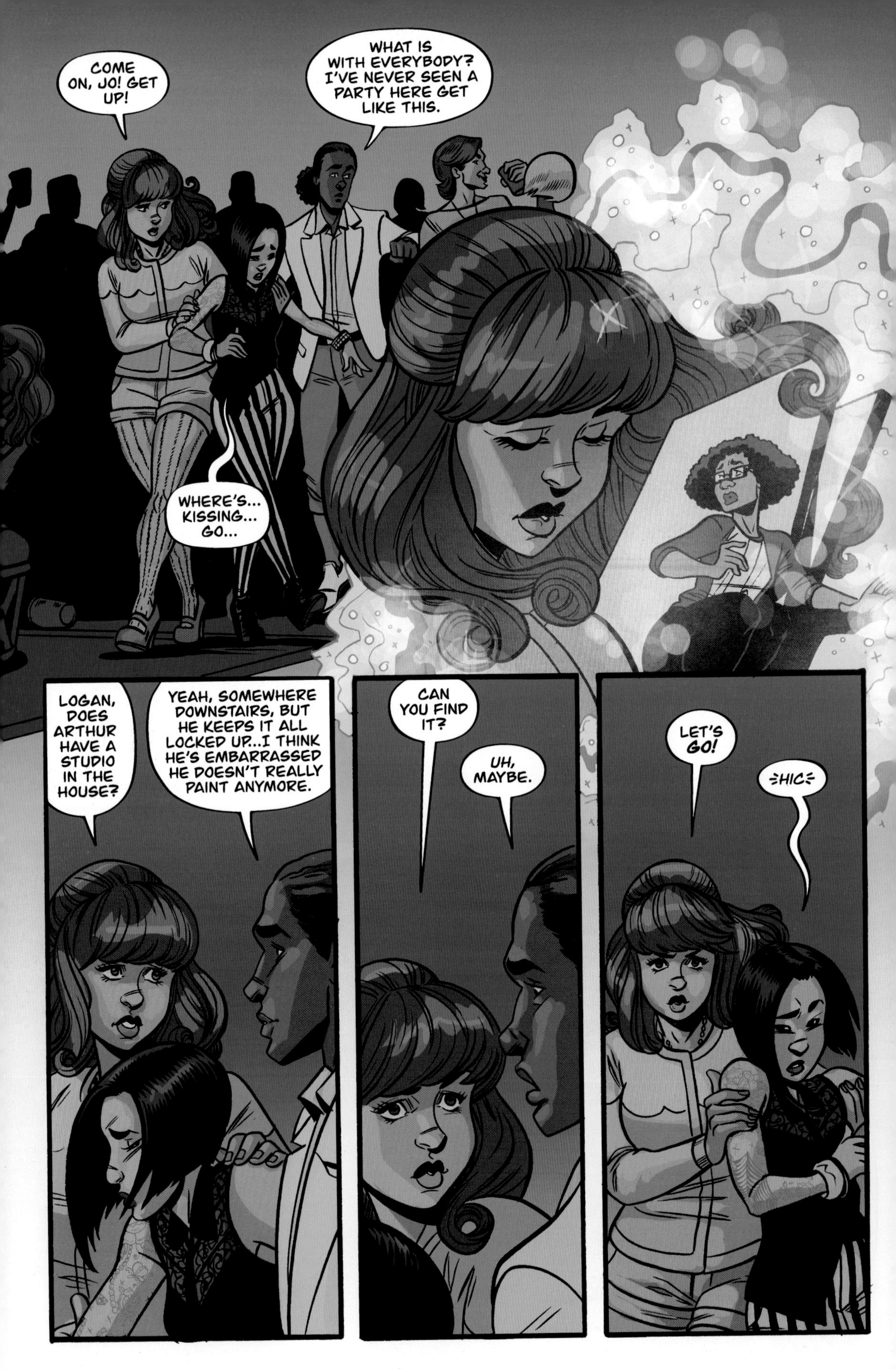
COME ON, JO! GET UP!
WHAT IS WITH EVERYBODY? I'VE NEVER SEEN A PARTY HERE GET LIKE THIS.
WHERE'S... KISSING... GO...
LOGAN, DOES ARTHUR HAVE A STUDIO IN THE HOUSE?
YEAH, SOMEWHERE DOWNSTAIRS, BUT HE KEEPS IT ALL LOCKED UP...I THINK HE'S EMBARRASSED HE DOESN'T REALLY PAINT ANYMORE.
CAN YOU FIND IT?
UH, MAYBE.
LET'S GO!
HIC

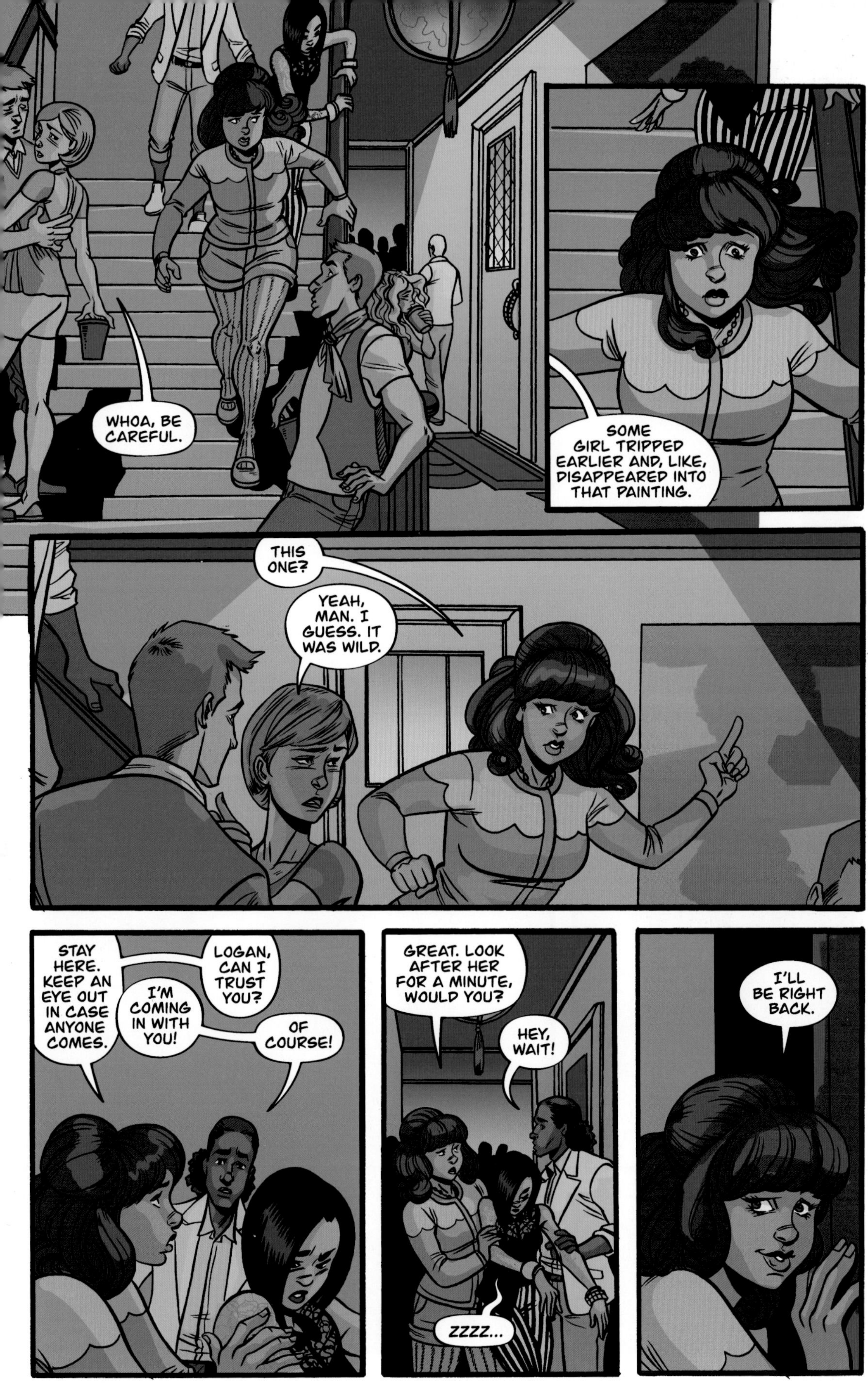
WHOA, BE CAREFUL.
SOME GIRL TRIPPED EARLIER AND, LIKE, DISAPPEARED INTO THAT PAINTING.
THIS ONE?
YEAH, MAN. I GUESS. IT WAS WILD.
STAY HERE. KEEP AN EYE OUT IN CASE ANYONE COMES.
LOGAN, CAN I TRUST YOU?
I'M COMING IN WITH YOU!
OF COURSE!
GREAT. LOOK AFTER HER FOR A MINUTE, WOULD YOU?
HEY, WAIT!
ZZZZ...
I'LL BE RIGHT BACK.

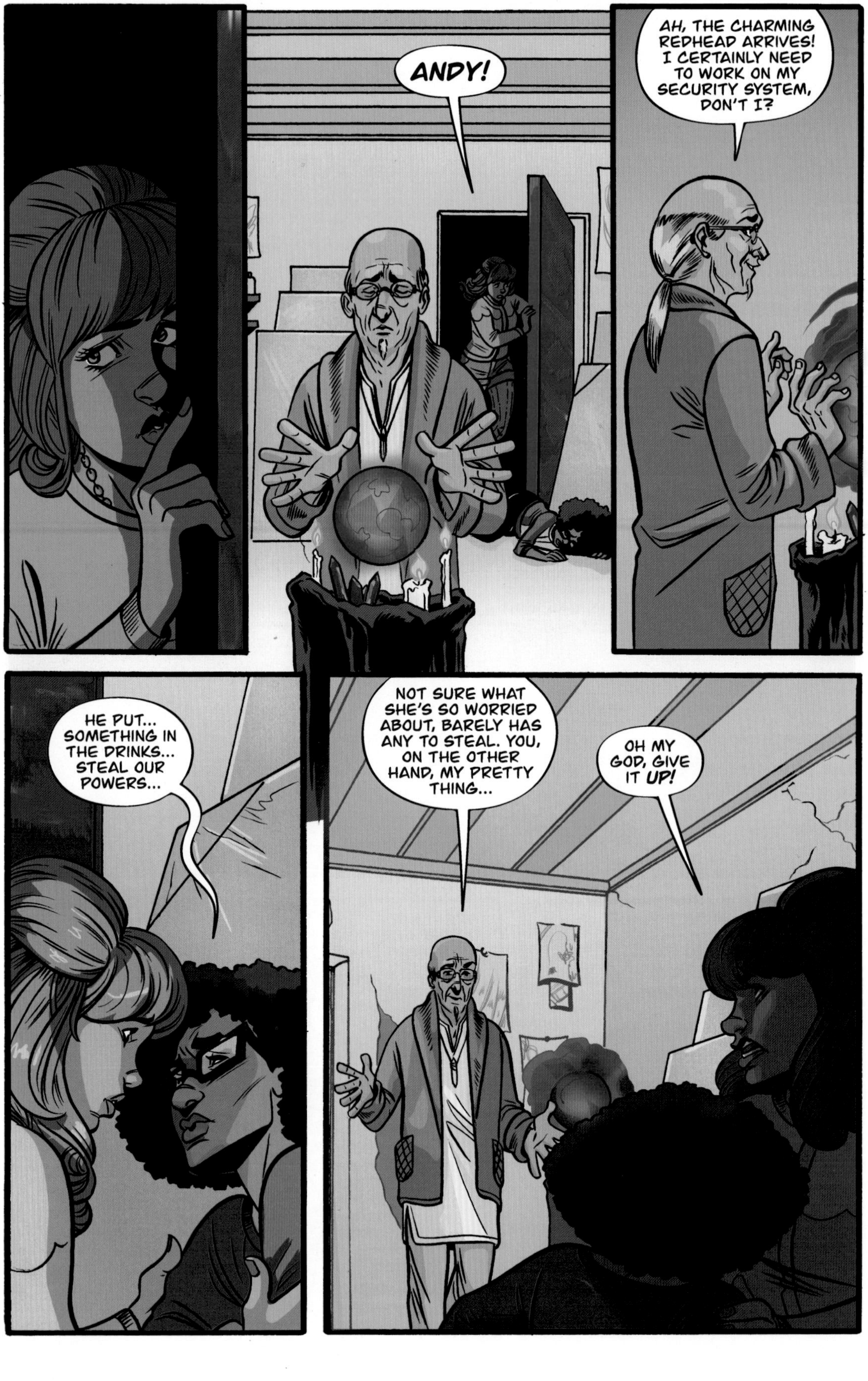
ANDY!
AH, THE CHARMING REDHEAD ARRIVES! I CERTAINLY NEED TO WORK ON MY SECURITY SYSTEM, DON'T I?
HE PUT... SOMETHING IN THE DRINKS... STEAL OUR POWERS...
NOT SURE WHAT SHE'S SO WORRIED ABOUT, BARELY HAS ANY TO STEAL. YOU, ON THE OTHER HAND, MY PRETTY THING...
OH MY GOD, GIVE IT UP!

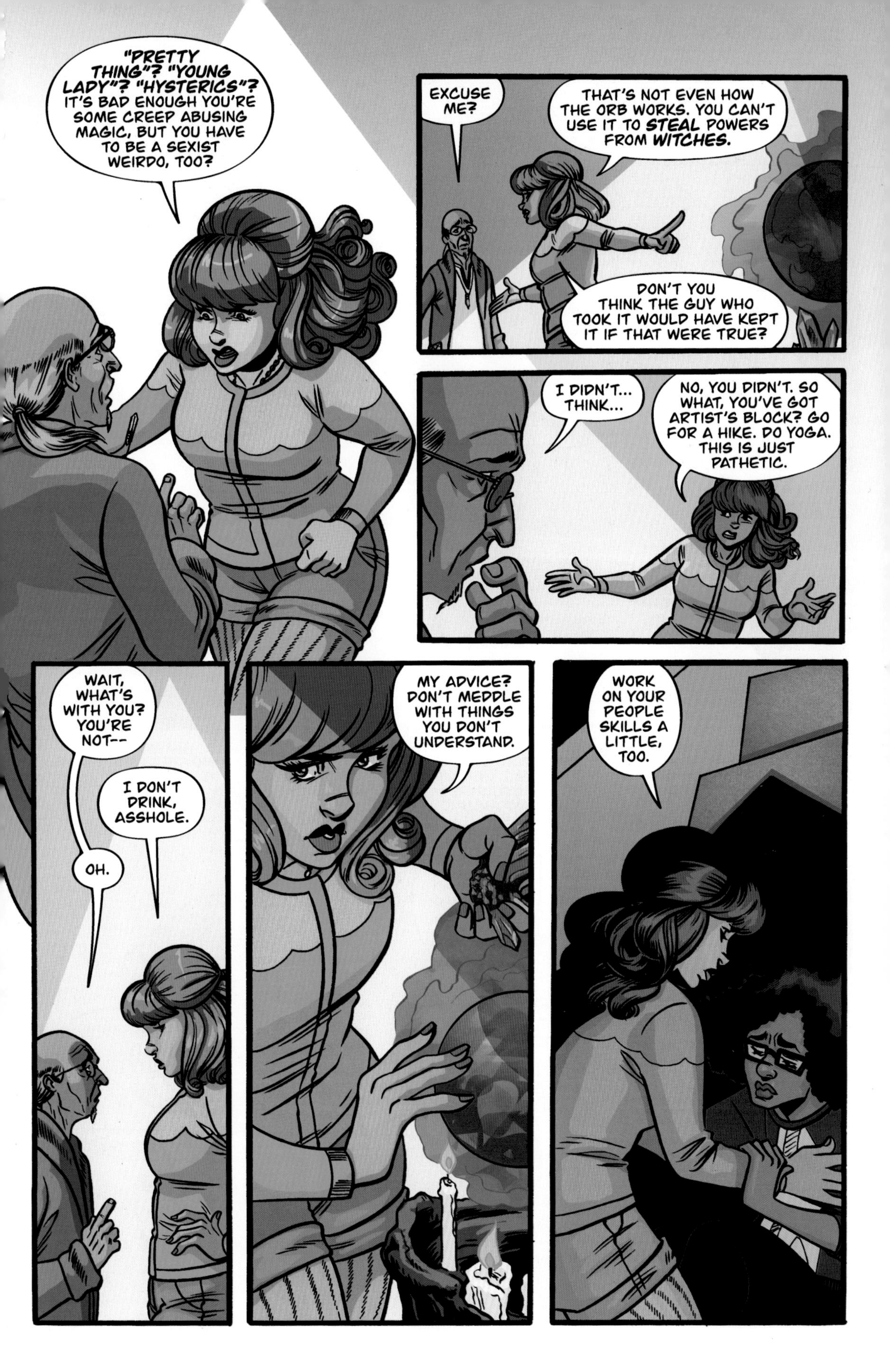
"PRETTY THING"? "YOUNG LADY"? "HYSTERICS"? IT'S BAD ENOUGH YOU'RE SOME CREEP ABUSING MAGIC, BUT YOU HAVE TO BE A SEXIST WEIRDO, TOO?
EXCUSE ME?
THAT'S NOT EVEN HOW THE ORB WORKS. YOU CAN'T USE IT TO STEAL POWERS FROM WITCHES.
DON'T YOU THINK THE GUY WHO TOOK IT WOULD HAVE KEPT IT IF THAT WERE TRUE?
I DIDN'T... THINK...
NO, YOU DIDN'T. SO WHAT, YOU'VE GOT ARTIST'S BLOCK? GO FOR A HIKE. DO YOGA. THIS IS JUST PATHETIC.
WAIT, WHAT'S WITH YOU? YOU'RE NOT--
I DON'T DRINK, ASSHOLE.
OH.
MY ADVICE? DON'T MEDDLE WITH THINGS YOU DON'T UNDERSTAND.
WORK ON YOUR PEOPLE SKILLS A LITTLE, TOO.

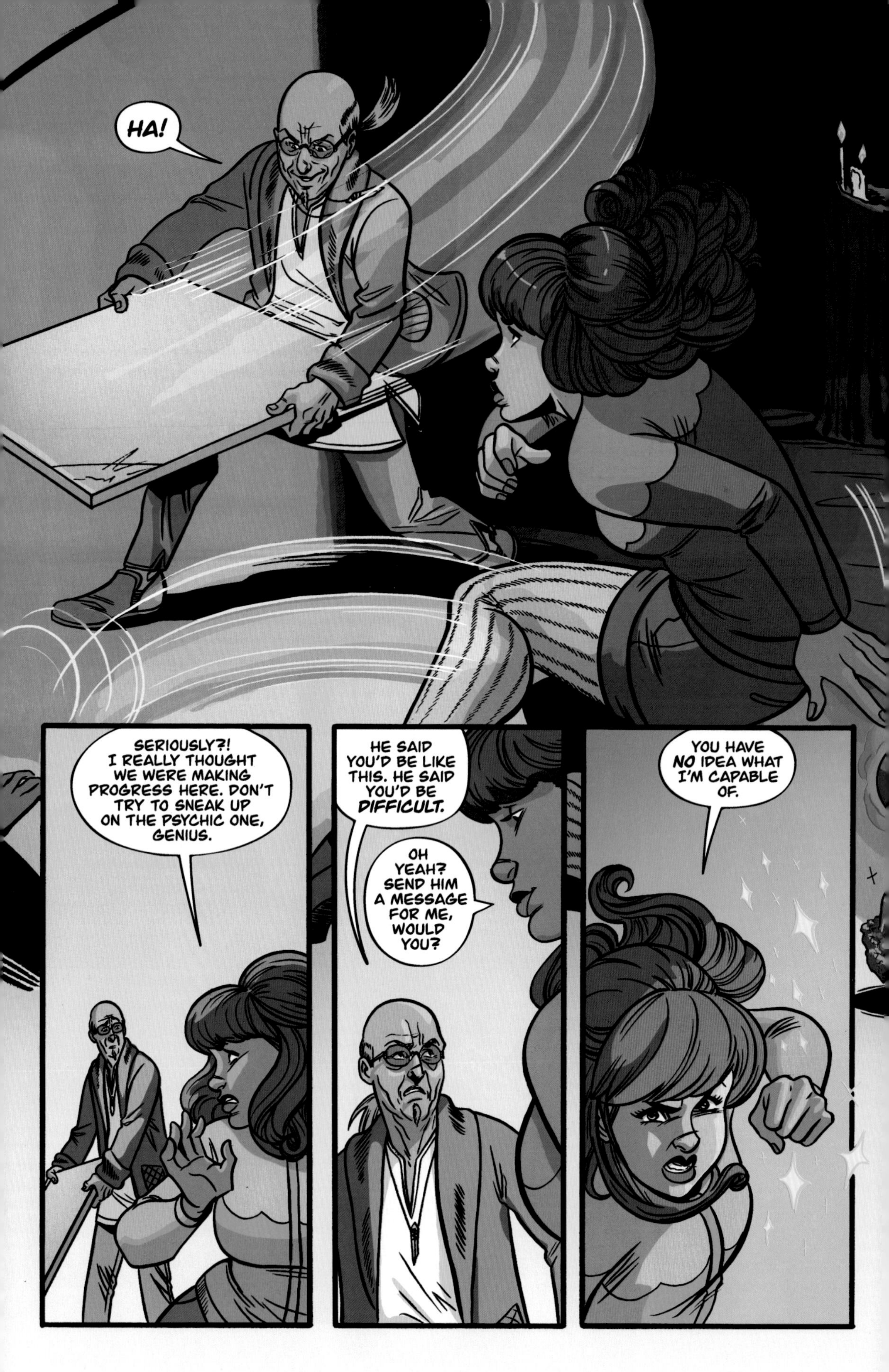
HA!
SERIOUSLY?! I REALLY THOUGHT WE WERE MAKING PROGRESS HERE. DON'T TRY TO SNEAK UP ON THE PSYCHIC ONE, GENIUS.
HE SAID YOU'D BE LIKE THIS. HE SAID YOU'D BE DIFFICULT.
OH YEAH? SEND HIM A MESSAGE FOR ME, WOULD YOU?
YOU HAVE NO IDEA WHAT I'M CAPABLE OF.

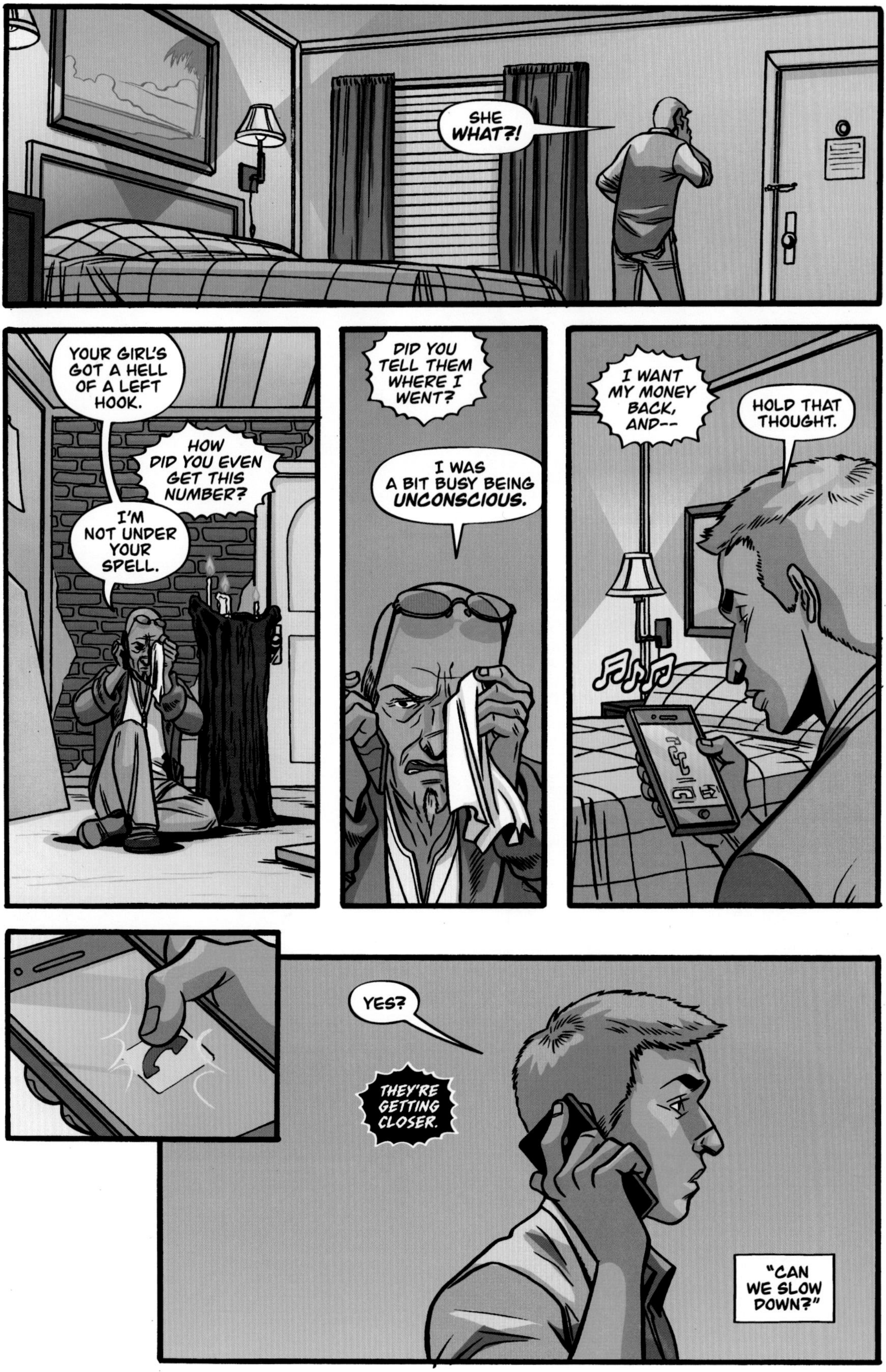
SHE WHAT?!
YOUR GIRL'S GOT A HELL OF A LEFT HOOK.
HOW DID YOU EVEN GET THIS NUMBER?
I'M NOT UNDER YOUR SPELL.
DID YOU TELL THEM WHERE I WENT?
I WAS A BIT BUSY BEING UNCONSCIOUS.
I WANT MY MONEY BACK, AND--
HOLD THAT THOUGHT.
YES?
THEY'RE GETTING CLOSER.
"CAN WE SLOW DOWN?"

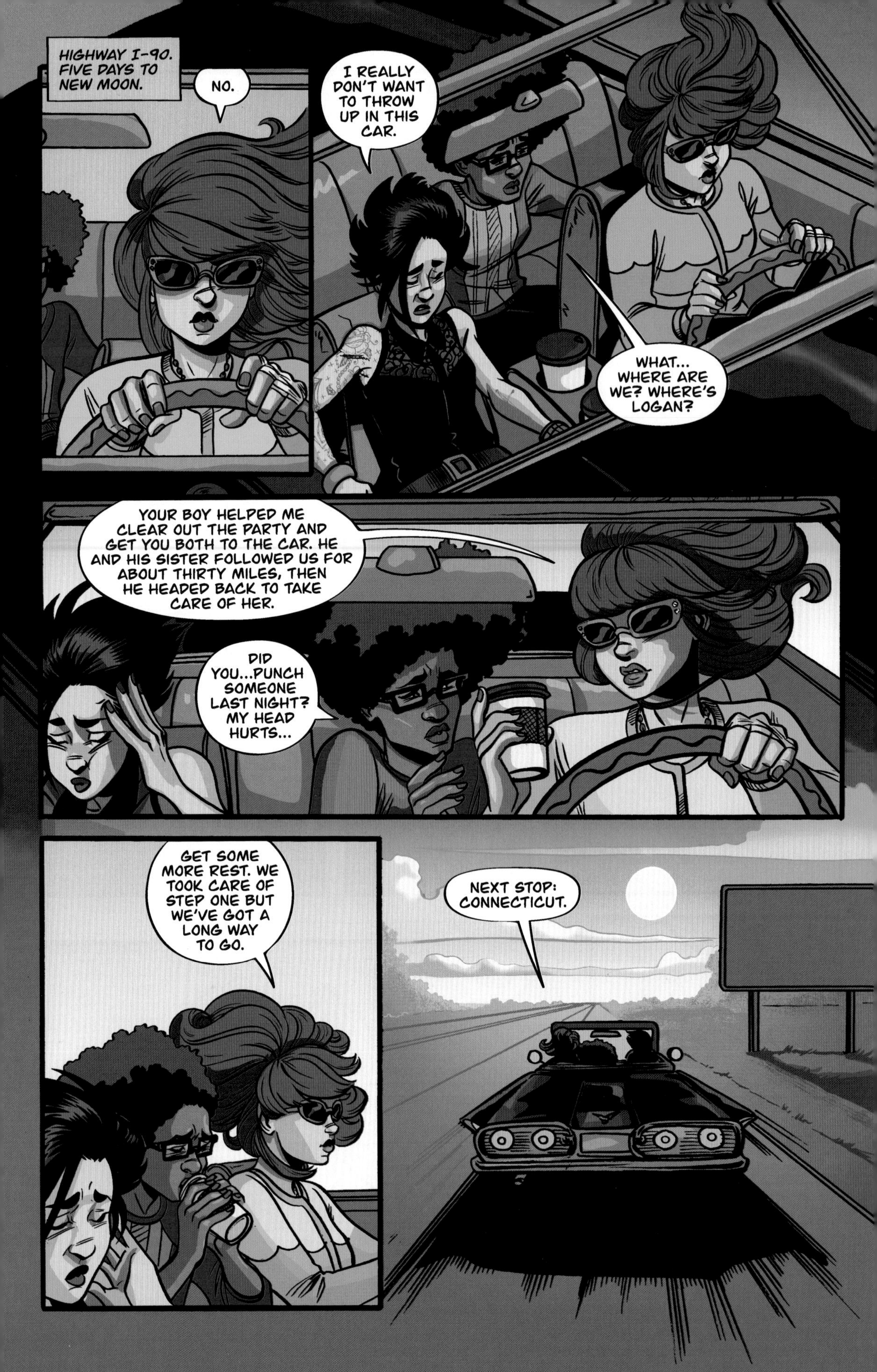
HIGHWAY I-90. FIVE DAYS TO NEW MOON.
NO.
I REALLY DON'T WANT TO THROW UP IN THIS CAR.
WHAT... WHERE ARE WE? WHERE'S LOGAN?
YOUR BOY HELPED ME CLEAR OUT THE PARTY AND GET YOU BOTH TO THE CAR. HE AND HIS SISTER FOLLOWED US FOR ABOUT THIRTY MILES, THEN HE HEADED BACK TO TAKE CARE OF HER.
DID YOU...PUNCH SOMEONE LAST NIGHT? MY HEAD HURTS...
GET SOME MORE REST. WE TOOK CARE OF STEP ONE BUT WE'VE GOT A LONG WAY TO GO.
NEXT STOP: CONNECTICUT.

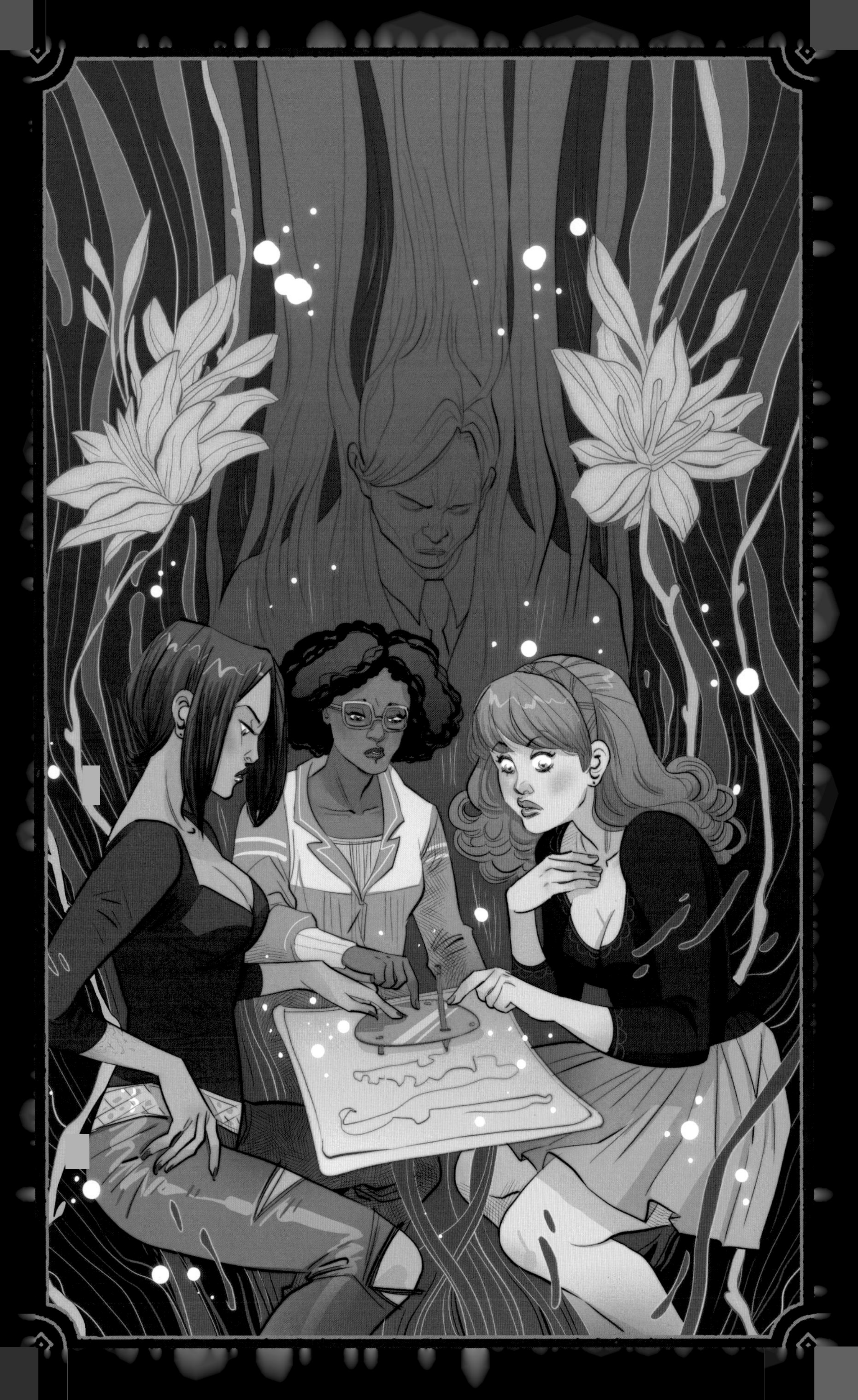

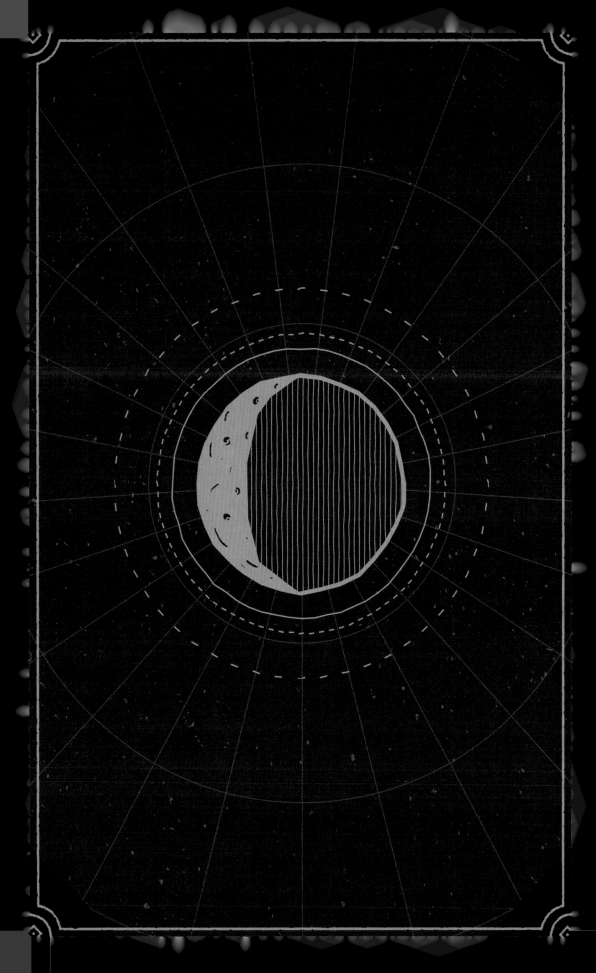

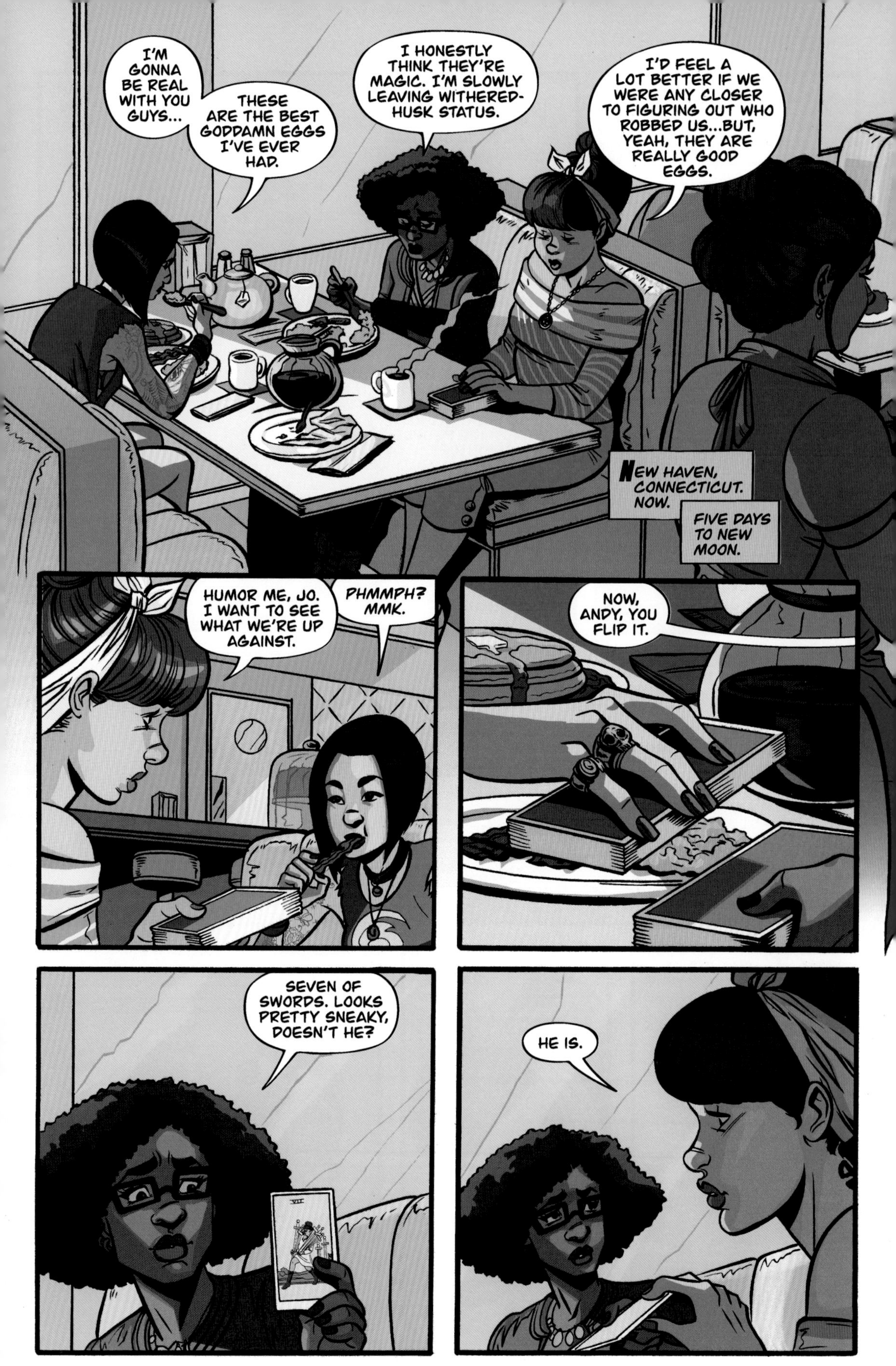
I'M GONNA BE REAL WITH YOU GUYS...
THESE ARE THE BEST GODDAMN EGGS I'VE EVER HAD.
I HONESTLY THINK THEY'RE MAGIC. I'M SLOWLY LEAVING WITHERED-HUSK STATUS.
I'D FEEL A LOT BETTER IF WE WERE ANY CLOSER TO FIGURING OUT WHO ROBBED US...BUT, YEAH, THEY ARE REALLY GOOD EGGS.
NEW HAVEN, CONNECTICUT. NOW.
FIVE DAYS TO NEW MOON.
HUMOR ME, JO. I WANT TO SEE WHAT WE'RE UP AGAINST.
PHMMPH? MMK.
NOW, ANDY, YOU FLIP IT.
SEVEN OF SWORDS. LOOKS PRETTY SNEAKY, DOESN'T HE?
HE IS.

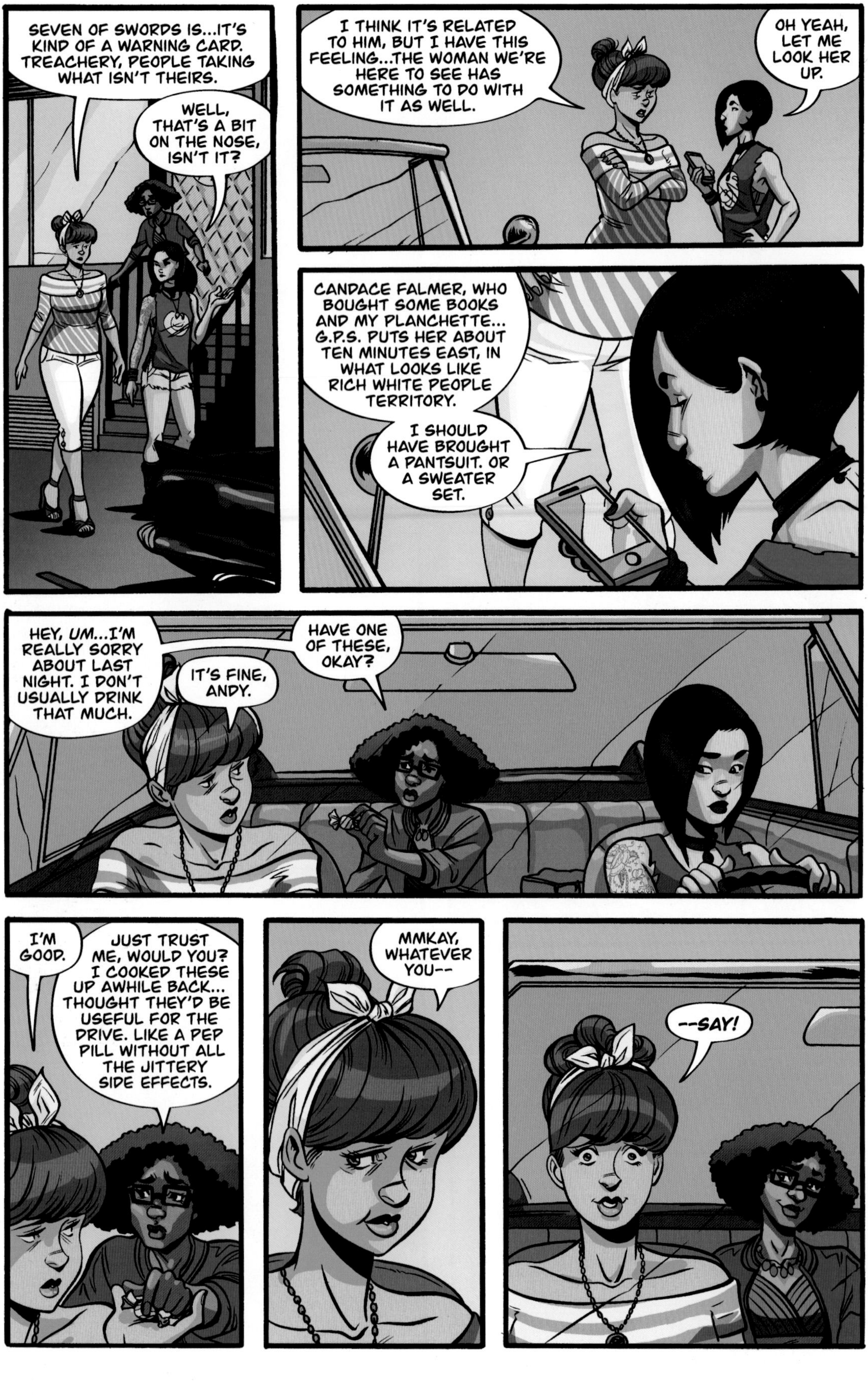
SEVEN OF SWORDS IS...IT'S KIND OF A WARNING CARD. TREACHERY, PEOPLE TAKING WHAT ISN'T THEIRS.
WELL, THAT'S A BIT ON THE NOSE, ISN'T IT?
I THINK IT'S RELATED TO HIM, BUT I HAVE THIS FEELING...THE WOMAN WE'RE HERE TO SEE HAS SOMETHING TO DO WITH IT AS WELL.
OH YEAH, LET ME LOOK HER UP.
CANDACE FALMER, WHO BOUGHT SOME BOOKS AND MY PLANCHETTE... G.P.S. PUTS HER ABOUT TEN MINUTES EAST, IN WHAT LOOKS LIKE RICH WHITE PEOPLE TERRITORY.
I SHOULD HAVE BROUGHT A PANTSUIT. OR A SWEATER SET.
HEY, UM...I'M REALLY SORRY ABOUT LAST NIGHT. I DON'T USUALLY DRINK THAT MUCH.
IT'S FINE, ANDY.
HAVE ONE OF THESE, OKAY?
I'M GOOD.
JUST TRUST ME, WOULD YOU? I COOKED THESE UP AWHILE BACK... THOUGHT THEY'D BE USEFUL FOR THE DRIVE. LIKE A PEP PILL WITHOUT ALL THE JITTERY SIDE EFFECTS.
MMKAY, WHATEVER YOU--
--SAY!

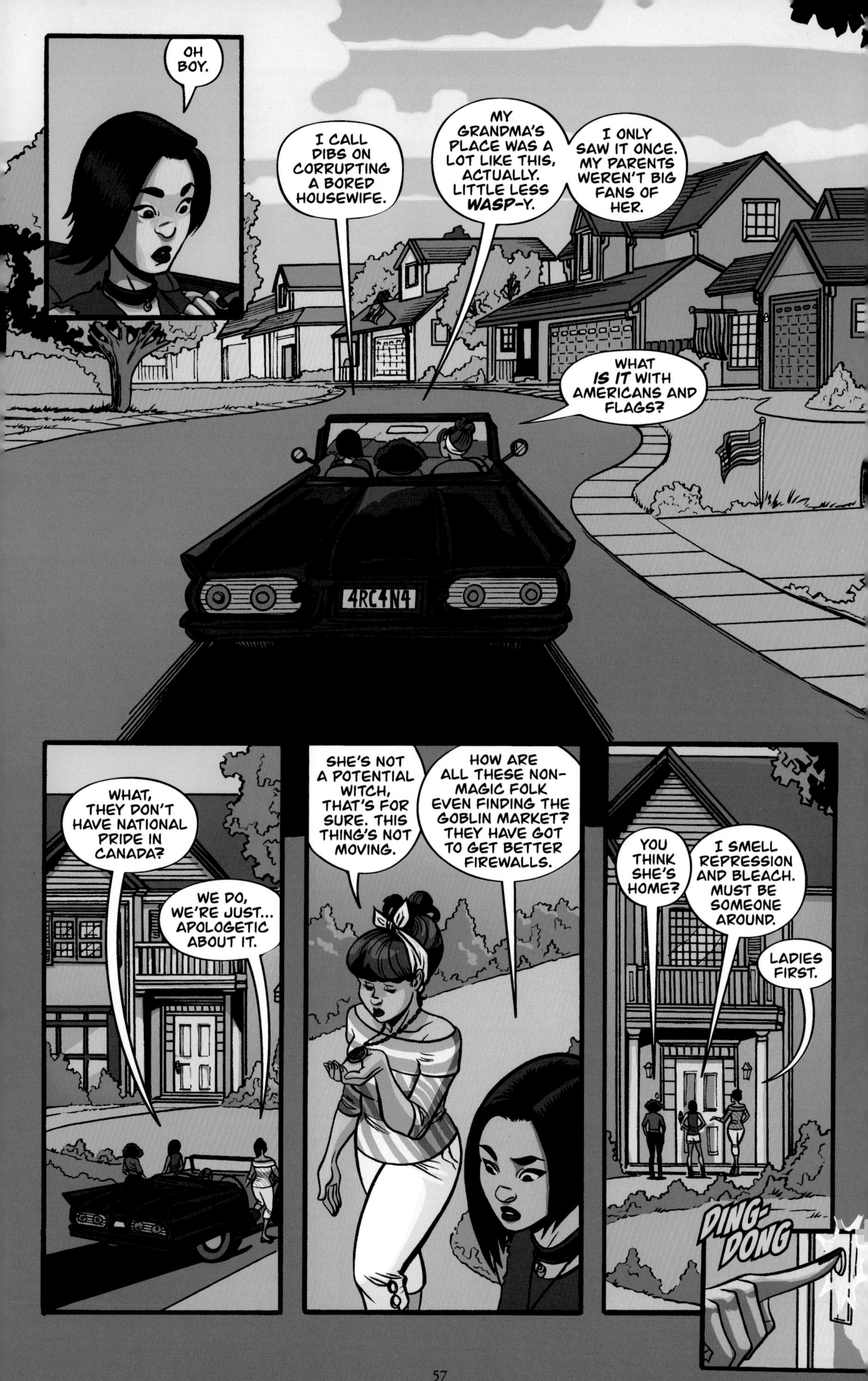
OH BOY.
I CALL DIBS ON CORRUPTING A BORED HOUSEWIFE.
MY GRANDMA'S PLACE WAS A LOT LIKE THIS, ACTUALLY. LITTLE LESS WASP-Y.
I ONLY SAW IT ONCE. MY PARENTS WEREN'T BIG FANS OF HER.
WHAT IS IT WITH AMERICANS AND FLAGS?
4RC4N4
WHAT, THEY DON'T HAVE NATIONAL PRIDE IN CANADA?
WE DO, WE'RE JUST... APOLOGETIC ABOUT IT.
SHE'S NOT A POTENTIAL WITCH, THAT'S FOR SURE. THIS THING'S NOT MOVING.
HOW ARE ALL THESE NON-MAGIC FOLK EVEN FINDING THE GOBLIN MARKET? THEY HAVE GOT TO GET BETTER FIREWALLS.
YOU THINK SHE'S HOME?
I SMELL REPRESSION AND BLEACH. MUST BE SOMEONE AROUND.
LADIES FIRST.
DING-DONG

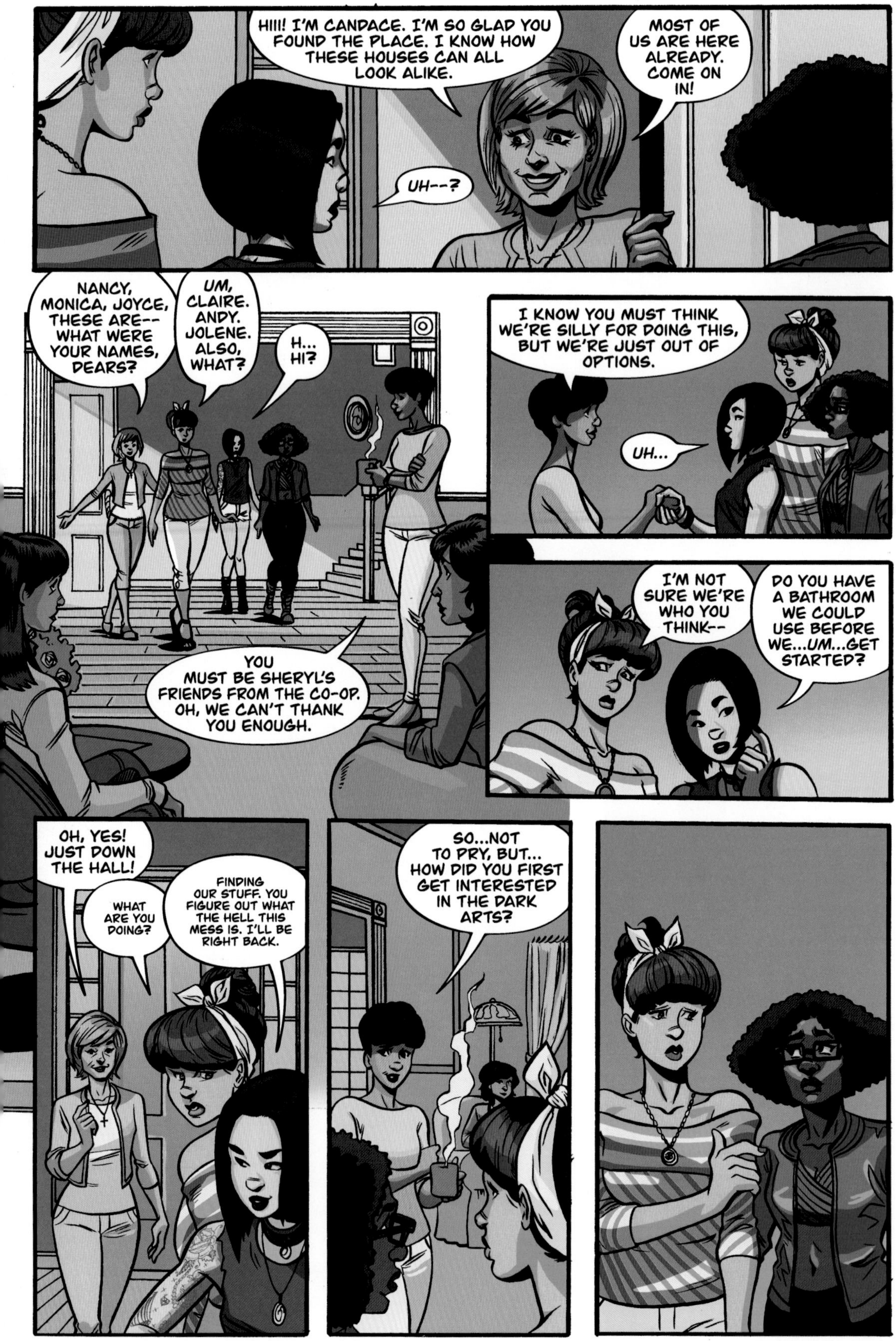
HIII! I'M CANDACE. I'M SO GLAD YOU FOUND THE PLACE. I KNOW HOW THESE HOUSES CAN ALL LOOK ALIKE.
MOST OF US ARE HERE ALREADY. COME ON IN!
UH--?
NANCY, MONICA, JOYCE, THESE ARE-- WHAT WERE YOUR NAMES, DEARS?
UM, CLAIRE. ANDY. JOLENE. ALSO, WHAT?
H... HI?
YOU MUST BE SHERYL'S FRIENDS FROM THE CO-OP. OH, WE CAN'T THANK YOU ENOUGH.
I KNOW YOU MUST THINK WE'RE SILLY FOR DOING THIS, BUT WE'RE JUST OUT OF OPTIONS.
UH...
I'M NOT SURE WE'RE WHO YOU THINK--
DO YOU HAVE A BATHROOM WE COULD USE BEFORE WE...UM...GET STARTED?
OH, YES! JUST DOWN THE HALL!
WHAT ARE YOU DOING?
FINDING OUR STUFF. YOU FIGURE OUT WHAT THE HELL THIS MESS IS. I'LL BE RIGHT BACK.
SO...NOT TO PRY, BUT... HOW DID YOU FIRST GET INTERESTED IN THE DARK ARTS?

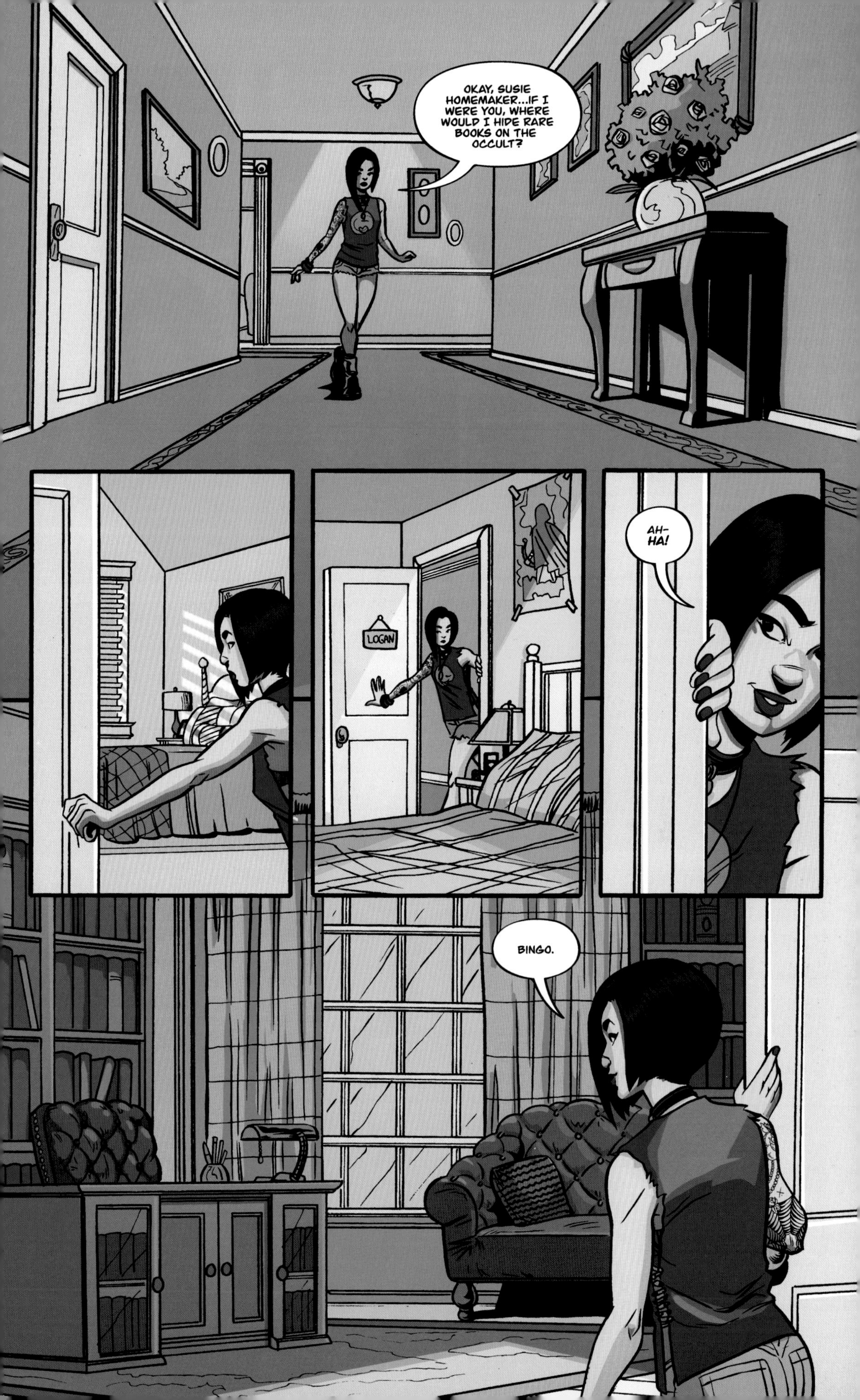
OKAY, SUSIE HOMEMAKER...IF I WERE YOU, WHERE WOULD I HIDE RARE BOOKS ON THE OCCULT?
LOGAN
AH-HA!
BINGO.

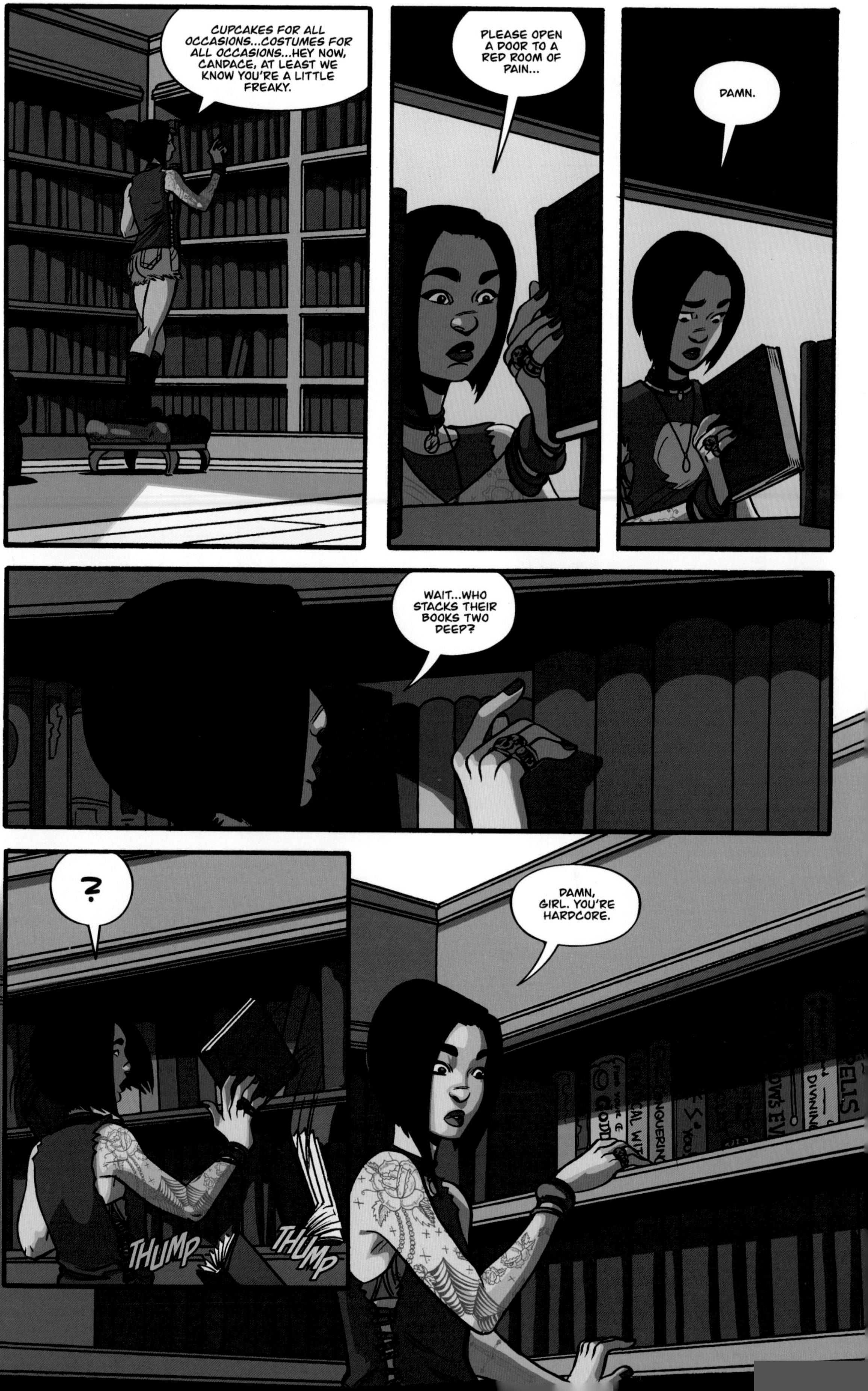
CUPCAKES FOR ALL OCCASIONS...COSTUMES FOR ALL OCCASIONS...HEY NOW, CANDACE, AT LEAST WE KNOW YOU'RE A LITTLE FREAKY.
PLEASE OPEN A DOOR TO A RED ROOM OF PAIN...
DAMN.
WAIT...WHO STACKS THEIR BOOKS TWO DEEP?
?
DAMN, GIRL. YOU'RE HARDCORE.
THUMP
THUMP

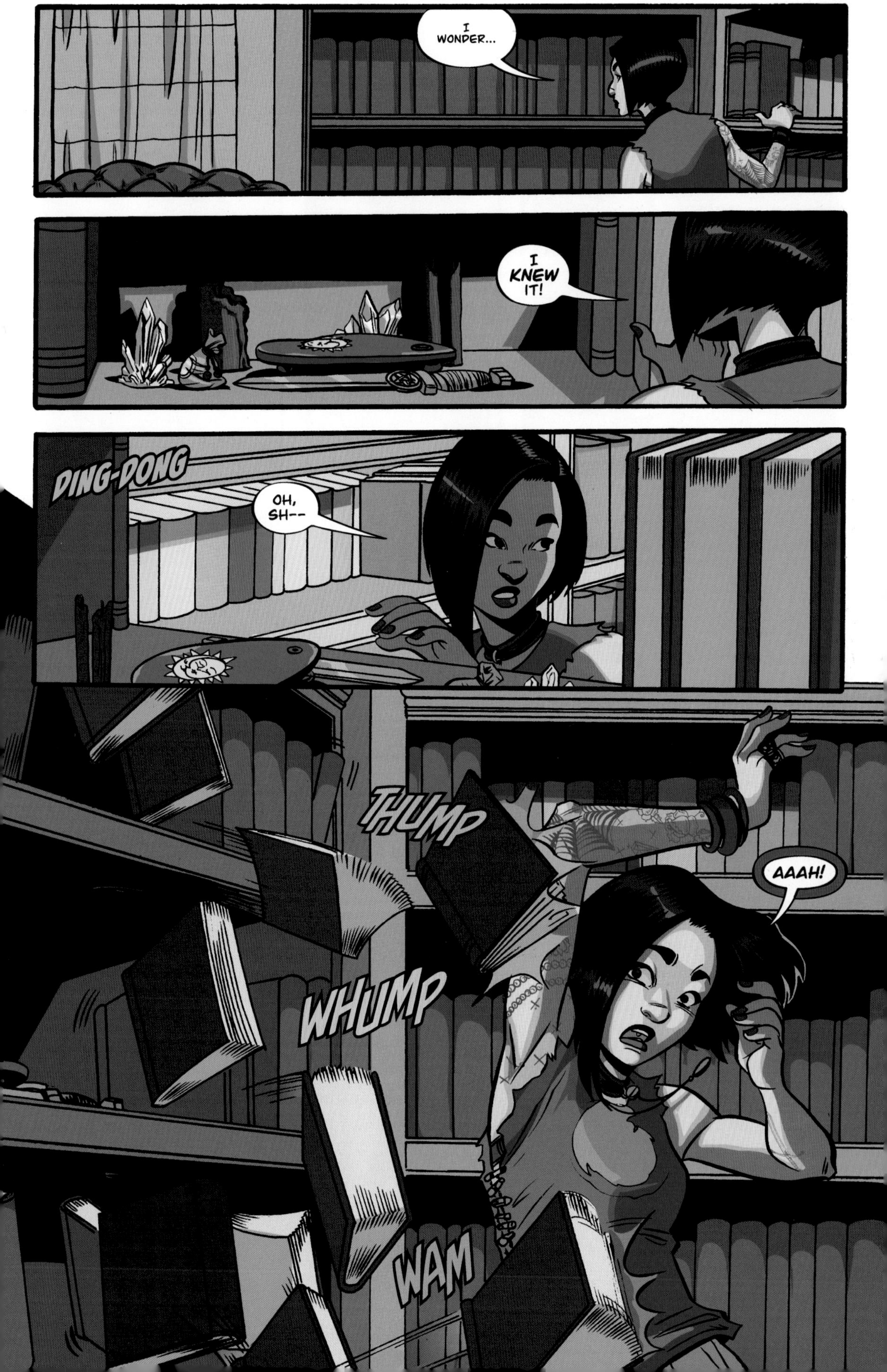
I WONDER...
I KNEW IT!
DING-DONG
OH, SH--
THUMP
AAAH!
WHUMP
WAM

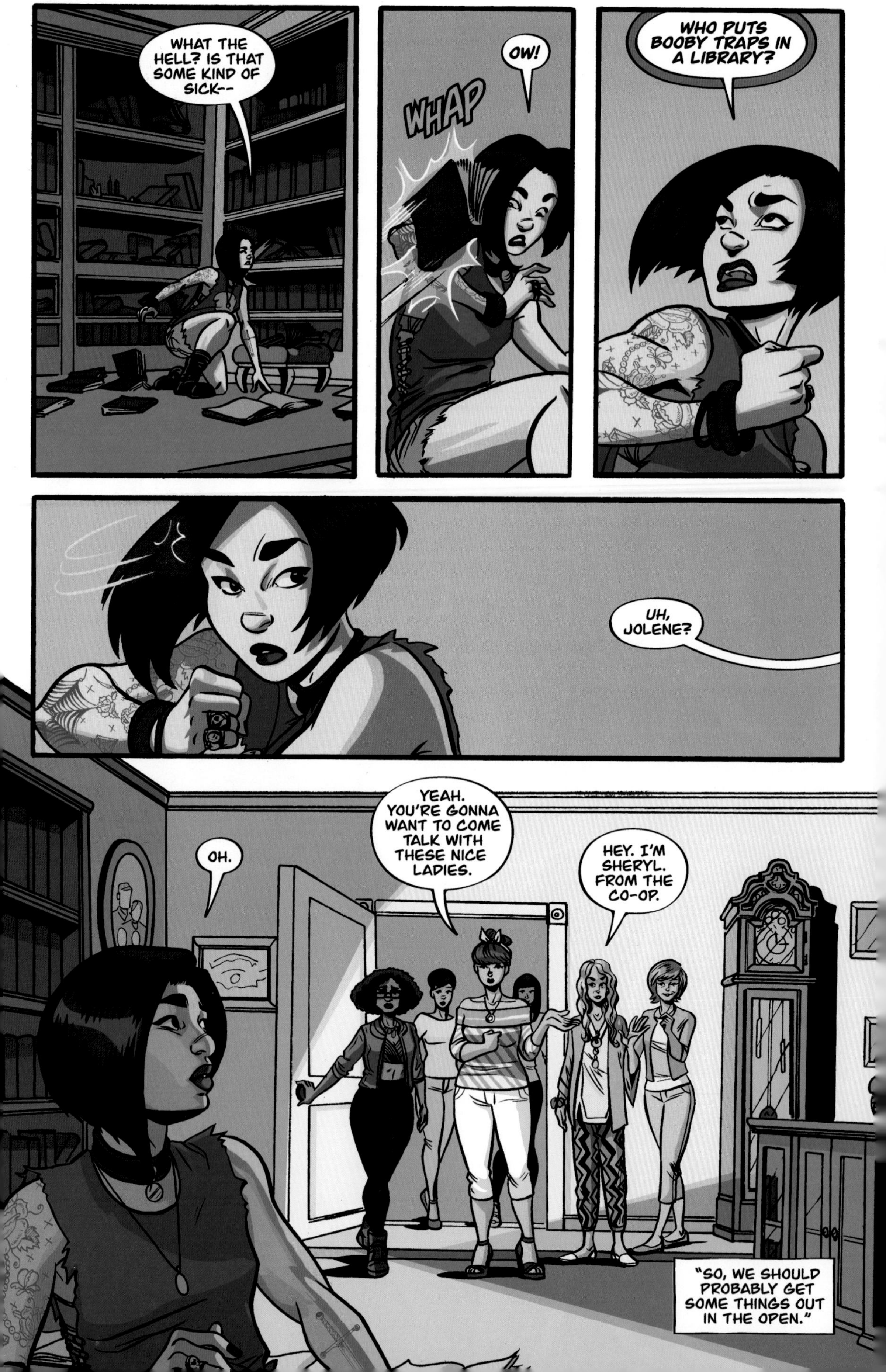
WHAT THE HELL? IS THAT SOME KIND OF SICK--
WHAP
OW!
WHO PUTS BOOBY TRAPS IN A LIBRARY?
UH, JOLENE?
OH.
YEAH. YOU'RE GONNA WANT TO COME TALK WITH THESE NICE LADIES.
HEY. I'M SHERYL. FROM THE CO-OP.
"SO, WE SHOULD PROBABLY GET SOME THINGS OUT IN THE OPEN."

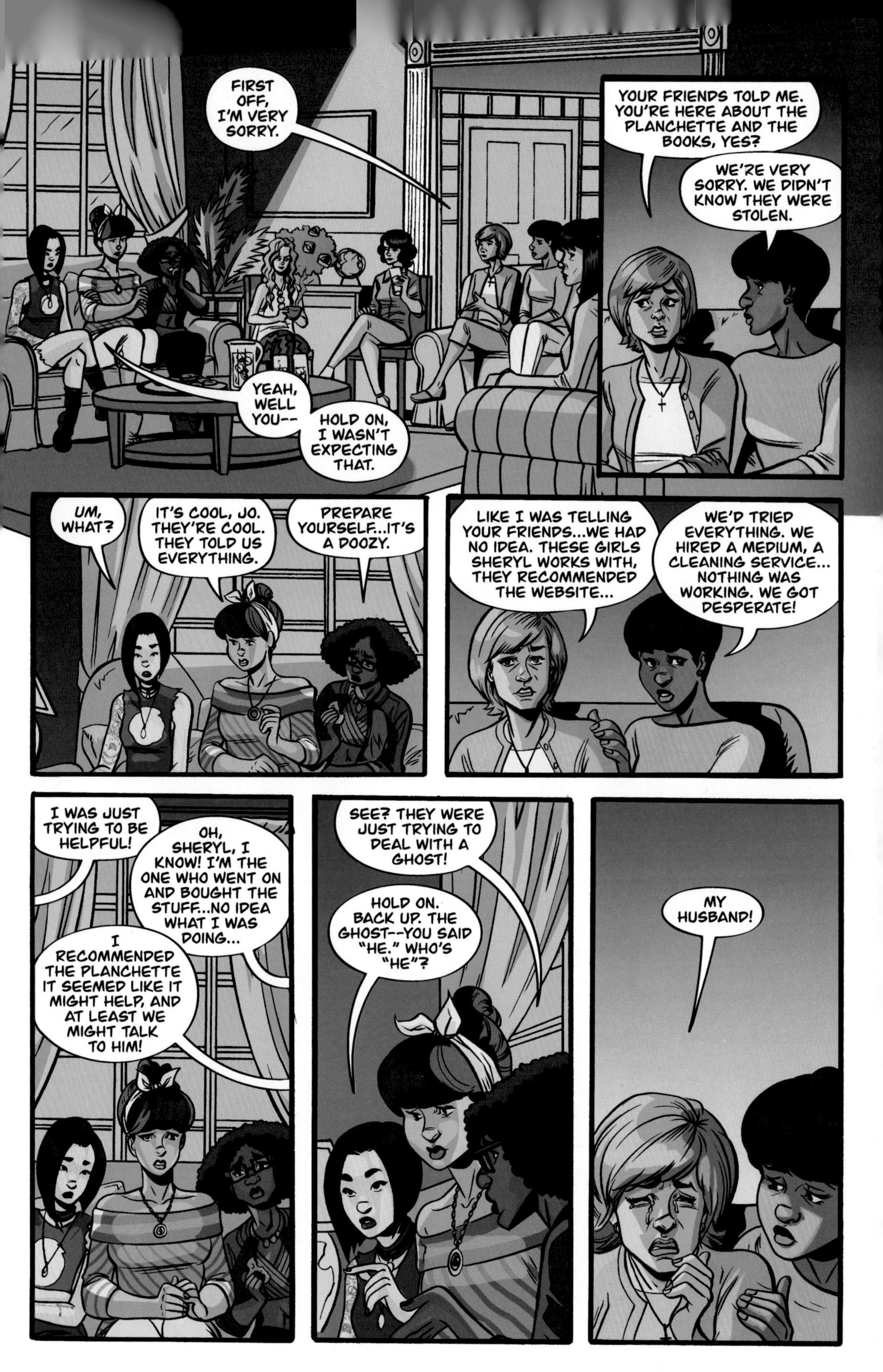
FIRST OFF, I'M VERY SORRY.
YEAH, WELL YOU--
HOLD ON, I WASN'T EXPECTING THAT.
YOUR FRIENDS TOLD ME. YOU'RE HERE ABOUT THE PLANCHETTE AND THE BOOKS, YES?
WE'RE VERY SORRY. WE DIDN'T KNOW THEY WERE STOLEN.
UM, WHAT?
IT'S COOL, JO. THEY'RE COOL. THEY TOLD US EVERYTHING.
PREPARE YOURSELF...IT'S A DOOZY.
LIKE I WAS TELLING YOUR FRIENDS...WE HAD NO IDEA. THESE GIRLS SHERYL WORKS WITH, THEY RECOMMENDED THE WEBSITE...
WE'D TRIED EVERYTHING. WE HIRED A MEDIUM, A CLEANING SERVICE... NOTHING WAS WORKING. WE GOT DESPERATE!
I WAS JUST TRYING TO BE HELPFUL!
OH, SHERYL, I KNOW! I'M THE ONE WHO WENT ON AND BOUGHT THE STUFF...NO IDEA WHAT I WAS DOING...
I RECOMMENDED THE PLANCHETTE IT SEEMED LIKE IT MIGHT HELP, AND AT LEAST WE MIGHT TALK TO HIM!
SEE? THEY WERE JUST TRYING TO DEAL WITH A GHOST!
HOLD ON. BACK UP. THE GHOST--YOU SAID "HE." WHO'S "HE"?
MY HUSBAND!

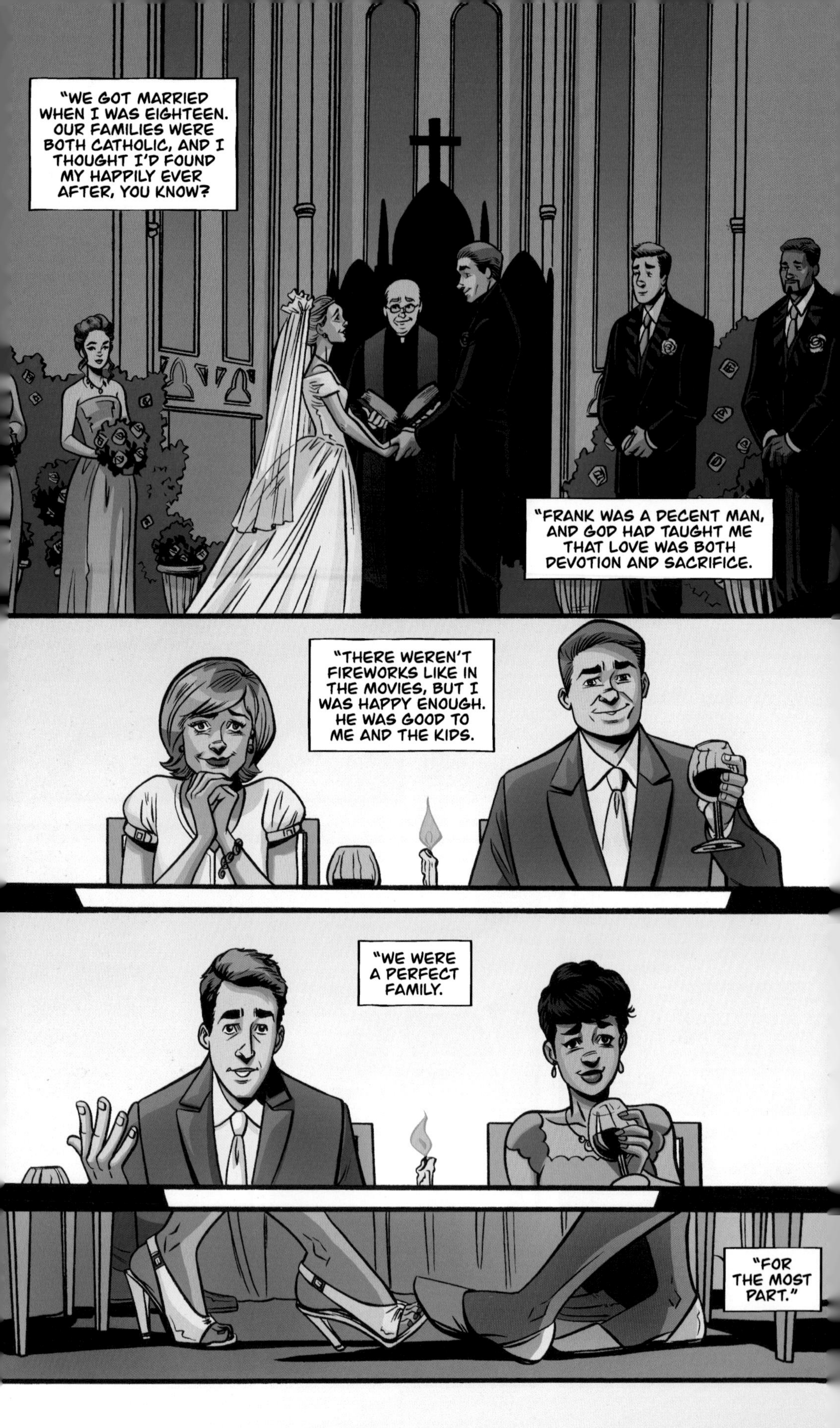
"WE GOT MARRIED WHEN I WAS EIGHTEEN. OUR FAMILIES WERE BOTH CATHOLIC, AND I THOUGHT I'D FOUND MY HAPPILY EVER AFTER, YOU KNOW?
"FRANK WAS A DECENT MAN, AND GOD HAD TAUGHT ME THAT LOVE WAS BOTH DEVOTION AND SACRIFICE.
"THERE WEREN'T FIREWORKS LIKE IN THE MOVIES, BUT I WAS HAPPY ENOUGH. HE WAS GOOD TO ME AND THE KIDS.
"WE WERE A PERFECT FAMILY.
"FOR THE MOST PART."

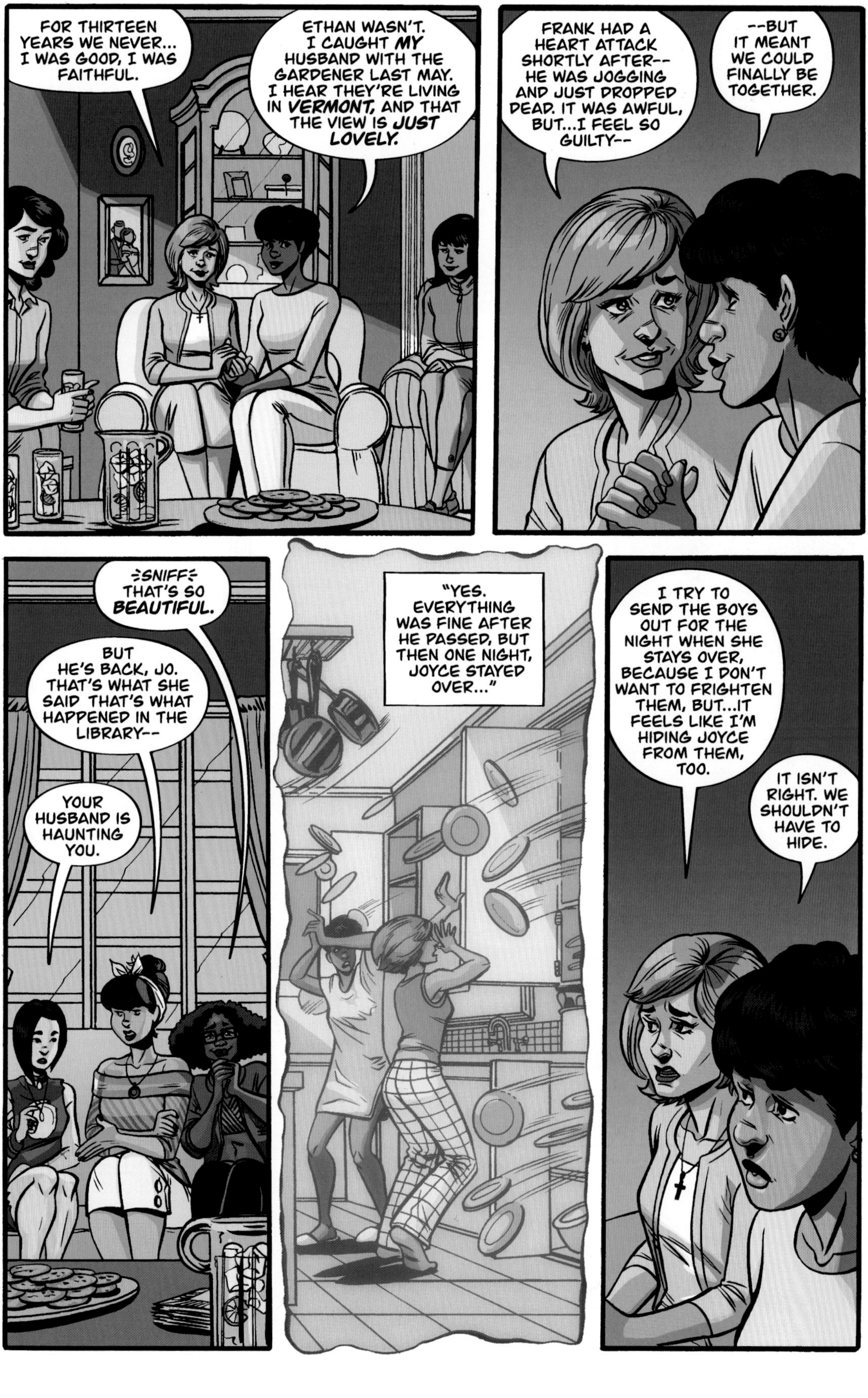

FOR THIRTEEN YEARS WE NEVER... I WAS GOOD, I WAS FAITHFUL.
ETHAN WASN'T. I CAUGHT MY HUSBAND WITH THE GARDENER LAST MAY. I HEAR THEY'RE LIVING IN VERMONT, AND THAT THE VIEW IS JUST LOVELY.
FRANK HAD A HEART ATTACK SHORTLY AFTER-- HE WAS JOGGING AND JUST DROPPED DEAD. IT WAS AWFUL, BUT...I FEEL SO GUILTY--
--BUT IT MEANT WE COULD FINALLY BE TOGETHER.
=SNIFF= THAT'S SO BEAUTIFUL.
BUT HE'S BACK, JO. THAT'S WHAT SHE SAID THAT'S WHAT HAPPENED IN THE LIBRARY--
YOUR HUSBAND IS HAUNTING YOU.
"YES. EVERYTHING WAS FINE AFTER HE PASSED, BUT THEN ONE NIGHT, JOYCE STAYED OVER..."
I TRY TO SEND THE BOYS OUT FOR THE NIGHT WHEN SHE STAYS OVER, BECAUSE I DON'T WANT TO FRIGHTEN THEM, BUT...IT FEELS LIKE I'M HIDING JOYCE FROM THEM, TOO.
IT ISN'T RIGHT. WE SHOULDN'T HAVE TO HIDE.

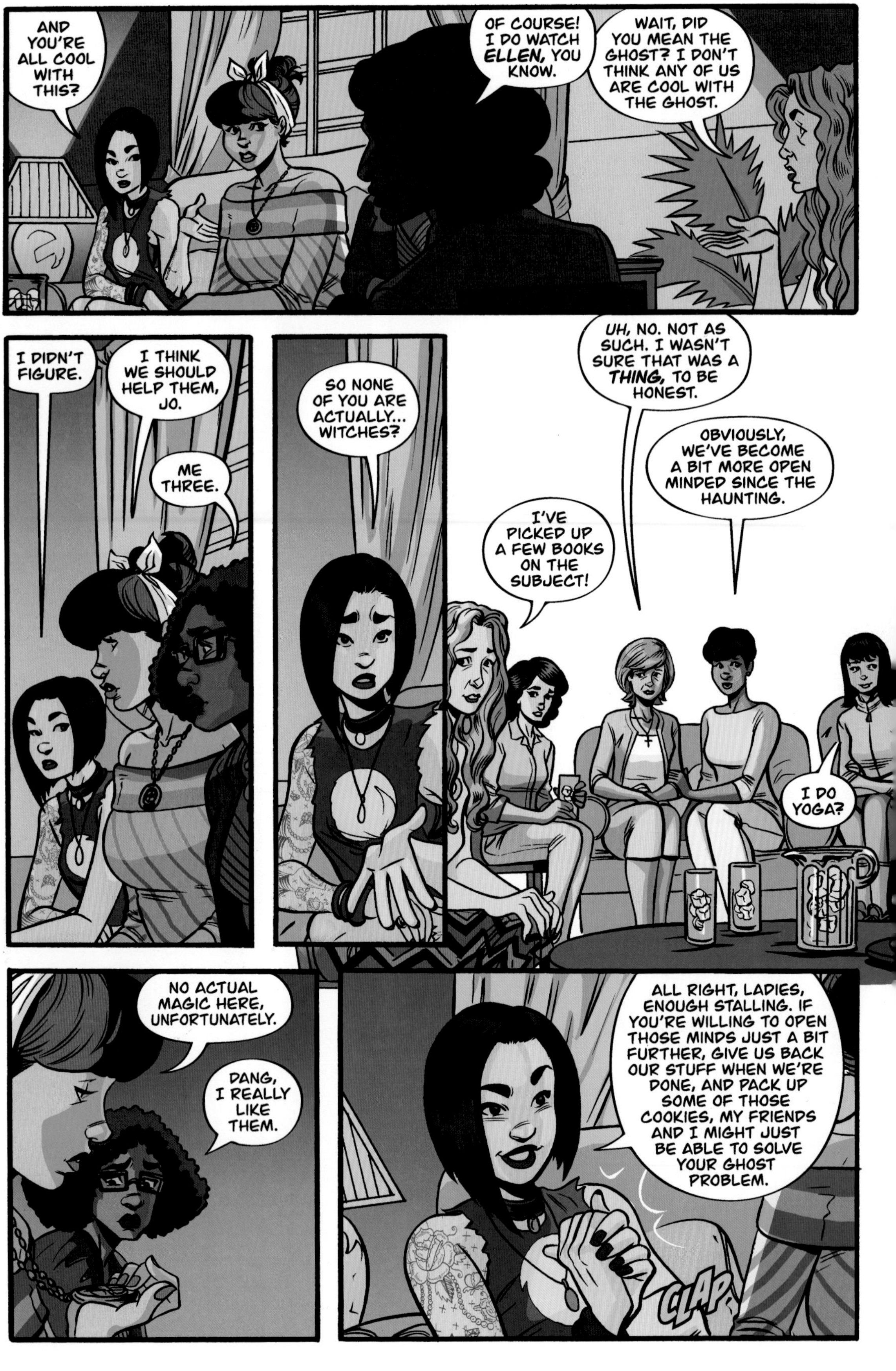
AND YOU'RE ALL COOL WITH THIS?
OF COURSE! I DO WATCH ELLEN, YOU KNOW.
WAIT, DID YOU MEAN THE GHOST? I DON'T THINK ANY OF US ARE COOL WITH THE GHOST.
I DIDN'T FIGURE.
I THINK WE SHOULD HELP THEM, JO.
ME THREE.
SO NONE OF YOU ARE ACTUALLY... WITCHES?
UH, NO. NOT AS SUCH. I WASN'T SURE THAT WAS A THING, TO BE HONEST.
OBVIOUSLY, WE'VE BECOME A BIT MORE OPEN MINDED SINCE THE HAUNTING.
I'VE PICKED UP A FEW BOOKS ON THE SUBJECT!
I DO YOGA?
NO ACTUAL MAGIC HERE, UNFORTUNATELY.
DANG, I REALLY LIKE THEM.
ALL RIGHT, LADIES, ENOUGH STALLING. IF YOU'RE WILLING TO OPEN THOSE MINDS JUST A BIT FURTHER, GIVE US BACK OUR STUFF WHEN WE'RE DONE, AND PACK UP SOME OF THOSE COOKIES, MY FRIENDS AND I MIGHT JUST BE ABLE TO SOLVE YOUR GHOST PROBLEM.
CLAP

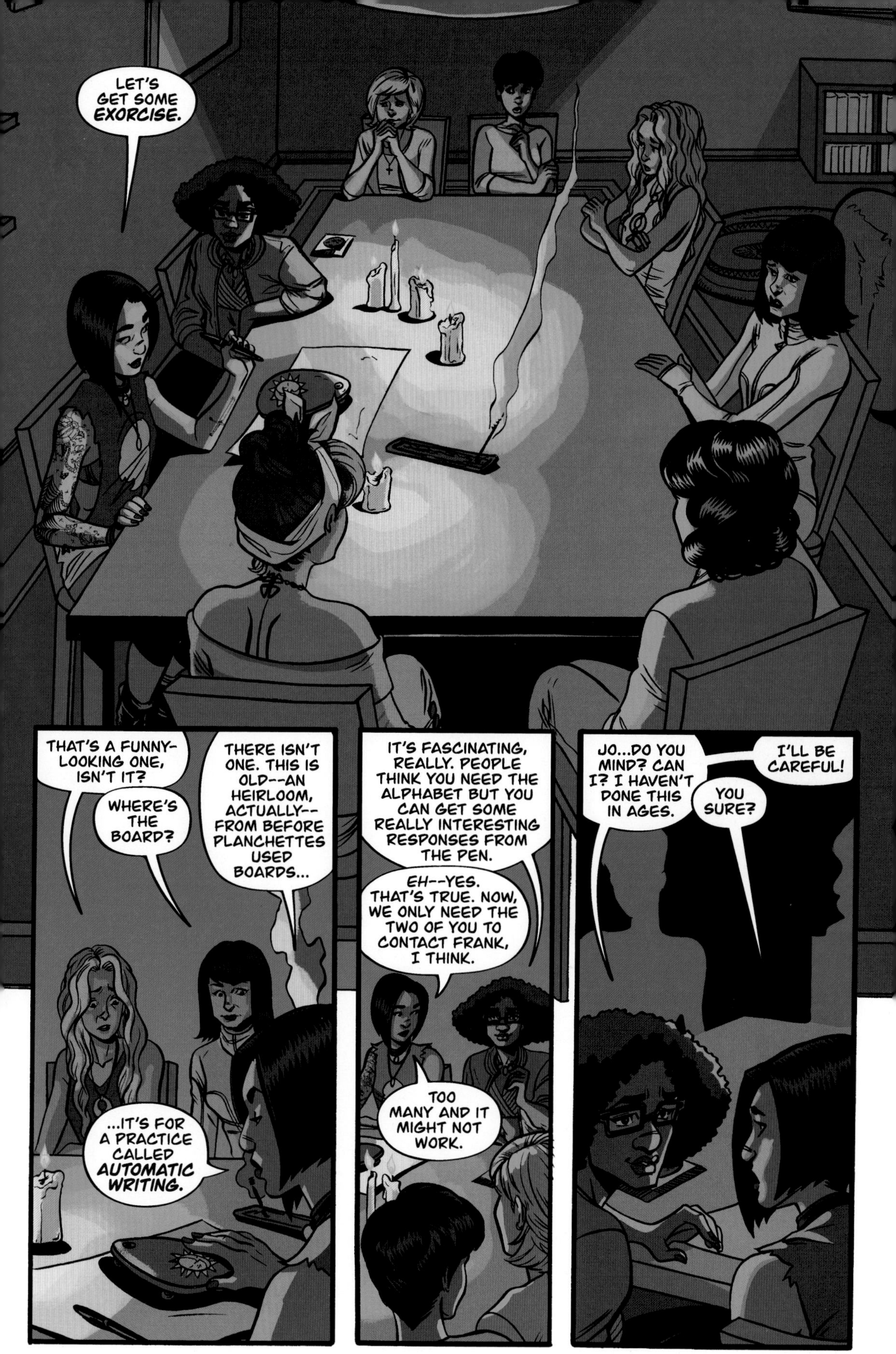
LET'S GET SOME EXORCISE.
THAT'S A FUNNY-LOOKING ONE, ISN'T IT?
WHERE'S THE BOARD?
THERE ISN'T ONE. THIS IS OLD--AN HEIRLOOM, ACTUALLY--FROM BEFORE PLANCHETTES USED BOARDS...
...IT'S FOR A PRACTICE CALLED AUTOMATIC WRITING.
IT'S FASCINATING, REALLY. PEOPLE THINK YOU NEED THE ALPHABET BUT YOU CAN GET SOME REALLY INTERESTING RESPONSES FROM THE PEN.
EH--YES. THAT'S TRUE. NOW, WE ONLY NEED THE TWO OF YOU TO CONTACT FRANK, I THINK.
TOO MANY AND IT MIGHT NOT WORK.
JO...DO YOU MIND? CAN I? I HAVEN'T DONE THIS IN AGES.
YOU SURE?
I'LL BE CAREFUL!

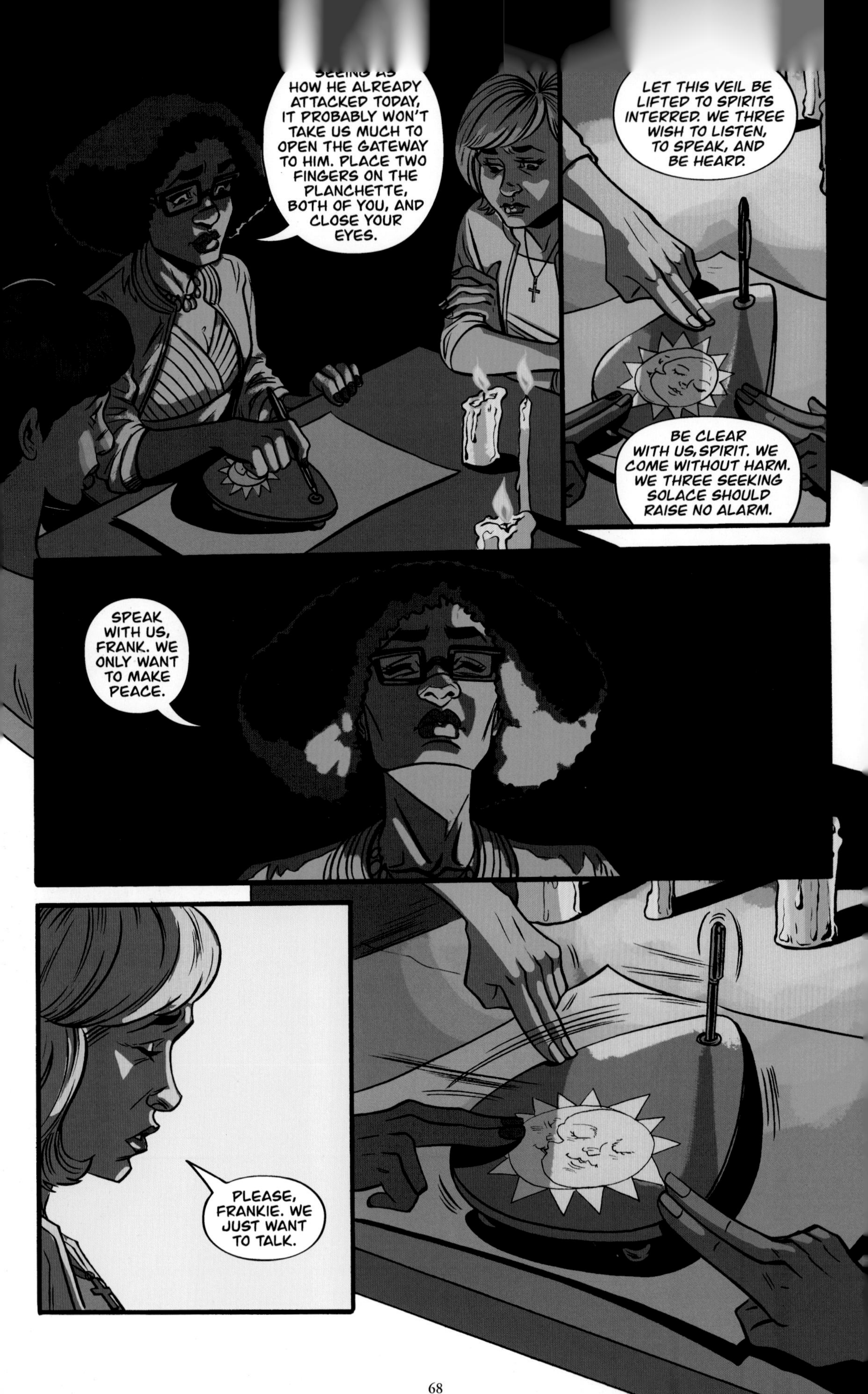
HOW HE ALREADY ATTACKED TODAY, IT PROBABLY WON'T TAKE US MUCH TO OPEN THE GATEWAY TO HIM. PLACE TWO FINGERS ON THE PLANCHETTE, BOTH OF YOU, AND CLOSE YOUR EYES.
LET THIS VEIL BE LIFTED TO SPIRITS INTERRED. WE THREE WISH TO LISTEN, TO SPEAK, AND BE HEARD.
BE CLEAR WITH US, SPIRIT. WE COME WITHOUT HARM. WE THREE SEEKING SOLACE SHOULD RAISE NO ALARM.
SPEAK WITH US, FRANK. WE ONLY WANT TO MAKE PEACE.
PLEASE, FRANKIE. WE JUST WANT TO TALK.

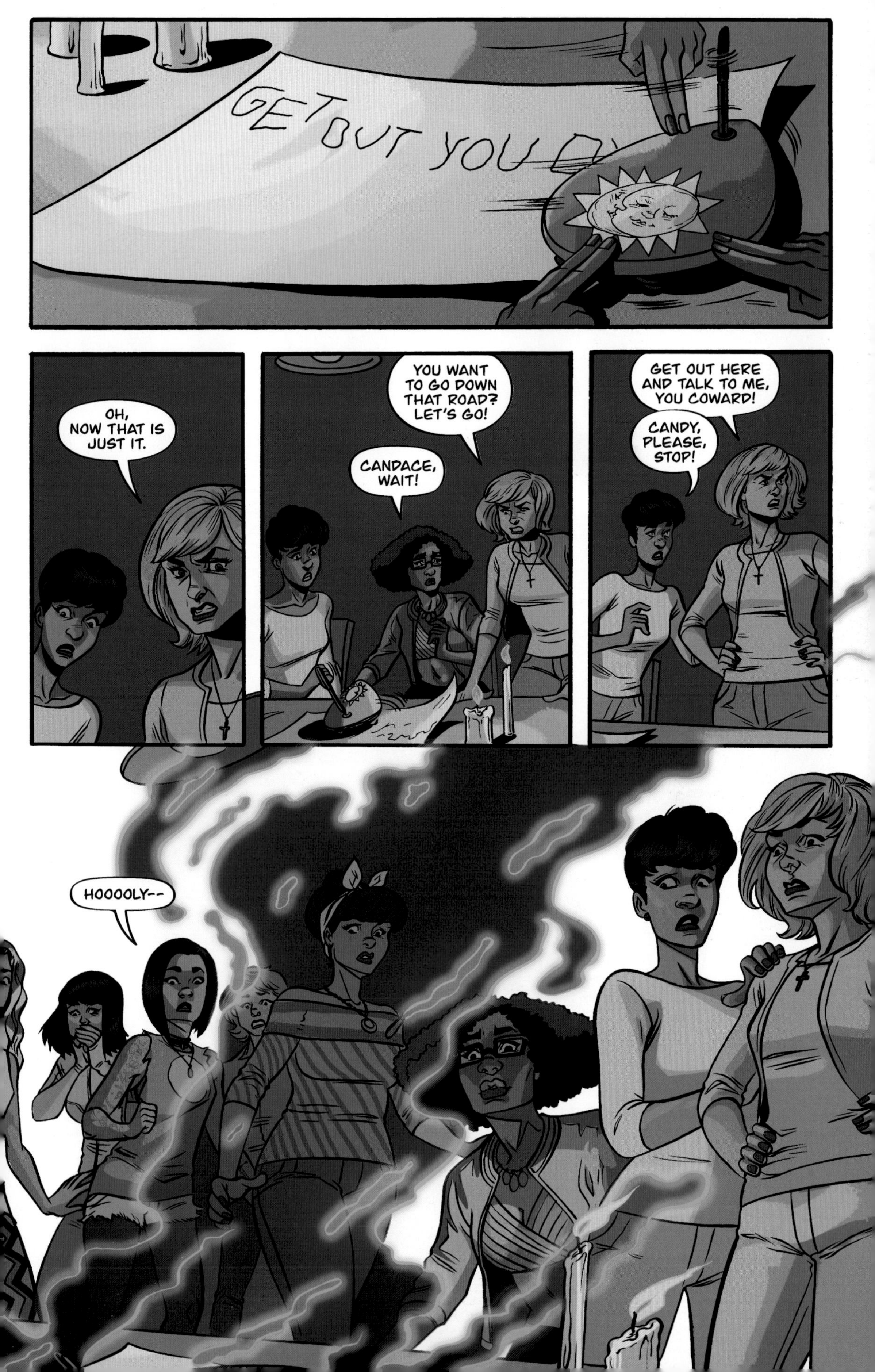
GET OUT YOU
OH, NOW THAT IS JUST IT.
YOU WANT TO GO DOWN THAT ROAD? LET'S GO!
CANDACE, WAIT!
GET OUT HERE AND TALK TO ME, YOU COWARD!
CANDY, PLEASE, STOP!
HOOOOLY--

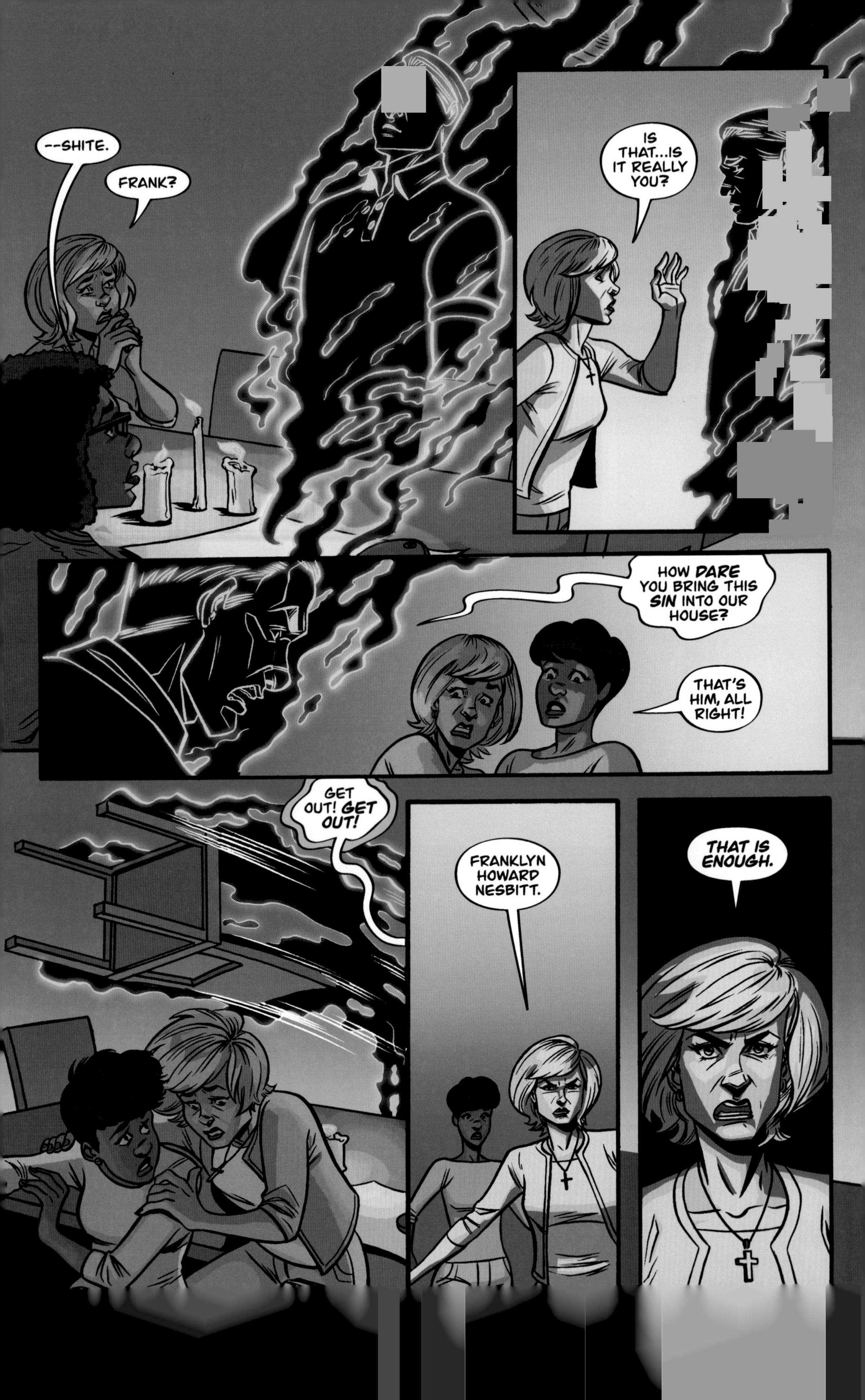
--SHITE.
FRANK?
IS THAT...IS IT REALLY YOU?
HOW DARE YOU BRING THIS SIN INTO OUR HOUSE?
THAT'S HIM, ALL RIGHT!
GET OUT! GET OUT!
FRANKLYN HOWARD NESBITT.
THAT IS ENOUGH.

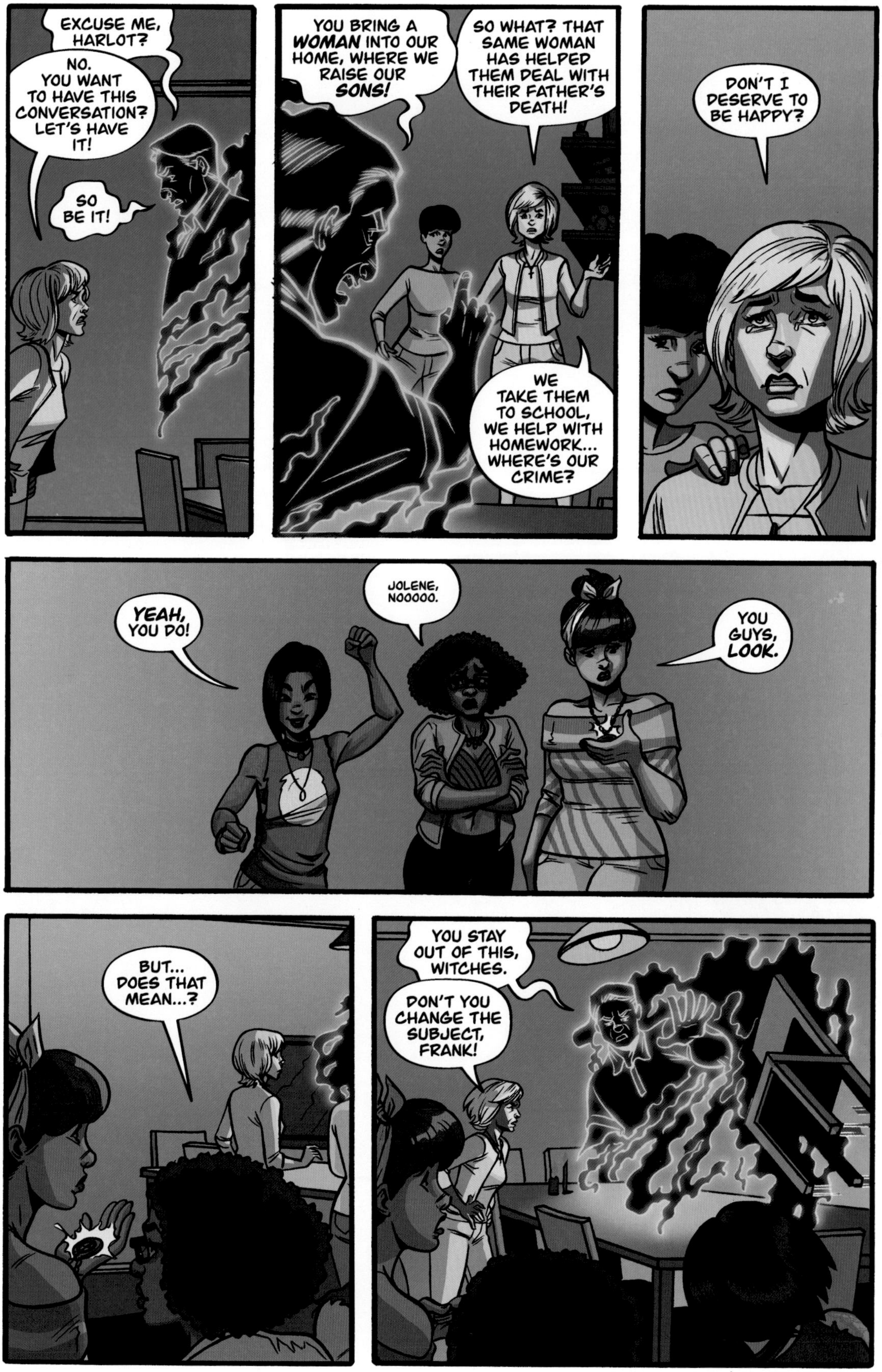
EXCUSE ME, HARLOT?
NO. YOU WANT TO HAVE THIS CONVERSATION? LET'S HAVE IT!
SO BE IT!
YOU BRING A WOMAN INTO OUR HOME, WHERE WE RAISE OUR SONS!
SO WHAT? THAT SAME WOMAN HAS HELPED THEM DEAL WITH THEIR FATHER'S DEATH!
WE TAKE THEM TO SCHOOL, WE HELP WITH HOMEWORK... WHERE'S OUR CRIME?
DON'T I DESERVE TO BE HAPPY?
YEAH, YOU DO!
JOLENE, NOOOOO.
YOU GUYS, LOOK.
BUT... DOES THAT MEAN...?
YOU STAY OUT OF THIS, WITCHES.
DON'T YOU CHANGE THE SUBJECT, FRANK!

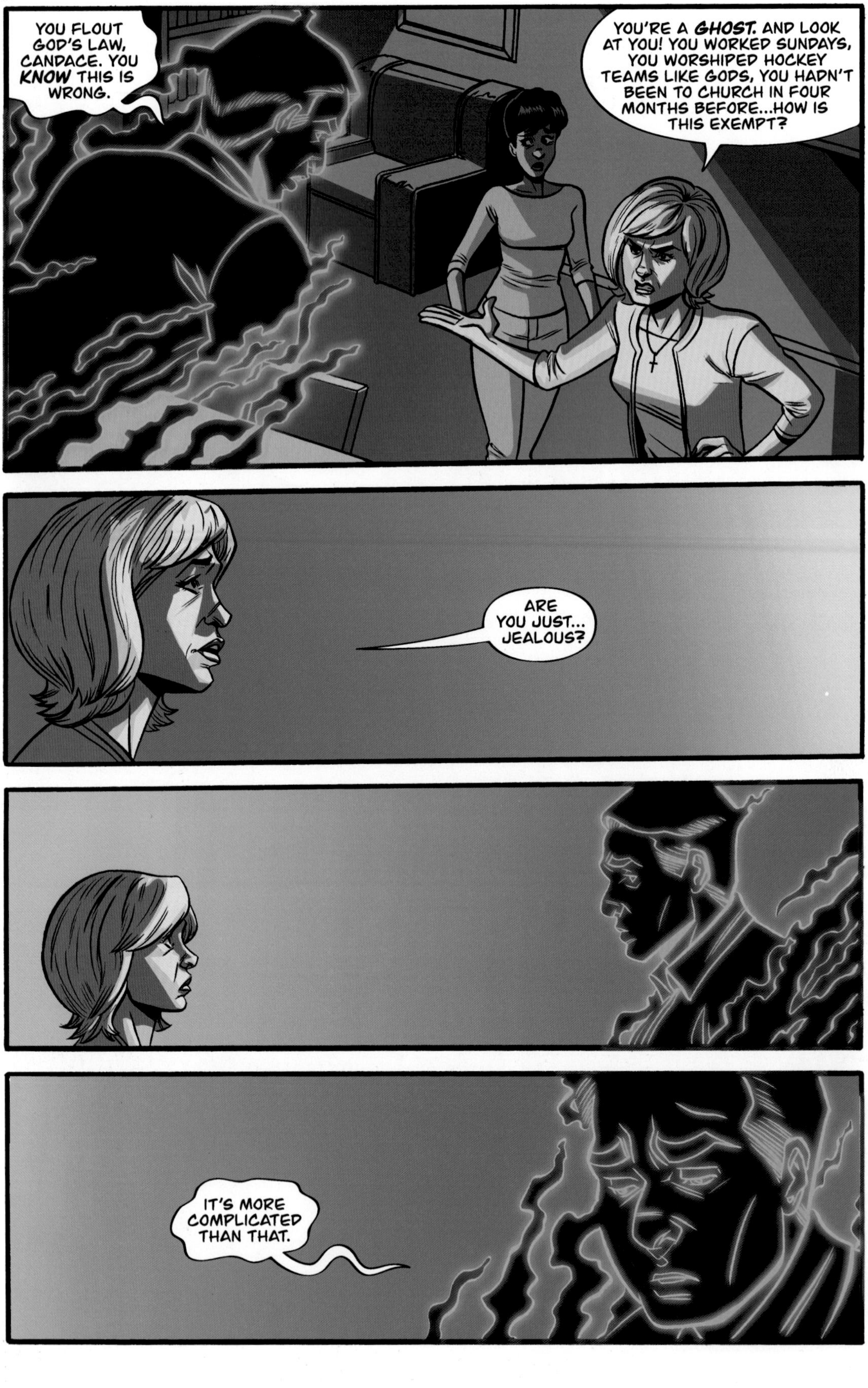
YOU FLOUT GOD'S LAW, CANDACE. YOU KNOW THIS IS WRONG.
YOU'RE A GHOST. AND LOOK AT YOU! YOU WORKED SUNDAYS, YOU WORSHIPED HOCKEY TEAMS LIKE GODS, YOU HADN'T BEEN TO CHURCH IN FOUR MONTHS BEFORE...HOW IS THIS EXEMPT?
ARE YOU JUST... JEALOUS?
IT'S MORE COMPLICATED THAN THAT.

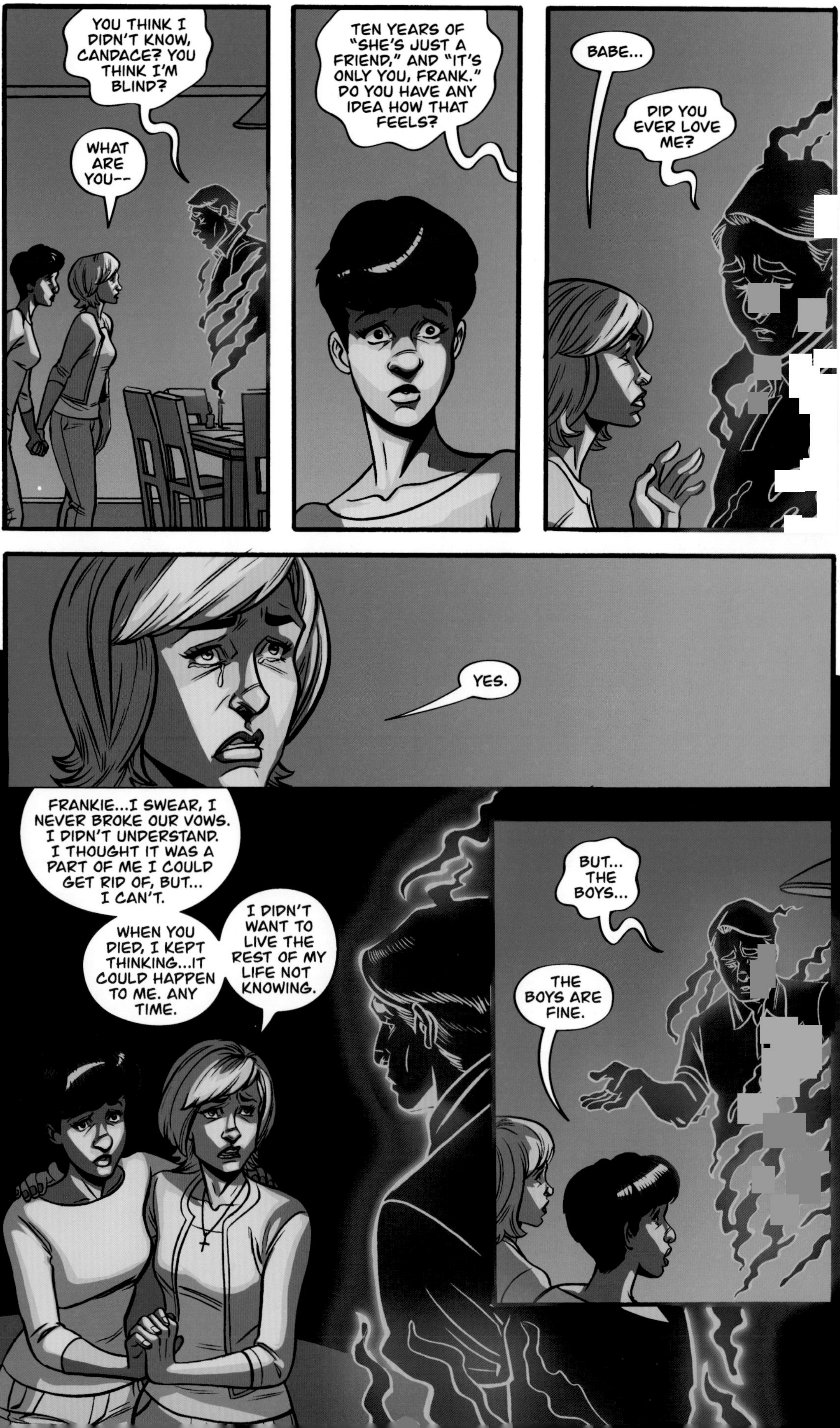
YOU THINK I DIDN'T KNOW, CANDACE? YOU THINK I'M BLIND?
WHAT ARE YOU--
TEN YEARS OF "SHE'S JUST A FRIEND," AND "IT'S ONLY YOU, FRANK." DO YOU HAVE ANY IDEA HOW THAT FEELS?
BABE...
DID YOU EVER LOVE ME?
YES.
FRANKIE...I SWEAR, I NEVER BROKE OUR VOWS. I DIDN'T UNDERSTAND. I THOUGHT IT WAS A PART OF ME I COULD GET RID OF, BUT... I CAN'T.
WHEN YOU DIED, I KEPT THINKING...IT COULD HAPPEN TO ME. ANY TIME.
I DIDN'T WANT TO LIVE THE REST OF MY LIFE NOT KNOWING.
BUT... THE BOYS...
THE BOYS ARE FINE.

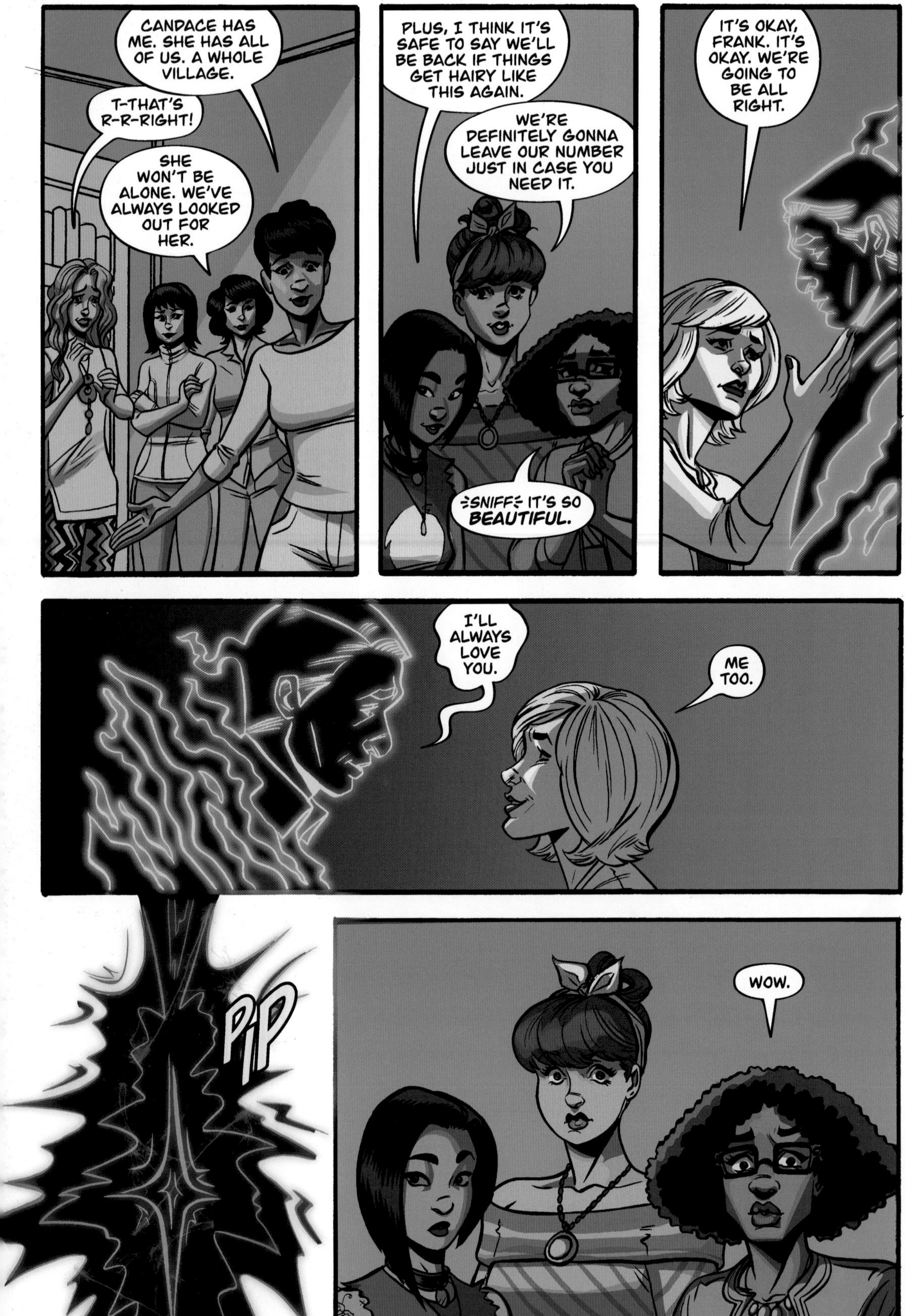

CANDACE HAS ME. SHE HAS ALL OF US. A WHOLE VILLAGE.
T-THAT'S R-R-RIGHT!
SHE WON'T BE ALONE. WE'VE ALWAYS LOOKED OUT FOR HER.
PLUS, I THINK IT'S SAFE TO SAY WE'LL BE BACK IF THINGS GET HAIRY LIKE THIS AGAIN.
WE'RE DEFINITELY GONNA LEAVE OUR NUMBER JUST IN CASE YOU NEED IT.
SNIFF IT'S SO BEAUTIFUL.
IT'S OKAY, FRANK. IT'S OKAY. WE'RE GOING TO BE ALL RIGHT.
I'LL ALWAYS LOVE YOU.
ME TOO.
PIP
WOW.

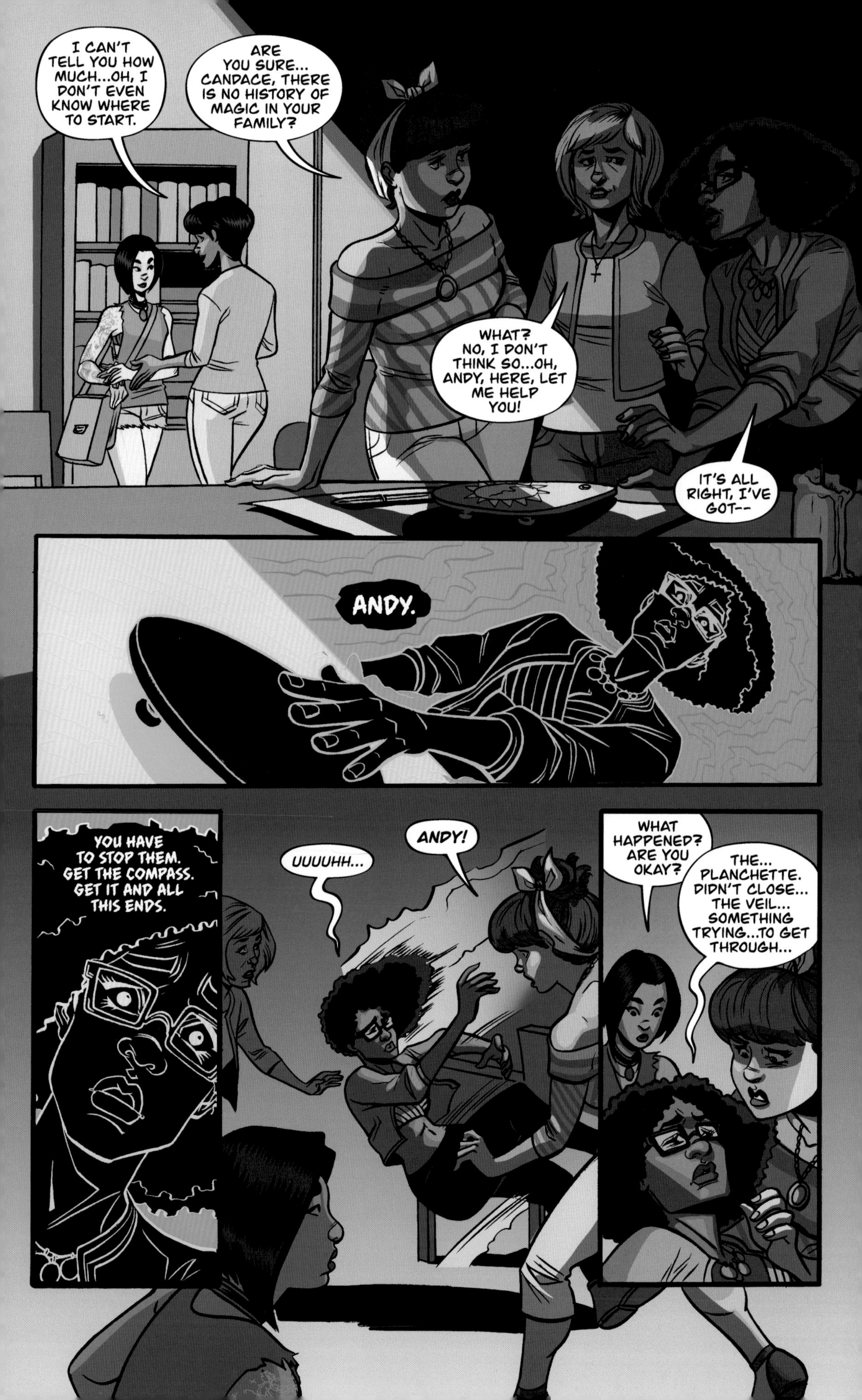
I CAN'T TELL YOU HOW MUCH...OH, I DON'T EVEN KNOW WHERE TO START.
ARE YOU SURE... CANDACE, THERE IS NO HISTORY OF MAGIC IN YOUR FAMILY?
WHAT? NO, I DON'T THINK SO...OH, ANDY, HERE, LET ME HELP YOU!
IT'S ALL RIGHT, I'VE GOT--
ANDY.
YOU HAVE TO STOP THEM. GET THE COMPASS. GET IT AND ALL THIS ENDS.
UUUUHH...
ANDY!
WHAT HAPPENED? ARE YOU OKAY?
THE... PLANCHETTE. DIDN'T CLOSE... THE VEIL... SOMETHING TRYING...TO GET THROUGH...

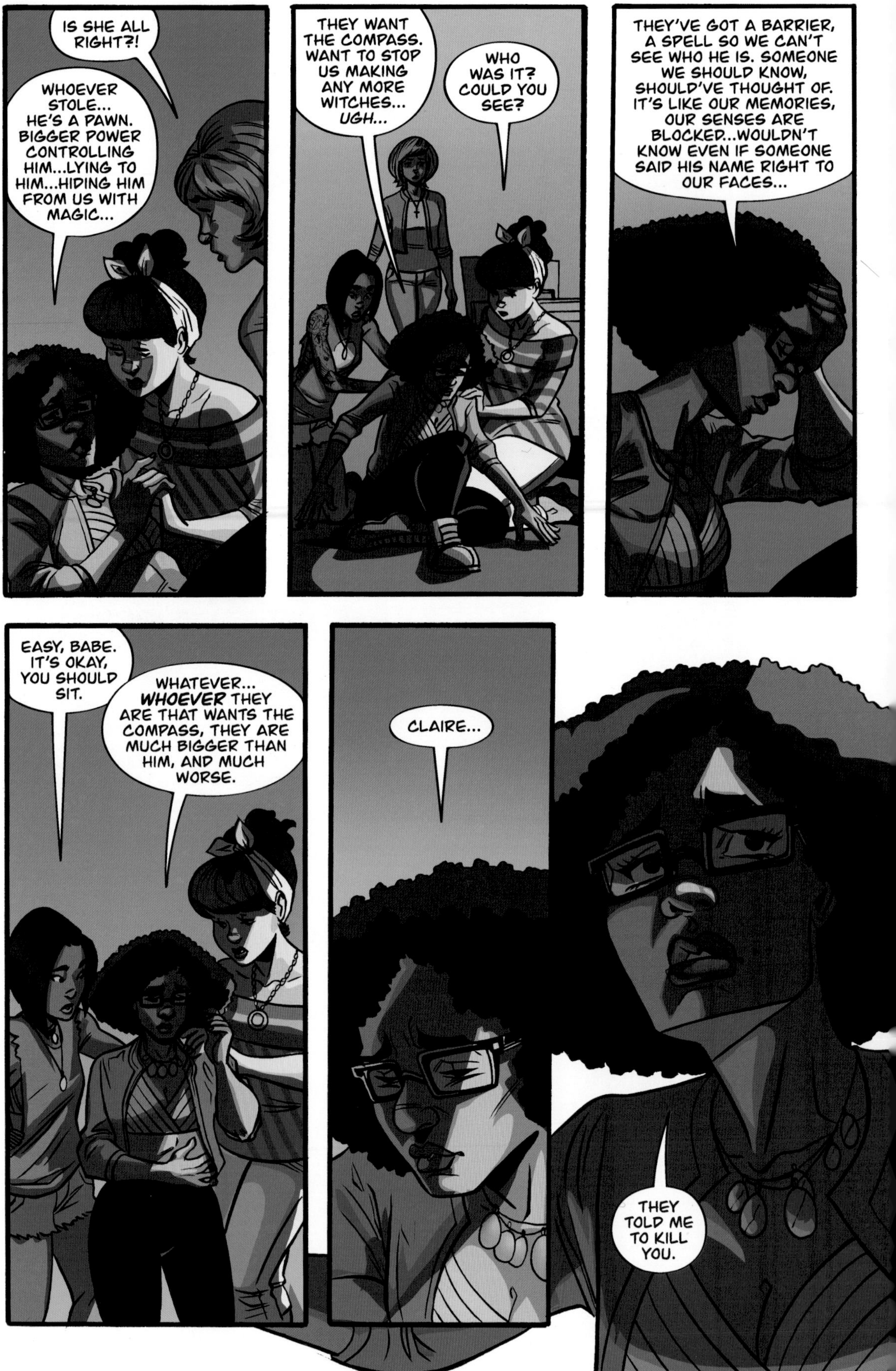
IS SHE ALL RIGHT?!
WHOEVER STOLE... HE'S A PAWN. BIGGER POWER CONTROLLING HIM...LYING TO HIM...HIDING HIM FROM US WITH MAGIC...
THEY WANT THE COMPASS. WANT TO STOP US MAKING ANY MORE WITCHES... UGH...
WHO WAS IT? COULD YOU SEE?
THEY'VE GOT A BARRIER, A SPELL SO WE CAN'T SEE WHO HE IS. SOMEONE WE SHOULD KNOW, SHOULD'VE THOUGHT OF. IT'S LIKE OUR MEMORIES, OUR SENSES ARE BLOCKED...WOULDN'T KNOW EVEN IF SOMEONE SAID HIS NAME RIGHT TO OUR FACES...
EASY, BABE. IT'S OKAY, YOU SHOULD SIT.
WHATEVER... **WHOEVER** THEY ARE THAT WANTS THE COMPASS, THEY ARE MUCH BIGGER THAN HIM, AND MUCH WORSE.
CLAIRE...
THEY TOLD ME TO KILL YOU.

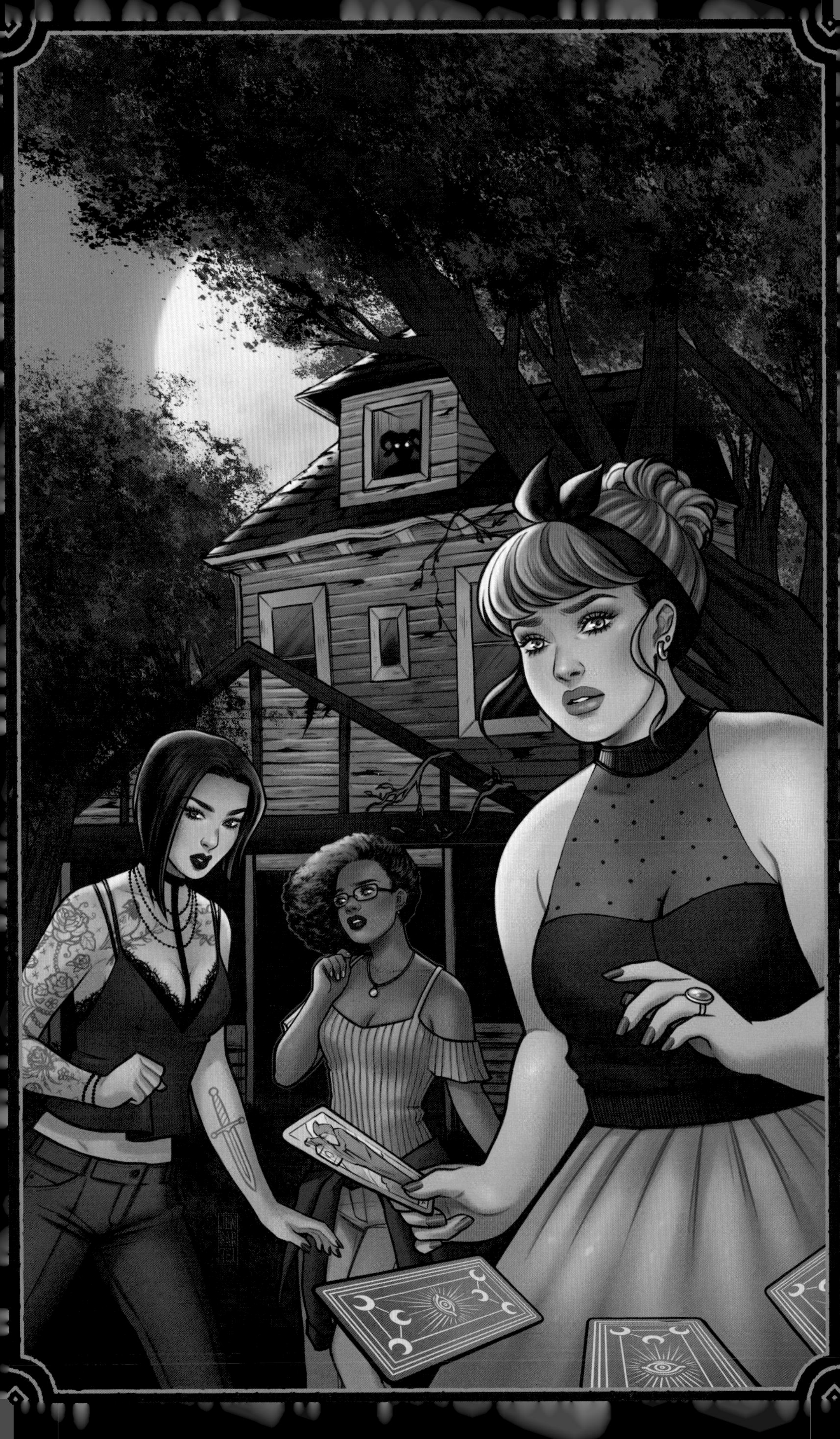

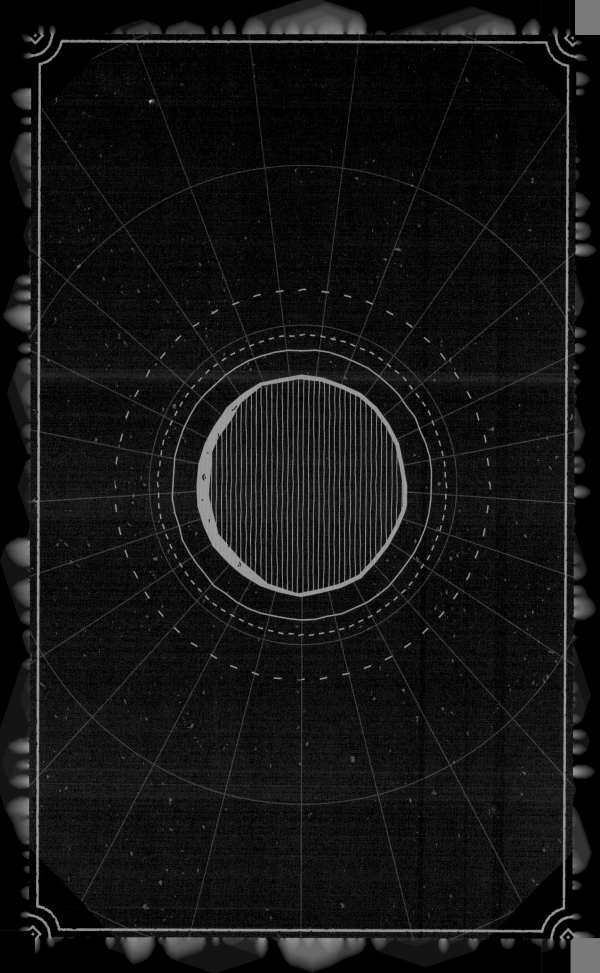

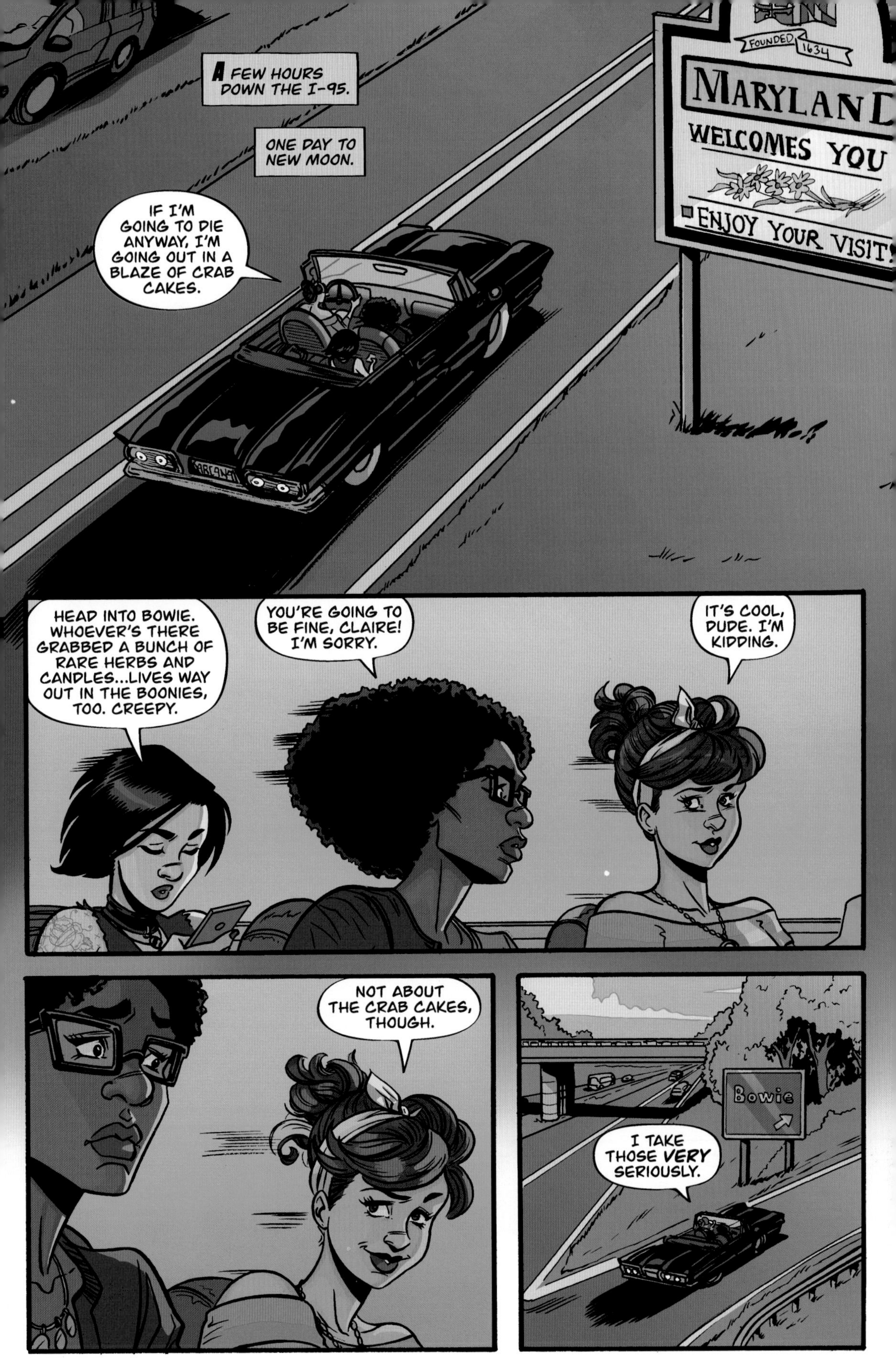
FOUNDED 1634
MARYLAND
WELCOMES YOU
ENJOY YOUR VISIT
A FEW HOURS DOWN THE I-95.
ONE DAY TO NEW MOON.
IF I'M GOING TO DIE ANYWAY, I'M GOING OUT IN A BLAZE OF CRAB CAKES.
HEAD INTO BOWIE. WHOEVER'S THERE GRABBED A BUNCH OF RARE HERBS AND CANDLES...LIVES WAY OUT IN THE BOONIES, TOO. CREEPY.
YOU'RE GOING TO BE FINE, CLAIRE! I'M SORRY.
IT'S COOL, DUDE. I'M KIDDING.
NOT ABOUT THE CRAB CAKES, THOUGH.
Bowie
I TAKE THOSE ***VERY*** SERIOUSLY.

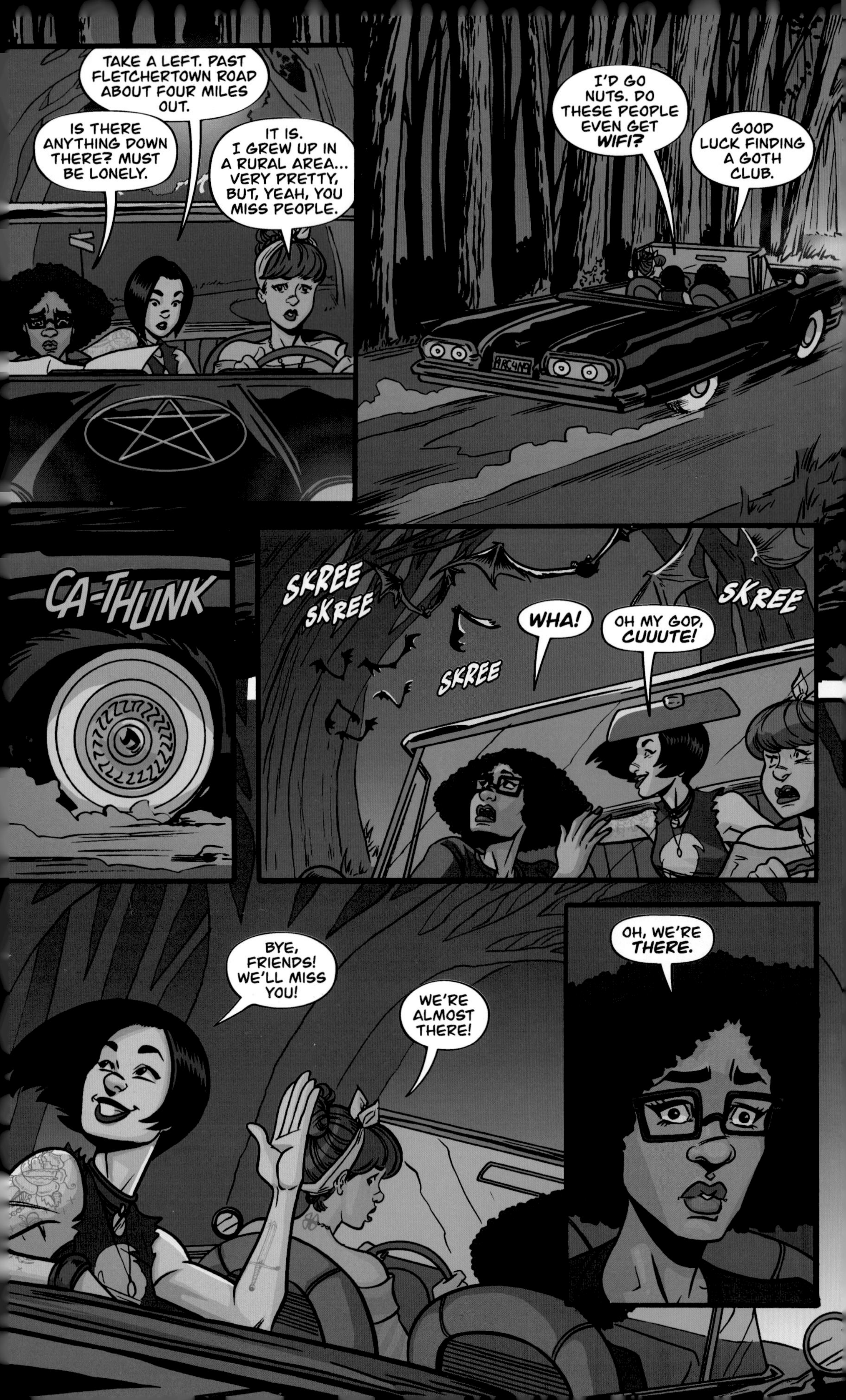
TAKE A LEFT. PAST FLETCHERTOWN ROAD ABOUT FOUR MILES OUT.
IS THERE ANYTHING DOWN THERE? MUST BE LONELY.
IT IS. I GREW UP IN A RURAL AREA... VERY PRETTY, BUT, YEAH, YOU MISS PEOPLE.
I'D GO NUTS. DO THESE PEOPLE EVEN GET WIFI?
GOOD LUCK FINDING A GOTH CLUB.
CA-THUNK
SKREE SKREE
WHA!
OH MY GOD, CUUUTE!
SKREE
SKREE
BYE, FRIENDS! WE'LL MISS YOU!
WE'RE ALMOST THERE!
OH, WE'RE THERE.

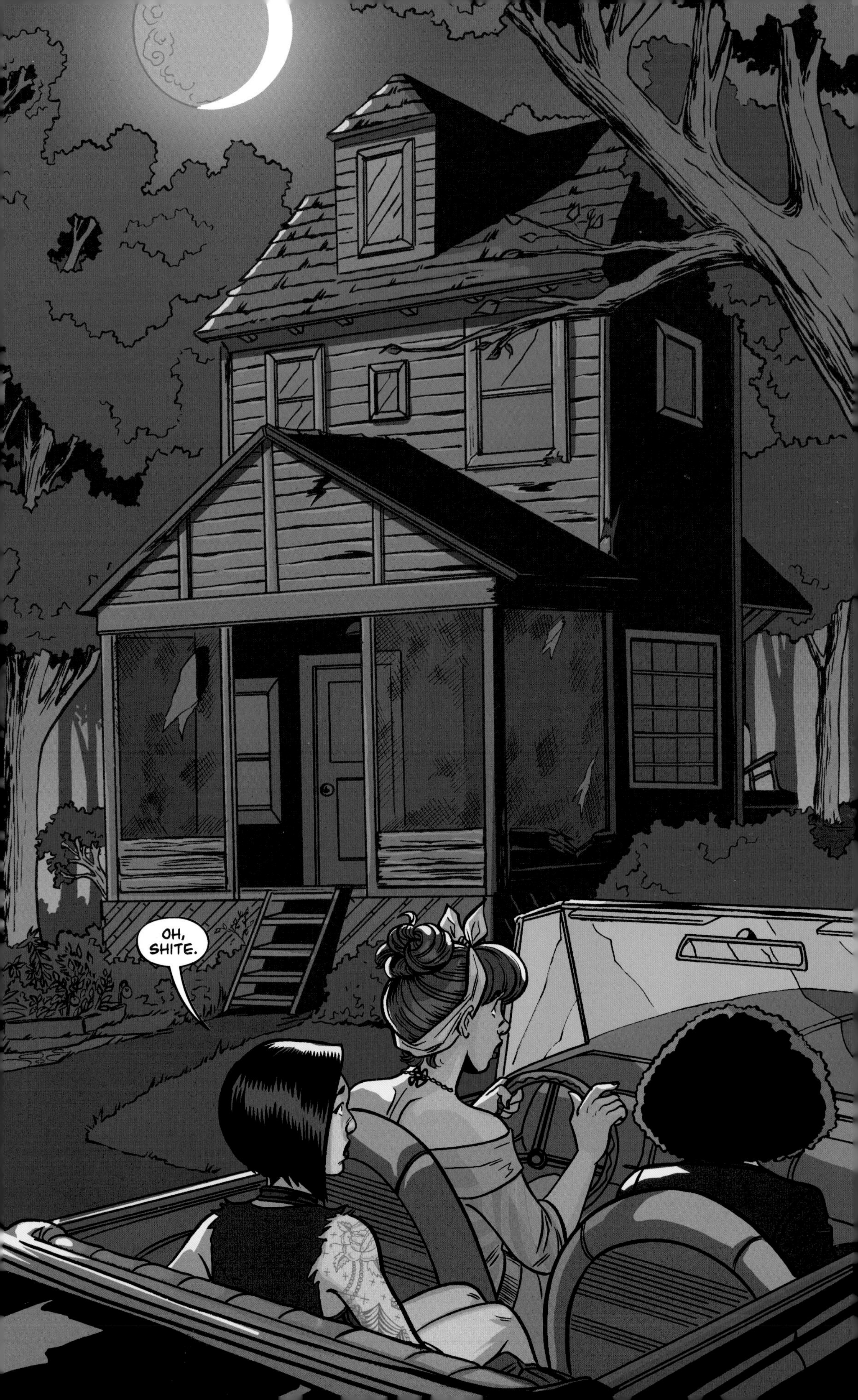
OH, SHITE.

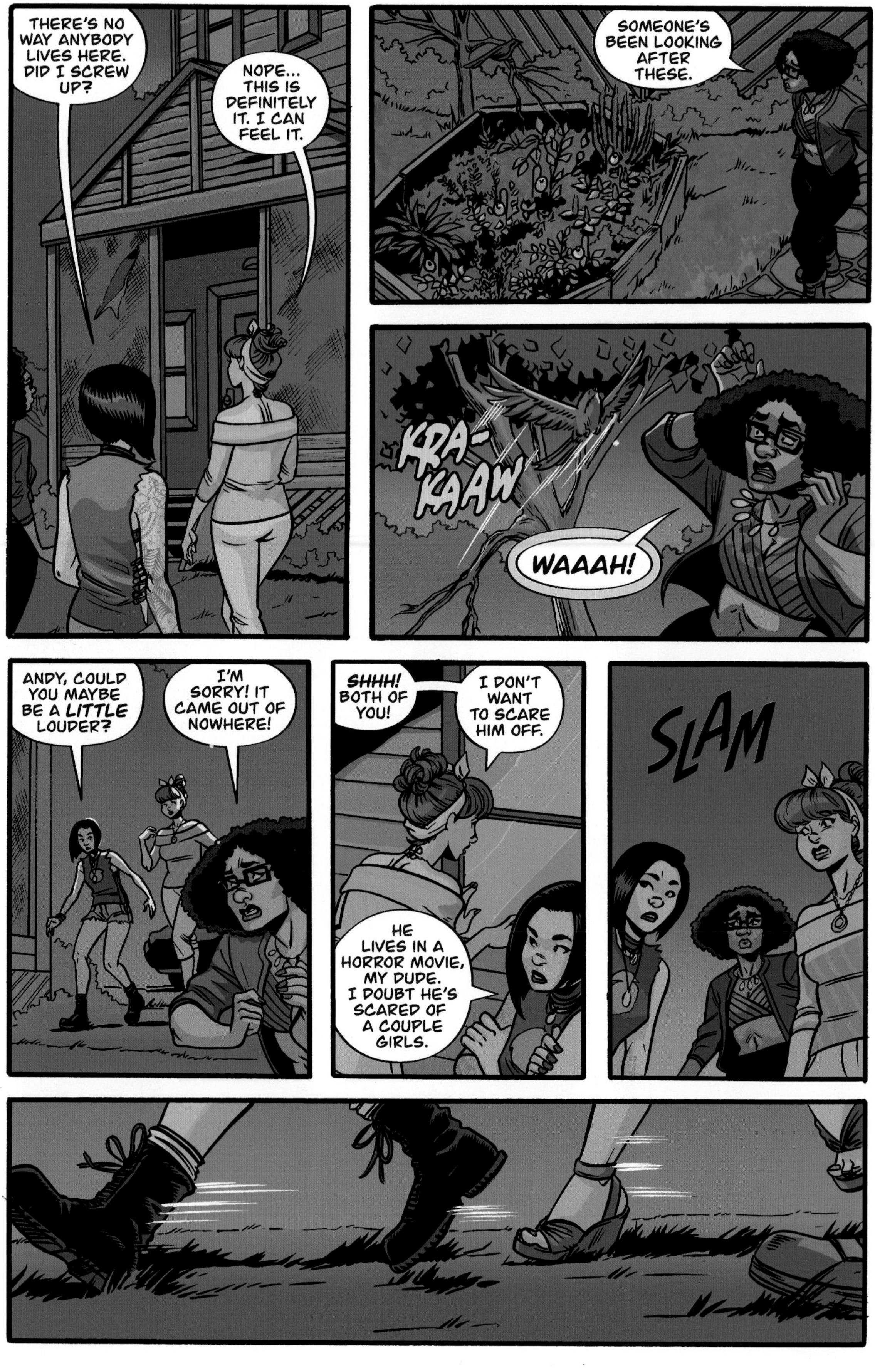
THERE'S NO WAY ANYBODY LIVES HERE. DID I SCREW UP?
NOPE... THIS IS DEFINITELY IT. I CAN FEEL IT.
SOMEONE'S BEEN LOOKING AFTER THESE.
KRA-KAAW
WAAAH!
ANDY, COULD YOU MAYBE BE A LITTLE LOUDER?
I'M SORRY! IT CAME OUT OF NOWHERE!
SHHH! BOTH OF YOU!
I DON'T WANT TO SCARE HIM OFF.
HE LIVES IN A HORROR MOVIE, MY DUDE. I DOUBT HE'S SCARED OF A COUPLE GIRLS.
SLAM

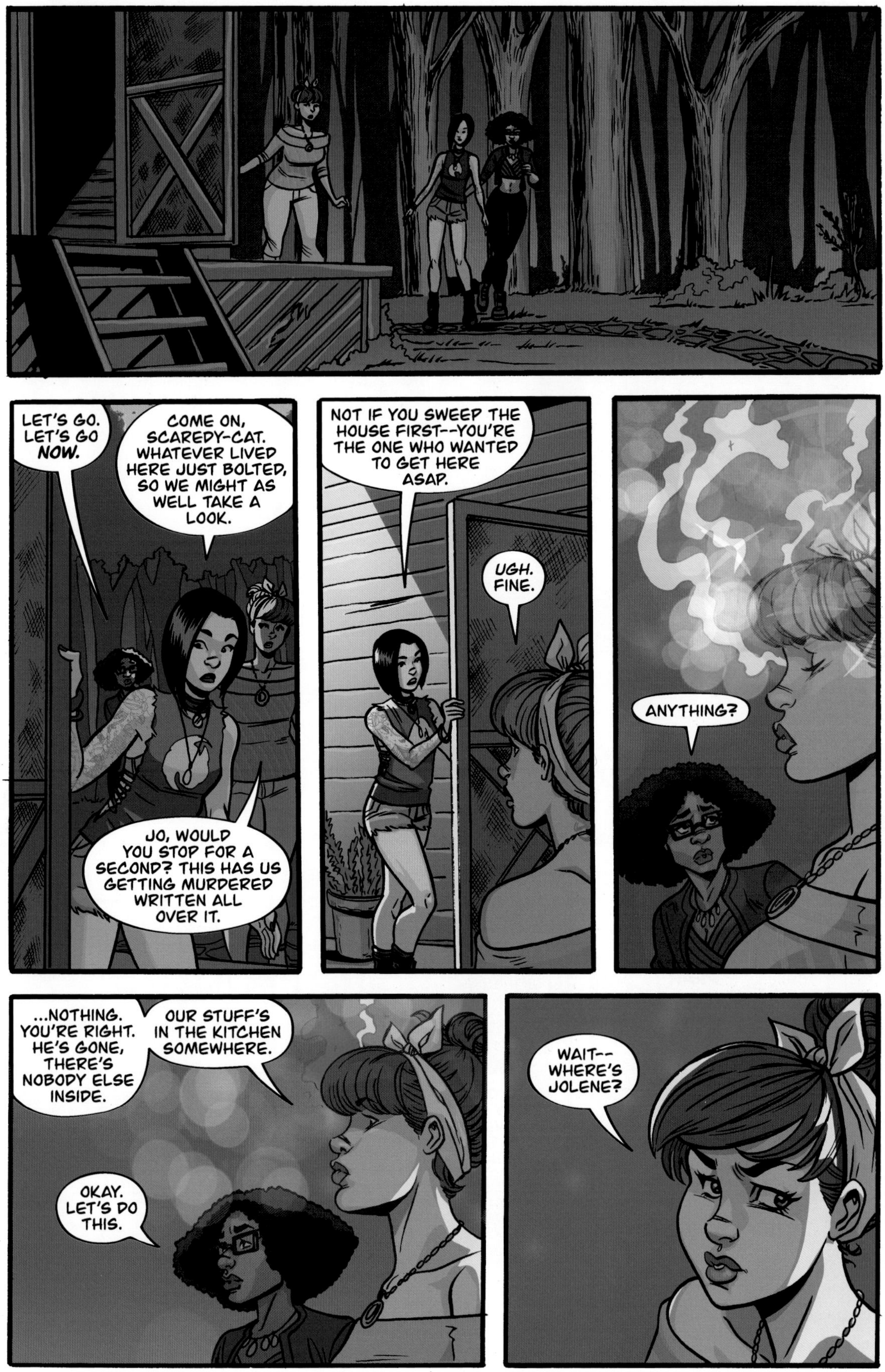
LET'S GO. LET'S GO NOW.
COME ON, SCAREDY-CAT. WHATEVER LIVED HERE JUST BOLTED, SO WE MIGHT AS WELL TAKE A LOOK.
JO, WOULD YOU STOP FOR A SECOND? THIS HAS US GETTING MURDERED WRITTEN ALL OVER IT.
NOT IF YOU SWEEP THE HOUSE FIRST--YOU'RE THE ONE WHO WANTED TO GET HERE ASAP.
UGH. FINE.
ANYTHING?
...NOTHING. YOU'RE RIGHT. HE'S GONE, THERE'S NOBODY ELSE INSIDE.
OUR STUFF'S IN THE KITCHEN SOMEWHERE.
OKAY. LET'S DO THIS.
WAIT-- WHERE'S JOLENE?

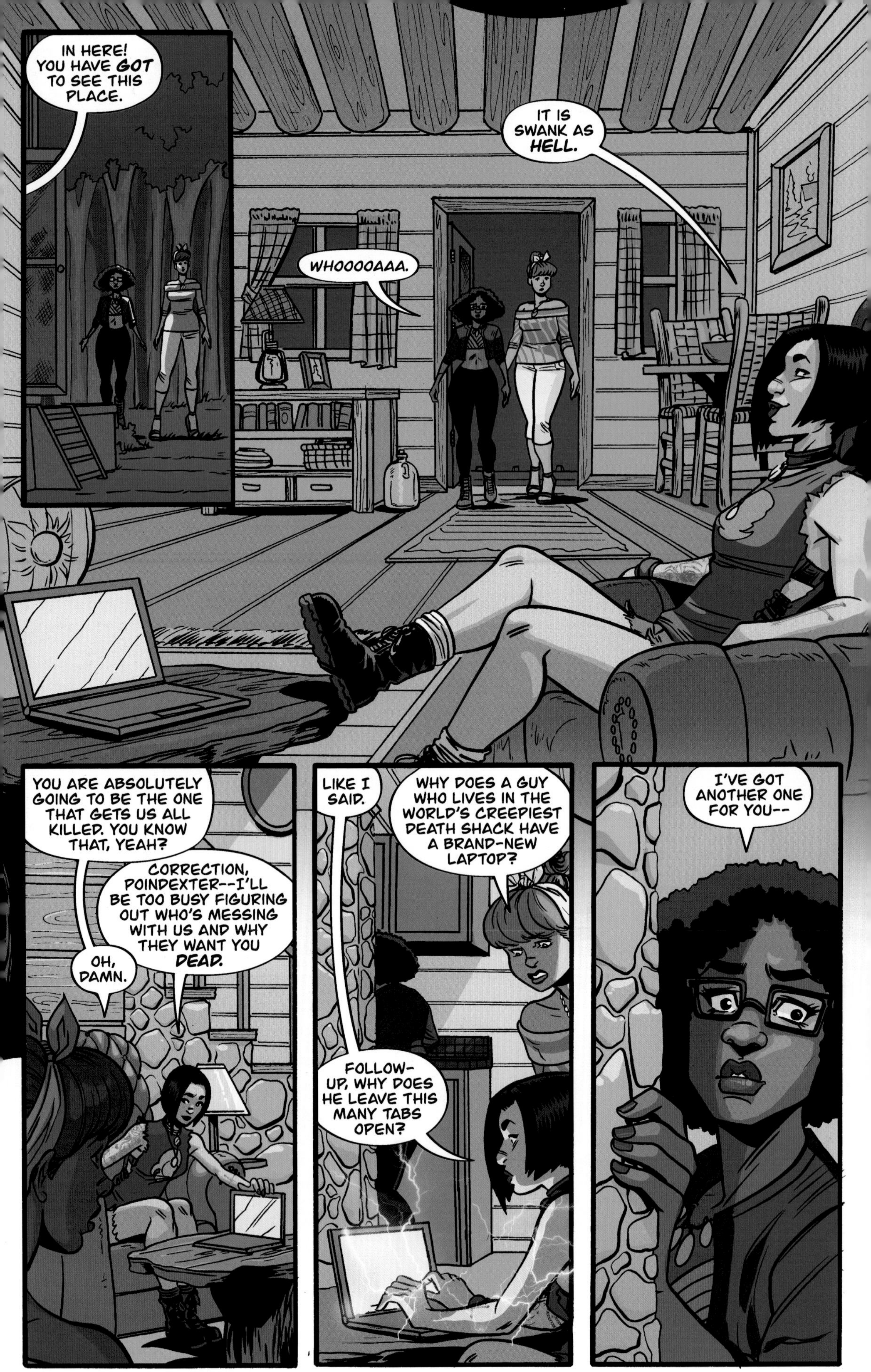
IN HERE! YOU HAVE GOT TO SEE THIS PLACE.
IT IS SWANK AS HELL.
WHOOOOAAA.
YOU ARE ABSOLUTELY GOING TO BE THE ONE THAT GETS US ALL KILLED. YOU KNOW THAT, YEAH?
CORRECTION, POINDEXTER--I'LL BE TOO BUSY FIGURING OUT WHO'S MESSING WITH US AND WHY THEY WANT YOU DEAD.
OH, DAMN.
LIKE I SAID.
WHY DOES A GUY WHO LIVES IN THE WORLD'S CREEPIEST DEATH SHACK HAVE A BRAND-NEW LAPTOP?
FOLLOW-UP, WHY DOES HE LEAVE THIS MANY TABS OPEN?
I'VE GOT ANOTHER ONE FOR YOU--

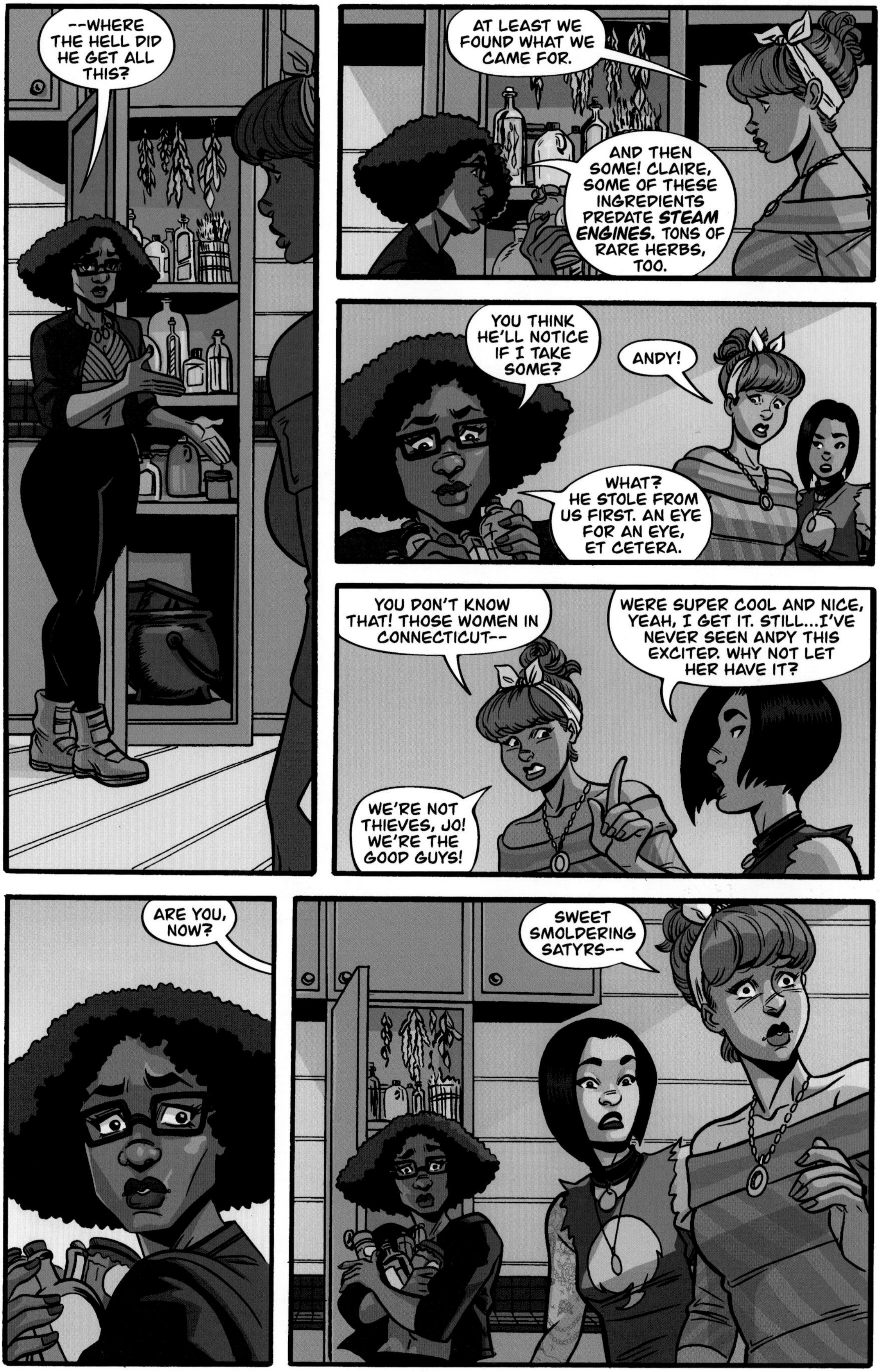
--WHERE THE HELL DID HE GET ALL THIS?
AT LEAST WE FOUND WHAT WE CAME FOR.
AND THEN SOME! CLAIRE, SOME OF THESE INGREDIENTS PREDATE STEAM ENGINES. TONS OF RARE HERBS, TOO.
YOU THINK HE'LL NOTICE IF I TAKE SOME?
ANDY!
WHAT? HE STOLE FROM US FIRST. AN EYE FOR AN EYE, ET CETERA.
YOU DON'T KNOW THAT! THOSE WOMEN IN CONNECTICUT--
WERE SUPER COOL AND NICE, YEAH, I GET IT. STILL...I'VE NEVER SEEN ANDY THIS EXCITED. WHY NOT LET HER HAVE IT?
WE'RE NOT THIEVES, JO! WE'RE THE GOOD GUYS!
ARE YOU, NOW?
SWEET SMOLDERING SATYRS--

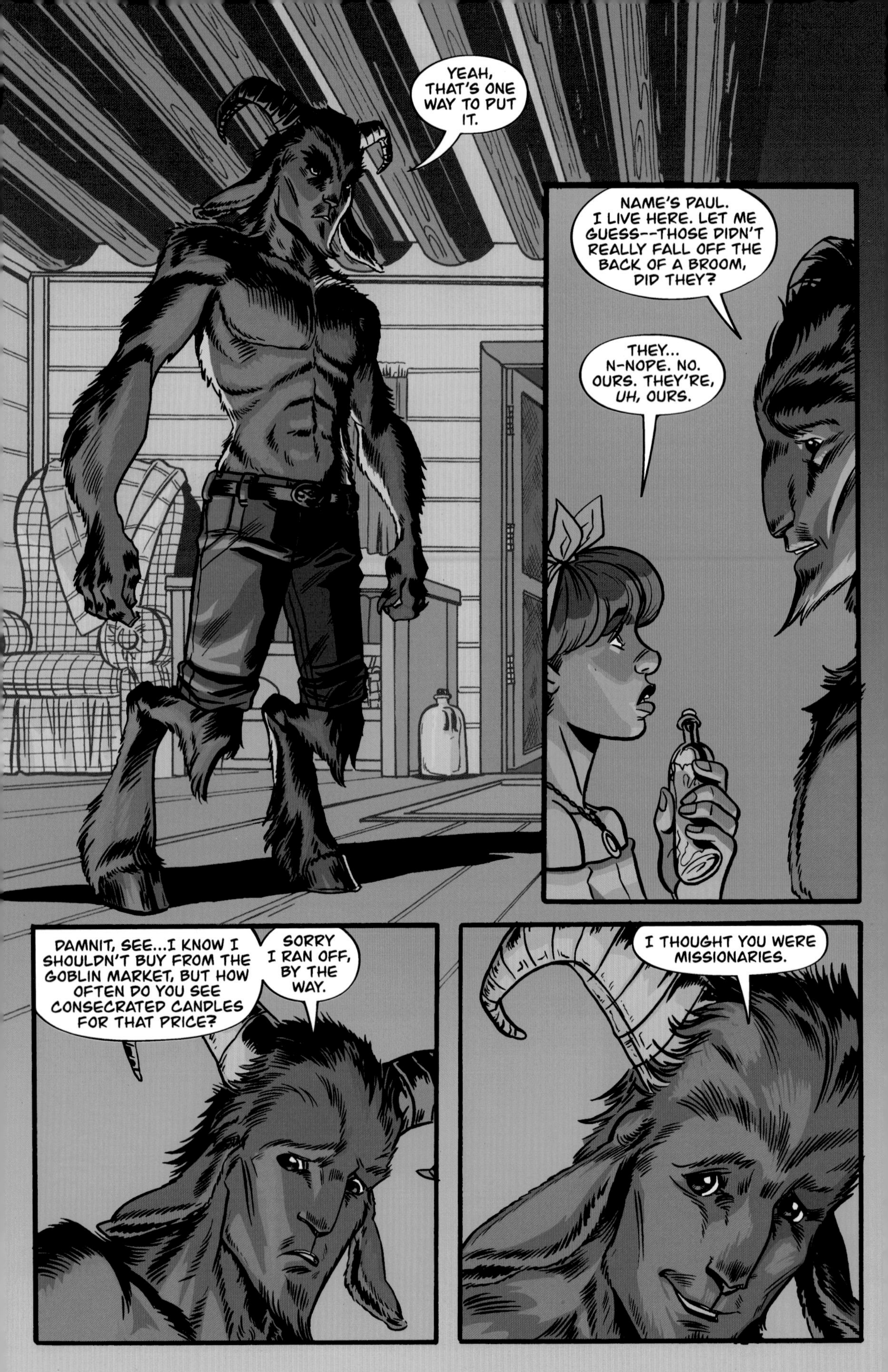
YEAH, THAT'S ONE WAY TO PUT IT.
NAME'S PAUL. I LIVE HERE. LET ME GUESS--THOSE DIDN'T REALLY FALL OFF THE BACK OF A BROOM, DID THEY?
THEY... N-NOPE. NO. OURS. THEY'RE, UH, OURS.
DAMNIT, SEE...I KNOW I SHOULDN'T BUY FROM THE GOBLIN MARKET, BUT HOW OFTEN DO YOU SEE CONSECRATED CANDLES FOR THAT PRICE?
SORRY I RAN OFF, BY THE WAY.
I THOUGHT YOU WERE MISSIONARIES.

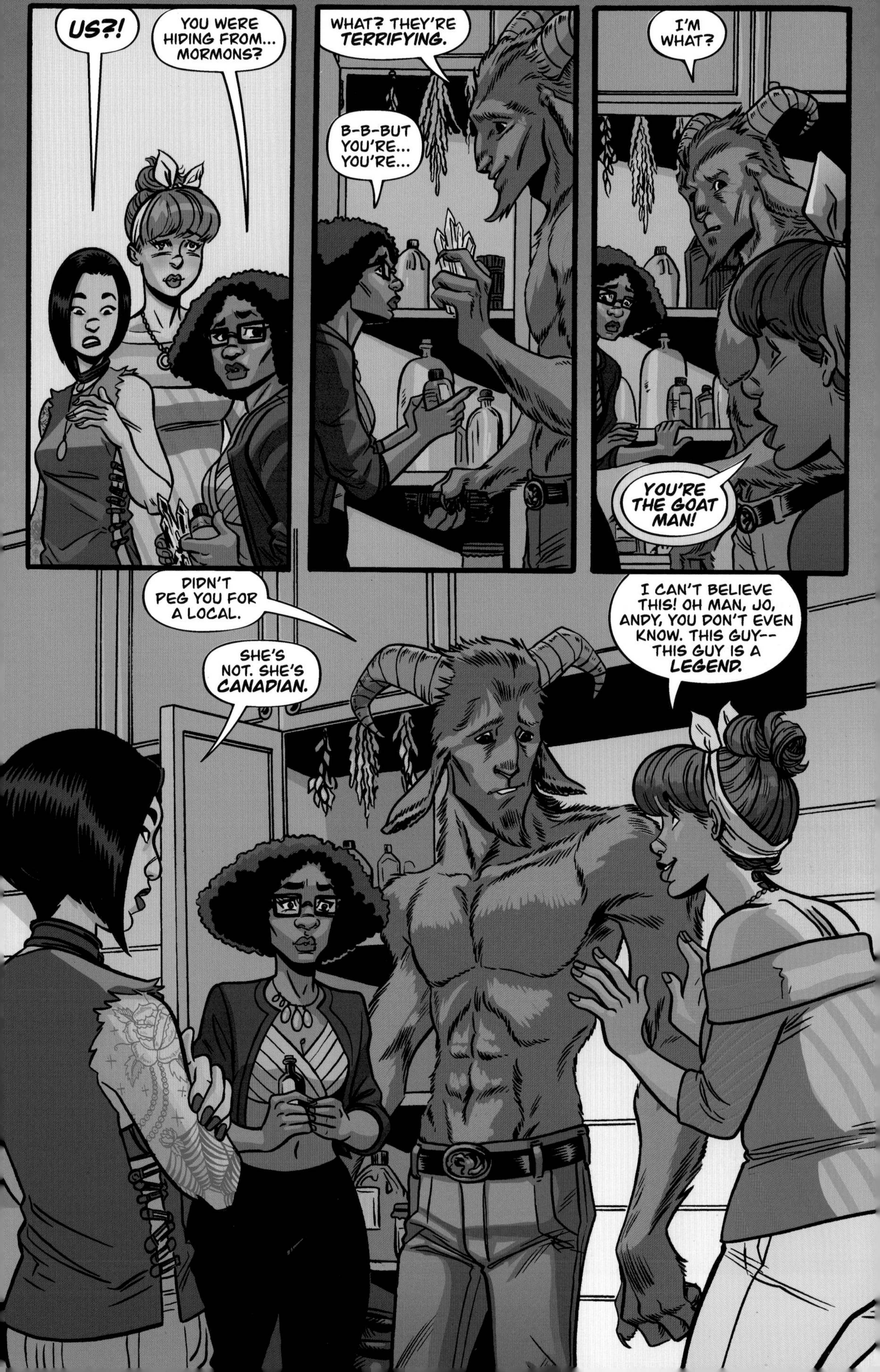
US?!
YOU WERE HIDING FROM... MORMONS?
WHAT? THEY'RE TERRIFYING.
B-B-BUT YOU'RE... YOU'RE...
I'M WHAT?
YOU'RE THE GOAT MAN!
DIDN'T PEG YOU FOR A LOCAL.
SHE'S NOT. SHE'S CANADIAN.
I CAN'T BELIEVE THIS! OH MAN, JO, ANDY, YOU DON'T EVEN KNOW. THIS GUY-- THIS GUY IS A LEGEND.

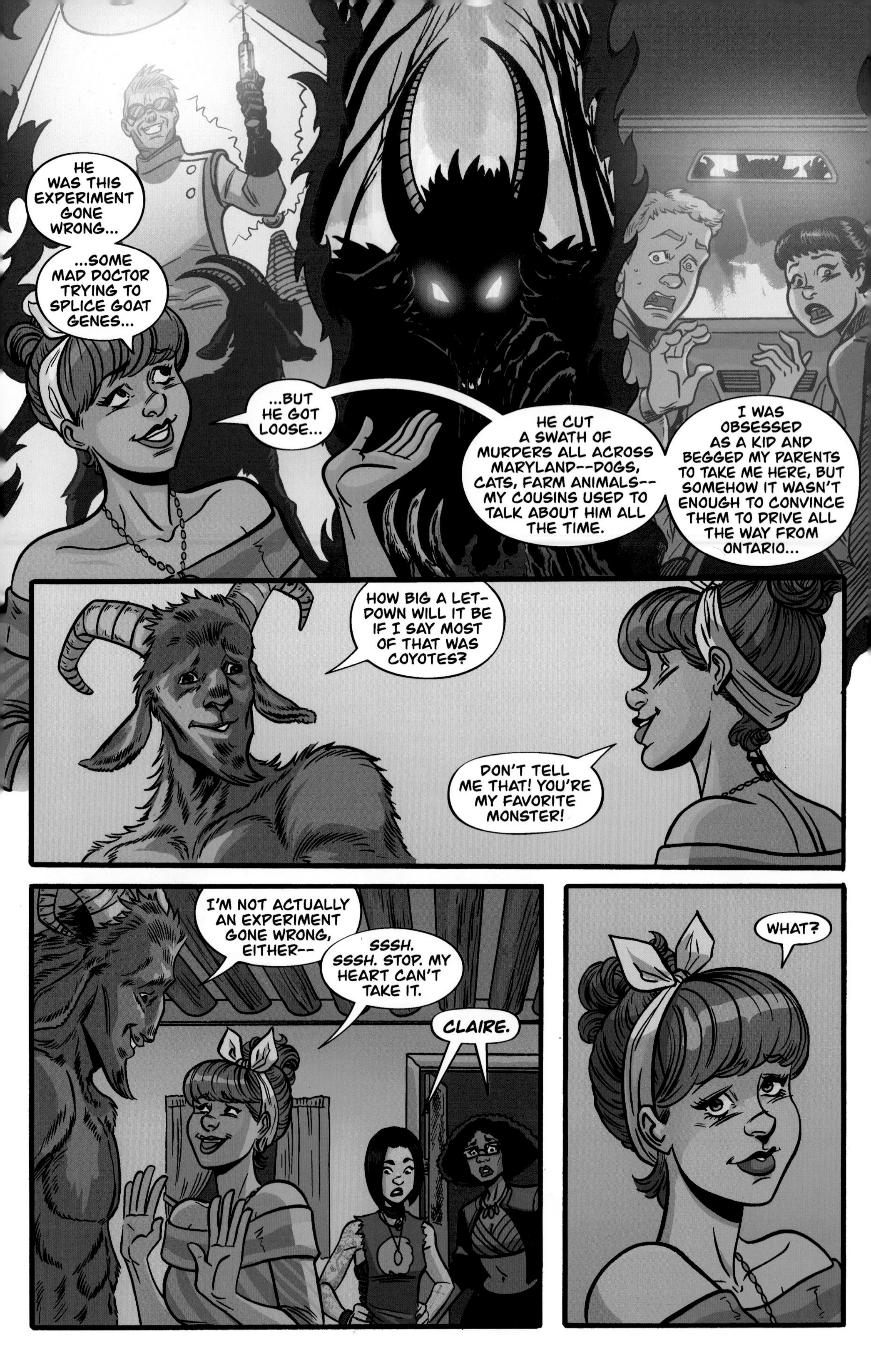
HE WAS THIS EXPERIMENT GONE WRONG...
...SOME MAD DOCTOR TRYING TO SPLICE GOAT GENES...
...BUT HE GOT LOOSE...
HE CUT A SWATH OF MURDERS ALL ACROSS MARYLAND--DOGS, CATS, FARM ANIMALS--MY COUSINS USED TO TALK ABOUT HIM ALL THE TIME.
I WAS OBSESSED AS A KID AND BEGGED MY PARENTS TO TAKE ME HERE, BUT SOMEHOW IT WASN'T ENOUGH TO CONVINCE THEM TO DRIVE ALL THE WAY FROM ONTARIO...
HOW BIG A LET-DOWN WILL IT BE IF I SAY MOST OF THAT WAS COYOTES?
DON'T TELL ME THAT! YOU'RE MY FAVORITE MONSTER!
I'M NOT ACTUALLY AN EXPERIMENT GONE WRONG, EITHER--
SSSH. SSSH. STOP. MY HEART CAN'T TAKE IT.
CLAIRE.
WHAT?

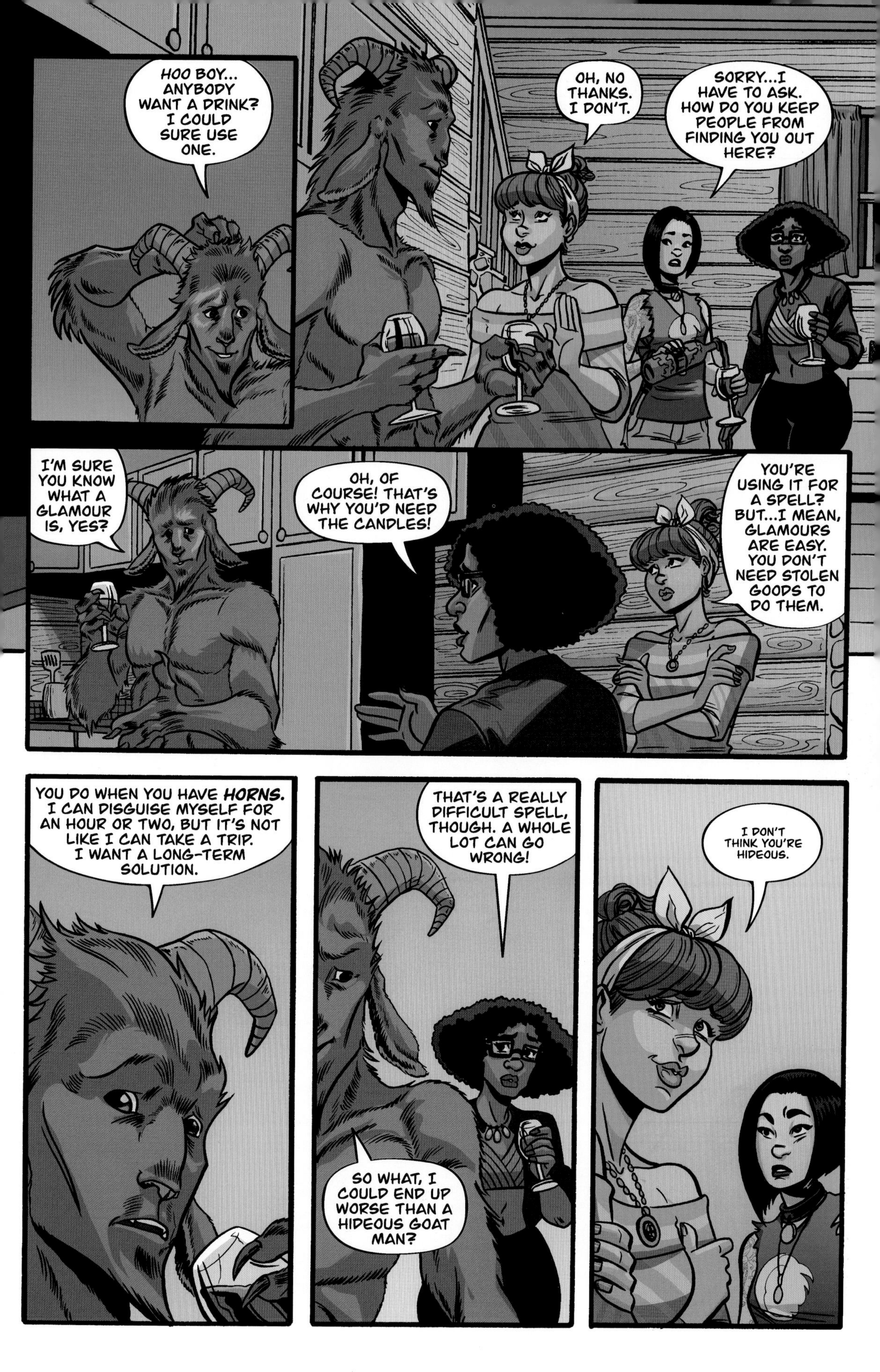
HOO BOY... ANYBODY WANT A DRINK? I COULD SURE USE ONE.
OH, NO THANKS. I DON'T.
SORRY...I HAVE TO ASK. HOW DO YOU KEEP PEOPLE FROM FINDING YOU OUT HERE?
I'M SURE YOU KNOW WHAT A GLAMOUR IS, YES?
OH, OF COURSE! THAT'S WHY YOU'D NEED THE CANDLES!
YOU'RE USING IT FOR A SPELL? BUT...I MEAN, GLAMOURS ARE EASY. YOU DON'T NEED STOLEN GOODS TO DO THEM.
YOU DO WHEN YOU HAVE HORNS. I CAN DISGUISE MYSELF FOR AN HOUR OR TWO, BUT IT'S NOT LIKE I CAN TAKE A TRIP. I WANT A LONG-TERM SOLUTION.
THAT'S A REALLY DIFFICULT SPELL, THOUGH. A WHOLE LOT CAN GO WRONG!
SO WHAT, I COULD END UP WORSE THAN A HIDEOUS GOAT MAN?
I DON'T THINK YOU'RE HIDEOUS.

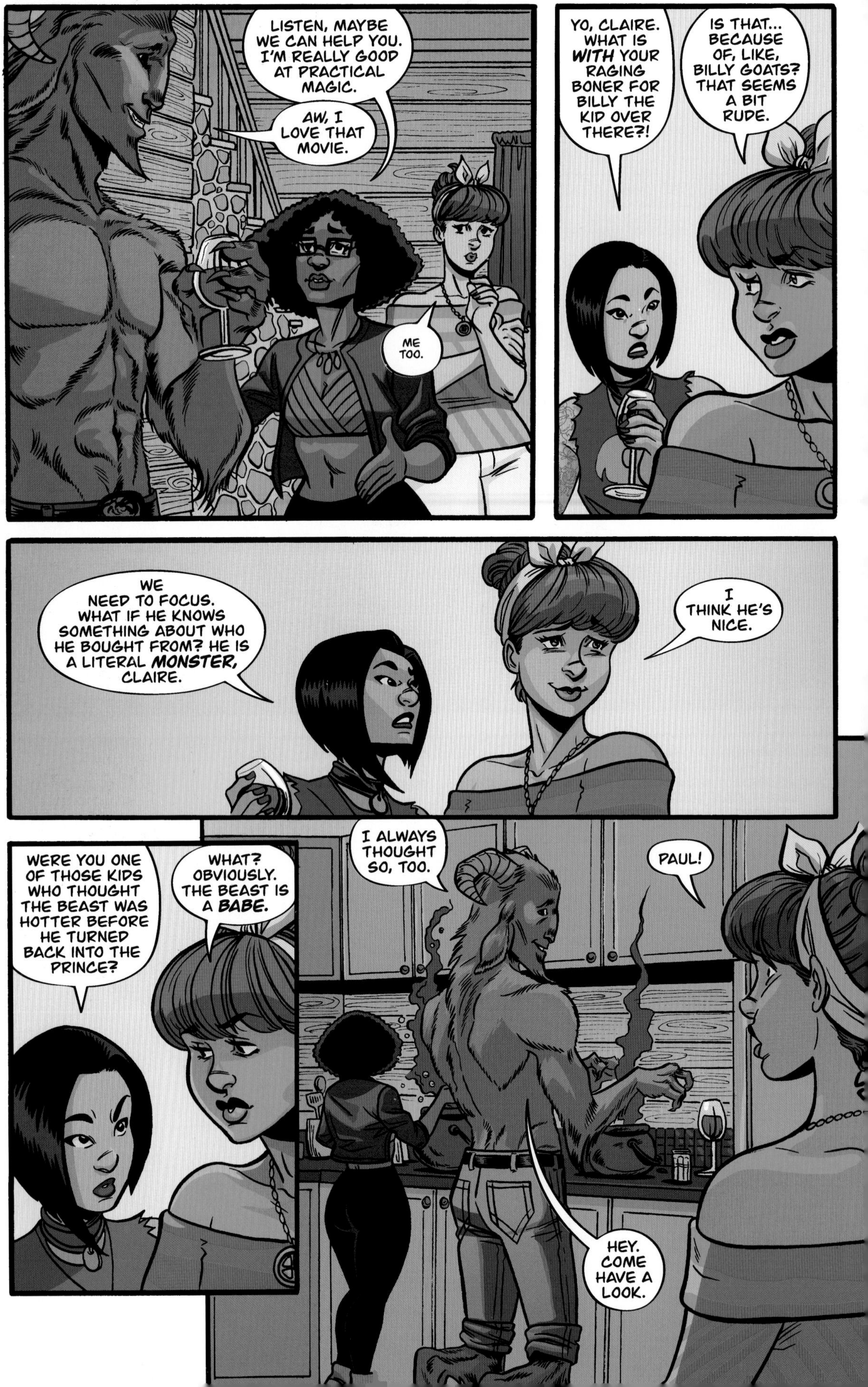
LISTEN, MAYBE WE CAN HELP YOU. I'M REALLY GOOD AT PRACTICAL MAGIC.
AW, I LOVE THAT MOVIE.
ME TOO.
YO, CLAIRE. WHAT IS WITH YOUR RAGING BONER FOR BILLY THE KID OVER THERE?!
IS THAT... BECAUSE OF, LIKE, BILLY GOATS? THAT SEEMS A BIT RUDE.
WE NEED TO FOCUS. WHAT IF HE KNOWS SOMETHING ABOUT WHO HE BOUGHT FROM? HE IS A LITERAL MONSTER, CLAIRE.
I THINK HE'S NICE.
WERE YOU ONE OF THOSE KIDS WHO THOUGHT THE BEAST WAS HOTTER BEFORE HE TURNED BACK INTO THE PRINCE?
WHAT? OBVIOUSLY. THE BEAST IS A BABE.
I ALWAYS THOUGHT SO, TOO.
PAUL!
HEY. COME HAVE A LOOK.

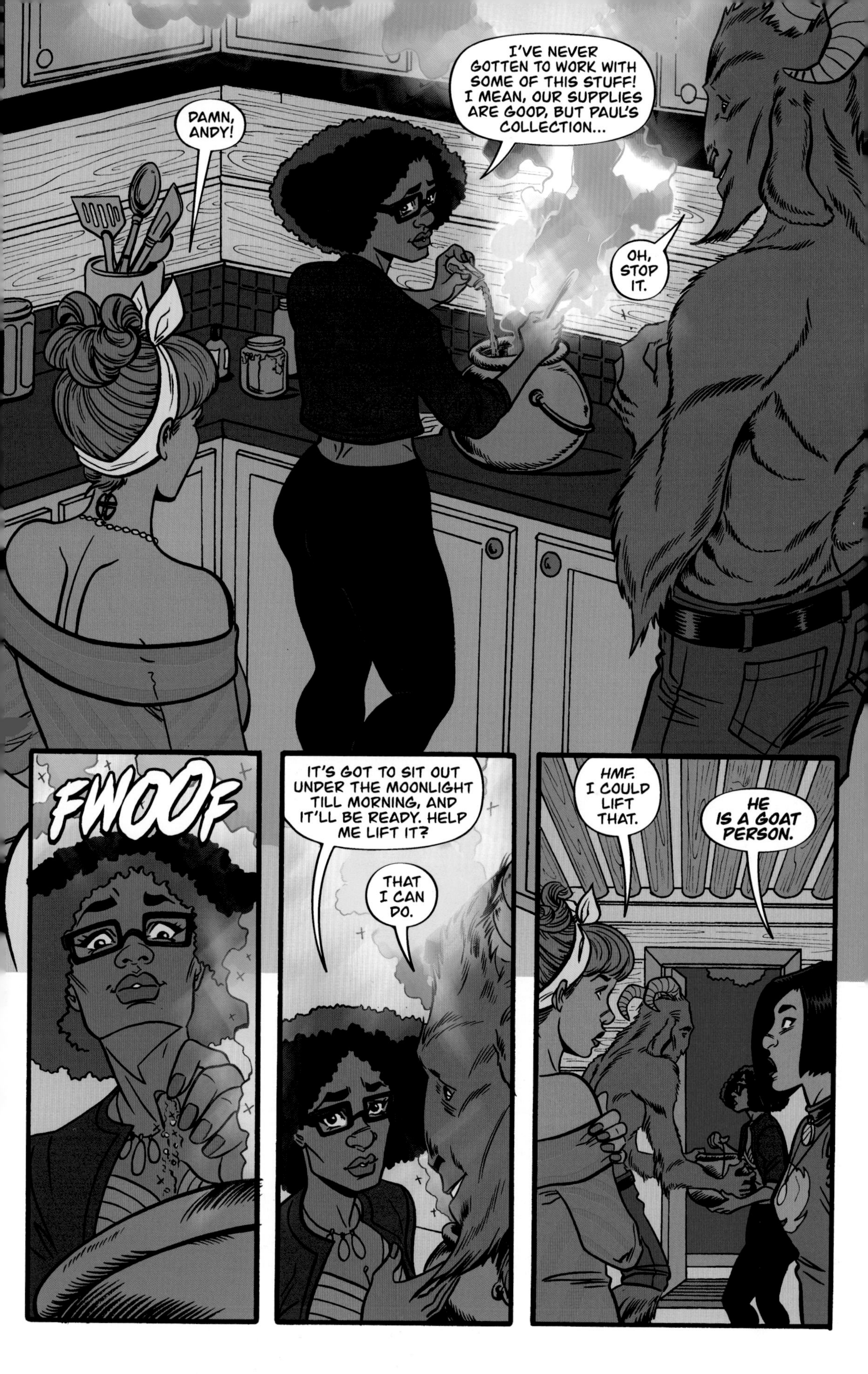
DAMN, ANDY!
I'VE NEVER GOTTEN TO WORK WITH SOME OF THIS STUFF! I MEAN, OUR SUPPLIES ARE GOOD, BUT PAUL'S COLLECTION...
OH, STOP IT.
FWOOF
IT'S GOT TO SIT OUT UNDER THE MOONLIGHT TILL MORNING, AND IT'LL BE READY. HELP ME LIFT IT?
THAT I CAN DO.
HMF. I COULD LIFT THAT.
HE IS A GOAT PERSON.

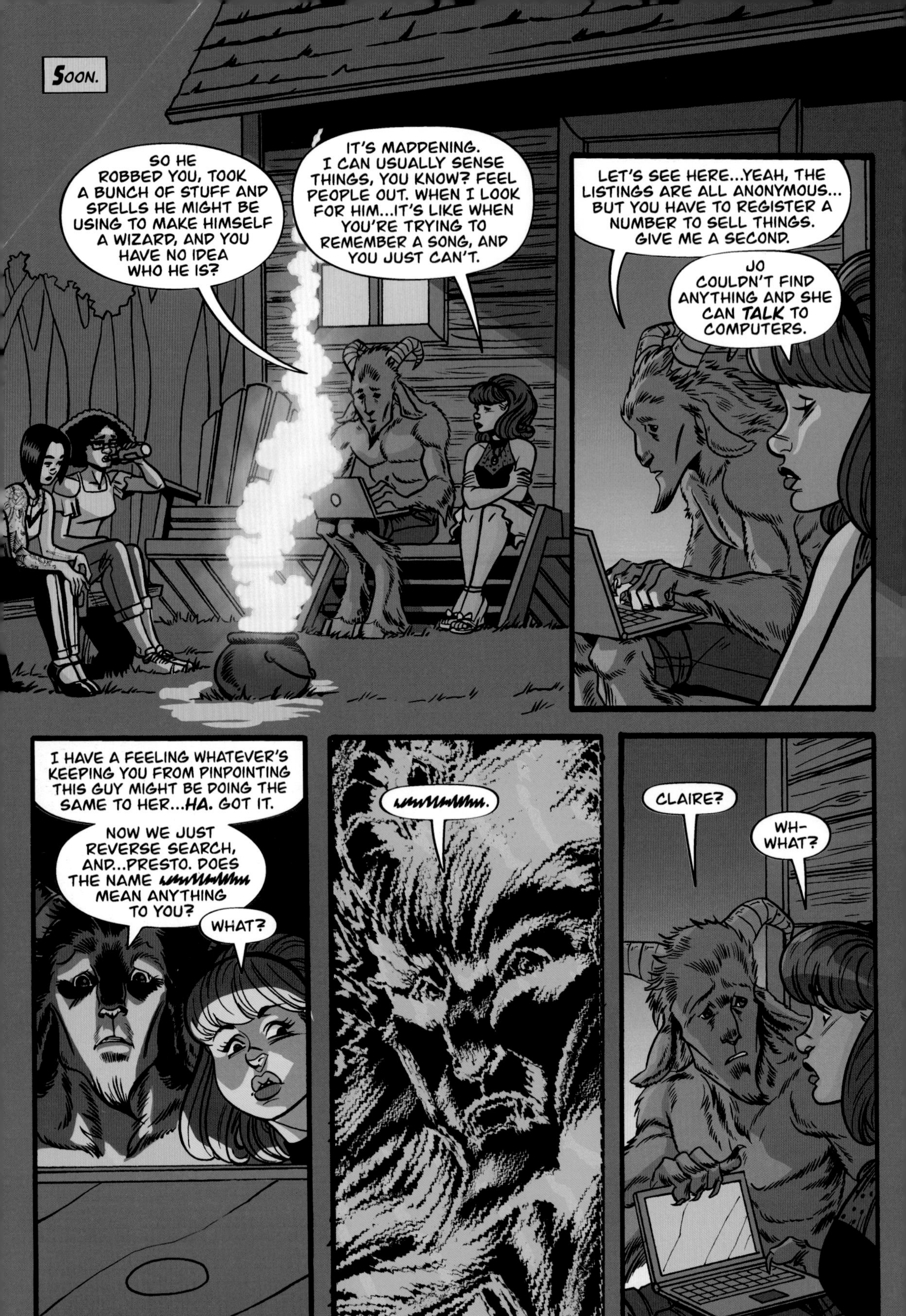
SOON.
SO HE ROBBED YOU, TOOK A BUNCH OF STUFF AND SPELLS HE MIGHT BE USING TO MAKE HIMSELF A WIZARD, AND YOU HAVE NO IDEA WHO HE IS?
IT'S MADDENING. I CAN USUALLY SENSE THINGS, YOU KNOW? FEEL PEOPLE OUT. WHEN I LOOK FOR HIM...IT'S LIKE WHEN YOU'RE TRYING TO REMEMBER A SONG, AND YOU JUST CAN'T.
LET'S SEE HERE...YEAH, THE LISTINGS ARE ALL ANONYMOUS... BUT YOU HAVE TO REGISTER A NUMBER TO SELL THINGS. GIVE ME A SECOND.
JO COULDN'T FIND ANYTHING AND SHE CAN TALK TO COMPUTERS.
I HAVE A FEELING WHATEVER'S KEEPING YOU FROM PINPOINTING THIS GUY MIGHT BE DOING THE SAME TO HER...HA. GOT IT.
NOW WE JUST REVERSE SEARCH, AND...PRESTO. DOES THE NAME MEAN ANYTHING TO YOU?
WHAT?
CLAIRE?
WH-WHAT?

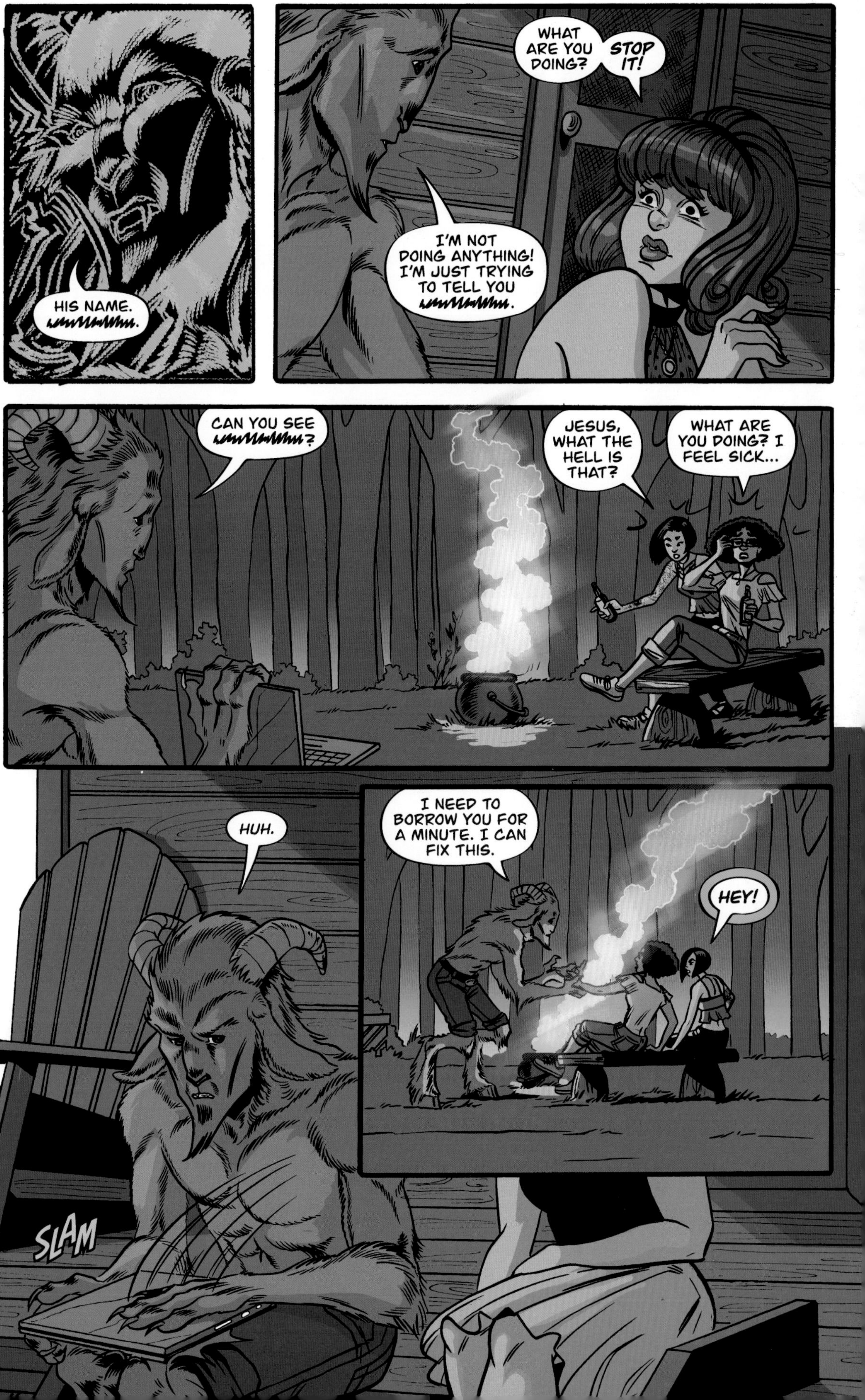
HIS NAME. ~~~~~~.
WHAT ARE YOU DOING?
STOP IT!
I'M NOT DOING ANYTHING! I'M JUST TRYING TO TELL YOU ~~~~~~.
CAN YOU SEE ~~~~~~?
JESUS, WHAT THE HELL IS THAT?
WHAT ARE YOU DOING? I FEEL SICK...
HUH.
I NEED TO BORROW YOU FOR A MINUTE. I CAN FIX THIS.
HEY!
SLAM

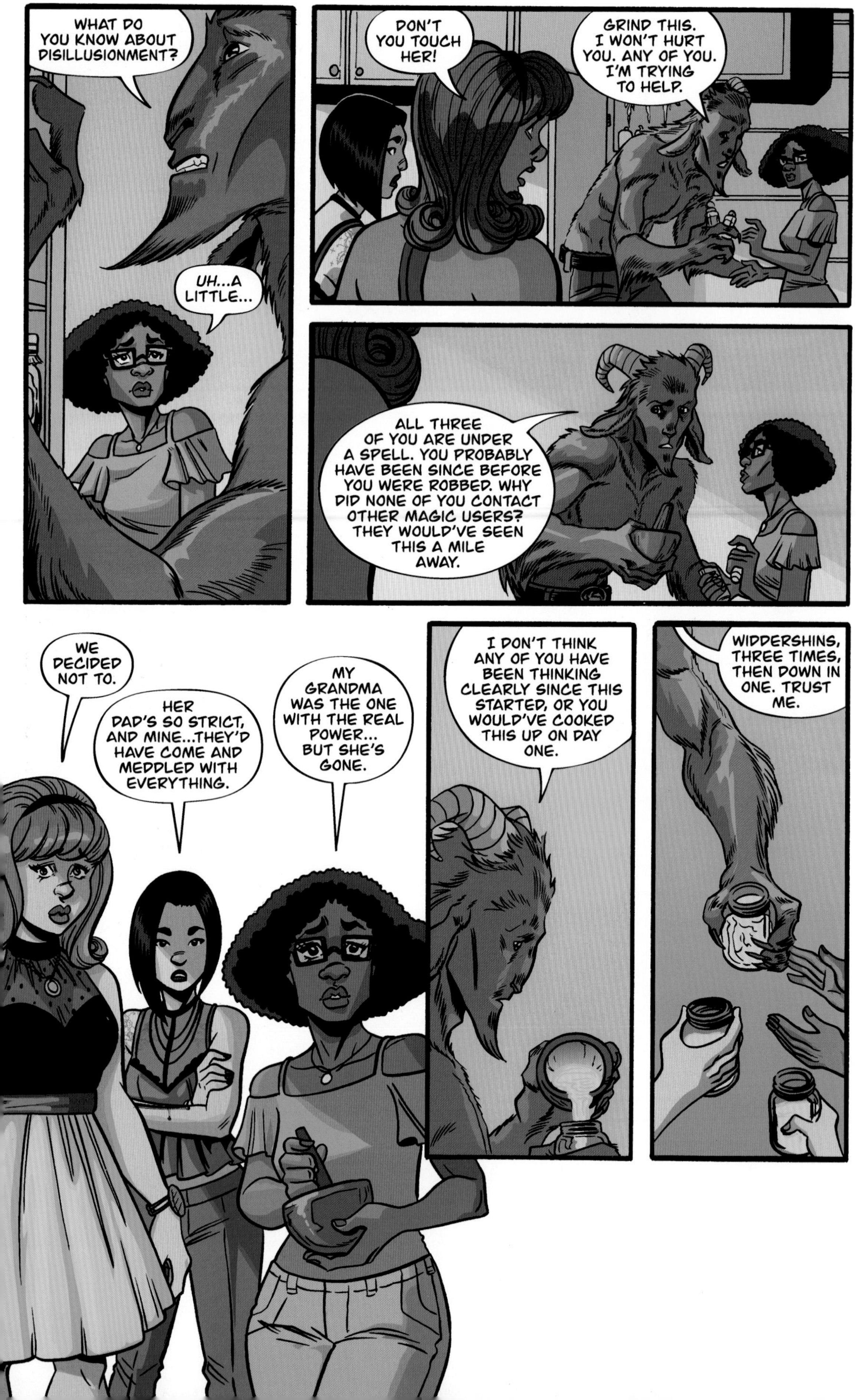
WHAT DO YOU KNOW ABOUT DISILLUSIONMENT?
UH...A LITTLE...
DON'T YOU TOUCH HER!
GRIND THIS. I WON'T HURT YOU. ANY OF YOU. I'M TRYING TO HELP.
ALL THREE OF YOU ARE UNDER A SPELL. YOU PROBABLY HAVE BEEN SINCE BEFORE YOU WERE ROBBED. WHY DID NONE OF YOU CONTACT OTHER MAGIC USERS? THEY WOULD'VE SEEN THIS A MILE AWAY.
WE DECIDED NOT TO.
HER DAD'S SO STRICT, AND MINE...THEY'D HAVE COME AND MEDDLED WITH EVERYTHING.
MY GRANDMA WAS THE ONE WITH THE REAL POWER... BUT SHE'S GONE.
I DON'T THINK ANY OF YOU HAVE BEEN THINKING CLEARLY SINCE THIS STARTED, OR YOU WOULD'VE COOKED THIS UP ON DAY ONE.
WIDDERSHINS, THREE TIMES, THEN DOWN IN ONE. TRUST ME.

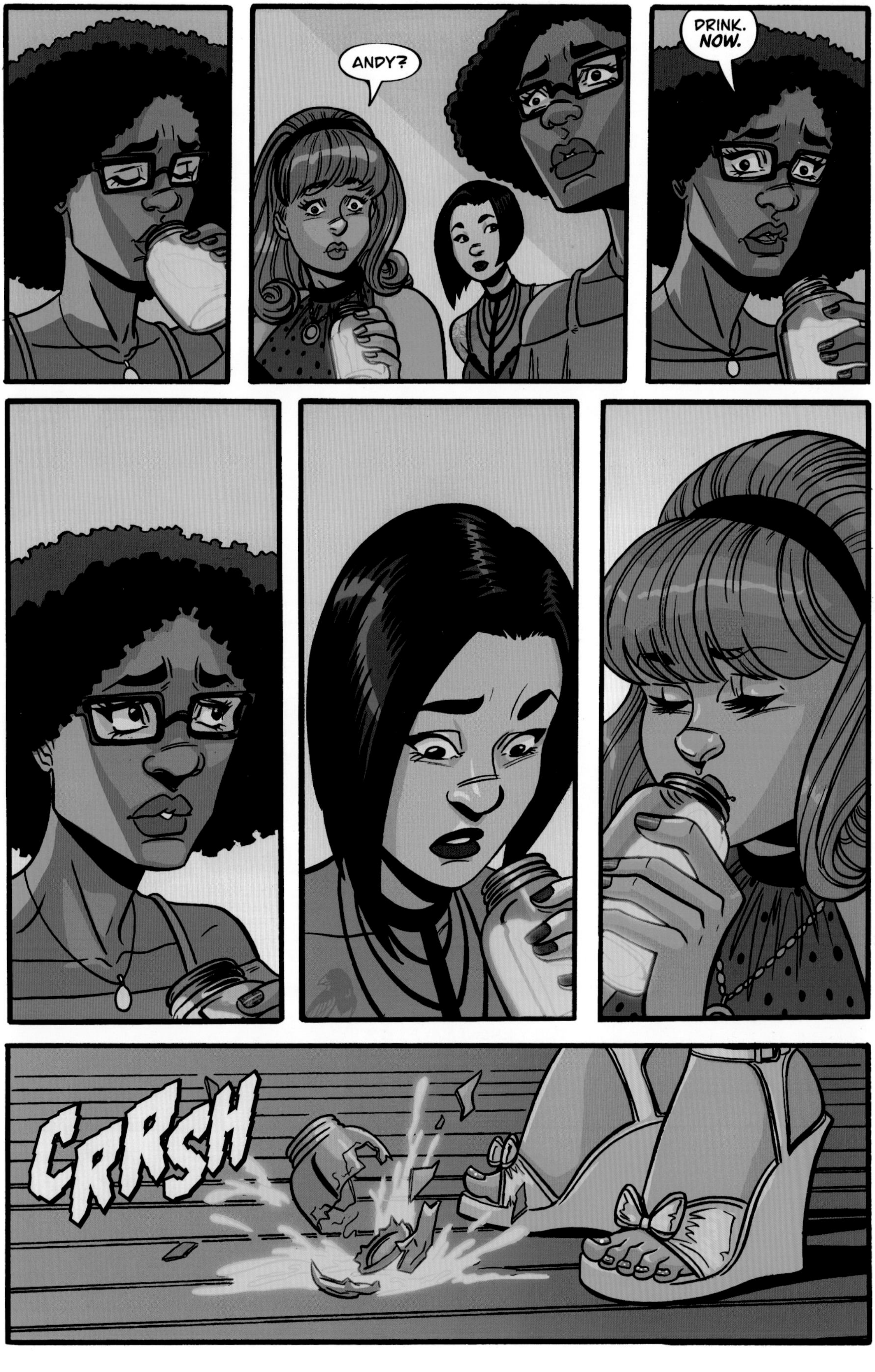
ANDY?
DRINK. NOW.
CRRSH

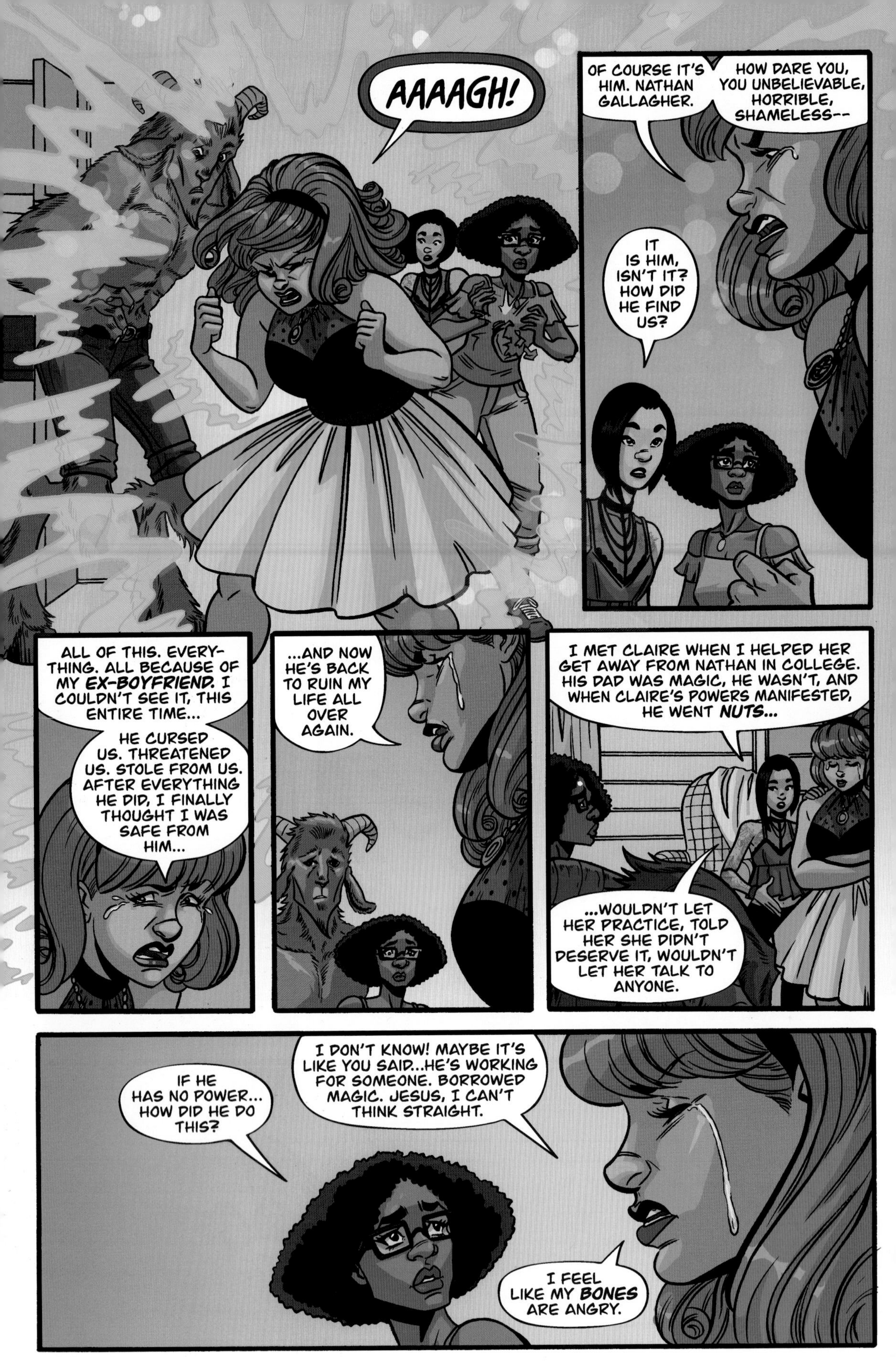
AAAAGH!
OF COURSE IT'S HIM. NATHAN GALLAGHER.
HOW DARE YOU, YOU UNBELIEVABLE, HORRIBLE, SHAMELESS--
IT IS HIM, ISN'T IT? HOW DID HE FIND US?
ALL OF THIS. EVERY-THING. ALL BECAUSE OF MY EX-BOYFRIEND. I COULDN'T SEE IT, THIS ENTIRE TIME...
HE CURSED US. THREATENED US. STOLE FROM US. AFTER EVERYTHING HE DID, I FINALLY THOUGHT I WAS SAFE FROM HIM...
...AND NOW HE'S BACK TO RUIN MY LIFE ALL OVER AGAIN.
I MET CLAIRE WHEN I HELPED HER GET AWAY FROM NATHAN IN COLLEGE. HIS DAD WAS MAGIC, HE WASN'T, AND WHEN CLAIRE'S POWERS MANIFESTED, HE WENT NUTS...
...WOULDN'T LET HER PRACTICE, TOLD HER SHE DIDN'T DESERVE IT, WOULDN'T LET HER TALK TO ANYONE.
IF HE HAS NO POWER... HOW DID HE DO THIS?
I DON'T KNOW! MAYBE IT'S LIKE YOU SAID...HE'S WORKING FOR SOMEONE. BORROWED MAGIC. JESUS, I CAN'T THINK STRAIGHT.
I FEEL LIKE MY BONES ARE ANGRY.

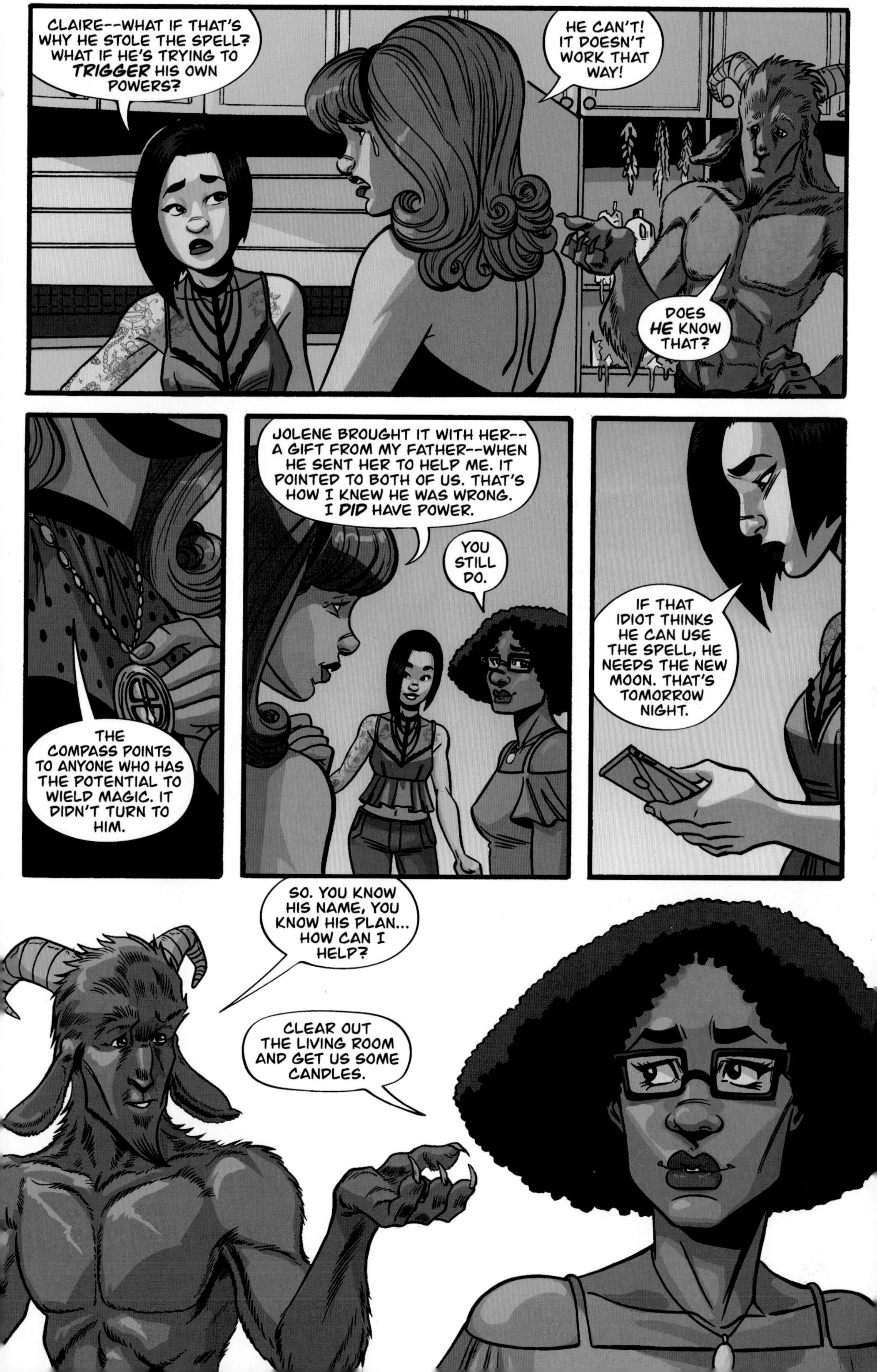
CLAIRE--WHAT IF THAT'S WHY HE STOLE THE SPELL? WHAT IF HE'S TRYING TO *TRIGGER* HIS OWN POWERS?
HE CAN'T! IT DOESN'T WORK THAT WAY!
DOES *HE* KNOW THAT?
THE COMPASS POINTS TO ANYONE WHO HAS THE POTENTIAL TO WIELD MAGIC. IT DIDN'T TURN TO HIM.
JOLENE BROUGHT IT WITH HER--A GIFT FROM MY FATHER--WHEN HE SENT HER TO HELP ME. IT POINTED TO BOTH OF US. THAT'S HOW I KNEW HE WAS WRONG. I *DID* HAVE POWER.
YOU STILL DO.
IF THAT IDIOT THINKS HE CAN USE THE SPELL, HE NEEDS THE NEW MOON. THAT'S TOMORROW NIGHT.
SO. YOU KNOW HIS NAME, YOU KNOW HIS PLAN... HOW CAN I HELP?
CLEAR OUT THE LIVING ROOM AND GET US SOME CANDLES.

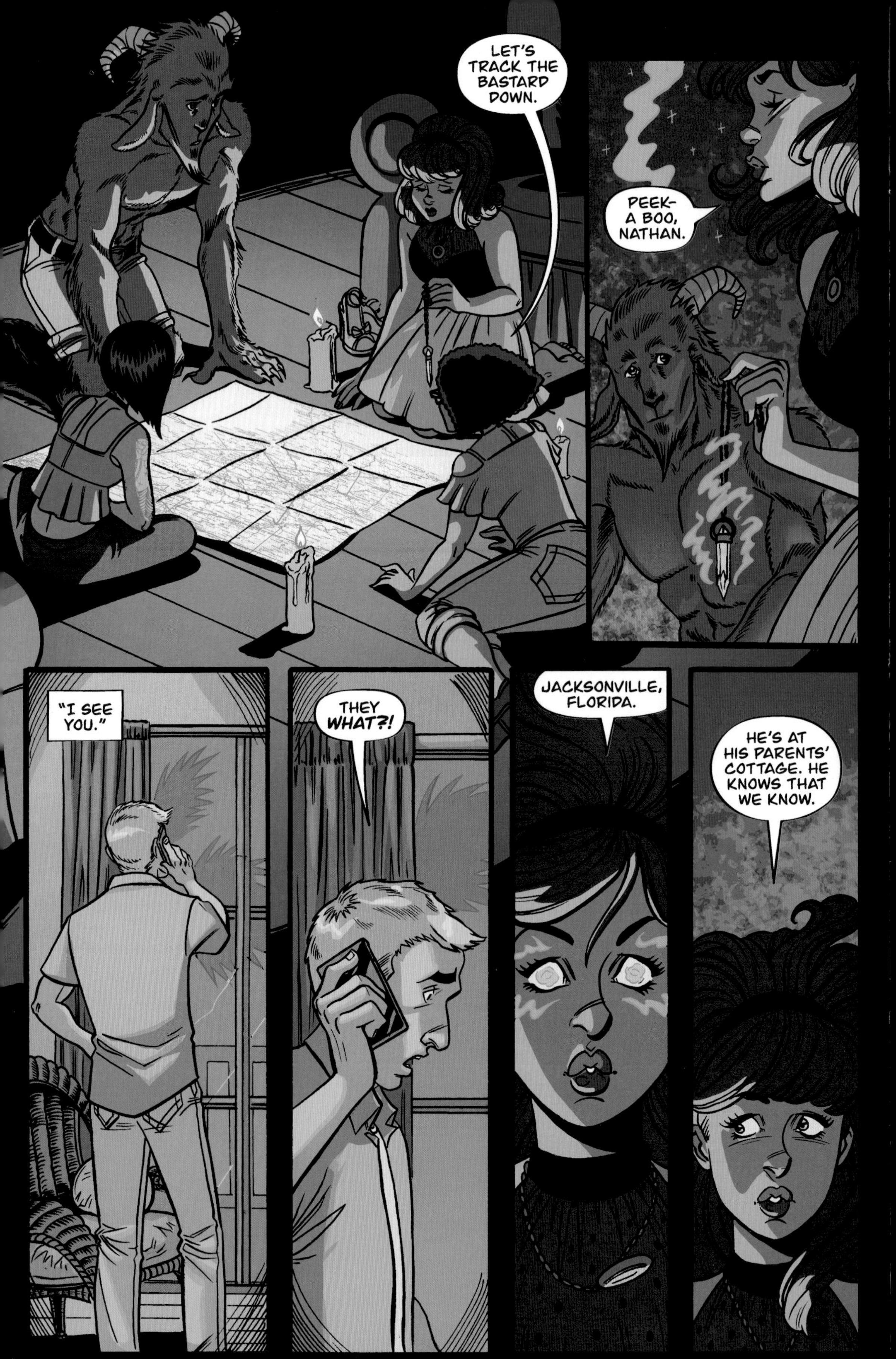
LET'S TRACK THE BASTARD DOWN.
PEEK-A BOO, NATHAN.
"I SEE YOU."
THEY WHAT?!
JACKSONVILLE, FLORIDA.
HE'S AT HIS PARENTS' COTTAGE. HE KNOWS THAT WE KNOW.

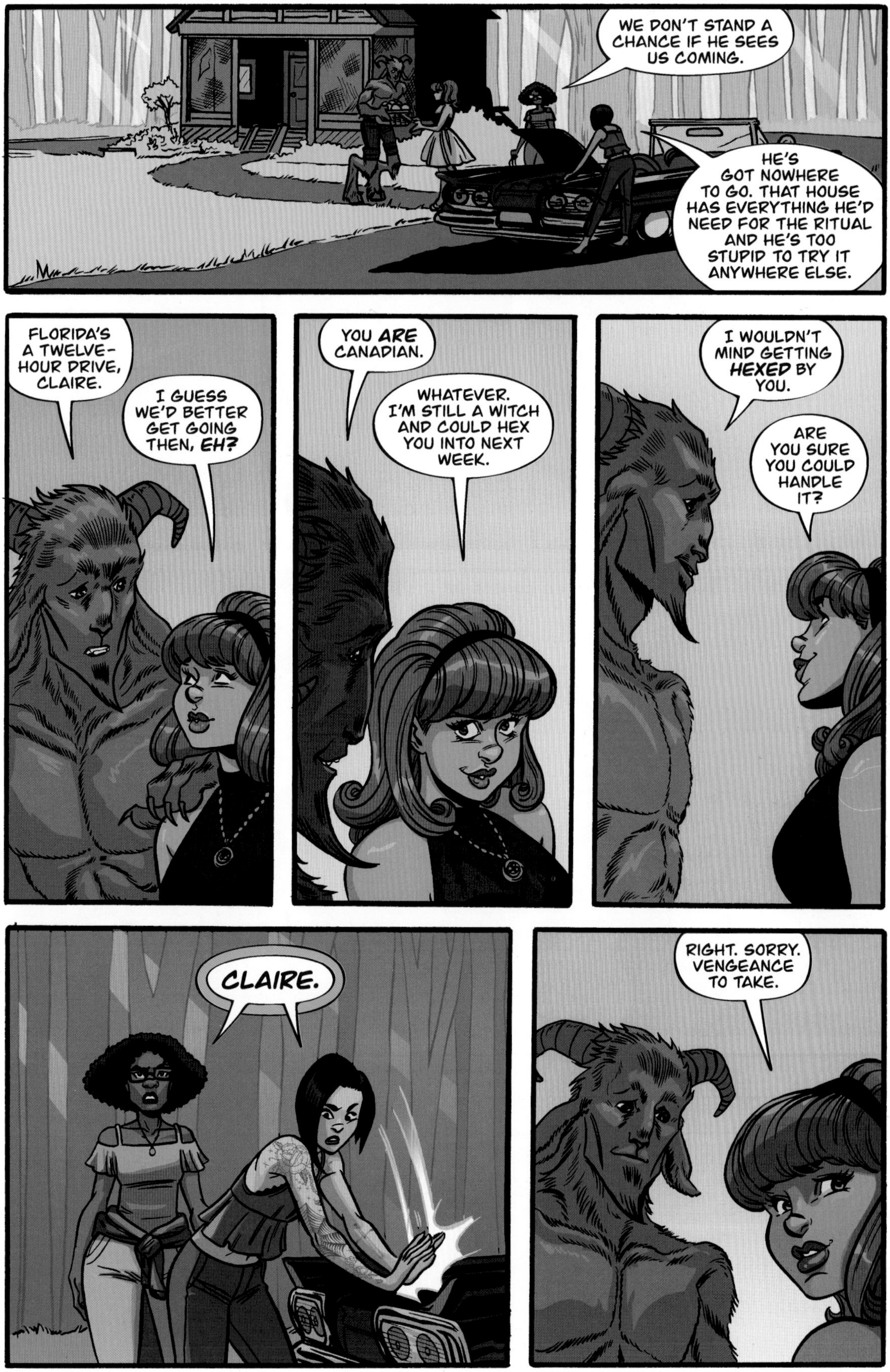
WE DON'T STAND A CHANCE IF HE SEES US COMING.
HE'S GOT NOWHERE TO GO. THAT HOUSE HAS EVERYTHING HE'D NEED FOR THE RITUAL AND HE'S TOO STUPID TO TRY IT ANYWHERE ELSE.
FLORIDA'S A TWELVE-HOUR DRIVE, CLAIRE.
I GUESS WE'D BETTER GET GOING THEN, EH?
YOU ARE CANADIAN.
WHATEVER. I'M STILL A WITCH AND COULD HEX YOU INTO NEXT WEEK.
I WOULDN'T MIND GETTING HEXED BY YOU.
ARE YOU SURE YOU COULD HANDLE IT?
CLAIRE.
RIGHT. SORRY. VENGEANCE TO TAKE.

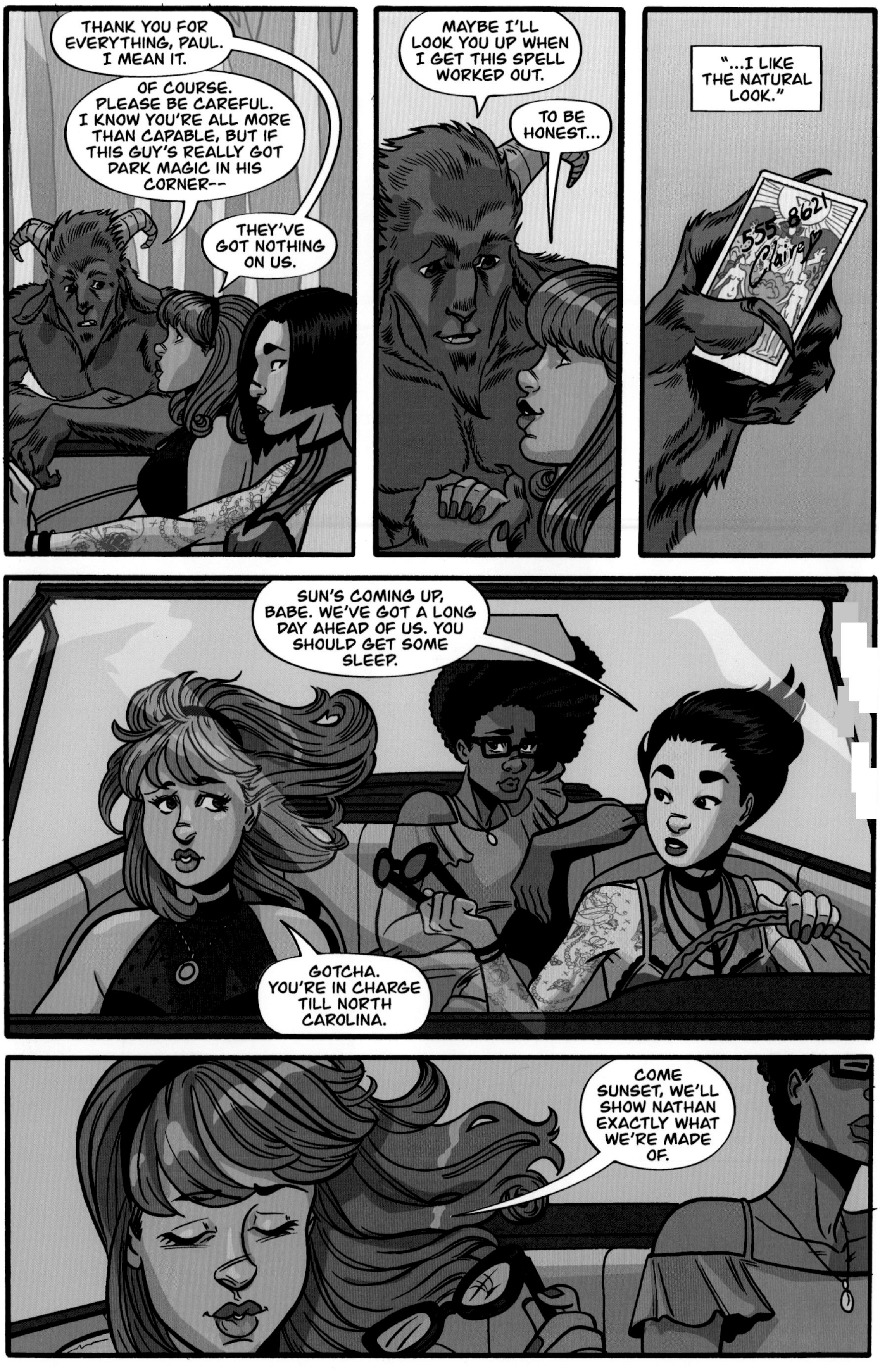
THANK YOU FOR EVERYTHING, PAUL. I MEAN IT.
OF COURSE. PLEASE BE CAREFUL. I KNOW YOU'RE ALL MORE THAN CAPABLE, BUT IF THIS GUY'S REALLY GOT DARK MAGIC IN HIS CORNER--
THEY'VE GOT NOTHING ON US.
MAYBE I'LL LOOK YOU UP WHEN I GET THIS SPELL WORKED OUT.
TO BE HONEST...
"...I LIKE THE NATURAL LOOK."
555-8621
Claire
SUN'S COMING UP, BABE. WE'VE GOT A LONG DAY AHEAD OF US. YOU SHOULD GET SOME SLEEP.
GOTCHA. YOU'RE IN CHARGE TILL NORTH CAROLINA.
COME SUNSET, WE'LL SHOW NATHAN EXACTLY WHAT WE'RE MADE OF.

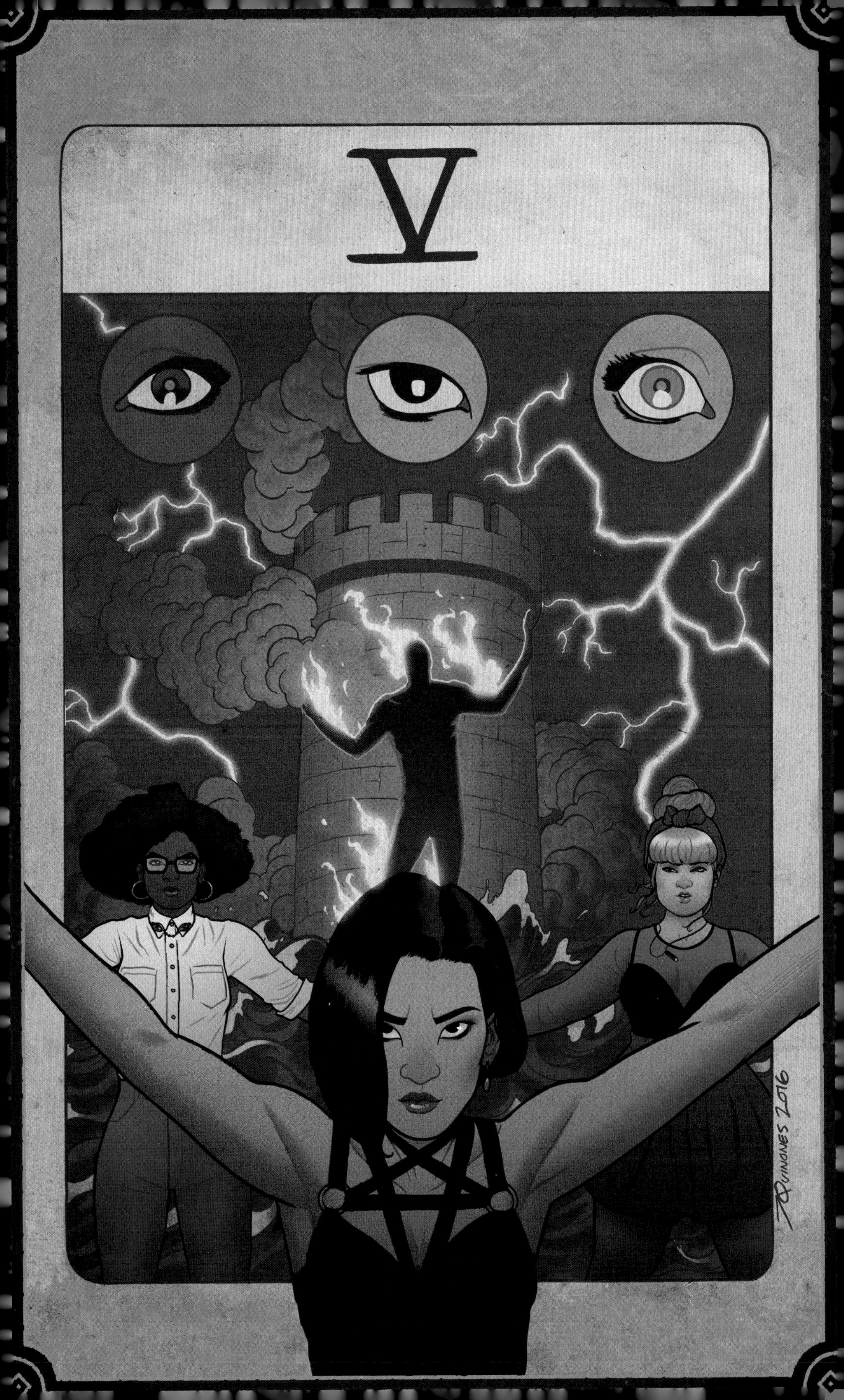
V
QUINONES 2016

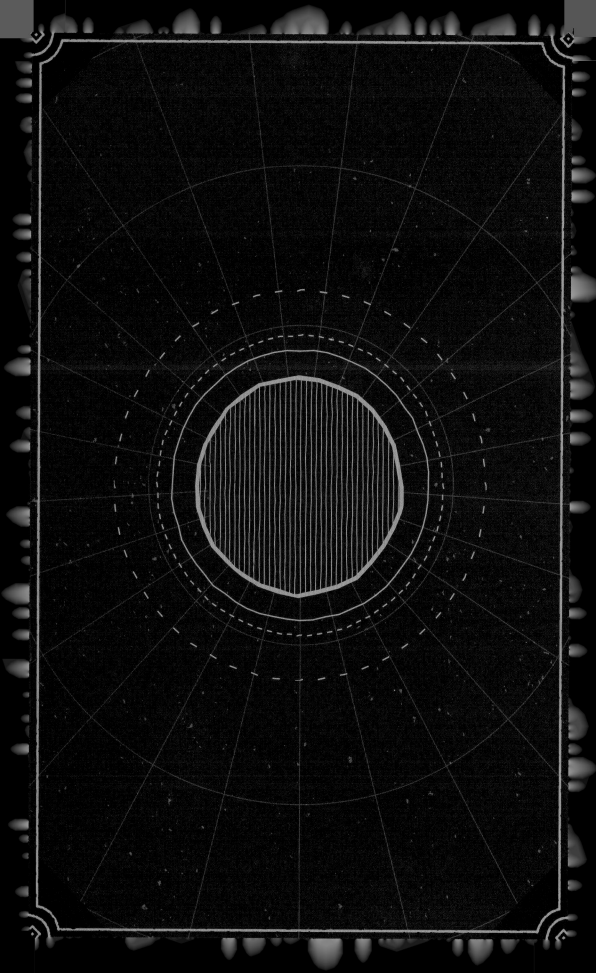

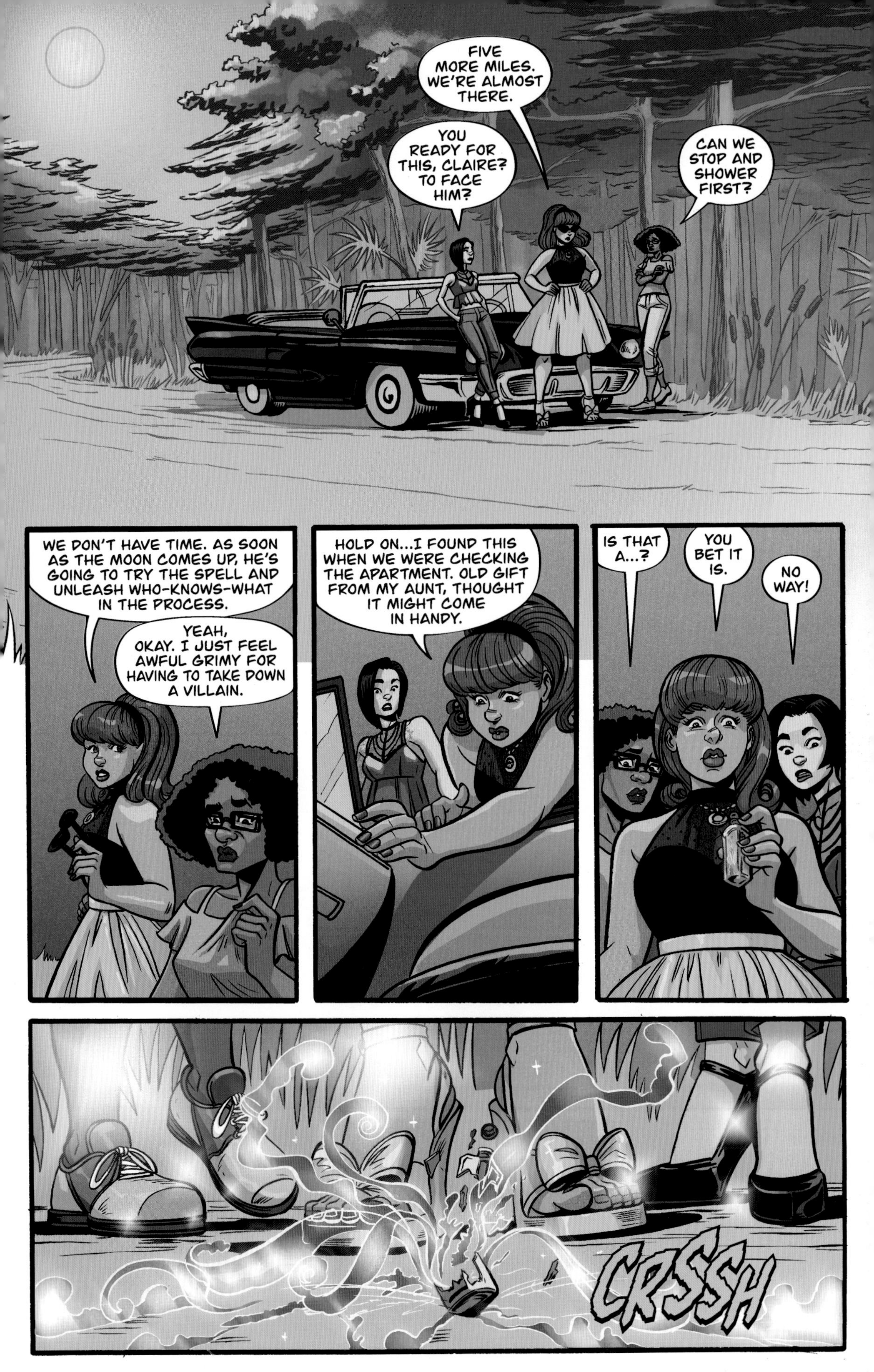
FIVE MORE MILES. WE'RE ALMOST THERE.
YOU READY FOR THIS, CLAIRE? TO FACE HIM?
CAN WE STOP AND SHOWER FIRST?
WE DON'T HAVE TIME. AS SOON AS THE MOON COMES UP, HE'S GOING TO TRY THE SPELL AND UNLEASH WHO-KNOWS-WHAT IN THE PROCESS.
YEAH, OKAY. I JUST FEEL AWFUL GRIMY FOR HAVING TO TAKE DOWN A VILLAIN.
HOLD ON...I FOUND THIS WHEN WE WERE CHECKING THE APARTMENT. OLD GIFT FROM MY AUNT, THOUGHT IT MIGHT COME IN HANDY.
IS THAT A...?
YOU BET IT IS.
NO WAY!
CRSSH

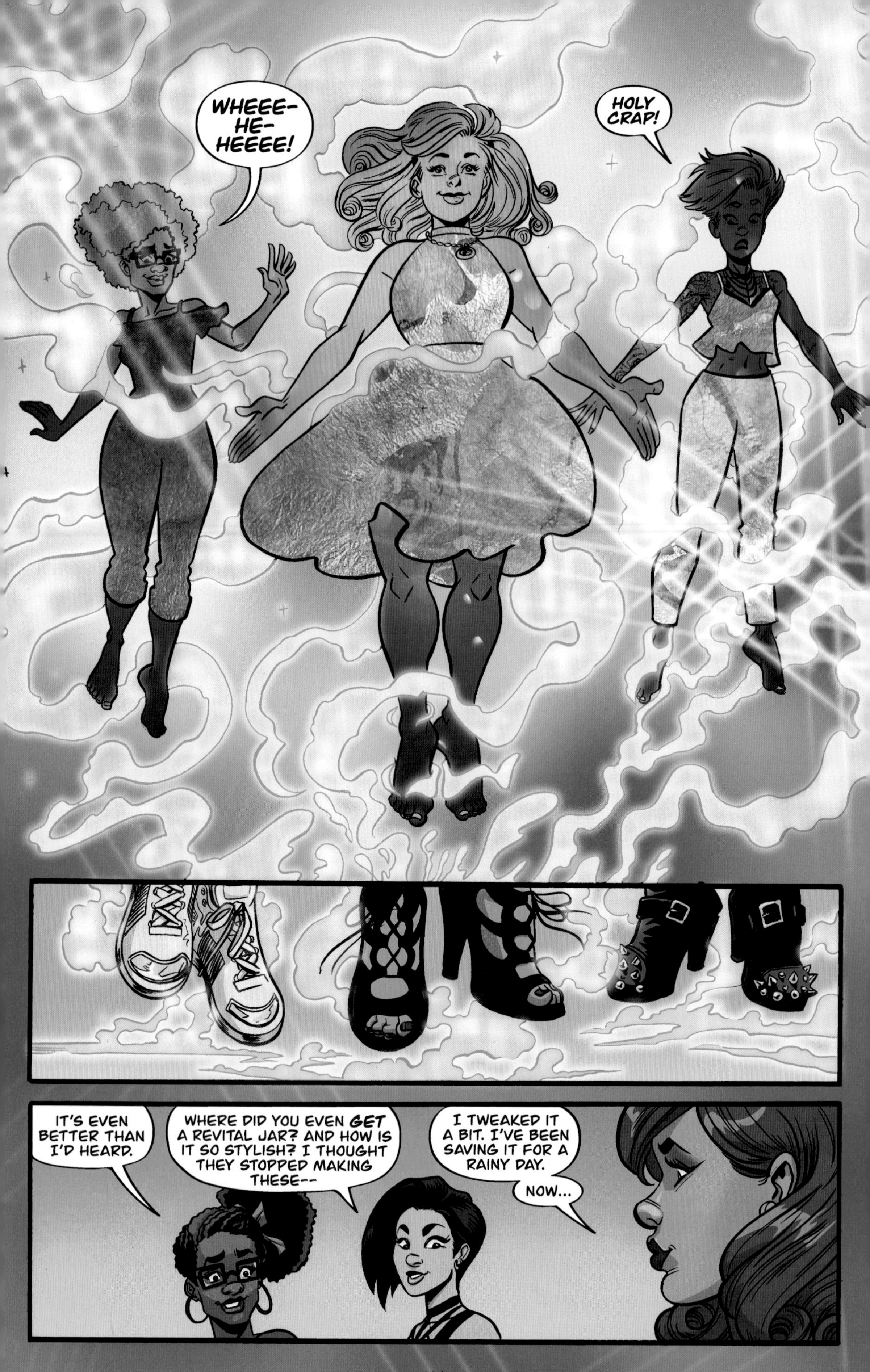
WHEEEE-HE-HEEEEE!
HOLY CRAP!
IT'S EVEN BETTER THAN I'D HEARD.
WHERE DID YOU EVEN **GET** A REVITAL JAR? AND HOW IS IT SO STYLISH? I THOUGHT THEY STOPPED MAKING THESE--
I TWEAKED IT A BIT. I'VE BEEN SAVING IT FOR A RAINY DAY.
NOW...

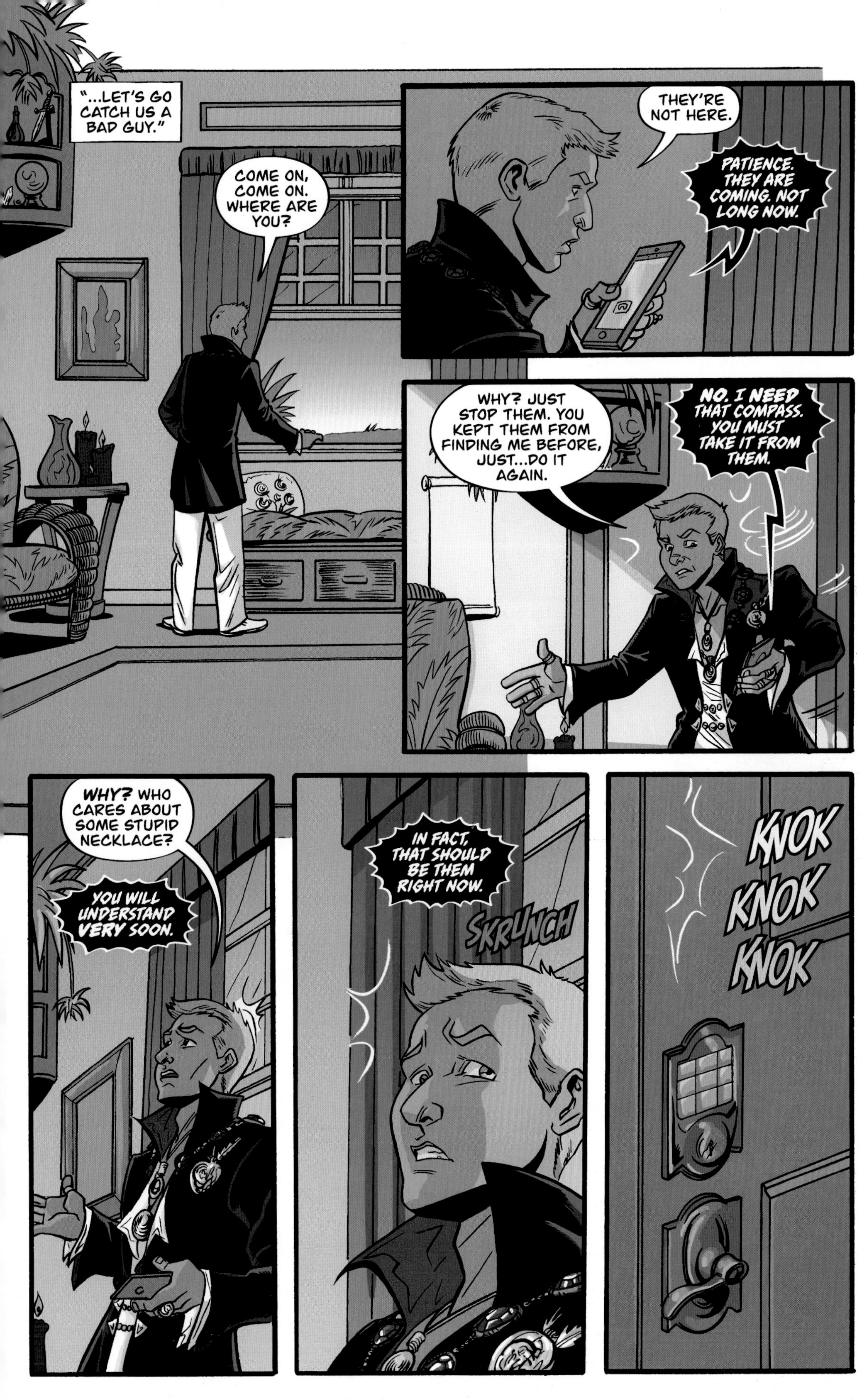

"...LET'S GO CATCH US A BAD GUY."
COME ON, COME ON. WHERE ARE YOU?
THEY'RE NOT HERE.
PATIENCE. THEY ARE COMING. NOT LONG NOW.
WHY? JUST STOP THEM. YOU KEPT THEM FROM FINDING ME BEFORE, JUST...DO IT AGAIN.
NO. I NEED THAT COMPASS. YOU MUST TAKE IT FROM THEM.
WHY? WHO CARES ABOUT SOME STUPID NECKLACE?
YOU WILL UNDERSTAND VERY SOON.
IN FACT, THAT SHOULD BE THEM RIGHT NOW.
SKRUNCH
KNOK
KNOK
KNOK

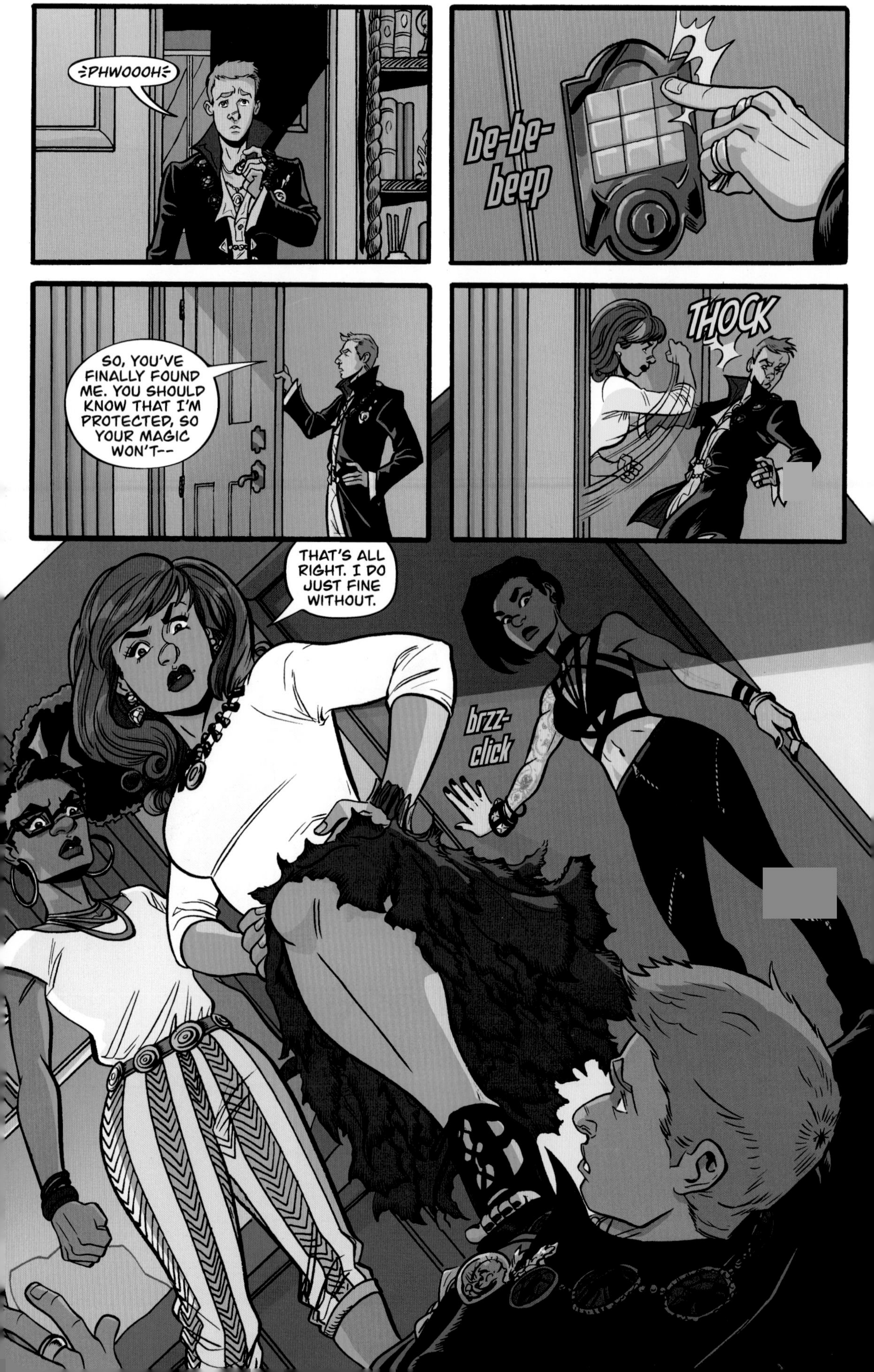
PHWOOOH
be-be-beep
SO, YOU'VE FINALLY FOUND ME. YOU SHOULD KNOW THAT I'M PROTECTED, SO YOUR MAGIC WON'T--
THOCK
THAT'S ALL RIGHT. I DO JUST FINE WITHOUT.
brzz-click

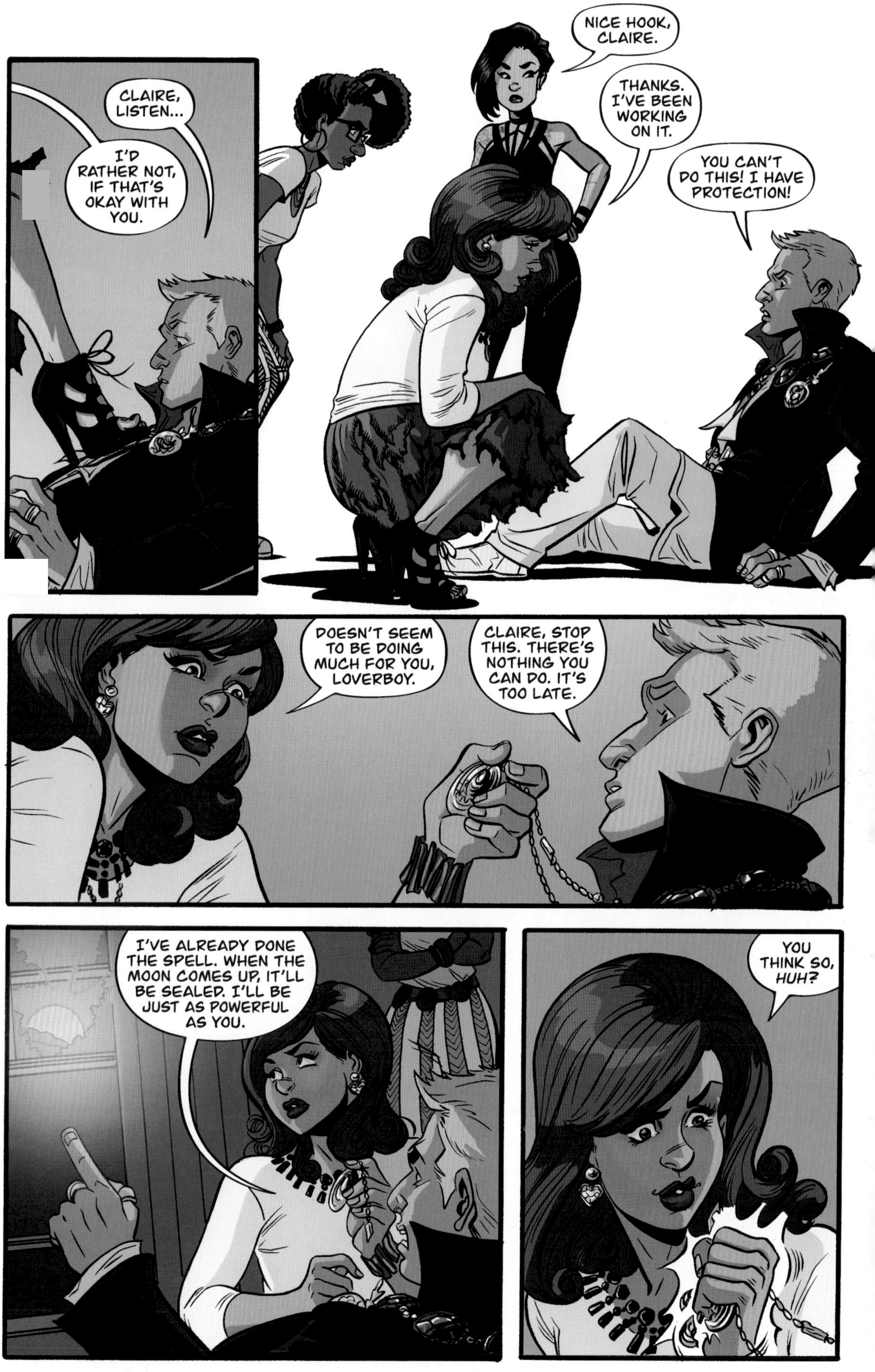
CLAIRE, LISTEN...
I'D RATHER NOT, IF THAT'S OKAY WITH YOU.
NICE HOOK, CLAIRE.
THANKS. I'VE BEEN WORKING ON IT.
YOU CAN'T DO THIS! I HAVE PROTECTION!
DOESN'T SEEM TO BE DOING MUCH FOR YOU, LOVERBOY.
CLAIRE, STOP THIS. THERE'S NOTHING YOU CAN DO. IT'S TOO LATE.
I'VE ALREADY DONE THE SPELL. WHEN THE MOON COMES UP, IT'LL BE SEALED. I'LL BE JUST AS POWERFUL AS YOU.
YOU THINK SO, HUH?

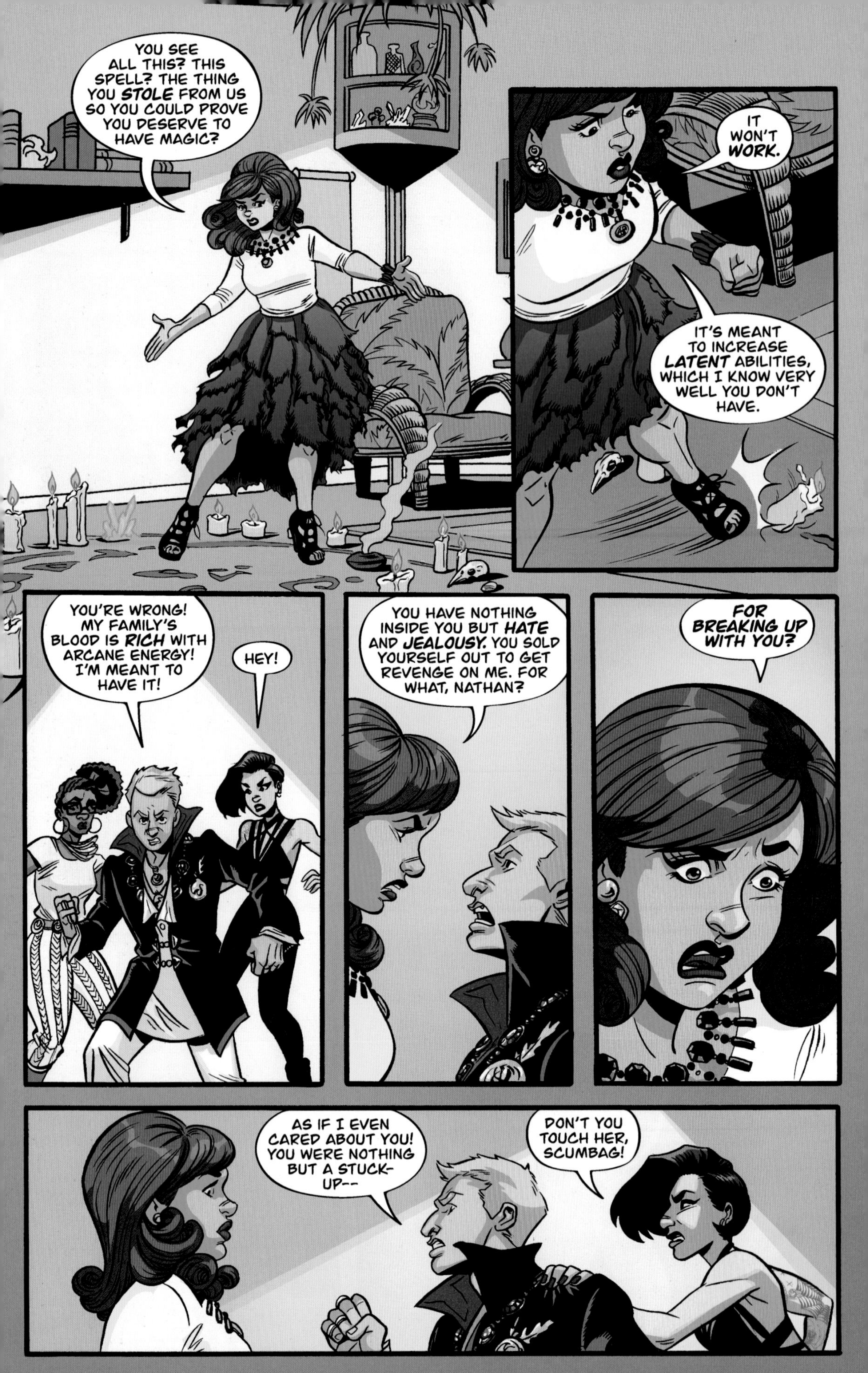
YOU SEE ALL THIS? THIS SPELL? THE THING YOU STOLE FROM US SO YOU COULD PROVE YOU DESERVE TO HAVE MAGIC?
IT WON'T WORK.
IT'S MEANT TO INCREASE LATENT ABILITIES, WHICH I KNOW VERY WELL YOU DON'T HAVE.
YOU'RE WRONG! MY FAMILY'S BLOOD IS RICH WITH ARCANE ENERGY! I'M MEANT TO HAVE IT!
HEY!
YOU HAVE NOTHING INSIDE YOU BUT HATE AND JEALOUSY. YOU SOLD YOURSELF OUT TO GET REVENGE ON ME. FOR WHAT, NATHAN?
FOR BREAKING UP WITH YOU?
AS IF I EVEN CARED ABOUT YOU! YOU WERE NOTHING BUT A STUCK-UP--
DON'T YOU TOUCH HER, SCUMBAG!

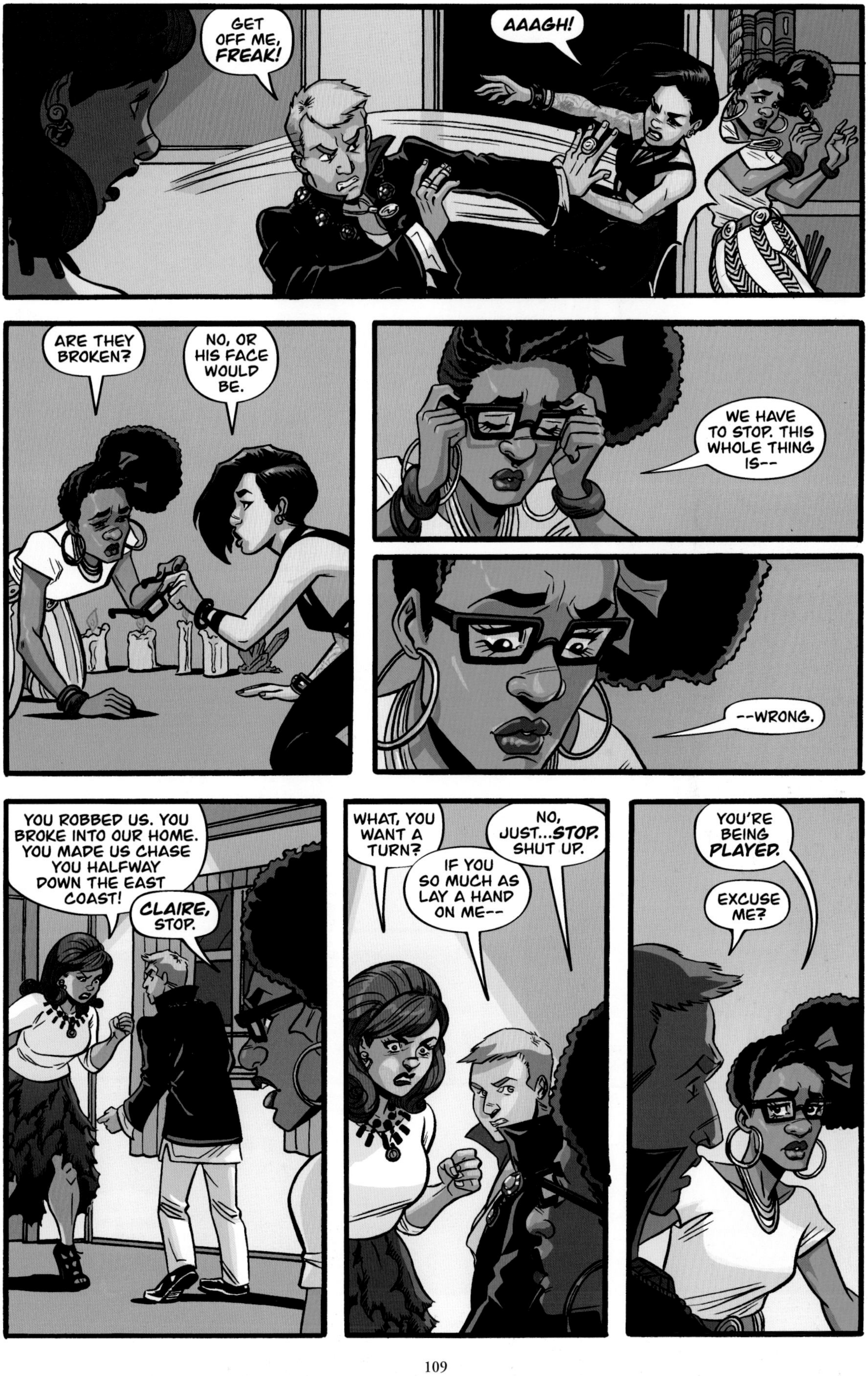
GET OFF ME, FREAK!
AAAGH!
ARE THEY BROKEN?
NO, OR HIS FACE WOULD BE.
WE HAVE TO STOP. THIS WHOLE THING IS--
--WRONG.
YOU ROBBED US. YOU BROKE INTO OUR HOME. YOU MADE US CHASE YOU HALFWAY DOWN THE EAST COAST!
CLAIRE, STOP.
WHAT, YOU WANT A TURN?
NO, JUST...STOP. SHUT UP.
IF YOU SO MUCH AS LAY A HAND ON ME--
YOU'RE BEING PLAYED.
EXCUSE ME?

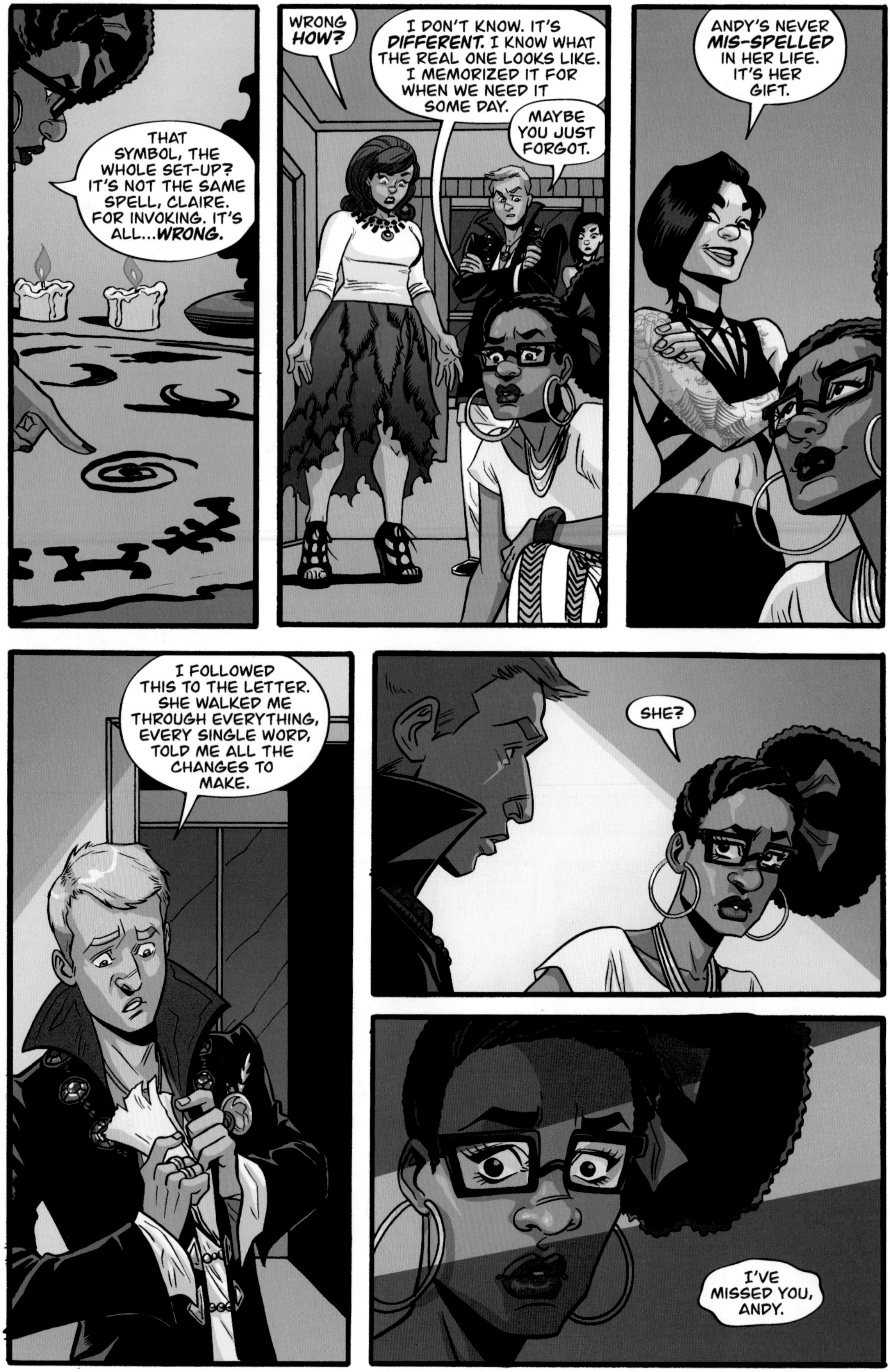
THAT SYMBOL, THE WHOLE SET-UP? IT'S NOT THE SAME SPELL, CLAIRE. FOR INVOKING. IT'S ALL...WRONG.
WRONG HOW?
I DON'T KNOW. IT'S DIFFERENT. I KNOW WHAT THE REAL ONE LOOKS LIKE. I MEMORIZED IT FOR WHEN WE NEED IT SOME DAY.
MAYBE YOU JUST FORGOT.
ANDY'S NEVER MIS-SPELLED IN HER LIFE. IT'S HER GIFT.
I FOLLOWED THIS TO THE LETTER. SHE WALKED ME THROUGH EVERYTHING, EVERY SINGLE WORD, TOLD ME ALL THE CHANGES TO MAKE.
SHE?
I'VE MISSED YOU, ANDY.

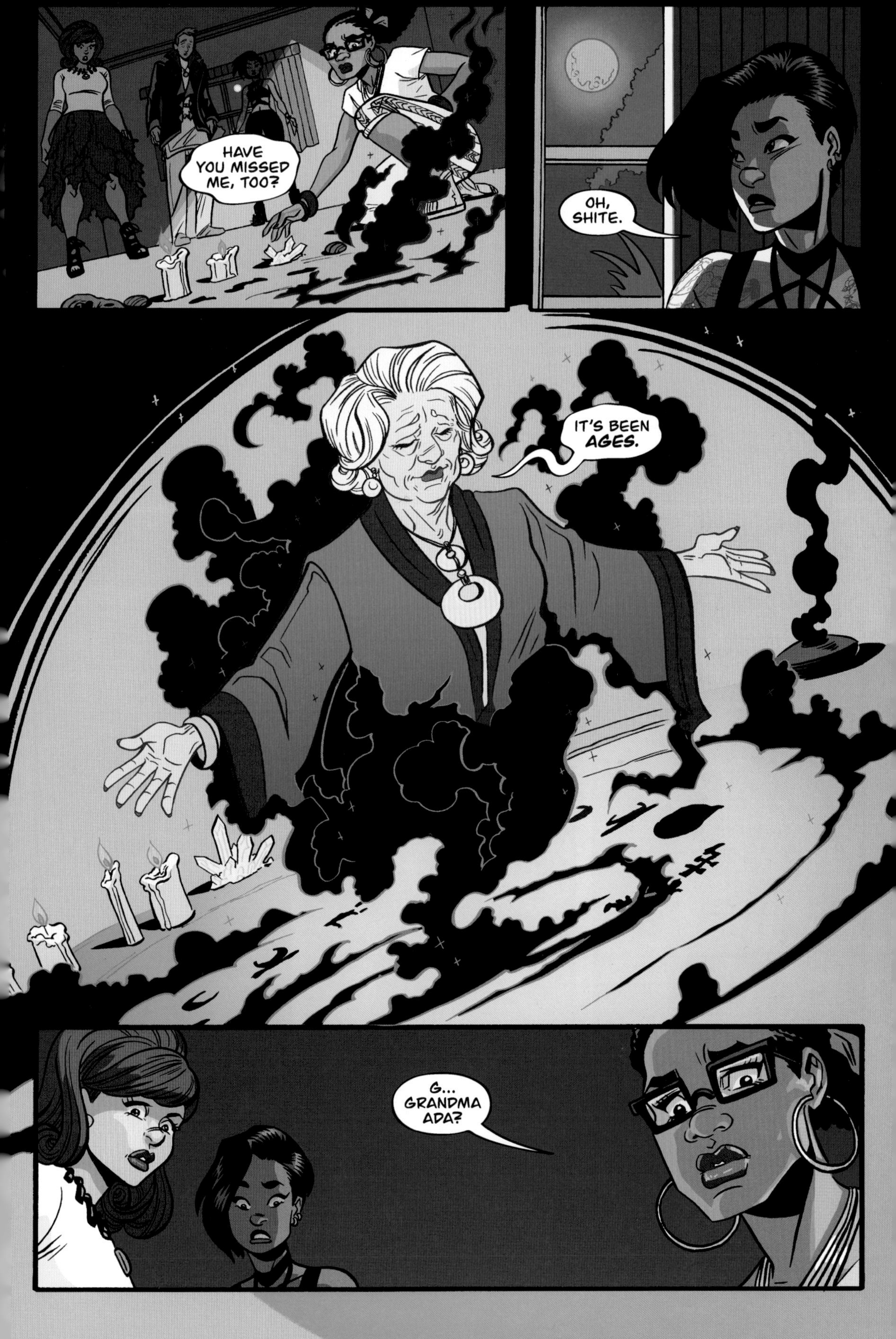
HAVE YOU MISSED ME, TOO?
OH, SHITE.
IT'S BEEN AGES.
G... GRANDMA ADA?

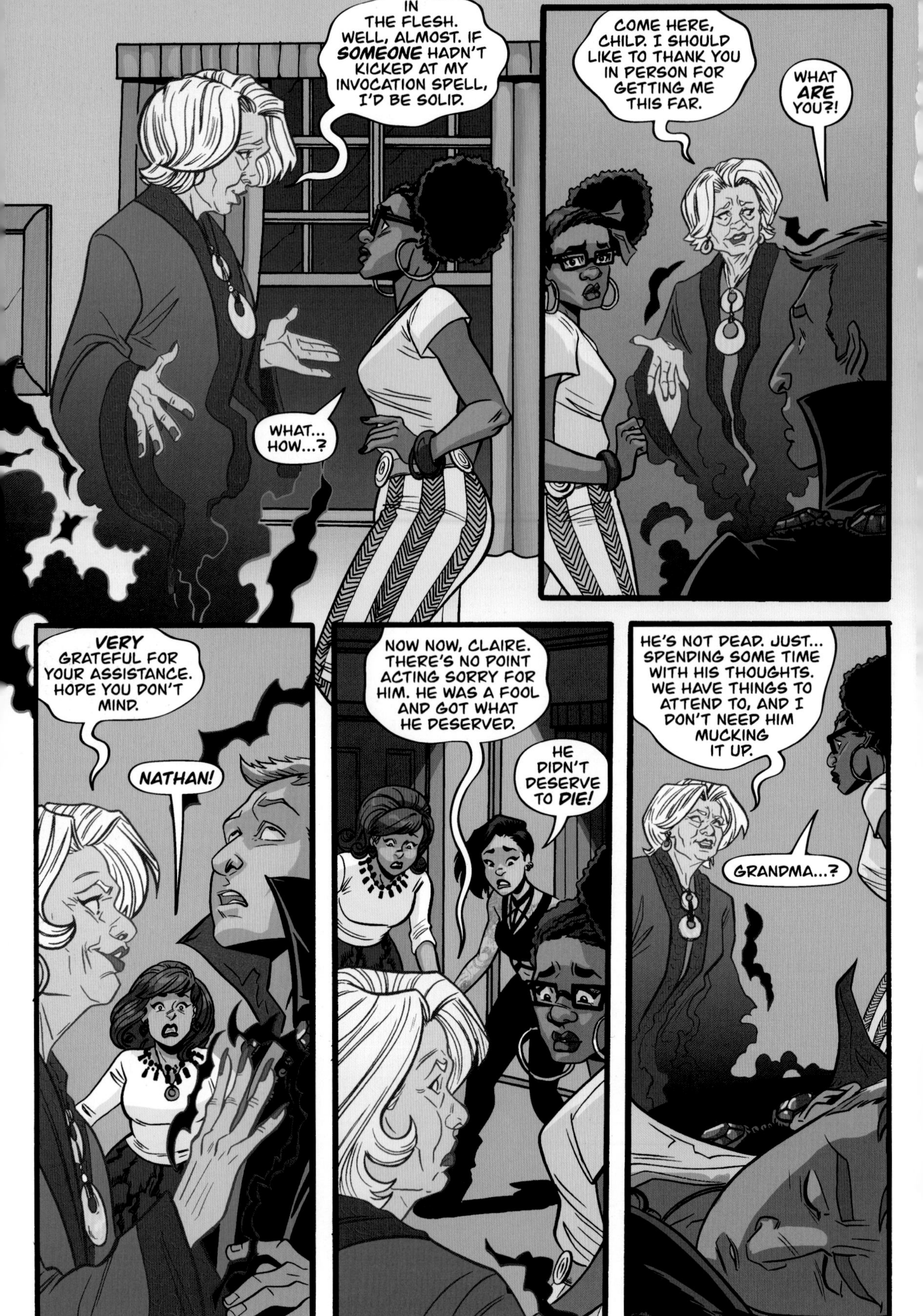
IN THE FLESH. WELL, ALMOST. IF **SOMEONE** HADN'T KICKED AT MY INVOCATION SPELL, I'D BE SOLID.
WHAT... HOW...?
COME HERE, CHILD. I SHOULD LIKE TO THANK YOU IN PERSON FOR GETTING ME THIS FAR.
WHAT **ARE** YOU?!
VERY GRATEFUL FOR YOUR ASSISTANCE. HOPE YOU DON'T MIND.
NATHAN!
NOW NOW, CLAIRE. THERE'S NO POINT ACTING SORRY FOR HIM. HE WAS A FOOL AND GOT WHAT HE DESERVED.
HE DIDN'T DESERVE TO **DIE!**
HE'S NOT DEAD. JUST... SPENDING SOME TIME WITH HIS THOUGHTS. WE HAVE THINGS TO ATTEND TO, AND I DON'T NEED HIM MUCKING IT UP.
GRANDMA...?

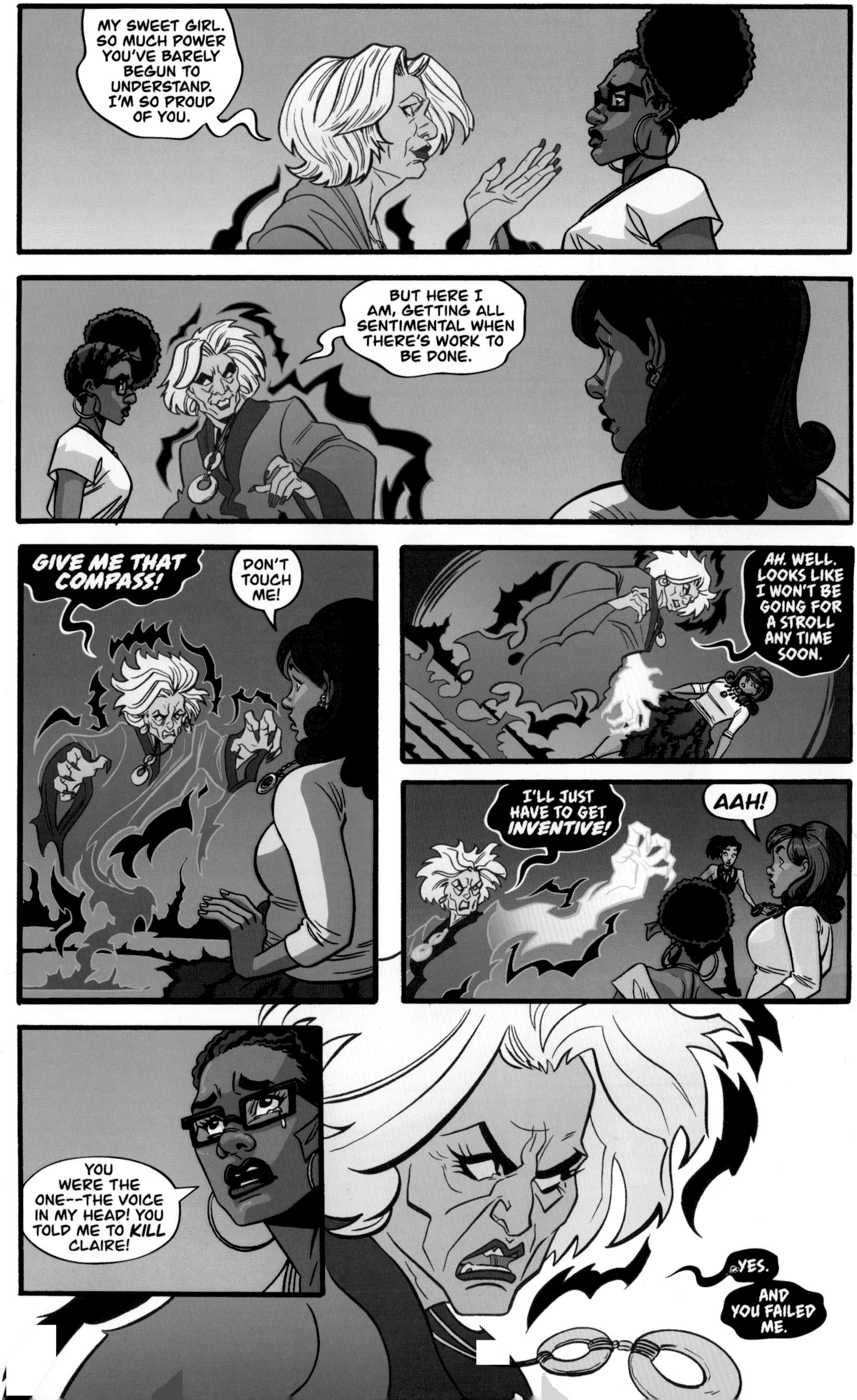
MY SWEET GIRL. SO MUCH POWER YOU'VE BARELY BEGUN TO UNDERSTAND. I'M SO PROUD OF YOU.
BUT HERE I AM, GETTING ALL SENTIMENTAL WHEN THERE'S WORK TO BE DONE.
GIVE ME THAT COMPASS!
DON'T TOUCH ME!
AH. WELL. LOOKS LIKE I WON'T BE GOING FOR A STROLL ANY TIME SOON.
I'LL JUST HAVE TO GET INVENTIVE!
AAH!
YOU WERE THE ONE--THE VOICE IN MY HEAD! YOU TOLD ME TO KILL CLAIRE!
YES.
AND YOU FAILED ME.

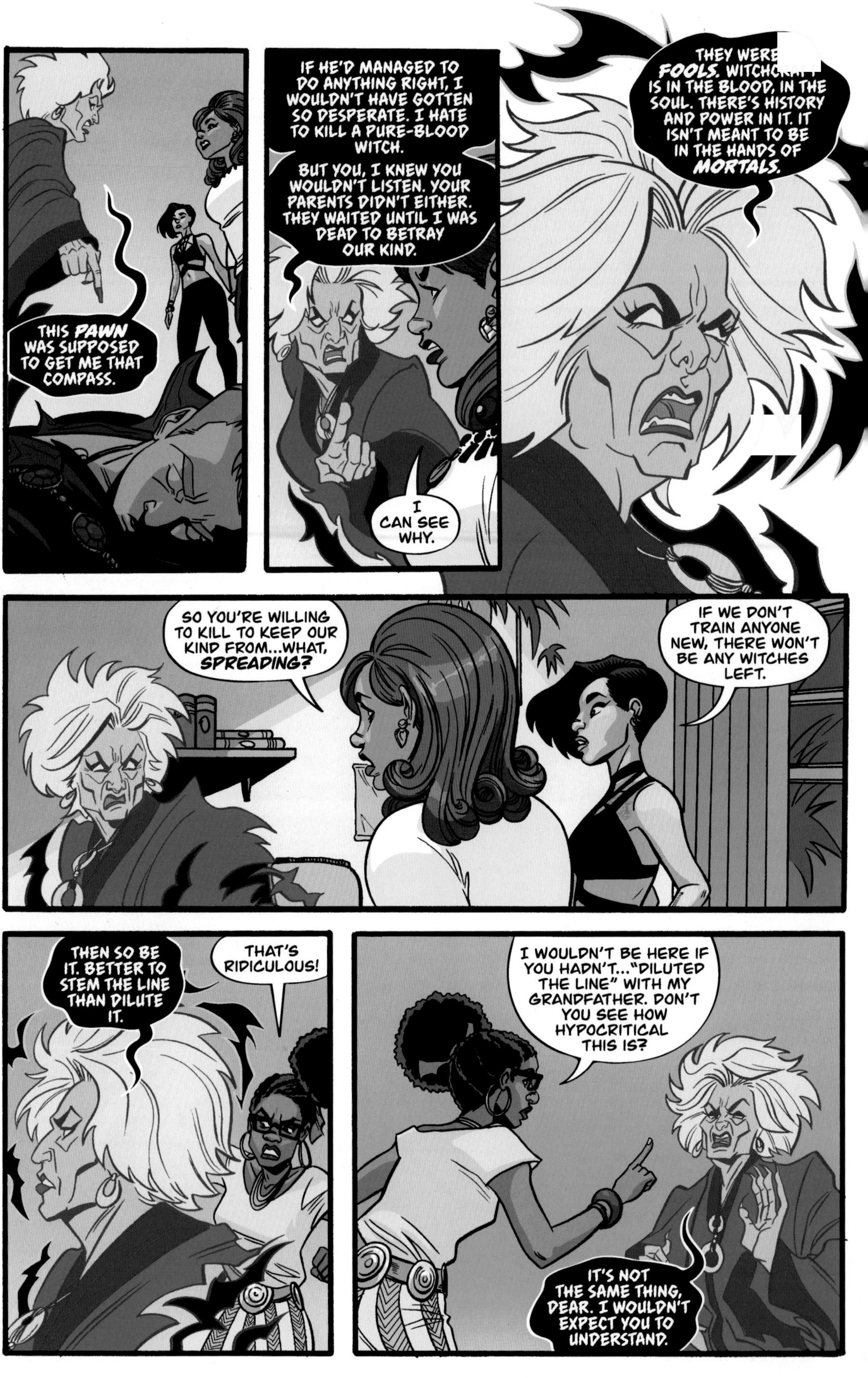
THIS PAWN WAS SUPPOSED TO GET ME THAT COMPASS.
IF HE'D MANAGED TO DO ANYTHING RIGHT, I WOULDN'T HAVE GOTTEN SO DESPERATE. I HATE TO KILL A PURE-BLOOD WITCH.
BUT YOU, I KNEW YOU WOULDN'T LISTEN. YOUR PARENTS DIDN'T EITHER. THEY WAITED UNTIL I WAS DEAD TO BETRAY OUR KIND.
I CAN SEE WHY.
THEY WERE FOOLS. WITCHCRA… IS IN THE BLOOD, IN THE SOUL. THERE'S HISTORY AND POWER IN IT. IT ISN'T MEANT TO BE IN THE HANDS OF MORTALS.
SO YOU'RE WILLING TO KILL TO KEEP OUR KIND FROM...WHAT, SPREADING?
IF WE DON'T TRAIN ANYONE NEW, THERE WON'T BE ANY WITCHES LEFT.
THEN SO BE IT. BETTER TO STEM THE LINE THAN DILUTE IT.
THAT'S RIDICULOUS!
I WOULDN'T BE HERE IF YOU HADN'T..."DILUTED THE LINE" WITH MY GRANDFATHER. DON'T YOU SEE HOW HYPOCRITICAL THIS IS?
IT'S NOT THE SAME THING, DEAR. I WOULDN'T EXPECT YOU TO UNDERSTAND.

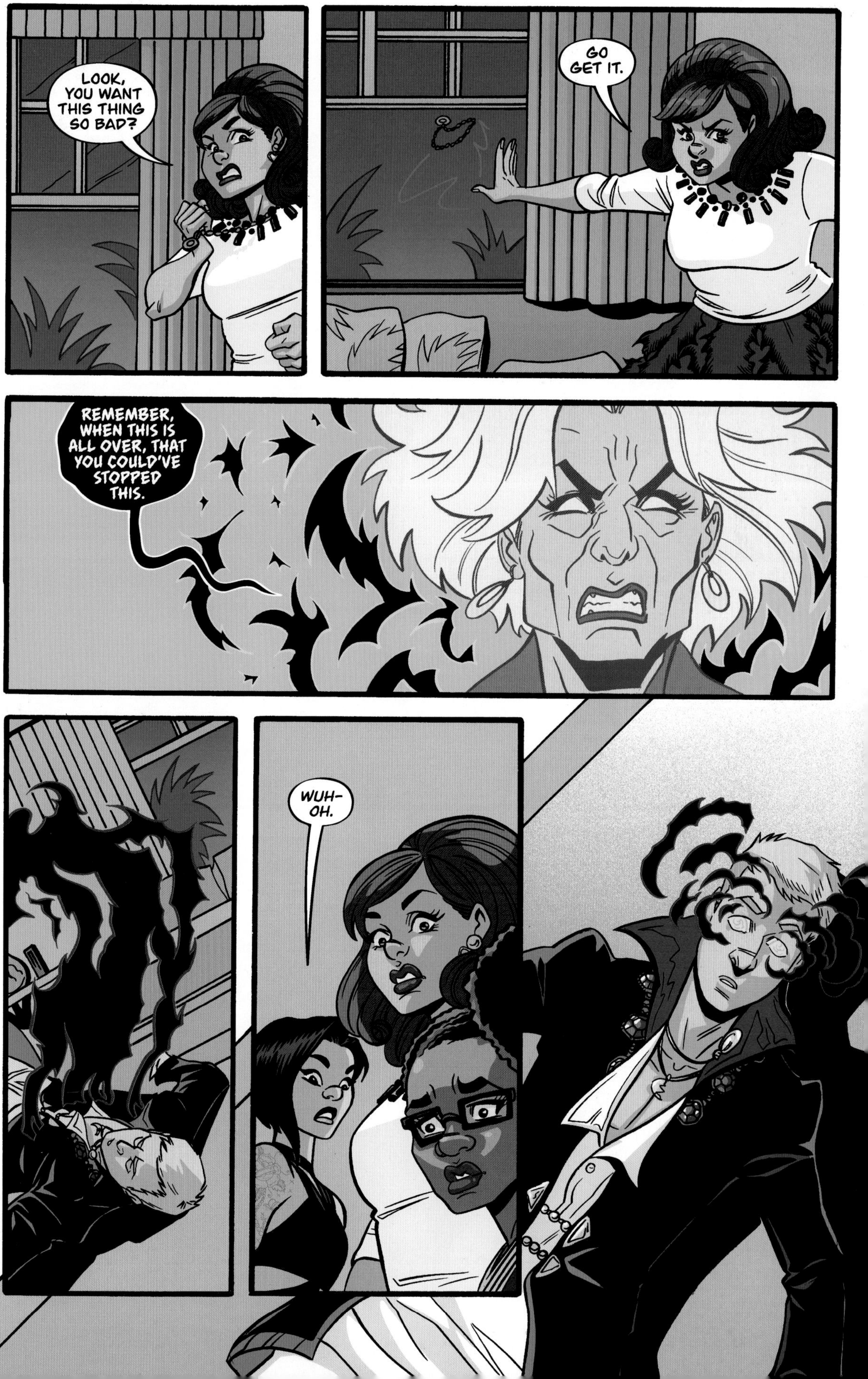
LOOK, YOU WANT THIS THING SO BAD?
GO GET IT.
REMEMBER, WHEN THIS IS ALL OVER, THAT YOU COULD'VE STOPPED THIS.
WUH-OH.

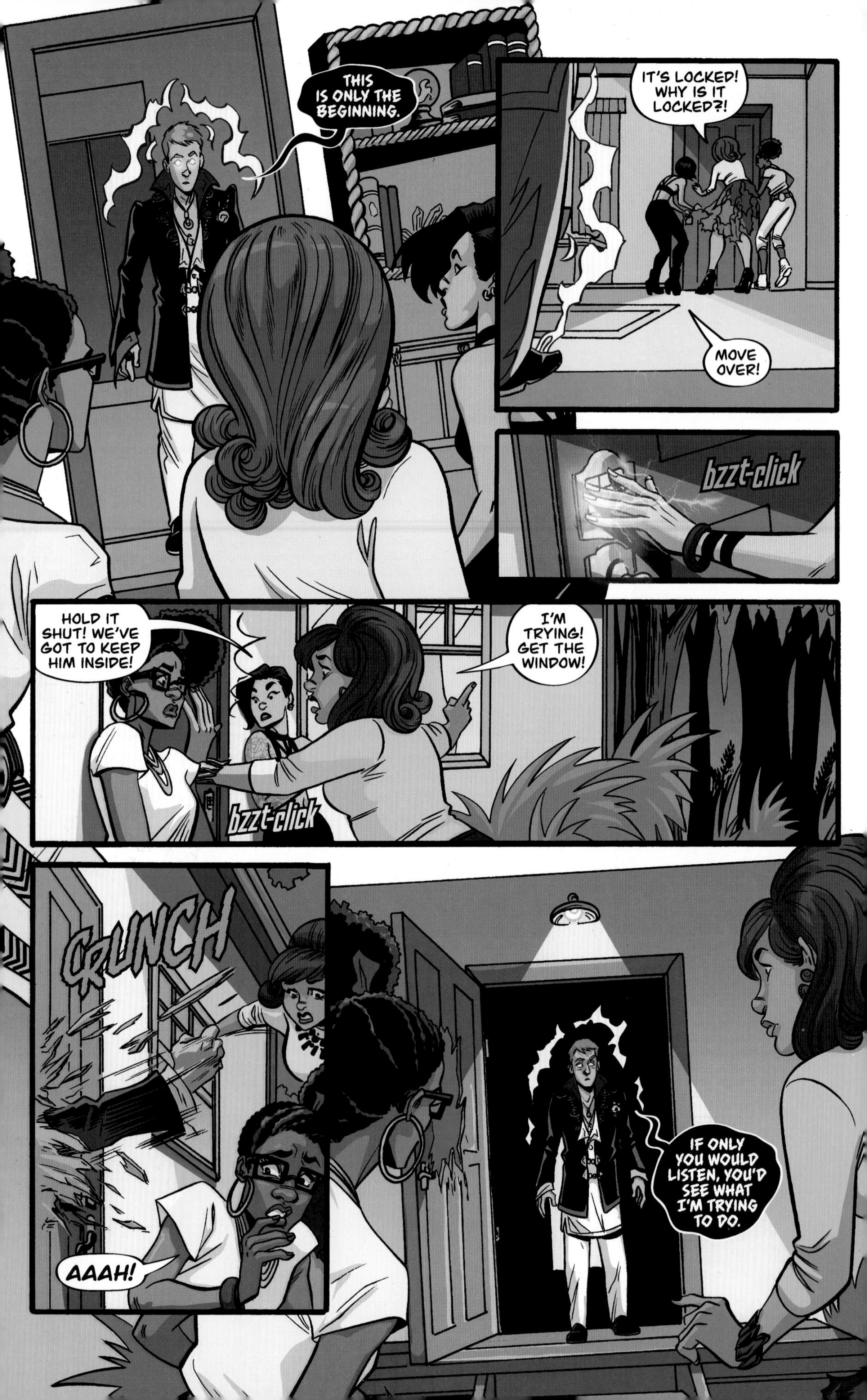
THIS IS ONLY THE BEGINNING.
IT'S LOCKED! WHY IS IT LOCKED?!
MOVE OVER!
bzzt-click
HOLD IT SHUT! WE'VE GOT TO KEEP HIM INSIDE!
I'M TRYING! GET THE WINDOW!
bzzt-click
CRUNCH
AAAH!
IF ONLY YOU WOULD LISTEN, YOU'D SEE WHAT I'M TRYING TO DO.

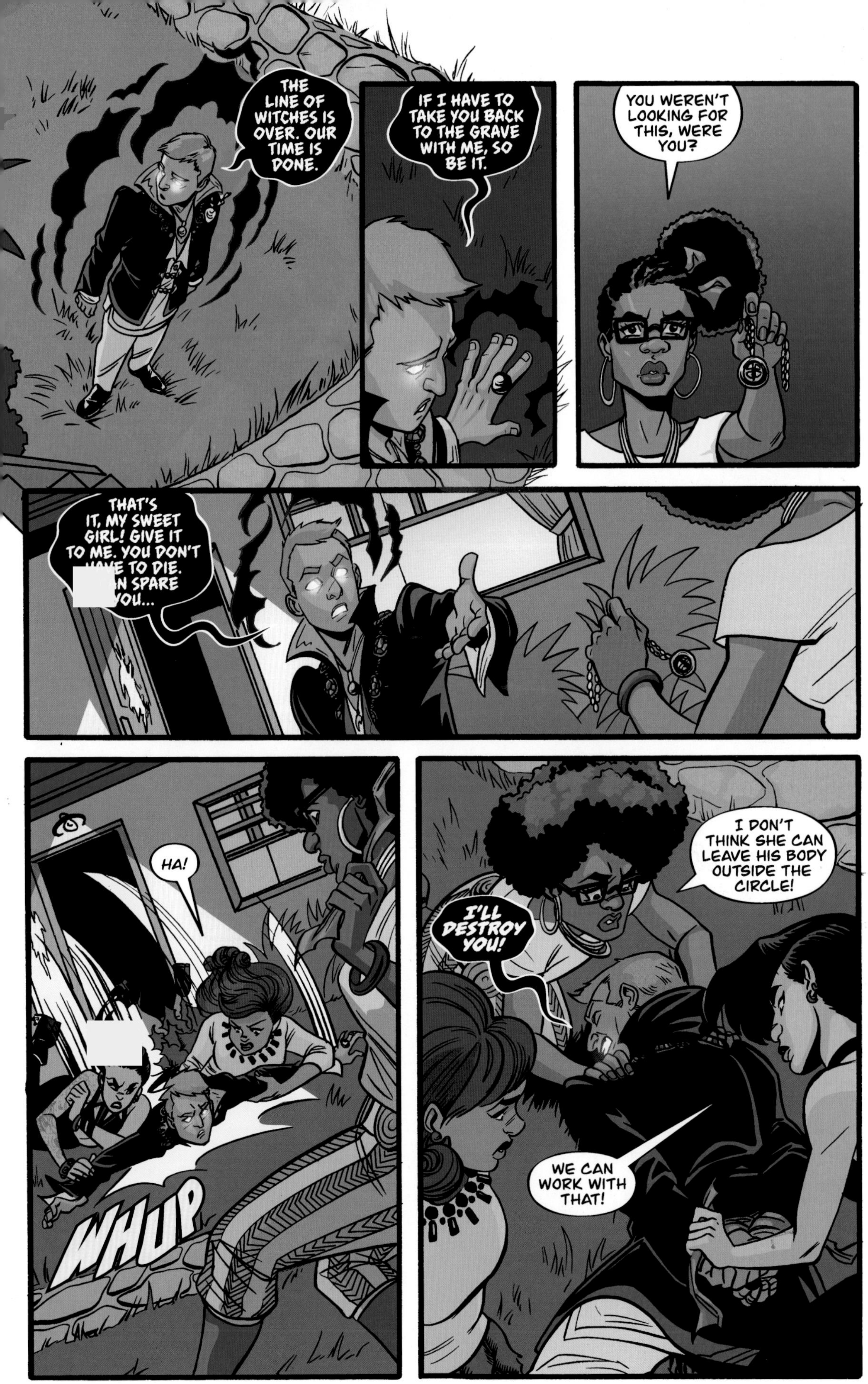
THE LINE OF WITCHES IS OVER. OUR TIME IS DONE.
IF I HAVE TO TAKE YOU BACK TO THE GRAVE WITH ME, SO BE IT.
YOU WEREN'T LOOKING FOR THIS, WERE YOU?
THAT'S IT, MY SWEET GIRL! GIVE IT TO ME. YOU DON'T … TO DIE. … SPARE YOU...
HA!
WHUP
I'LL DESTROY YOU!
I DON'T THINK SHE CAN LEAVE HIS BODY OUTSIDE THE CIRCLE!
WE CAN WORK WITH THAT!

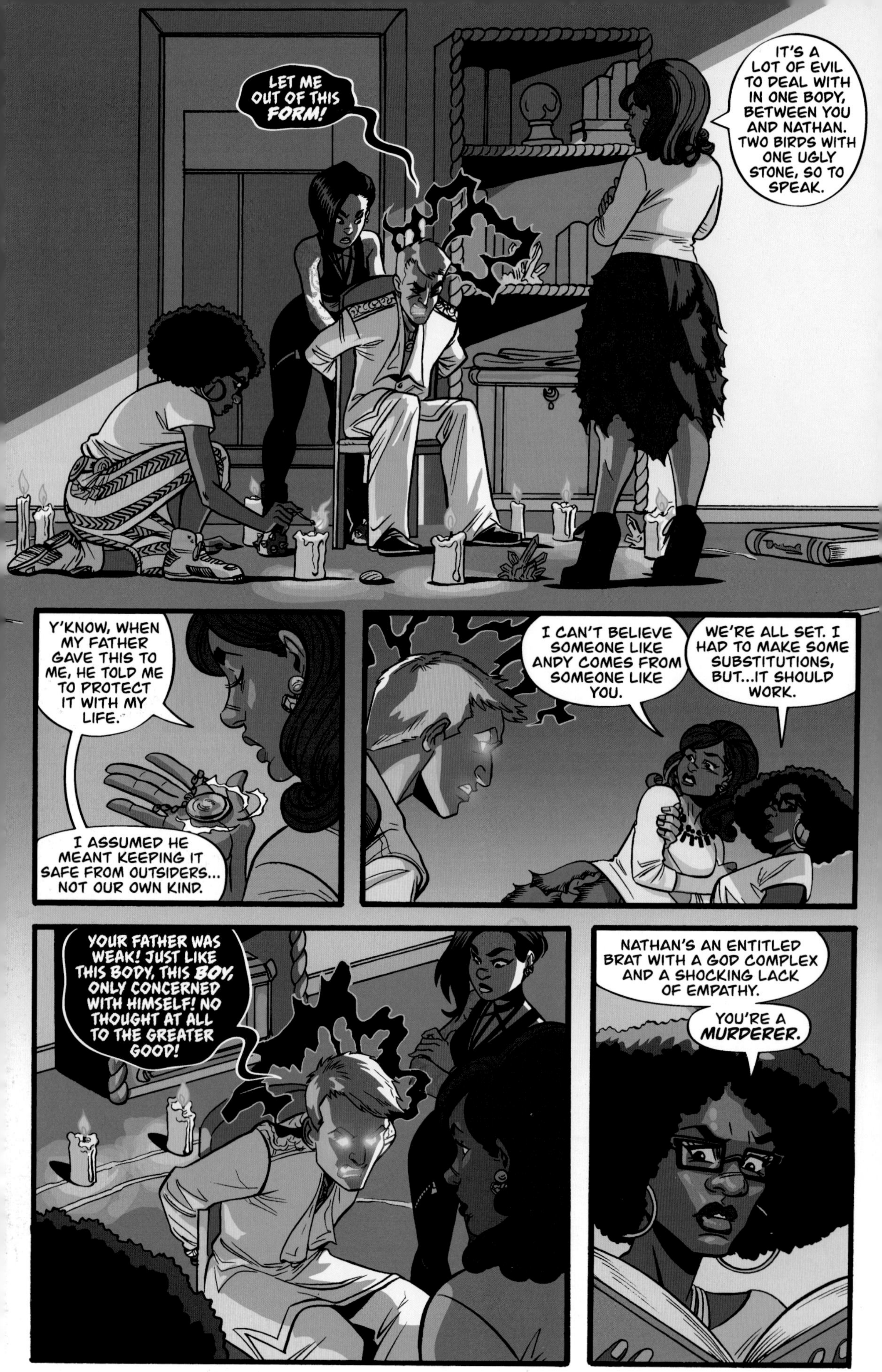
LET ME OUT OF THIS *FORM!*
IT'S A LOT OF EVIL TO DEAL WITH IN ONE BODY, BETWEEN YOU AND NATHAN. TWO BIRDS WITH ONE UGLY STONE, SO TO SPEAK.
Y'KNOW, WHEN MY FATHER GAVE THIS TO ME, HE TOLD ME TO PROTECT IT WITH MY LIFE.
I ASSUMED HE MEANT KEEPING IT SAFE FROM OUTSIDERS... NOT OUR OWN KIND.
I CAN'T BELIEVE SOMEONE LIKE ANDY COMES FROM SOMEONE LIKE YOU.
WE'RE ALL SET. I HAD TO MAKE SOME SUBSTITUTIONS, BUT...IT SHOULD WORK.
YOUR FATHER WAS WEAK! JUST LIKE THIS BODY, THIS *BOY,* ONLY CONCERNED WITH HIMSELF! NO THOUGHT AT ALL TO THE GREATER GOOD!
NATHAN'S AN ENTITLED BRAT WITH A GOD COMPLEX AND A SHOCKING LACK OF EMPATHY.
YOU'RE A *MURDERER.*

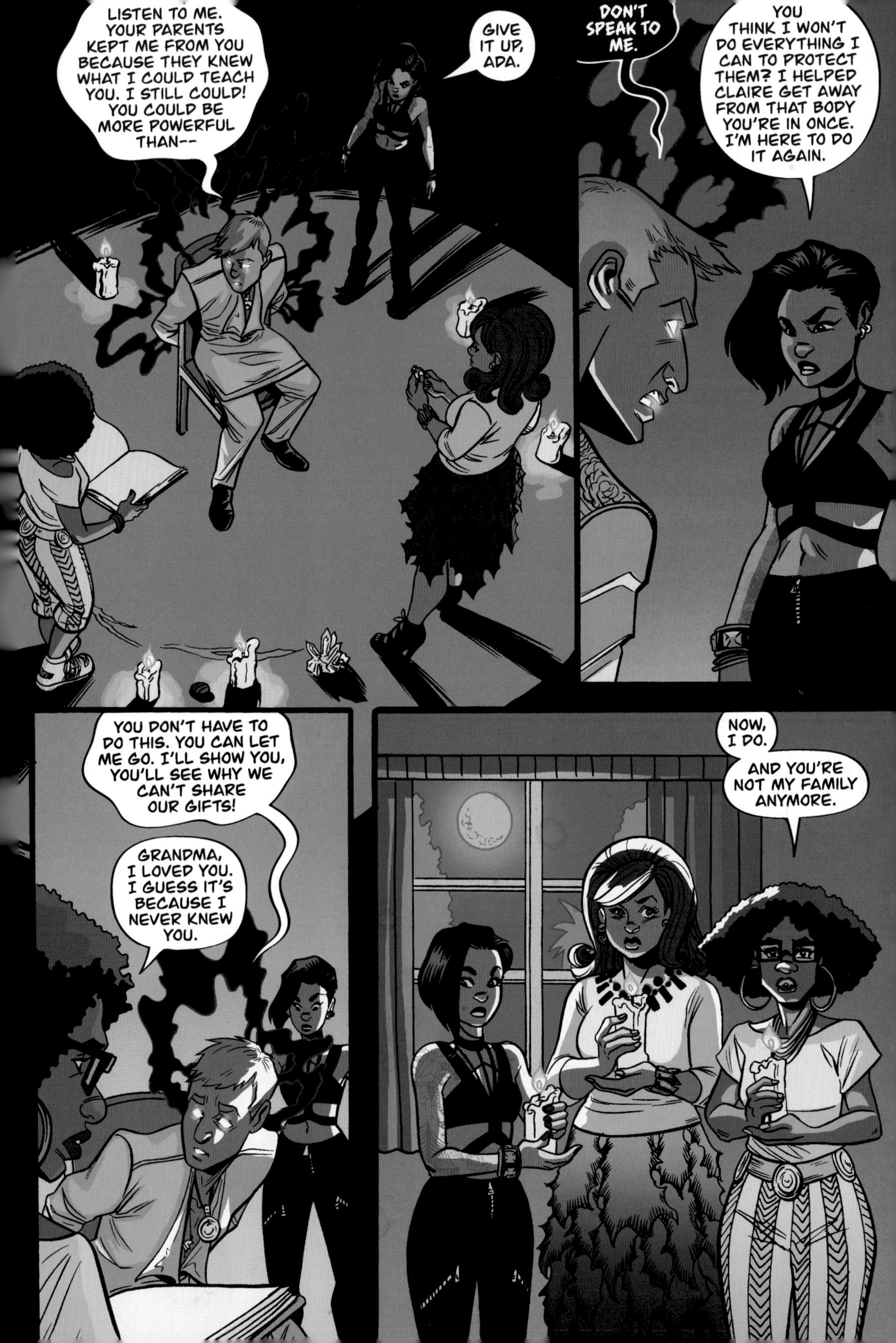
LISTEN TO ME. YOUR PARENTS KEPT ME FROM YOU BECAUSE THEY KNEW WHAT I COULD TEACH YOU. I STILL COULD! YOU COULD BE MORE POWERFUL THAN--
GIVE IT UP, ADA.
DON'T SPEAK TO ME.
YOU THINK I WON'T DO EVERYTHING I CAN TO PROTECT THEM? I HELPED CLAIRE GET AWAY FROM THAT BODY YOU'RE IN ONCE. I'M HERE TO DO IT AGAIN.
YOU DON'T HAVE TO DO THIS. YOU CAN LET ME GO. I'LL SHOW YOU, YOU'LL SEE WHY WE CAN'T SHARE OUR GIFTS!
GRANDMA, I LOVED YOU. I GUESS IT'S BECAUSE I NEVER KNEW YOU.
NOW, I DO.
AND YOU'RE NOT MY FAMILY ANYMORE.

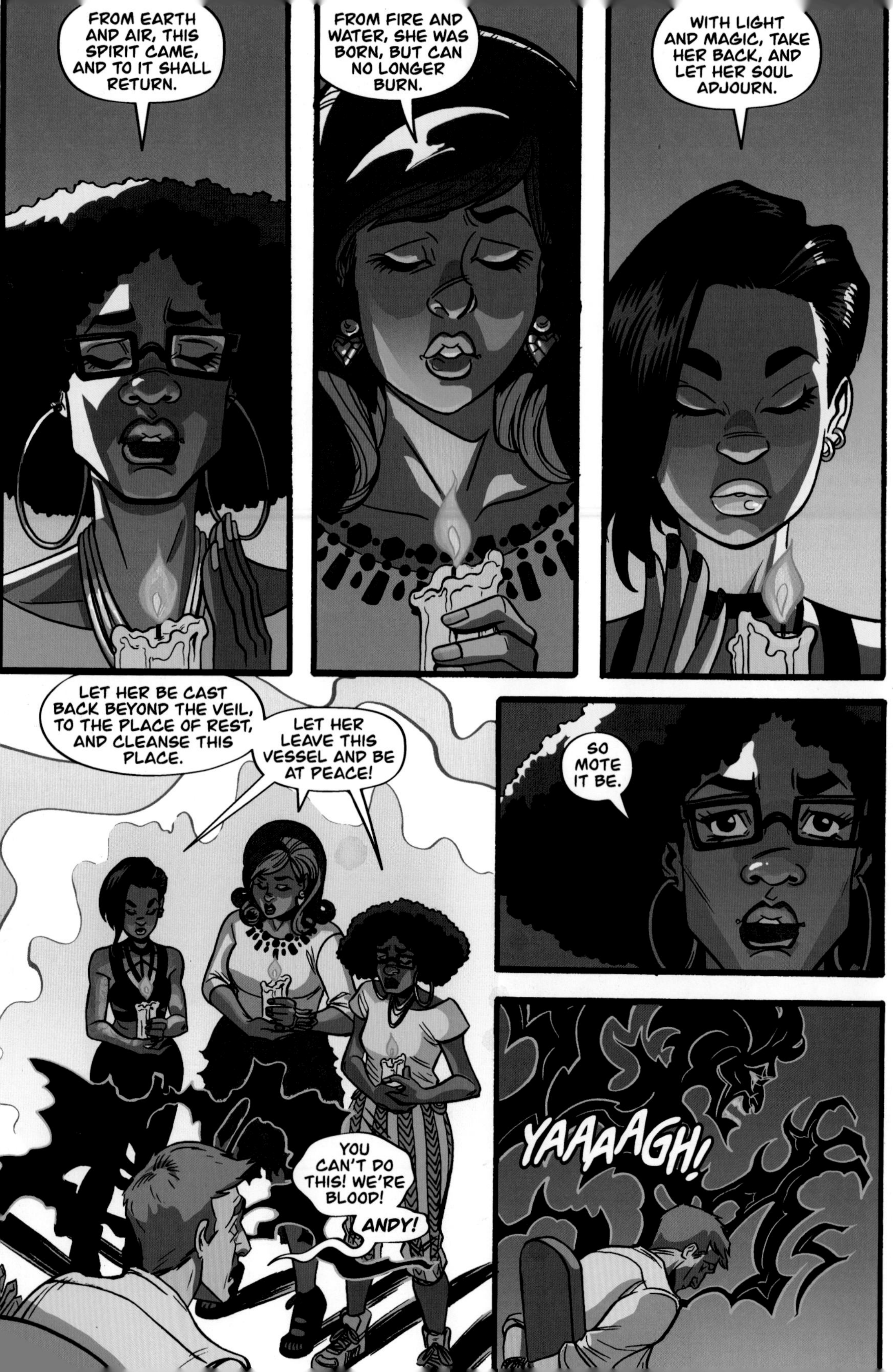

FROM EARTH AND AIR, THIS SPIRIT CAME, AND TO IT SHALL RETURN.
FROM FIRE AND WATER, SHE WAS BORN, BUT CAN NO LONGER BURN.
WITH LIGHT AND MAGIC, TAKE HER BACK, AND LET HER SOUL ADJOURN.
LET HER BE CAST BACK BEYOND THE VEIL, TO THE PLACE OF REST, AND CLEANSE THIS PLACE.
LET HER LEAVE THIS VESSEL AND BE AT PEACE!
YOU CAN'T DO THIS! WE'RE BLOOD!
ANDY!
SO MOTE IT BE.
YAAAAGH!

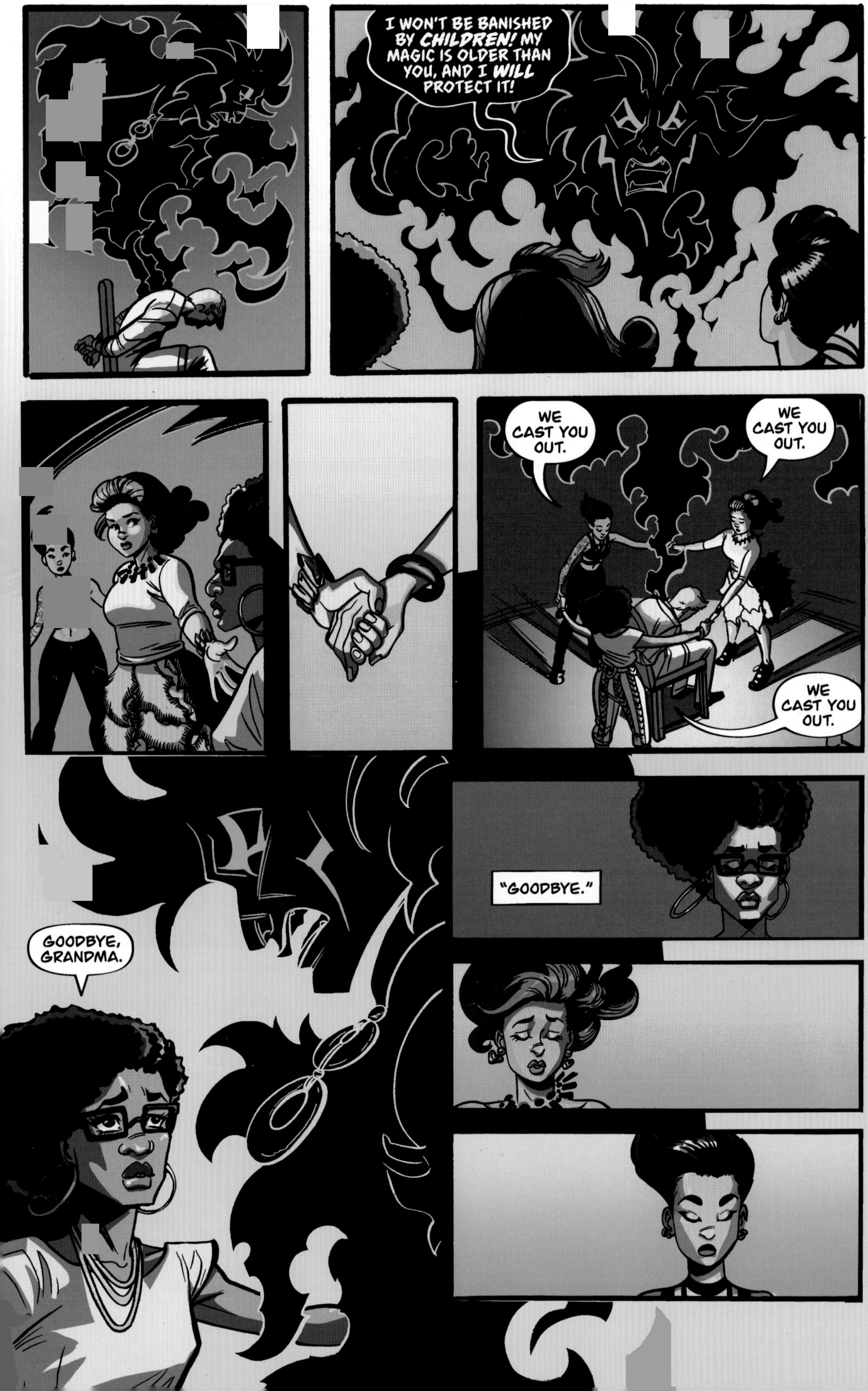

I WON'T BE BANISHED BY CHILDREN! MY MAGIC IS OLDER THAN YOU, AND I WILL PROTECT IT!
WE CAST YOU OUT.
WE CAST YOU OUT.
WE CAST YOU OUT.
"GOODBYE."
GOODBYE, GRANDMA.

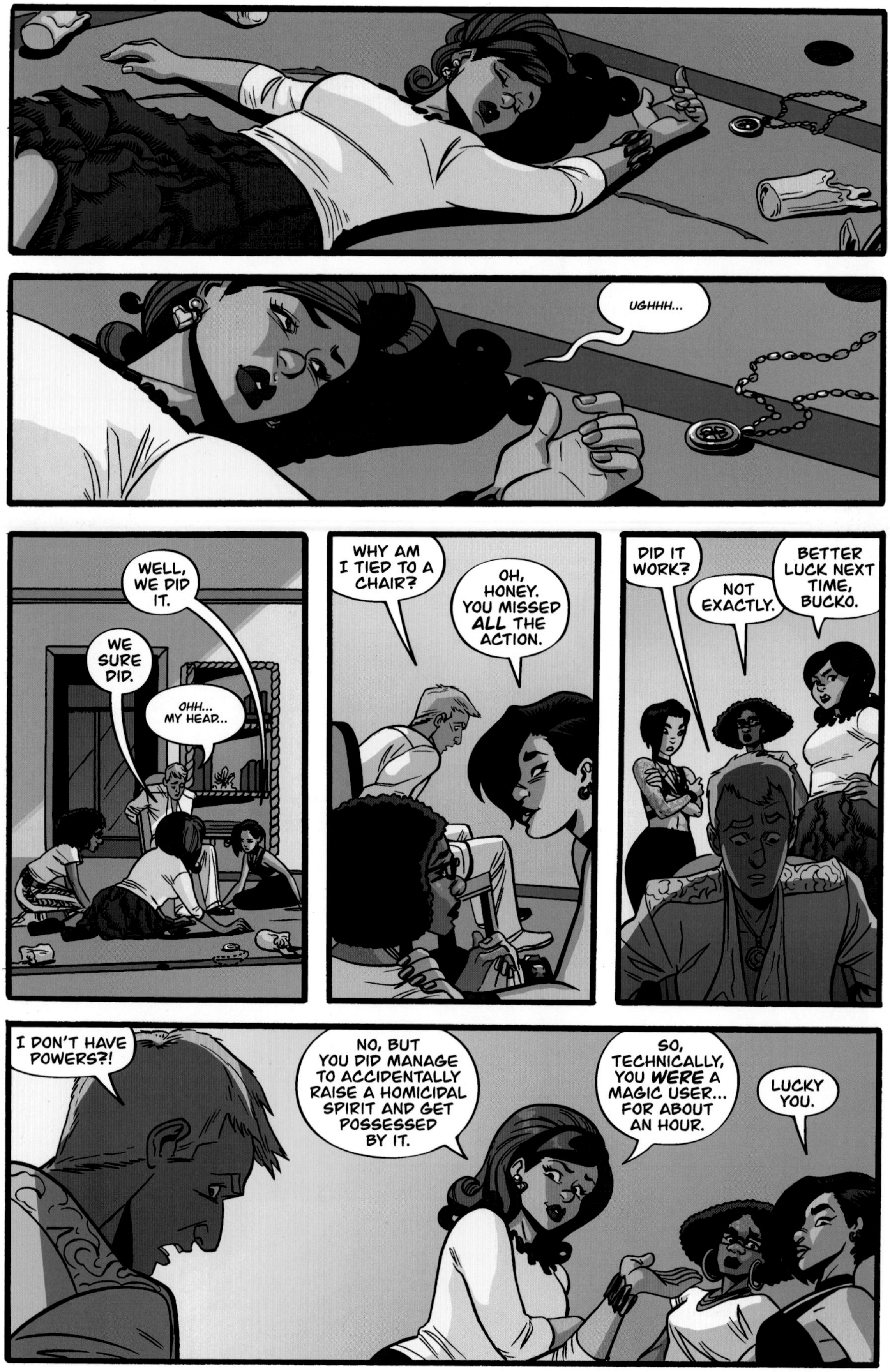
UGHHH...
WELL, WE DID IT.
WE SURE DID.
OHH... MY HEAD...
WHY AM I TIED TO A CHAIR?
OH, HONEY. YOU MISSED ALL THE ACTION.
DID IT WORK?
NOT EXACTLY.
BETTER LUCK NEXT TIME, BUCKO.
I DON'T HAVE POWERS?!
NO, BUT YOU DID MANAGE TO ACCIDENTALLY RAISE A HOMICIDAL SPIRIT AND GET POSSESSED BY IT.
SO, TECHNICALLY, YOU WERE A MAGIC USER... FOR ABOUT AN HOUR.
LUCKY YOU.

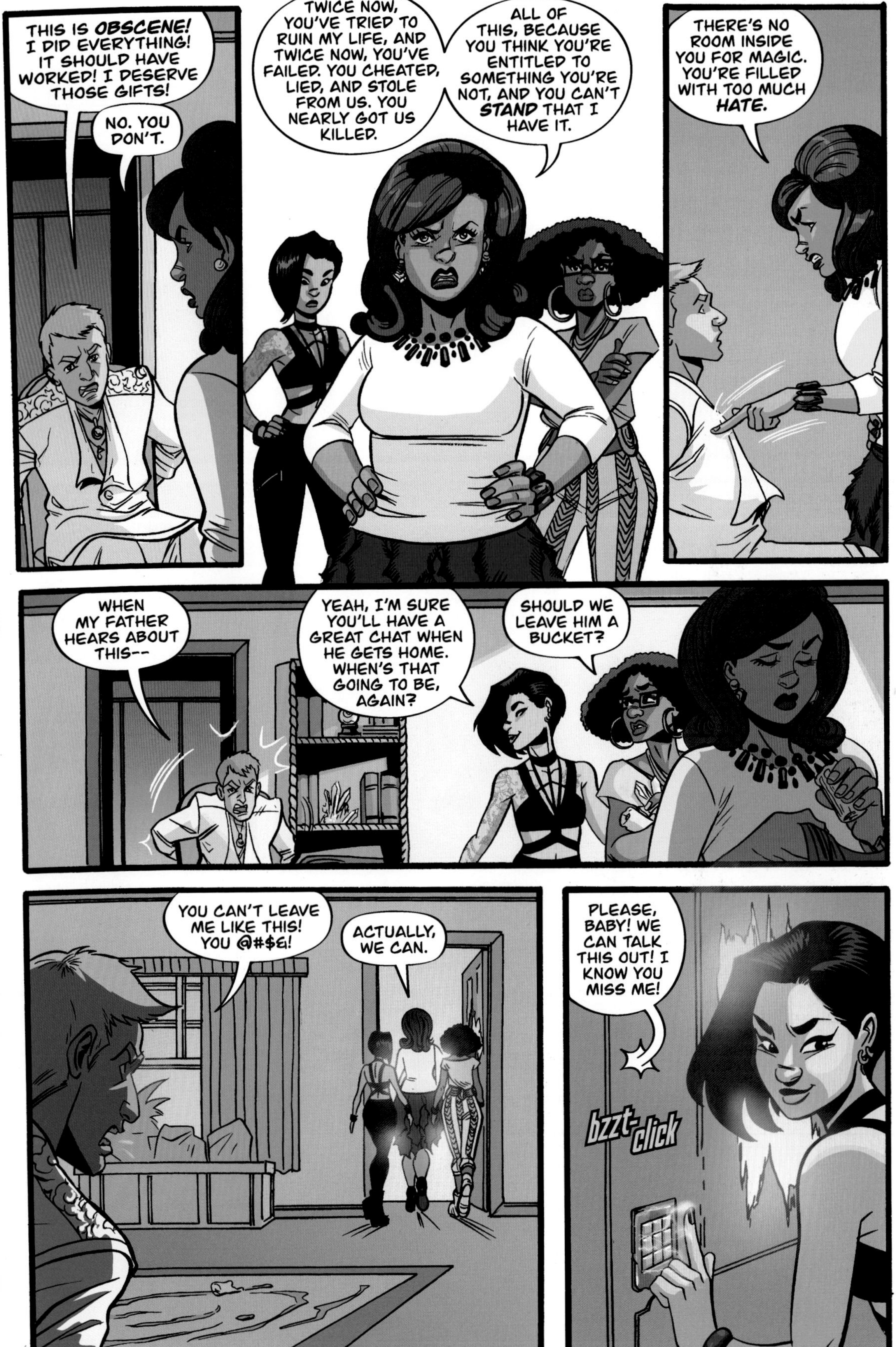
THIS IS OBSCENE! I DID EVERYTHING! IT SHOULD HAVE WORKED! I DESERVE THOSE GIFTS!
NO. YOU DON'T.
TWICE NOW, YOU'VE TRIED TO RUIN MY LIFE, AND TWICE NOW, YOU'VE FAILED. YOU CHEATED, LIED, AND STOLE FROM US. YOU NEARLY GOT US KILLED.
ALL OF THIS, BECAUSE YOU THINK YOU'RE ENTITLED TO SOMETHING YOU'RE NOT, AND YOU CAN'T STAND THAT I HAVE IT.
THERE'S NO ROOM INSIDE YOU FOR MAGIC. YOU'RE FILLED WITH TOO MUCH HATE.
WHEN MY FATHER HEARS ABOUT THIS--
YEAH, I'M SURE YOU'LL HAVE A GREAT CHAT WHEN HE GETS HOME. WHEN'S THAT GOING TO BE, AGAIN?
SHOULD WE LEAVE HIM A BUCKET?
YOU CAN'T LEAVE ME LIKE THIS! YOU @#$&!
ACTUALLY, WE CAN.
PLEASE, BABY! WE CAN TALK THIS OUT! I KNOW YOU MISS ME!
bzzt-click

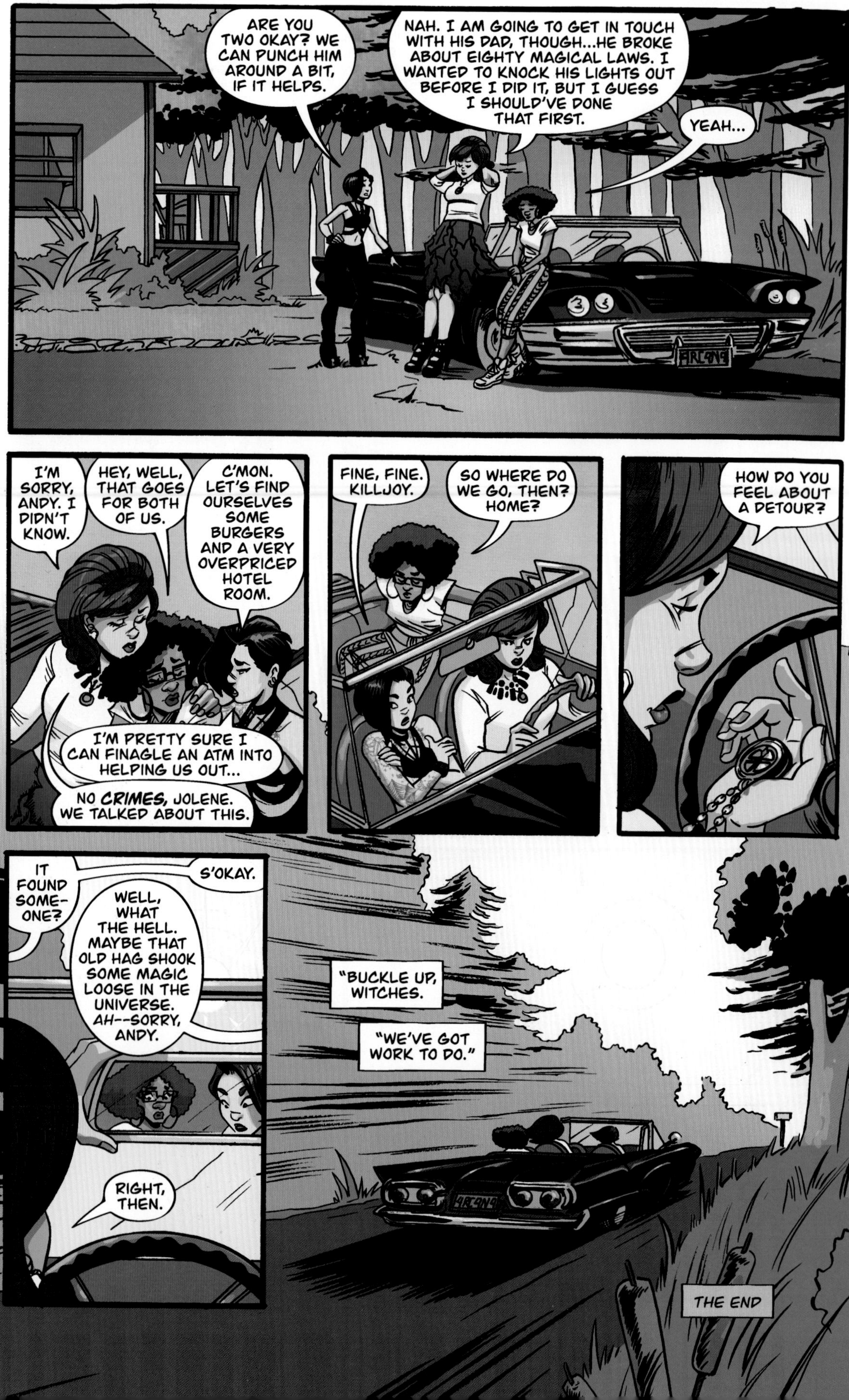
ARE YOU TWO OKAY? WE CAN PUNCH HIM AROUND A BIT, IF IT HELPS.
NAH. I AM GOING TO GET IN TOUCH WITH HIS DAD, THOUGH...HE BROKE ABOUT EIGHTY MAGICAL LAWS. I WANTED TO KNOCK HIS LIGHTS OUT BEFORE I DID IT, BUT I GUESS I SHOULD'VE DONE THAT FIRST.
YEAH...
I'M SORRY, ANDY. I DIDN'T KNOW.
HEY, WELL, THAT GOES FOR BOTH OF US.
C'MON. LET'S FIND OURSELVES SOME BURGERS AND A VERY OVERPRICED HOTEL ROOM.
I'M PRETTY SURE I CAN FINAGLE AN ATM INTO HELPING US OUT...
NO *CRIMES*, JOLENE. WE TALKED ABOUT THIS.
FINE, FINE. KILLJOY.
SO WHERE DO WE GO, THEN? HOME?
HOW DO YOU FEEL ABOUT A DETOUR?
IT FOUND SOME-ONE?
S'OKAY.
WELL, WHAT THE HELL. MAYBE THAT OLD HAG SHOOK SOME MAGIC LOOSE IN THE UNIVERSE. AH--SORRY, ANDY.
RIGHT, THEN.
"BUCKLE UP, WITCHES.
"WE'VE GOT WORK TO DO."
THE END

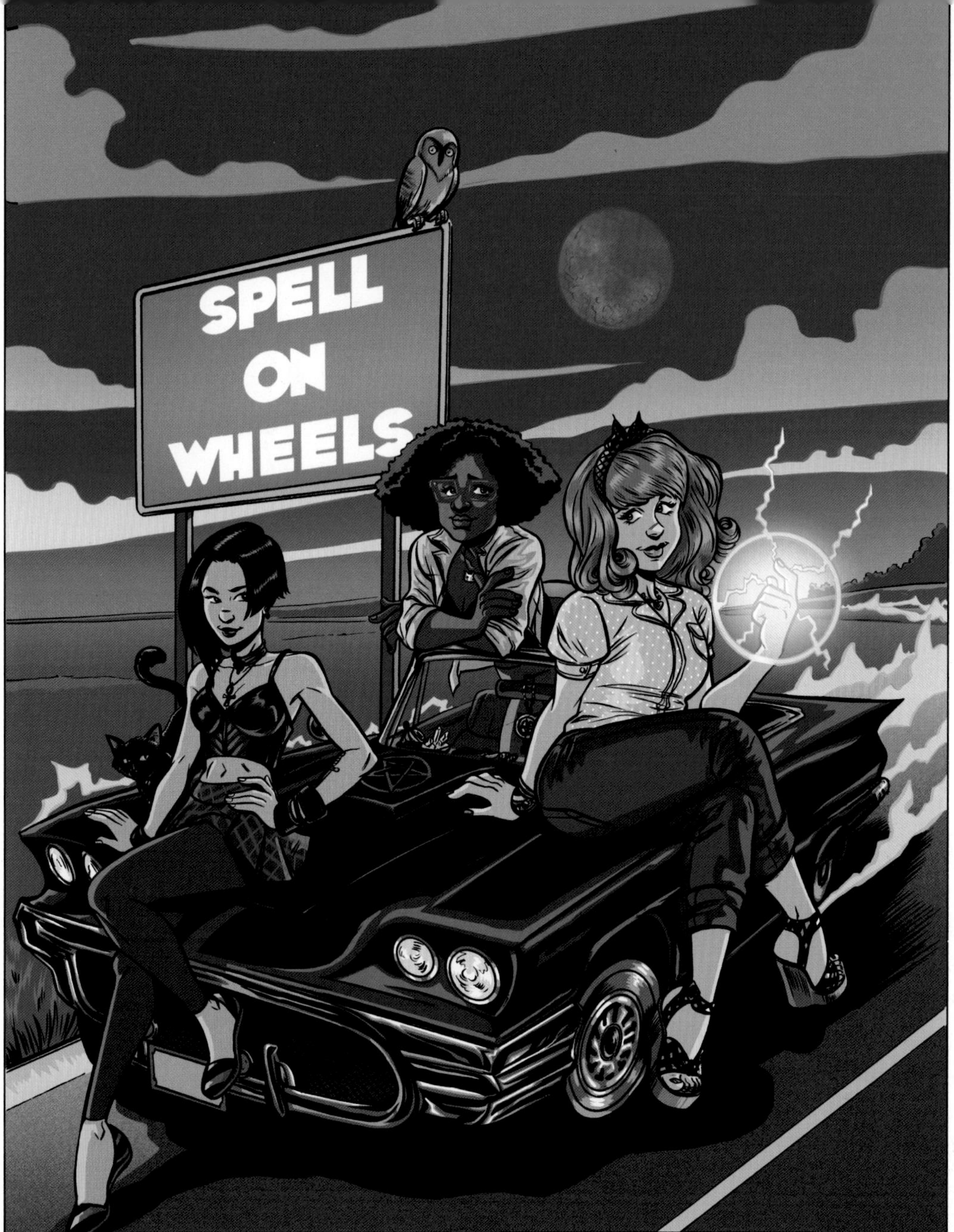
SPELL
ON
WHEELS

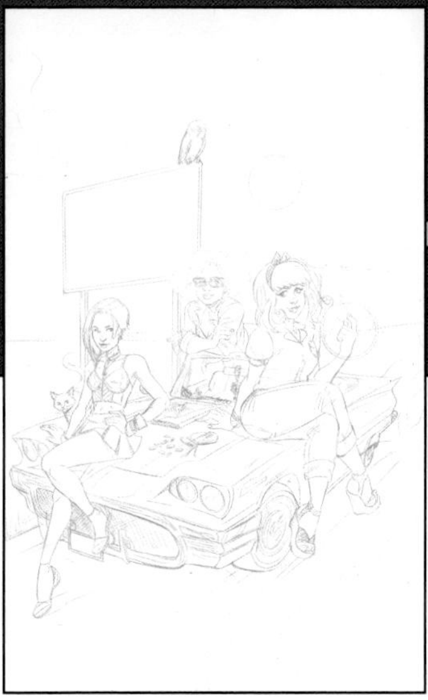

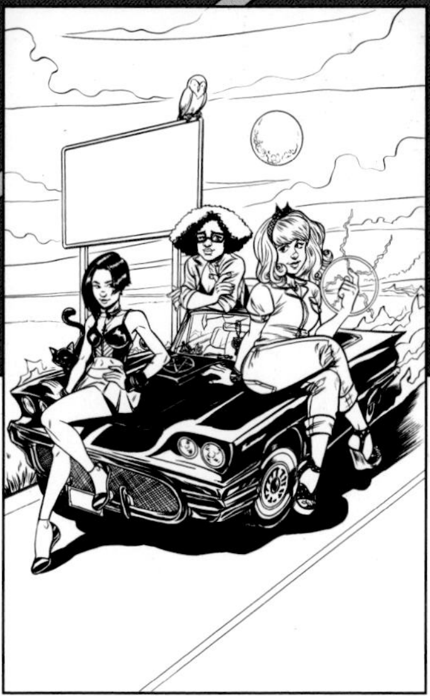

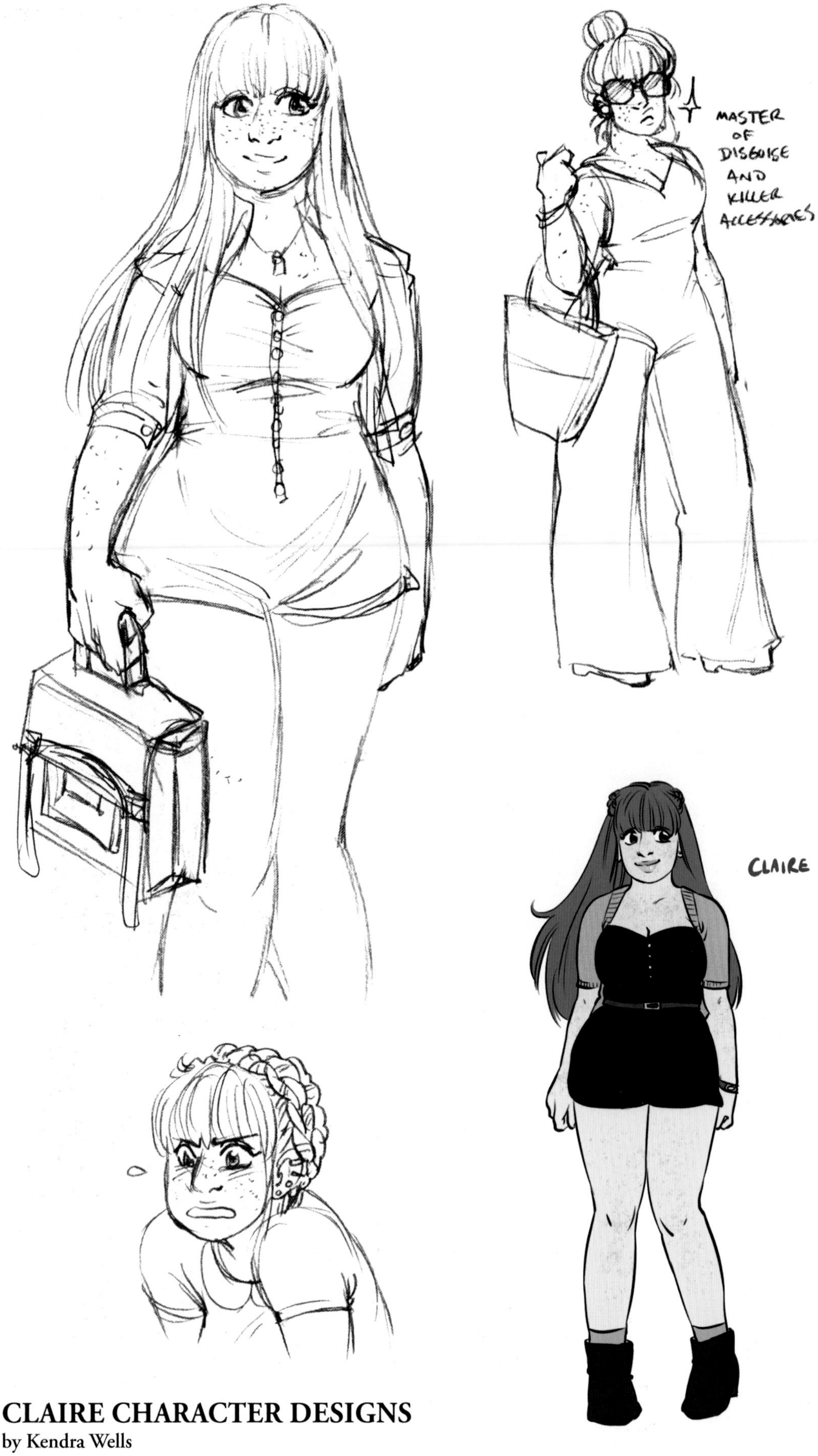
MASTER OF DISGUISE AND KILLER ACCESSORIES
CLAIRE

CLAIRE CHARACTER DESIGNS
by Kendra Wells

CLAIRE SKETCHES
by Megan

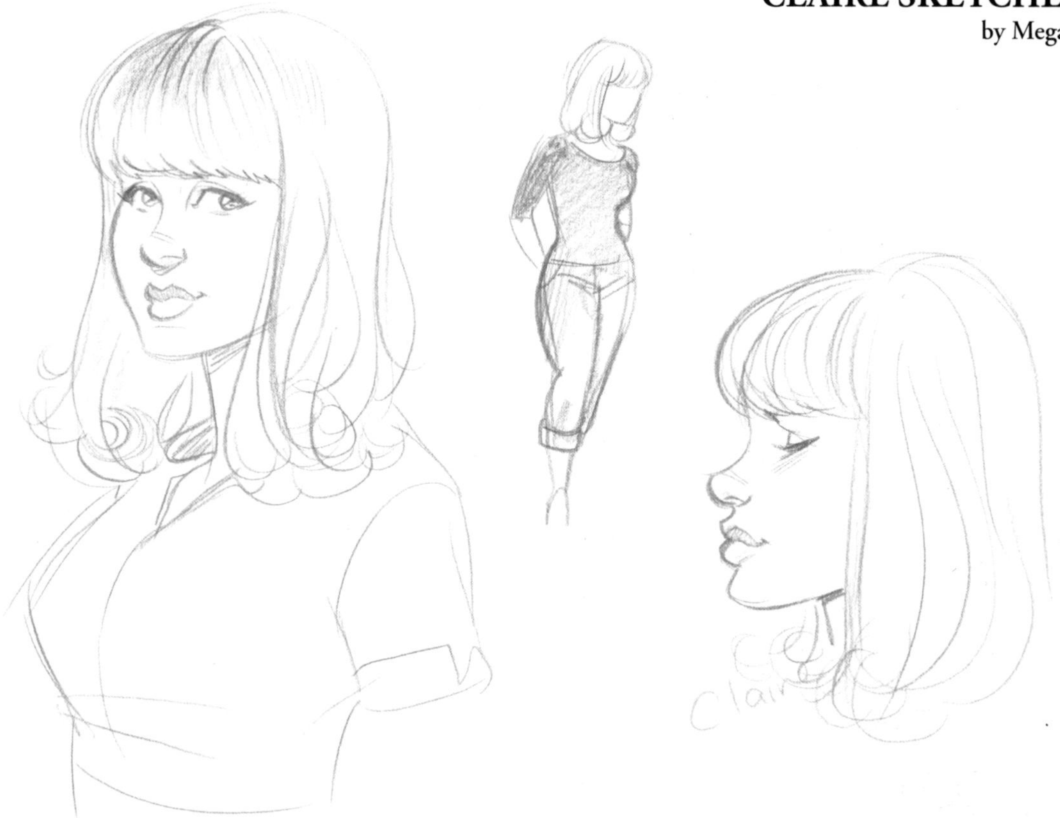
Claire

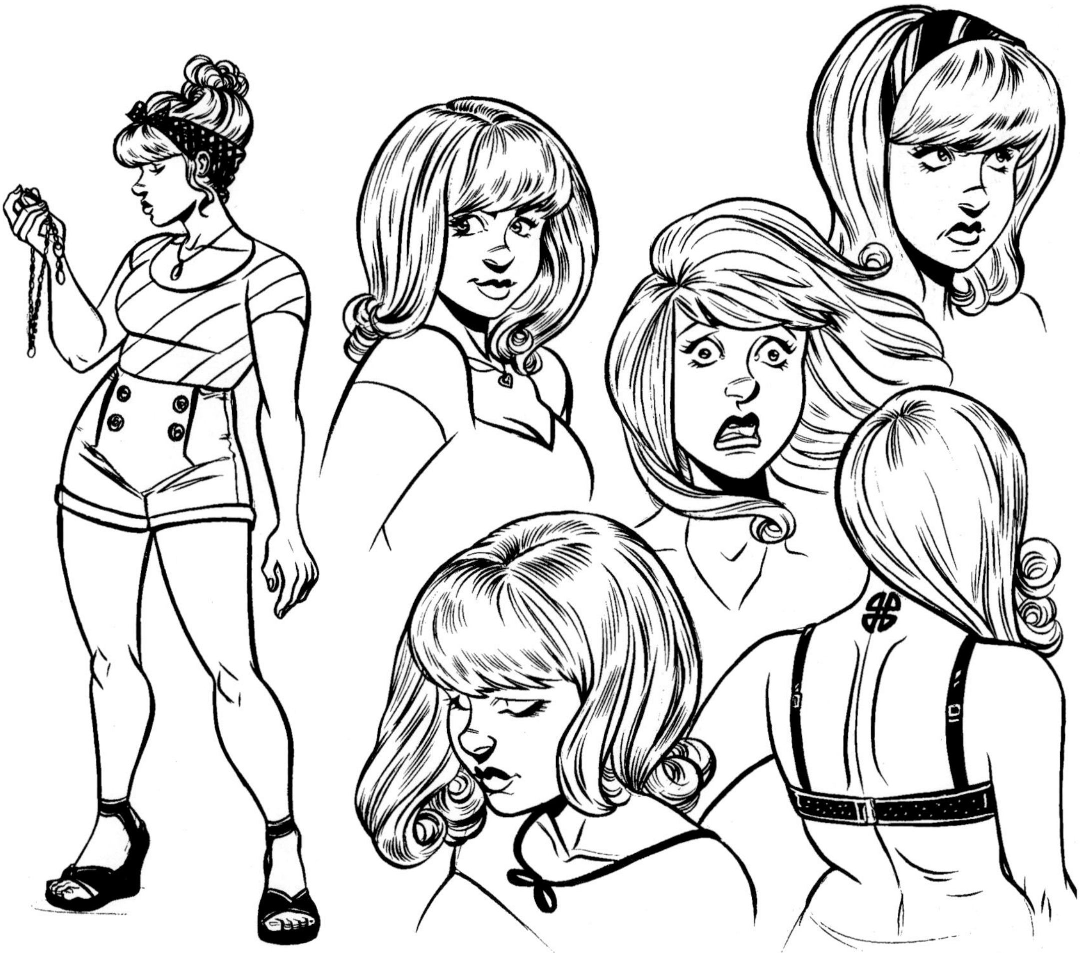

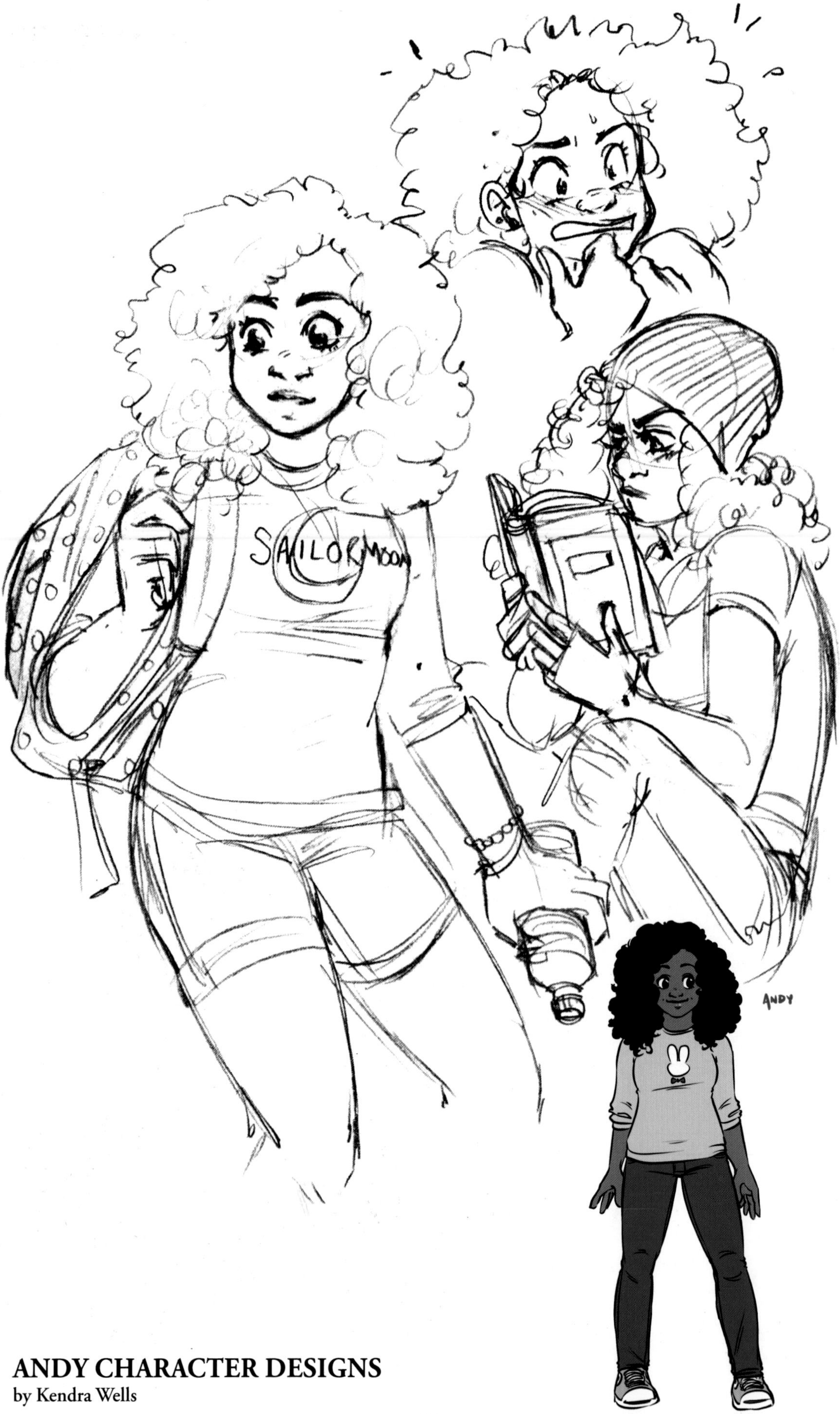
SAILOR MOON
ANDY

ANDY CHARACTER DESIGNS
by Kendra Wells

ANDY SKETCHES
by Megan

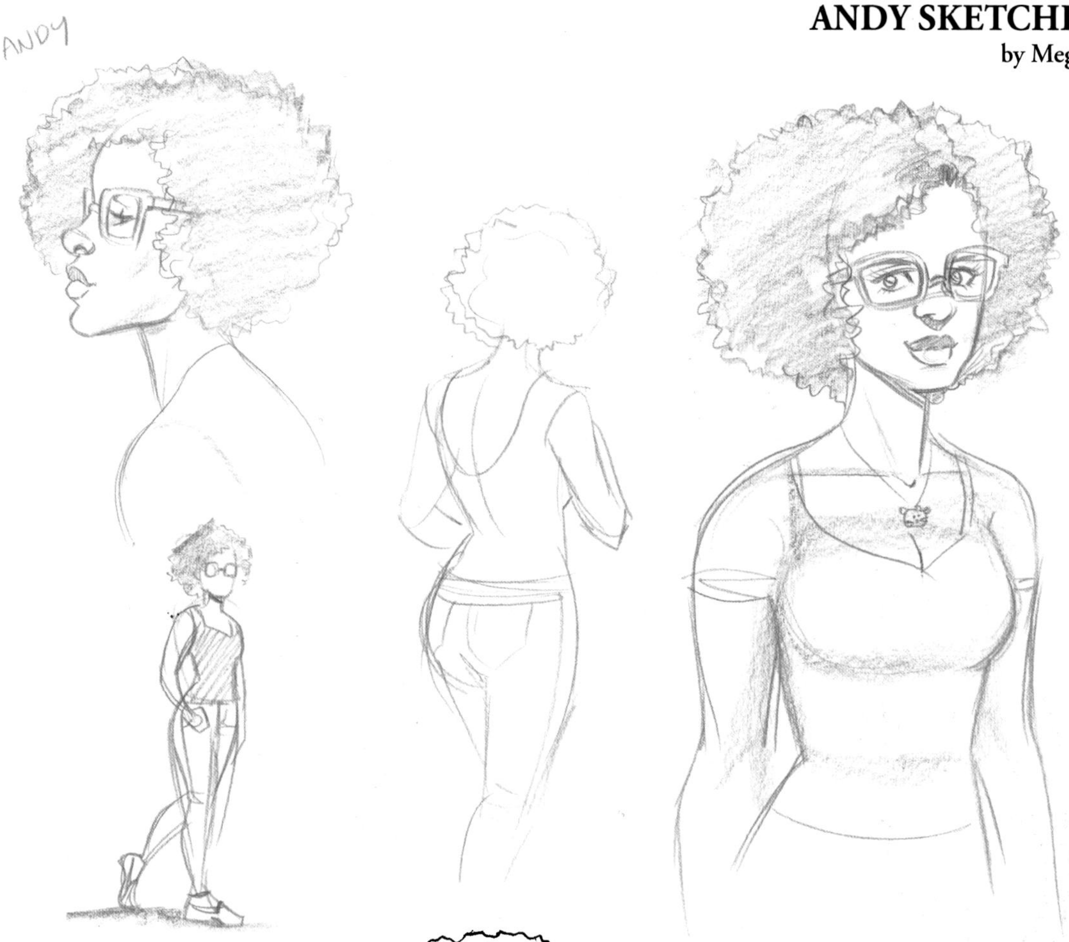
ANDY

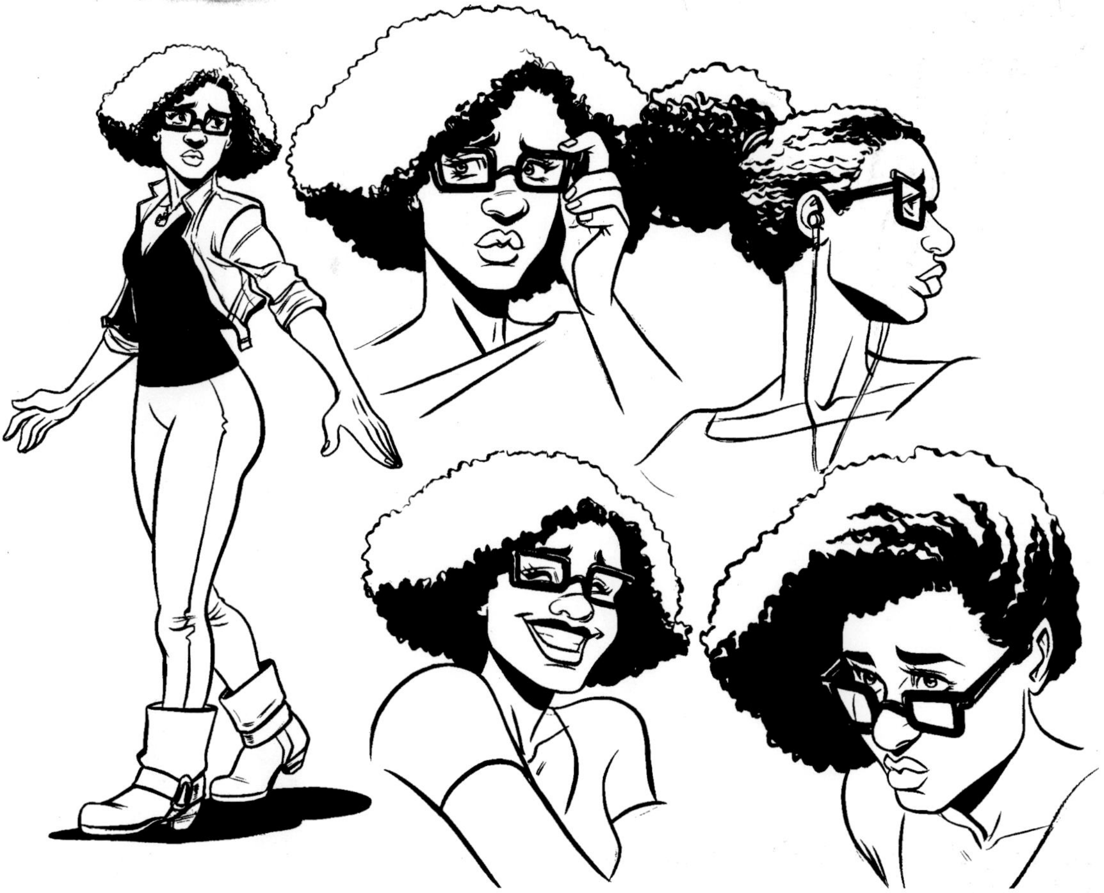

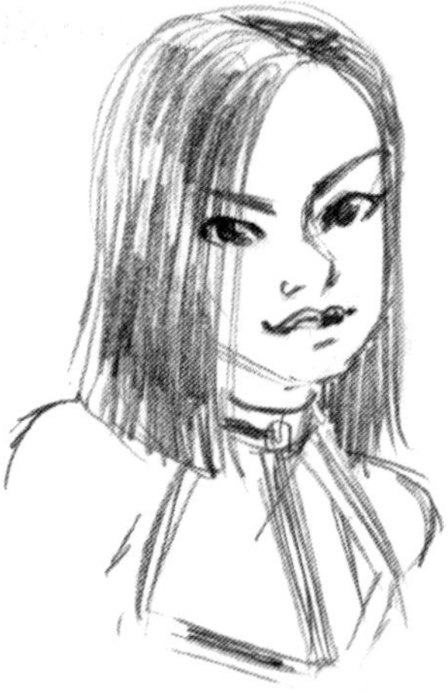

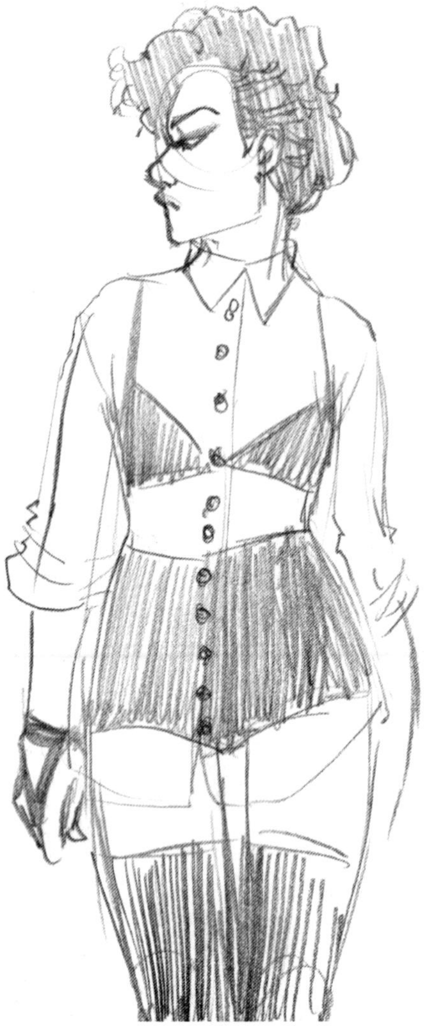

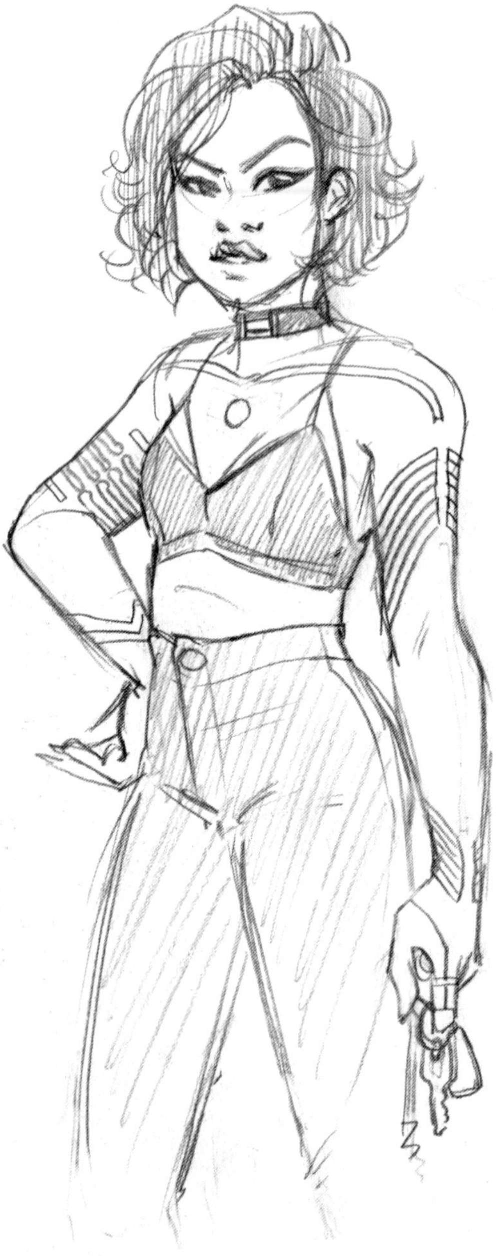

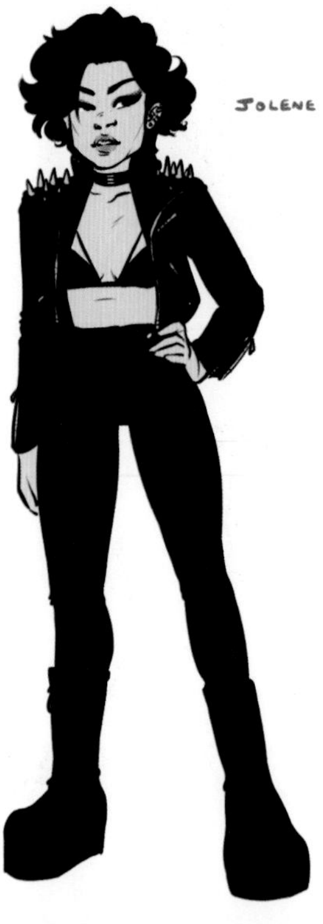
JOLENE

JOLENE CHARACTER DESIGN
by Kendra Wells

JOLENE SKETCHES
by Megan

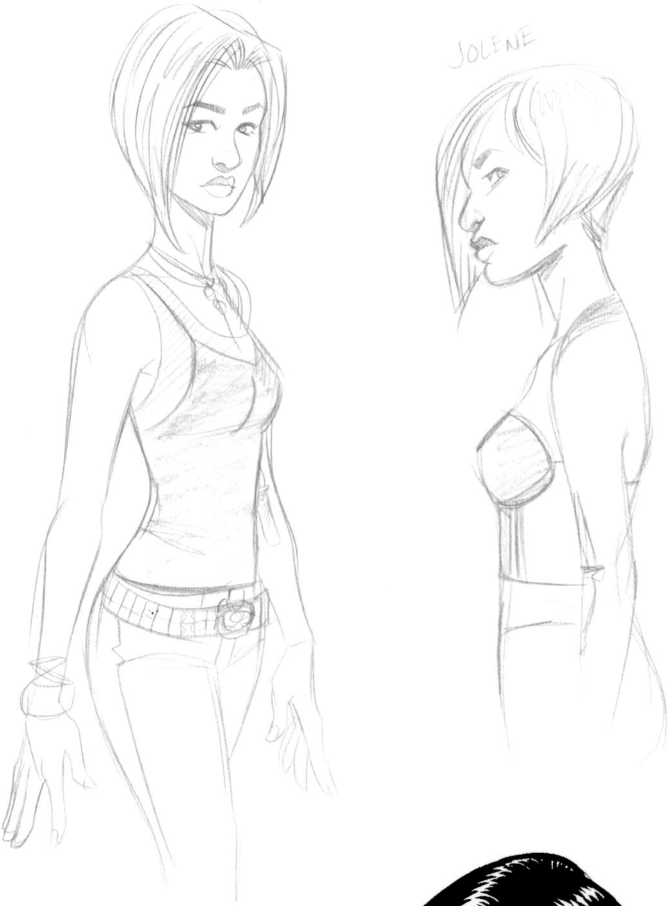
JOLENE

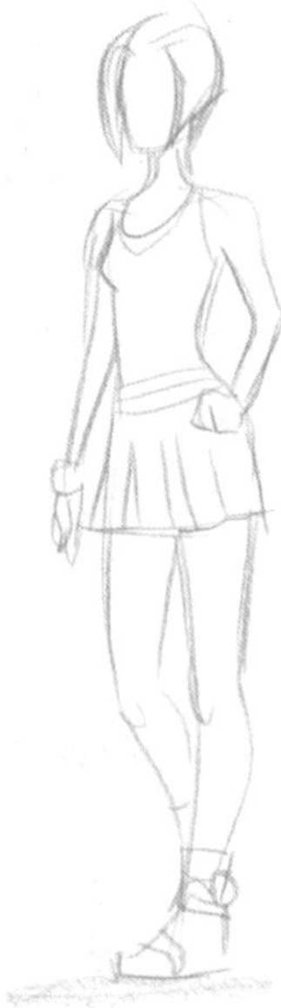

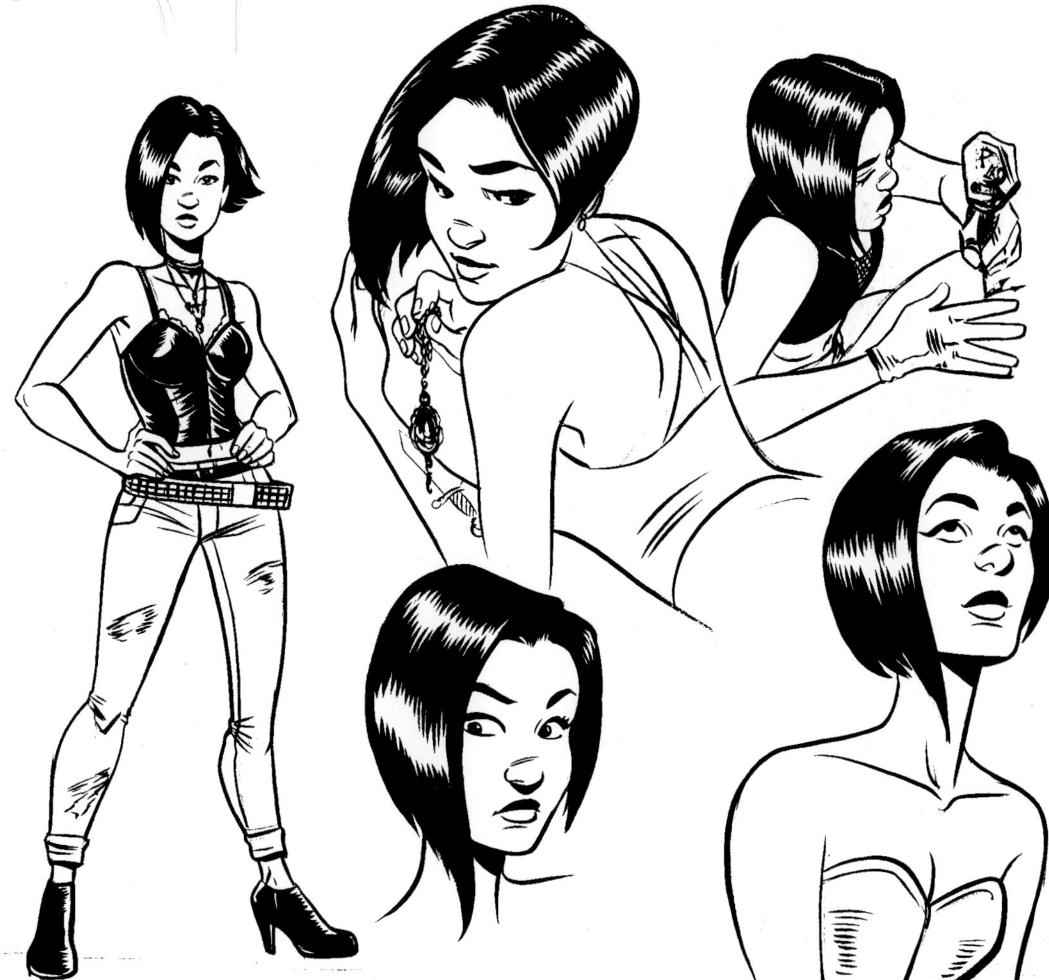

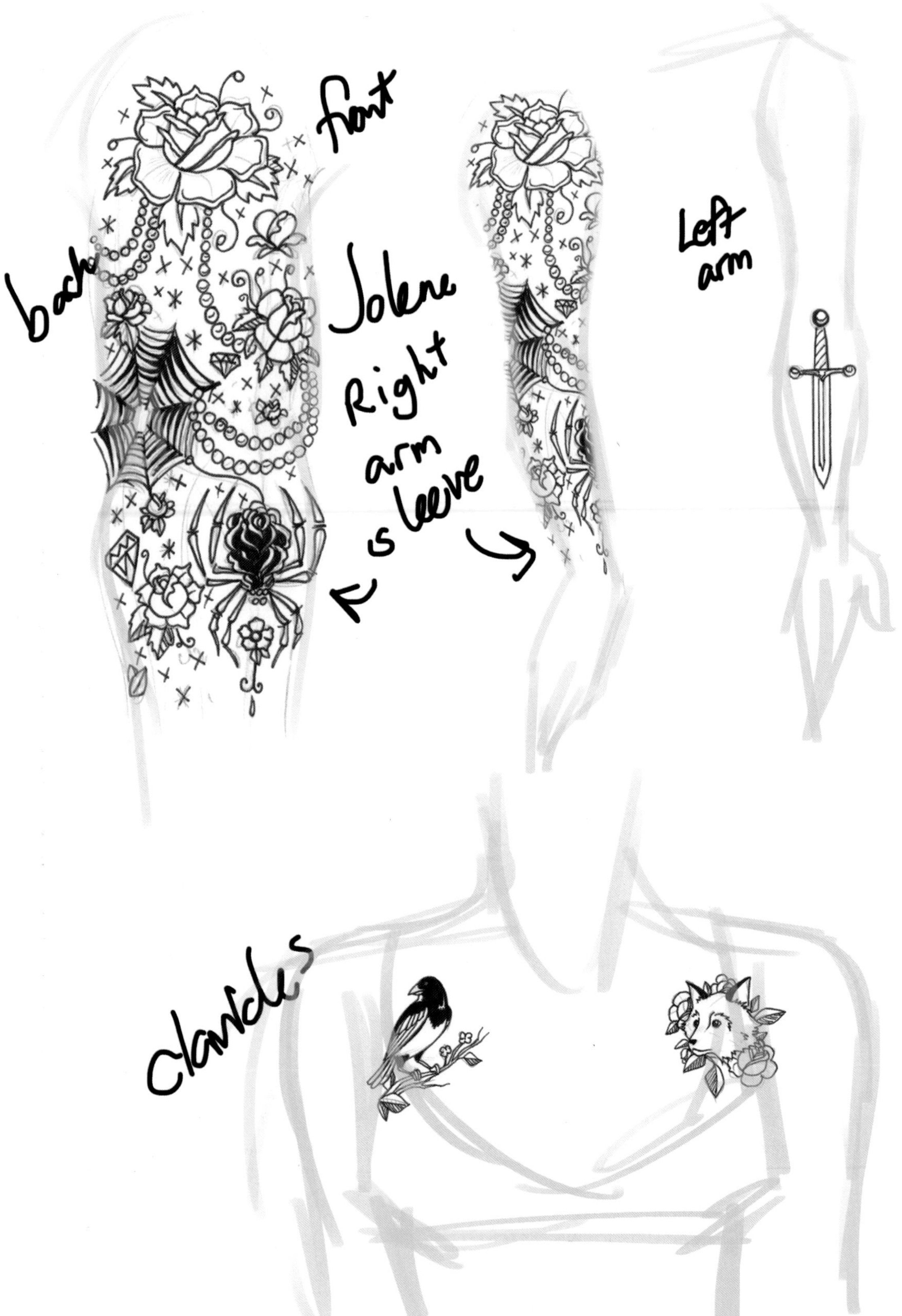
back
front
Jolene
Right
arm
sleeve
Left
arm
clavicles

JOLENE'S TATTOO DESIGNS

by Megan and Kate

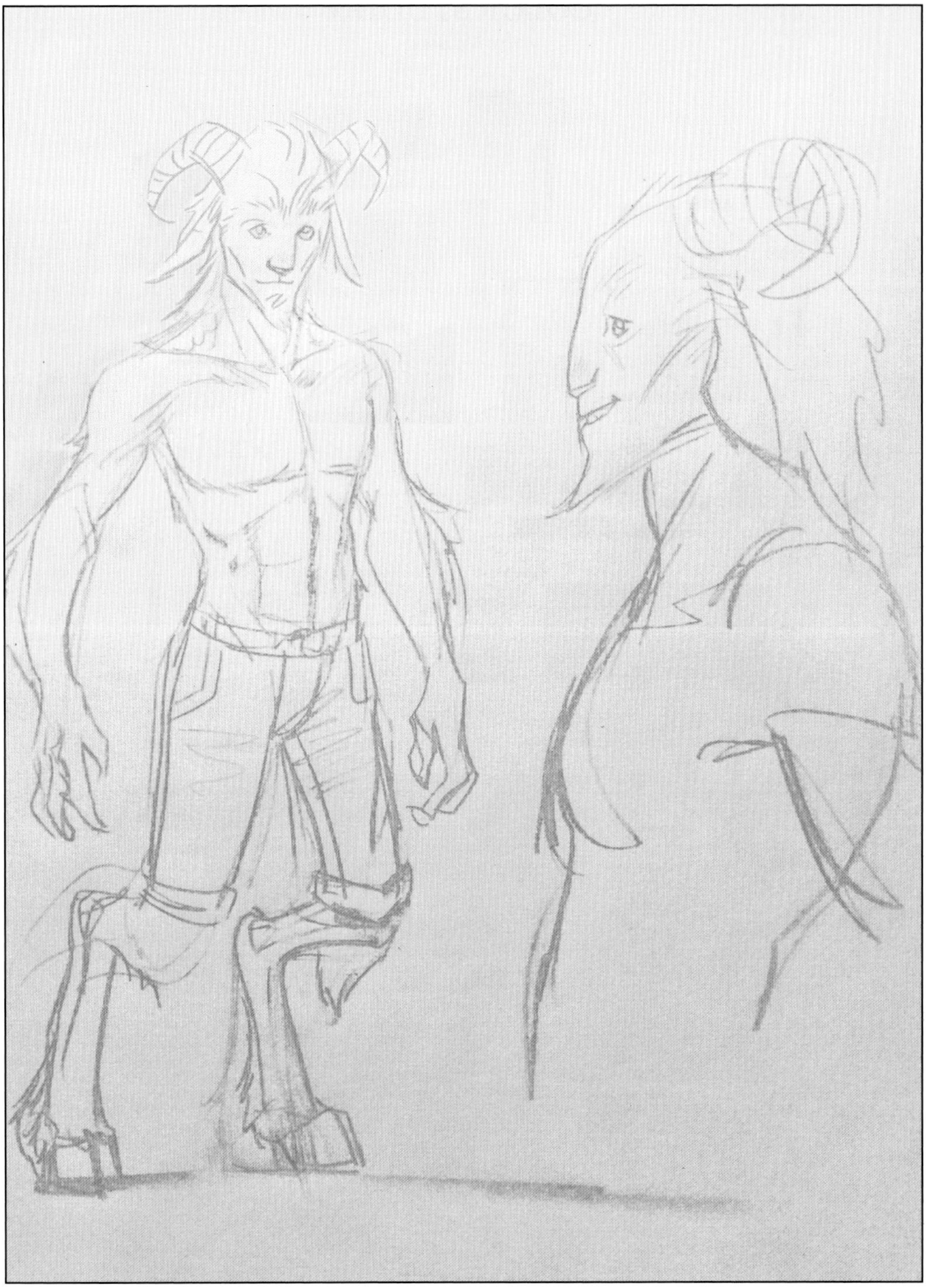

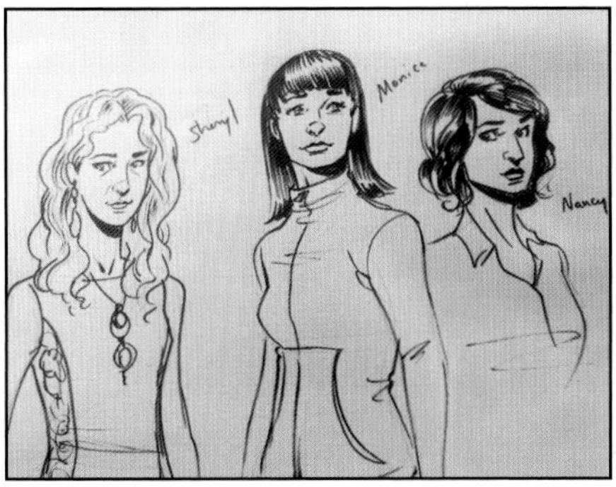
Sheryl
Monica
Nancy

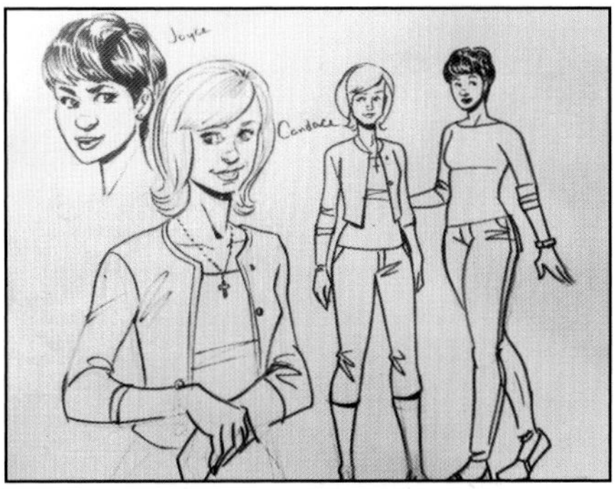
Joyce
Candace

The housewives' character designs from issue #2 and Paul's design for issue #4

COLOR STUDIES

by Marissa

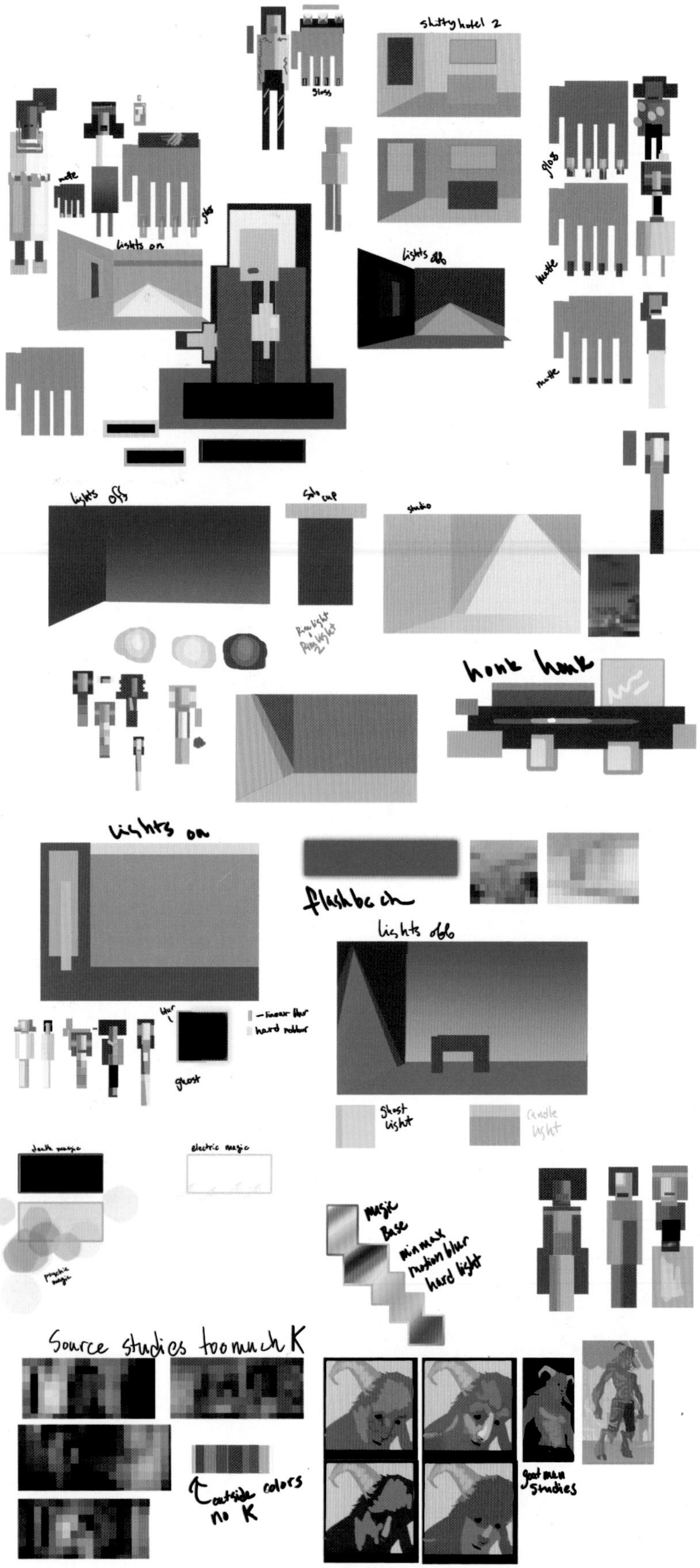
shitty hotel 2
gloss
matte
lights on
lights off
studio
honk honk
lights on
flashback
lights off
ghost
ghost light
candle light
death magic
electric magic
psychic magic
magic
Base
min max
motion blur
hard light
Source studies too much K
outside colors no K
goat man studies